MISTAKEN

An Arranged Marriage Bratva Romance

Arianna Fraser

STA, LLC

D1514358

FREE BOOKS!

If you love the organized crime bad boys and the women who - at least a little - redeem them, I'd love to offer you a free download for The Reluctant Spy for joining my email list.

Kindly copy and paste this link in your browser:

https://dl.bookfunnel.com/6xud62rmg0.bookfunnel

To Lynda, the best of cousins, the most ruthless of editors.

And to you; a sincere thank you to everyone who's bought this book or read it on Kindle. Proceeds from this book benefit the two crisis nurseries in my city. The crisis nurseries here are non-profits who exist to serve families where the parents are overwhelmed and in desperate need of help. Their little people can be lovingly and safely cared for while the parents get connected with services for everything from housing, to employment, to mental health assistance and more. Thanks to your kindness, I've had the chance to purchase much-needed items from their wish lists, like cases of diapers, industrial-sized boxes of goldfish crackers, books, formula, toys...

And socks. Those kiddos can never hold on to a pair of socks.

CONTENTS

PREFACE

Mistaken: An Arranged Marriage Bratva Romance is set in the brutal world of organized crime. These Russians are not messing around.

As such, there is violence, torture, explicit sex between adult married partners, kidnapping, forced marriage and profanity. Oh, so much profanity.

If these things are not to your taste, please find something you're more comfortable with, but I thank you for stopping by.

Still here? Excellent! Grab a glass of wine or a bag of Cheetos and let's get started. As always, thank you for reading.

-Arianna

CHAPTER 1 - YOU JUST CAN'T KEEP YOUR MOUTH SHUT.

In which a mistaken identity and Ella's complete inability to keep her smart mouth shut have disastrous consequences.

Maksim...

"You don't have a choice, Maksim."

Yuri had been my *Sovietnik* for five years. That - and being my younger brother - were the only reasons he was still drawing breath. But my hand still moved instinctively to the gun holster hidden under my suit jacket.

He saw this, of course. "Kill me, don't kill me *Pakhan*, the answer is still the same. Sokolov is circling. If you do not accept his proposition, he will take it as a serious insult. He's the last man in New York City that you want to insult. You know this."

Rubbing my forehead, I paced in front of the fireplace. I avoided an arranged marriage while our father was Pakhan, and I've escaped getting entangled for the five years I've been in power. "Facing life with one of these lunatic Bratva princesses isn't worth the power of joining in with another family," I snarled, "Sokolov wants to absorb our territory, not combine forces."

"His daughter Katya is very pretty," Yuri observed.

"She put out her cigarette on the face of her maid because she didn't get her an ashtray quickly enough," I scoffed. "I wouldn't want her near my children, much less bearing them."

"I completely understand your concern," he agreed, "but the meeting Sokolov has been requesting cannot be put off any longer. I am told he intends to block your access to three of our key shipping docks if you do not agree to the meeting next week."

I never questioned Yuri's information; his spies were rarely wrong. His careful, formal phrasing told me that he did not enjoy offering this information any more than I wanted to hear it. I lifted the vodka bottle again, gesturing to him. After his nod, I poured us both a drink. "So..." returning to my pacing, "Sokolov is going to force this meeting next week. He will use the opportunity to demand an alliance between our families, using a marriage to his daughter."

"Correct," Yuri said cautiously.

"And if I refuse, I'm bringing down an all-out war."

"That's likely," he agreed. Looking at me more closely, Yuri started laughing, "I know this expression of yours. It usually means trouble for me."

"Not at all. But if I am engaged already, and with wedding plans underway within eight days, there is no discussion to be had, yes?"

"While you are extremely popular with the ladies," Yuri said tactfully, "are you seeing anyone who could be considered marriageable? You do realize it has to be someone who understands this world and that this commitment would be for life?"

Mentally running through any potential candidates, I realized immediately that I associated with them primarily for sex.

Occasionally, there was a woman whose intelligence and wit made her a pleasure to spend time with. But for a wife? This required a different set of criteria. Smiling at my *Sovietnik*, I watched his face fall.

"*Ебать*, why are your most ambitious plans so filled with potential for disaster?" Yuri moaned.

"Not at all," I said haughtily. "I'll select an American. A professional. Embracing our new heritage as a US-based Bratva."

He sighed, rising to his feet and buttoning his suit jacket. "I recall the Second from the Corporation's London office doing this very thing when they were negotiating with the Solntsevskaya Bratva. You know how insistent they are about doing business with married men. Thomas Williams, I believe. He married the daughter of a CEO from one of their U.S. companies. She must have been good luck. He managed to take over the entire European region, without the Russian partners."

"You see? Already, a blueprint for success," I pointed out, "it's not traditional. But since I'm not yet bound to anyone, I'll have to make use of the next week to block Sokolov's plans."

"I'll do some research, *Pakhan*." Nodding, Yuri left the room, footsteps heavy. Sometimes, my little brother could just not see how my plans fit into the big picture.

Ella...

"If I have to spend another Friday night listening to you bitch and moan, I swear I'm going to cut you."

Tania is my best friend, and I have to admit, she's right. However, her memory is somewhat selective. She apparently didn't remember crying on my couch after her last six failed relationships.

So of course, my big mouth spouted out, "Oh, like our month-long grieving period for Jake, the biker who left you to follow the Ghost concert tour? Or Mikal, your boyfriend who wanted an open relationship with you and your cousin? Or-"

"Fine," Tania snarled, "but you know that loser Luka is out there getting some tonight. Why let him have all the fun?"

"True." I agree gloomily, "That little cockalorum would absolutely be out there, somewhere. Sleazing his way through the female population of lower Manhattan."

"Cocka- what?" Tania laughed, "Is this the word of the day on your British Insults calender?"

"Cockalorum," I told her, "a boastful and self-important person, a strutting little fellow."

"Yeah, he's definitely that," she agreed.

"And I was dumb enough to get engaged to him."

"Who's stupid enough to get oral sex from his secretary while on a Zoom call with his fiancée?" Tania said, shaking her head in disgust. It was one of her finest talents, the immediate outrage when I was hurt and then her ability to cheer me up. We'd been best friends since we were ten, and she was the social butterfly who dragged me out of my own cocoon, kicking and screaming.

Tania is watching me with concern now, which is almost worse than her pushing me to be an extrovert. "Honey, I know that assface broke your heart, but he does not deserve the mourning period you've given him. I'm not telling you to take a guy home - only because I know you won't - but... just dance. Have a cocktail. A lot of cocktails," she amended. "Flirt a little and remember that other men find you attractive and charming and blah, blah blah."

I'm laughing, "Isn't this the speech I give you every time you get your heart broken?"

"Ah, ah!" Tania corrects me. "They never break my heart. They just…" she tried to think of the right explanation. "They irritated me." She laughs at my look of skepticism. "It's not like I was ever going to marry Mikal the *artiste*, who squatted in an abandoned building to 'live his art,' except for when he was clearing out my fridge and perving after my cousin. But you? You're all sincere. You're *choosy*."

"You're too good to me," I'm still laughing at her description of me, but it really is the truth; she *is* too good to me. Tania moved to Manhattan with me, even though she worked from home and didn't need the extra expense and hassle of downtown. She brought me takeout during the endless days of finishing my Ph.D. And she was the only one in the audience for me when I graduated.

"Men are trash," she said, "but I'm your wing woman until you find one you want. As long as we're outside of your apartment and away from your freezer full of ice cream cakes. I've gained fifteen pounds from *your* breakup." Oh, please. Tania's a curvy, bouncing ball of energy with wild brown hair and golden-brown eyes. Men always gravitated to her first.

"Fair enough," I sighed, getting out of the Uber. The line to get into this club had to be two miles long. "But can we hit another place? Somewhere that isn't clogged with Instagram influencers and second-tier soccer players?"

"No way," gloated Tania, "we're on the list, baby! I stole my boss's invitation to the grand opening tonight!"

"Uh…" my steps slowed, "your boss Marcel? The one you think is involved in insider trading?"

"I was just joking!" Tania protested, "Probably… anyway, what do you care? You're one of the Beautiful People tonight!"

The club was amazing, I had to admit; four floors, two celebrity DJs, chrome and suede booths, and stupidly expensive cocktails. And three of those overpriced Mojitos later, Tania and I were swirling on the Trance Floor, my arms waving above my head like seaweed and feeling so good about myself.

Oh, wait. Now Tania is grinding up against some Wall Street guy and I am apparently on my own. "I'm getting another drink," I shouted at her, and she waved, nodding. But I knew I couldn't peel her off Mr. $2,000 Suit just for a cocktail.

Leaning over the polished mahogany bar, I tried to get the bartender's attention, but he was too busy flirting with the hot guy four stools down to notice.

"One Mojito and a Glenlivet," a deep voice growled behind me as my back nearly felt scorched by a wall of body heat. Like magic, the bartender hustled down to me with my drink in one hand and a bottle of alarmingly expensive Scotch in the other.

"Here you go, Mr. Morozov," he stammered, carefully pouring the drink into a square glass.

Angling to the right, I looked up, and up, and up some more to stare at this giant's face. The guy was *built* - not like a lot of time in the gym built - but like he was born this way, with a broad chest and thick arms in his clearly expensive and custom grey suit. Dark hair, high cheekbones, tasty full lips. But the eyes... this guy was trouble. Twinkling blue eyes, but the twinkle looked tarnished and he had the flat gaze of a predator.

"And for you, darling," he said, bending down to speak to me as he handed me my Mojito.

"How did you know I was drinking Mojitos?"

The giant chuckled indulgently. "I might have been watching you for a while."

How did this man make a compliment sound like a threat? He was still smiling with a shark grin, like he wanted to eat me up as he put his hand was out. "Maksim Morozov."

He was examining me closely, like he thought the name should mean something to me, maybe he was one of those second-tier soccer players?

"Ella Givens," I managed, gingerly shaking his hand and stifling a little girlie noise when he lifted my hand to his lips to kiss it lingeringly.

"You are quite beautiful, Ella Givens." His voice was gorgeous; deep and rumbling through his chest, and his tinge of a Russian accent was pretty sexy.

So I smiled back. "Oh, you sweet talker. Well, thank you for the drink, Maksim. I should go find my friend-"

He nodded over my head. "She's dancing with a friend of mine. They look cozy."

I turned to see Tania giggling as Mr. Wall Street snaked up and down her body. "Yeah... that would be her, all right," I sighed, taking a gulp of my Mojito. "So, is this your first time here, too?"

He laughed. It was condescending, even though he was clearly making an effort to be pleasant. "Oh, no. *Gehenna* is my club. Why don't you join me in the VIP lounge?" It sounded less like an invitation and more like an order.

"That's really sweet, uh, Maksim, but I have an early morning." I took another gulp of my Mojito, hoping to get it finished and thus become my excuse to leave. "I'm going to have to drag my girl off your buddy there, so..." Rubbing my stinging eyes, I asked, "So, what does the name *Gehenna* mean?"

He leaned down to murmur in my ear. "It is the Russian word for Hell."

I put the cocktail down, and it made a loud, obnoxious clinking sound and some of the drink splashed over the side. I was going to make an embarrassed little chuckle but my tongue suddenly seemed to feel too big to fit in my mouth. The room was bulging oddly and whatever ubiquitous trance tune this was from Armin van Buuren was slowing down and speeding up.

Oh, no, nononono... I moaned silently.

Clumsily stepping back from the bar, I pointed angrily at the expressionless Maksim. "W- wait. I saw the buh...uh, the bartender make this?"

He leaned in close again with a whisper. "My bar. My bartender."

I should have screamed for help. I should have punched his pretty face. What I definitely should not have done was open my big mouth and sneer, "Your drinks are boring and overpriced."

Enormous hands fastened over my arms like shackles, squeezing cruelly. "Oh, darling, you have much worse things to worry about." Before I could come up with a snappy retort, my body slumped bonelessly and everything faded away.

CHAPTER 2 - RUN, RACHEL, RUN!

In which Ella just cannot catch a break.

Maksim...

An hour before...

"Boss, I'm sorry to bother you but I knew you would want to be made aware of this."

Patrick was one of the few non-Russians in my Bratva's leadership, just one step under my *Obshchak.* He spoke Russian fluently but enjoyed pretending he didn't know the language since a surprising number of other rival Brigadiers would speak openly in front of him.

"Come in, Patrick. What's on your mind?" The grand opening of my new nightclub *Gehenna* was doing just fine without me, and I preferred the silence of my office overlooking the numerous dance floors.

He couldn't wait to sit down, blurting, "Remember Rachel Marx, the bodega owner in Queens who disappeared with all the merchandise from our weapons storage under her store?"

My lip curled. We'd paid that traitor a generous sum for her basement storage and for the simple matter of looking the other way. With all the surveillance in place, we still couldn't figure out how she pulled it off.

"Oh, yes. I remember. I'm looking forward to killing her myself."

"You just got your chance, Boss. She's been sighted."

Patrick jumped a little as I shouted, "Where?"

"Right here," he pointed down at the club. "She's on the third level, the trance floor. Short black dress."

Pushing past him, I searched briefly before spotting her. Waist-length black hair, pale skin, tall.

There she was, walking into hell all by herself. "She's never met me," I said thoughtfully, "I'm going to buy her a drink. Make sure there are two men on the periphery in case she recognizes me or tries to make a run for it."

Striding down the private stairway, I cracked my knuckles. It had been a long and infuriating day, fighting a power grab from other Bratva families. I was going to enjoy this.

Ella...

Currently...

Regaining consciousness as my head was knocked painfully against the spare tire in the trunk of a speeding car will not make my list of top ten ways to wake up. I moaned and clutched my skull, trying to keep my brain from leaking out. What the hell just happened to me? Okay, I was freaking out. My memory was mush and I started shaking. Who did this? What happened to me? The trunk may have been cold, but I was sweating. Swiping my hand over my wet face, I tried to concentrate.

We were at a new club...

Tania was dirty dancing with a Wall Street rich boy...

The hot Russian guy bought me a Mojito...

"Are you kidding me?" I rasped painfully, "That slime roofied me!"

It was clear that the driver did not have my comfort in mind when they took another sharp turn, rolling me right over something that felt like a crowbar and into the trunk latch.

Trunk latch... I was almost sure it was a latch to the trunk because it was a sharp metal piece digging into my ribs. Of course, the roofie or whatever poison that Russian had dosed me with was still making forming a coherent thought difficult, but I was pretty sure. Cursing under my breath, my hands pushed against the surface of the trunk, trying to squirm into a position where I could maybe open the latch.

"Wh- what did they say in the "Y" safety class?"

The heel of my hand slammed down on the latch as I stifled a shriek, feeling the shock reverberate up to my elbow. "Was it push the tail lights out and wave your hand through the opening?" The image of a wildly flapping hand at a stop sign made me choke out a hysterical laugh, but it reminded me that the car had not stopped once since I'd regained consciousness. Which meant... I was not in Manhattan anymore.

I abandoned the latch to desperately hit the tail light, trying to get a look at wherever the hell this car was speeding through. Ignoring the cut on the heel of my hand as the red plastic finally broke loose, I wedged my face against the opening.

"How long was I out?" I wheezed, "What.. am I in Nova Scotia or something? Keep it together!" I didn't have the luxury of freaking out again. "Be rational, just..."

There was forest as far as I could see, stately pines lining the road and turning into an impenetrable mass past the car's headlights. Hands fumbling back at the trunk latch, I took advantage of the dim light coming in from outside, shoving at it as hard as I could.

"You evil son of a bitch! Screw you and screw your stupid club!" So much for staying calm, but my rage gave me strength, and the latch cleared the locking mechanism. Holding on to the trunk to keep it from flying open, I shivered as the frigid night air slipped in like searching fingers. "I just need this guy to turn a corner or get off an exit…" On the bright side, the chilly breeze was helping me wake up, bolstered by my fury. "Is this some messed-up grand opening special? A little, 'Welcome to my stupid nightclub' by way of a dose of Ketamine?"

The chance to escape finally came as the car slowed, making a turn onto a dirt road. "Okay, okay," I coached myself, "you got this." Perching on the lip of the trunk, I gritted my teeth and rolled out.

Any thought I'd had about rolling gracefully free from the automotive clutches of that roofie-giving lunatic was squashed by my acutely painful thump onto the roadside. I kept rolling until I hit a ditch. Thank god, the car's brake lights never flashed.

Scraping the gravel out of my palms, I turned in a circle, trying to figure out where I was. "Will they go after me if I head back, or if I keep going?" Looking up at the stars fading from the early morning sky, I really wished I'd paid more attention the last time a date took me to the Hayden Planetarium for a star show.

I didn't know what was ahead of me, but back there is Manhattan. Somewhere. Or a police station. Or someone who will lend me their cell phone. Or a baseball bat. My Jimmy Choo's heels had flown free some time during my ungraceful escape, so with a sigh, I headed back the way I came, barefoot.

It's funny, after the acute terror dies down and you're focused on the business of getting out of whatever mess you've gotten into? It's really tedious.

"This suuuucks," I was sort of singing my complaints in time to my steps, feet blistering and I was pretty sure I was going to lose the toenail on my left big toe. Cars had passed me a couple of times, but I'd jumped into the woods to hide. I had no idea if that sociopathic supermodel was looking for me yet, but I wasn't taking any chances.

Crap! What about Tania? She'd been dancing with that douchey Wall Street guy that Maksim said was a friend of his. Was she safe? Did they roofie her, too?

"No panicking," I lectured myself, limping along. "Given that I woke up alone in the trunk of that car, I'm going to believe she went home with Mr. $2,000 Suit and she's already kicked him out of the apartment so she wouldn't have to make him breakfast."

Unreasonably cheered by this, I forced myself to walk a little faster on the uncooperatively rocky asphalt. "How far is this? A couple of miles?" I ran six miles in Central Park nearly every day, but I'd been wearing shoes then and hadn't thrown myself from a moving car. "I bet it's about two miles."

"Two point three miles."

Nightclub owner and roofie expert Maksim Morozov stepped out from the shelter of the trees, all 6"6 of him, biceps bulging as he folded his arms. "Or, three point seven kilometers. Not bad on bare feet." He was freshly showered, hair still wet, and dressed in jeans and a t-shirt.

I reeled backward. "Th- there's no reason to count in kilometers unless we're in Canada. Did you kidnap me to Canada? Oh, and nice shirt, there. So tight. Didn't they have one in your size?"

He was on me in two strides of his stupidly long legs. "You just don't know when it's in your best interests to keep quiet, do you?" His massive shoulder dug into my stomach, breath huffing out on impact as he threw me over it and marched over to a jeep hidden in the trees. When I dragged back in enough air to scream and start kicking him, a hand the size of a dinner plate came down on my butt with a resounding 'thwack!' and hurt so much that it felt like my thigh was on fire. It hurt so much, in fact, that I didn't even notice the sting in my other butt cheek until once again, the forest faded to black.

Maksim...

Two hours ago...

"What do you mean, you lost her?" I roared at the *Идиот* shaking in front of me.

"I- I don't know, Pakhan, there was no disturbance from the trunk, I thought she was still out. But when I opened the lid, she was gone."

I punched him in the face. "You're lucky I'm not shooting you." He was rolling on his back, groaning and cradling what was likely a broken jaw. As he was dragged out of the room, I turned to Grigoriy. "Your man is useless."

Folding his arms over his chest, my *Brigadier* frowned. "My apologies, we will find her and he will be demoted to cleaning the warehouse shit stalls."

"Pull the traffic cameras from the club to here. She couldn't have regained consciousness until very recently. Send up a drone along the route with a body heat sensor."

Grigoriy nodded and left immediately as I threw the glass I'd been holding at the wall, enjoying the sound of the crystal shattering. She was not getting away from me again.

By the time I'd showered and had dinner, Grigoriy's men had caught the image of Rachel rolling out of the trunk at the turn onto the road to my hunting lodge. The drone tracked her marching back down the highway, hiding when cars passed by. She was certainly a stealthy little thing. How she'd managed to steal my weapons inventory in her bodega's basement was beginning to make more sense.

Driving down the dirt frontage road from the lodge, I drove just past her location and parked the jeep. Prepping the syringe, I grinned, listening to her muttering as she headed up the highway. So that smart mouth of hers was always in gear, even when she was talking to herself.

"...This suuuucks.... How far is this? A couple of miles? I bet it's about two miles."

"Two point three miles." I corrected, stepping out of the trees. Her fury at seeing me made me want to laugh, but I had to look stern.

She looked pretty rough, scrapes and bruises from her plunge into the ditch from the car, but still beautiful, pale green eyes flashing and those pretty, pink lips snarling at me.

"You just don't know when it's in your best interests to keep quiet, do you?" I chuckled, on her in two steps and throwing her over my shoulder, enjoying her little pained grunt as her stomach landed on me, knocking the breath out of her. I could feel her angry little feet and fists hammering on me, but she was too tired to make it feel like anything more than a tap. Still, I slapped her hard on the ass, enjoying her outraged shriek before plunging the needle through her skin and knocking this mouthy little thief out again.

Back at the lodge, I had my housekeeper Megumi clean her up and get her dressed again. Megumi gave me her usual hostile stare. She was the only one of my employees who got away with that look, but she'd been with the Morozov family for years. I'd rescued her from a human trafficking ring when she was sixteen and made her a member of our staff, the only one who wasn't Russian.

But now that I had Rachel back, I was in the mood to play. And I had the perfect opponent.

Ella...

At least I'm more comfortable this time.

Groggily sitting up, I held my forehead and looked around. *Yeah, an optimist, that's me,* I thought bitterly. It was a big room, it had the hunting lodge feel: big timbered beams, old-world plastered walls, and a ton of dead animal heads nailed to the wall. At least I was warm, the fireplace was blazing and I thought it looked really cheerful. Stumbling a bit, I stood up, rubbing my eyes and looking for a door.

"The door's locked, Rachel."

And there he was, lounging in a huge wingback chair by the fire. "What, no velvet smoking jacket, Maksim?"

The gigantic lunatic had the nerve to chuckle indulgently. "You're very focused on my wardrobe, Rachel."

"I find my humor deflects from more serious issues, like getting kidnapped. And my name's not Rachel, it's- what am I wearing?"

Maksim made a stern tsk'ing sound. "Well, I couldn't leave you in that dress, as pretty as it was."

I didn't answer, too distracted by this outfit. I looked like a model at a Survival Con, all dressed up in boots, cargo pants and some stretchy turtleneck thing.

Rising from his giant, stupid ostentatious leather chair, Maksim strolled over. He towered over me with a scary little grin. "Here," handing me a cold bottle of water, "you must be very thirsty. Three Mojitos...."

"Two roofies..." I added, slowly taking the bottle. There were beads of condensation on the surface of the bottle and I was seconds away from just licking them right off the plastic. He was right, I was dying of thirst and the water bottle in my hand made it so much worse. I gingerly tried the cap. Was the seal broken?

He caught the movement, chuckling again. "I wouldn't bother to spike the water, Rachel. I've already knocked you out twice. And you need your strength."

With that ominous statement, I cracked the bottle and drank thirstily, aware that Maksim was watching every movement of my throat with unsettling intensity. Putting the back of my hand against my wet lips, I managed, "Uh, thank you, Maksim."

"I want you in top shape for what comes next." He leaned in closer as I stifled a desperate need to start weeping and begging for my life. He smelled good, like expensive cologne and minty toothpaste.

It was silent for a moment, the only sound was the crackling of the blaze in the fireplace, and I realized he was waiting for me to fearfully ask, "What comes next?"

So, I didn't.

Grinning as if he could read my mind, Maksim pulled away, strolling over to the fireplace. "You're stubborn, I like that. Usually, *predatel'* - traitors - are begging for their lives right now, trying to volunteer information."

A weak puff of air escaped my slack lips as I watched him pull on a heavy glove and lift an iron poker, red-hot from the fireplace.

I should be seeking an immediate exit from this room, I knew that. I also knew this beefy mental patient would be on me before I could take more than three steps. So, my stupid mouth opened again.

"You know, you're going to get ash all over this paramilitary outfit if you get too close with that thing."

"Still concerned about the clothes, I see." He shook his head in mock reproach, coming closer with the poker in his gloved hand.

"Cl- clothes make the man, Maksim."

"And red-hot pokers severely disfigure the traitor, Rachel."

I tried to chuckle but it lodged in my throat. The gargantuan thug expertly spun the poker once and I stifled a scream as I felt the heat pass by my face. "It s- seems to me, that you went to a fair amount of trouble to drug and kidnap me-"

"Oh, and I did," he interrupted sourly. "I had to stab your driver for losing you so easily."

"Is he okay?" I almost slapped the back of my own head for that idiotic comment.

"No, Rachel. He's dead. But I stabbed him in the stomach, so it took a while. Do you know how excruciatingly painful it is to die from a stomach wound? How long it can take in the hands of someone who knows how?"

"N... not personally, Maksim," I managed.

Casually twirling the blazing-hot poker again, he grinned a little, watching me stifle a shriek. "The point here, is had you been a man, I would be using this poker on you right now. But since you're a woman..." He shook his head, "There are some things that are against our code." He was strolling around the room, still keeping between me and the door.

"Can you explain exactly what it is you're looking for, here?" Now that I was - sort of - sure the red-hot poker was no longer the main threat, I had to find out who he thought I was and why he was calling me a traitor. My big mouth just had to open again. "Why do you think I'm a traitor? Is this wartime? Am I a spy?"

Shockingly, this just makes him smile at me. Fondly. Like he's picturing all the tortures that they must save up for women. His massive shoulders shrugged. "So many more serious repercussions can be avoided if you tell me now where you've hidden my weapons that you stole from me."

Okay, just when I think this couldn't get any weirder, he just took a left turn into What The Hell Is Happeningville, I thought. "What weapons? What are you talking about?"

Am I insane? I thought, *Is this some kind of mental break?*

He shook his head, as if deeply disappointed with me, "you're wasting time. You *will* tell me where the weapons are - and if you've offloaded them already, you will tell me who has them now. If you give me the location, and the weapons stash is there, I'll let you live. If they're not..." he smiled at me fondly, "it will be so much worse. I will have to make an example of you, darling."

I was seconds away from sobbing and flopping on the floor like a terrified, boneless chicken. "I feel terrible about your dilemma, and your uh, your weapons stash, but you've got the wrong girl. Check my purse. There's ID. For Ella Givens."

He shrugged negligently, "Anyone can make a false ID, Rachel. But as we review this evening, you've lied to me, you won't tell me where my weapons are and you ran away from me. That was bad. Very bad. So..." Maksim twirled that poker again and the iron tip was still a sullen, glowing red. "So, I will reevaluate my plans. If you're a runner, why then, let's play."

"You're clearly athletic," he was walking and talking in his lecturing voice again, "you're still in great shape after rolling out of a car and walking a few miles on bare feet."

Swallowing, I wished I had another bottle of water as my dry throat made a clicky noise. "So what's the plan here, Maksim?"

He absently stirred the cheerfully burning wood in the fireplace. "Well, Rachel, I'm going to give you a chance. You like running." He was in front of me in an instant, backing me up against the wall. "I like chasing," he continued with an unholy gleam in his eyes. "I used to track men through the forests around St. Petersburg, it makes the blood sing."

I know my mouth dropped open and I'm making little gasping noises. I probably look like a goldfish. This certifiable hoodlum was vibrating with some dark, insane energy. The idea of chasing me through a forest was *making his blood sing?* I was looking at a tall, gorgeous bag of crazy.

"I'll give you a head start of say… thirty minutes," he continued pleasantly. "Then, I'm coming after you. If you make it to the highway first, you will tell me where the weapons are and you will go free, with no repercussions. Of course, I'll blindfold you so you can't tell anyone about this location, but I will let you go. If I catch you, we're going to do all of those things I talked about before."

"Is there a second option here?" Could I talk him out of this? This lunatic was built like an offensive lineman for the New York Jets. And what was his blathering about weapons? Why wouldn't he listen when I told him I knew nothing about them?

"Yes," he offered, "I begin your questioning now. It will be very unpleasant. You *will* tell me what I need to know, though you may not last long after that. Unless you would prefer to go with option one."

My chest began to heave in that ridiculous paramilitary outfit. "Yeah, I think your original plan is a good one."

Dropping the poker back into the fire, he spread his arms wide. "Excellent! I thought you'd agree." Turning to the curtains, he pulled them back and opened a set of French doors leading to the garden. Tapping his stainless-steel Rolex, he looked up at me. Grinning in a way that showed off all of his white, even teeth, he inclined his head to the open door.

"Run, Rachel. RUN!"

CHAPTER 3 - THIS IS A VERY-SELF DESTRUCTIVE WAY TO AVOID ME.

In which Ella asks the question; why does this stuff always happen to me?

Maksim...

Rachel was a good little actress, she looked genuinely confused when I questioned her. Why did she bother to deny knowing anything about the weapons theft? But this was dragging on, and I was in the mood to play. I'd been trained - along with several others under my father's command - in escape maneuvers in the thick forests on the family estate near St. Petersburg, First by being the prey, and then the predator. The consequences for being caught were severe; I still had a burn mark on my lower back to prove it. But I was never caught, and I never lost my quarry again.

This chase, however, would actually be enjoyable.

Ah, clever girl, I thought, watching her make a speedy loop around the lodge. She'd successfully deduced which direction was east, which was also a straight shot to the highway. Not that she'd get there. Lacing on my boots, I stood and stretched. Grigoriy was finishing the vodka we'd shared while counting down Rachel's thirty-minute head start.

"You know, sir, that I am absolutely certain you will catch the thief before she can make it to the highway, but should I have a couple of men stationed along the property line, just in case?"

"I am almost hurt by your doubts, *Brigadier.* But I will catch her. Call Patrick and Yuri, have them ready to mobilize men to retrieve the weapons stash as soon as I have her confession."

"I understand," he rose, nodding to me respectfully. "May I ask something?"

"Of course."

"You aren't... really going to let her go, are you? Was that merely psychological, like waving the red-hot poker in her face and telling her you stabbed the driver in the stomach?"

"A Pakhan is only as good as his word, even to a *predatel'.* If she's clever enough to evade me, she deserves her freedom," I answered, opening the French doors. My blood was surging, and I felt a long-forgotten sense of excitement. Life as Pakhan was often drudgery, with sudden moments of intense danger. Tilting my head to the skies and taking a deep breath of the night air, I smiled. This was good.

Ella...

I may be a runner, but there is a difference between a well-lit path in Central Park and the dense forest I was tearing through. The sun had set before Maksim let me loose and branches were slapping me in the face. The boots were good on the rough terrain, but they made me clomp around like I was a Shetland pony.

My foot caught under a root and I nearly went sprawling before I caught myself on the huge trunk of a pine tree. The bark scratched my arms but I hugged it like a long-lost brother, wheezing, trying to drag more air into my tortured lungs. The only clue I'd had about the highway was that when he captured me - for the second time - the sun was rising on my right. So that was east. When I'd glanced out the window of his trophy room, I'd watched the sun set. So… that would be west. When I flew out the doors after Maksim's terrifying kickstart, I'd circled the gigantic lodge first thing and headed in what I hoped was the easterly direction and back to the highway.

So was that lunatic really going to honor the thirty-minute thing?

Trusting his promise seemed really stupid, but he seemed like he enjoyed his twisted little games. I thought I'd been running for maybe an hour or so. Sometimes, when there was a certain twist or bend in the path, I swear I could see the glow of what must be the lights along the highway.

Hiking up those stupid cargo pants, I pushed off the trunk and kept running. Trying to come up with something happy to keep me from freaking out wasn't as easy as I'd hoped. The thoughts of what could happen if he caught me before I got to the highway kept getting worse the longer I ran. "Okay, okay," I wheezed, "here's my happy place; I'm gonna find Tania back in the city, we're going to have brunch and she is going to *freak out* about-"

A penetrating whistle ripped through the pines.

"Rachel! I'm on your trail! Do you want to surrender and just tell me what I want to know?"

His whistle felt like it just drilled through my cerebellum, and wincing, I pushed my exhausted, shaking legs into a run again. I was highly motivated by the vision of what would happen to me if he actually caught me.

I can do this...

I tried to cut through the terror, but it clogged my thoughts like mud. *If he catches me, I'm never getting out of here. I won't even live long enough to see the highway ever again. He's going to cut me up, he's going to get that red-hot poker and-*

"BOO!"

Screaming, I fell on my butt, sticks poking painfully against my bare hands.

Chuckling, Maksim strolled out from behind a thicket of brambles. "Oh, honey," he said, his faux sympathy infuriating, "did I scare you?" He stepped closer, slowly, deliberately, enjoying my terror. His full lips were pursed as he leaned down. "Are you having trouble catching your breath?" The sickle moon was behind him, and this Russian nutjob's sheer height and bulk blocked the feeble light, casting me into darkness. "You're crying?" Maksim crooned, leaning down. "Do you want to beg me not to hurt you?"

Tears were pouring down my cheeks, making muddy trails in the dirt smeared on my face. My left hand clenched into a fist, and it closed around a nice, thick branch. Heavy enough to cause some damage, I was pretty sure I could swing it, even with my shaking arms.

"I- is that what you want?" The words were choking me, my smart mouth suddenly deserting me. "You want me to beg you?"

Maksim's hugely wide shoulders shuddered a little in pleasure, his head tipped back. "Yes, darling. I want you on your knees. I want you to beg." His stupid designer jeans were still spotless, no smears of dirt or lashings of pine sap. Did he *fly* here? Did he watch me on some hidden camera?

I forced a watery smile. "Could you please help me up?"

Brushing his hair off his forehead with one hand, the monster of these woods examined me. "Give me your hand."

My filthy right hand gripped his and my left swung up with all my strength. I must have totally telegraphed it. He casually grabbed the branch just before it made contact with one of his prominent cheekbones. He was laughing, the sound was deep and echoing through the woods and I knew I was going to die when he leaned in close. Maksim Morozov's eyes were a kaleidoscope of fury, adrenaline, and something else. Something really scary.

"You just can't stop, can you, Rachel? Not with the smart mouth and the feeble evasion moves and your terrible acting skills? Why do I find you so tempting?" I yelped as his terrifying face was suddenly next to mine, noses almost touching. "Because, at this point? I just want to hurt you. Very much so. Almost more than I want the answers. Almost more than I want my guns back. So let go of the branch, and we'll-"

Later, I remembered it as a one-two kind of punch; he jerked his arm back sharply, yanking my feeble weapon free from my clenched fist and... The jolt made my boots slip out from under me in the mud and ripped my arm loose from his grip.

Falling backward, my scream was cut short as I landed with a thump, slipping down an embankment, sliding first like a turtle in the mud and then rolling. Rolling faster and faster, rocks digging into my back and ribs and branches and roots tearing at my clothes and hair until the last freefall of five feet or so, right into the water.

Fighting to the surface, I coughed up a throatful of river water, flailing and thrashing in an attempt to get to the bank. I'd known there was a river, I'd heard it earlier but I didn't know where it went and I was pretty sure I knew what direction east was but probably none of that mattered now because I was just going to drown. There was something wrong with my shoulder and I could only move my right arm, battered legs still kicking.

"RAAACHEL!" I could still hear that certifiable freak shouting over the roar of the river. "THIS IS A VERY SELF-DESTRUCTIVE WAY TO AVOID ME! BUT IT'S STILL NOT GOING TO WORK!"

Spitting up more rank water, I tried to kick to the bank on the opposite side. This was going to hurt *so* much when it all hit me. "Shut up," I garbled, "just shut up for five minutes. You're givin' me... Uh... giving me a... It's so..." I felt the cool mud against my cheek and this time, I passed out all by myself.

Maksim...

Blyad'!

How in the hell did this infuriating woman manage to end up in the river? Cursing all the way down, I quickly traversed the muddy bank, leaping over boulders and keeping an eye on her flailing hands. I would not allow her to die in any way other than by my hand, and at this point, strangling her was all I could think about.

"Raaachel!" I roared, "This is a very self-destructive way to avoid me! But it's not going to work!"

There she was.... Of course, she managed to make her way onto the opposite side of the river, just to spite me, I was sure. I watched as she collapsed on the muddy bank before she could climb any further. Fortunately, there was a wider, more shallow area just down from her where I could cross easily.

Holding up my phone to keep it from getting wet, I dialed Grigoriy. "I'm going to need a pickup, she's not only a thief and a traitor, she's unbelievably irritating. She managed to fall into the river." I heard him chuckle softly as I sent the coordinates.

Slinging her limp body over my shoulder for the second time today, I wondered how Rachel Marx could get in this kind of trouble and not have been murdered by now.

Back at the lodge, I dumped her limp body on my bed, calling for Megumi. "Clean her up."

Megumi's mouth tightened as if I'd waved a skunk under her nose. "Again?"

"Megumi?"

"Yes, Pakhan?"

"You do realize that my patience with you has an expiration date, and it is rapidly approaching?"

"Understood, Pakhan."

I left the room as she removed the shredded, soggy cargo pants from Rachel, muttering in Cantonese.

My good mood instantly vanished with a phone call from Patrick.

"Uh, Pakhan?"

This must be serious, Patrick always insisted on calling me boss, instead of my Russian designation.

My voice lowered threateningly. "Yes?"

"This is unacceptable and I submit myself to your discipline, I have no excuse-"

"What?" I snapped.

He took a deep breath. "The woman you are holding is not Rachel Marx. The real Rachel Marx was found dead tonight, dumped at the door of one of our safe houses. This girl that you have - she looked identical - we were sure-"

"Patrick?"

"Y- yes Pakhan?"

"Shut up and make sure the mess with the body is sanitized and not under police investigation. Then tell your *Obshchak* I will be speaking with him in the morning."

"Yes, Pakhan."

He gratefully ended the call, and I slouched back in my chair, tapping my fingers together. Punching in another number, I smiled as Yuri picked up instantly.

"I am guessing you're calling to tell me that you know Patrick completely mangled this business with Rachel Marx."

"Yes, he did."

Yuri was silent for a moment, no doubt waiting for me to start shouting and throwing things. "You seem very calm about this," he ventured.

"Do you know the phrase, when life hands you lemons, make lemonade?"

"I do," he answered, clearly puzzled. I took a moment to enjoy this; since I had rarely witnessed my *Sovietnik* being confused.

"The thieving *predatel'* may be dead, and the guns are lost. But there is a beautiful, though somewhat shaken up woman in my bed who has shown impressive intelligence and determination over the last twenty-four hours. And I do require a bride." Yuri's dispirited sigh made me grin. "Find out everything you can about Ella Givens, we'll talk tomorrow."

predatel' - traitor

ARIANNA FRASER

blyad' - fuck

CHAPTER 4 - WHEN LIFE GIVES YOU LEMONS...

In which Maksim is such a dick.

Ella...

For two blissful seconds - maybe as many as five or so but definitely two - I was completely comfortable. I was resting on a cloud, or something super fluffy like a wisp of angel's wings and I was perfectly warm.

Then, I opened my eyes.

I hadn't seen this room before but it bore the unmistakable stamp of Maksim Morozov. More dead animal heads nailed to the walls. A nice fire in the gigantic hearth - no poker in the flames this time, thank god - and of course, the gigantic Russian is sitting casually in another wingback chair by the fireplace, he's only wearing thin sleep pants and there's a laptop open on the table next to him as he spoke into a headset.

"I am not interested in what he told you. The senator is about to come home to find his house on fire if he doesn't come up with those files in a big hur-" He looked over at me with a grin. "I'll get back to you," he said before pulling off the headset.

"Well, look at you, *plokhaya devochka.* And you were worried about me hurting you? You did a fine job all by yourself."

There were so many things I wanted to say. First, a stern commentary about how blatantly he was showing off his bare, gorgeous chest, with those sculpted pectorals and massive biceps. It was almost desperate.

Also, at this point, I was totally rooting for my tragic disappearance as opposed to one more second in the company of this heartless lunatic.

Then, the fact that whatever he was drinking smelled like ass and it was not helping my mild nausea at all.

But I settled on, "What're... what... uh... are you drinking? It looks like puréed lizard."

Chuckling indulgently, Maksim rose and strolled over to me. "How are you feeling, my sweet little invalid?"

Trying to rub my stinging eyes with the back of my hand, I noticed it had an IV taped to it. "No, seriously. Is that lizard in that glass?"

Taking a huge swig, he clearly enjoyed watching my face turn green. "It's delicious. Do you want a sip? It's flaxseed, kale, chia seeds, spinach, swiss chard, and cinnamon."

"Oh, god..." I gagged a little. "I'd rather drink the lizard."

He shrugged, tapping the clear bag dripping something into my veins. "That's fine. You're getting all your nutrients from this bag right now. My personal physician made a stop to check on you and she's rehydrating you with an IV fluid."

I ignored him as contemplating the horror of a kale-sucking, sociopathic, serial killer made tears come to my eyes.

"I'm not a serial killer," Maksim corrected me.

"Oh, did I say that out loud?" I sniffled, "That wasn't planned."

"Yes, well..." he clicked his tongue thoughtfully, "Did my doctor add something extra in your IV? But, back to the point, I'm not a serial killer, I..." he paused, as if finding something terribly amusing. "I run the family business."

"Which apparently includes killing people," I croaked.

Shrugging, he straightened my IV tubing and took my pulse. "Well, that's not all of it. I do start and end wars. Deliver weapons and explosives. Retrieve desired objects and desired people. I golf."

For the first time in my life, I didn't know what to say. I was a swollen, bruised bag of skin and not much else. I don't think I have ever been this beat up and so exhausted. I couldn't run. He hadn't even bothered to shackle me, he knew I'd be lucky to flee as far as the bathroom. I just...

God, I hope he isn't going to sleep in here.

"No, I'm not going to sleep in the same bed with you," he had the nerve to look offended. "Yes, you said it out loud. Don't take this personally, but you're not at your most enticing. Get some rest. We'll talk tomorrow when you're not quite so fragile."

"There's something to look forward to," I mumbled, so exhausted that being terrified seemed like too much work.

"Rise and shine!"

It could have been Maksim's irritating good cheer or the fact that the sun was shining aggressively right in my face, but I opened my eyes. He was lounging on the bed, the IV was out of my hand and there was a stern-looking older woman in an honest-to-god maid's outfit standing at the foot of my bed, holding a tray.

"Megumi's got your lunch and then she's going to help you tidy up. I have a couple of calls to make."

I eyed Megumi. Megumi eyed me. She looked like she might be perfectly willing to hurt me, even in my fragile condition, so I wasn't sure whose company I feared more.

Megumi was not interested in conversation. She snapped a cloth napkin over my lap and plonked the tray on top. The salmon and risotto were delicious and I would have definitely enjoyed my first meal in three days if she hadn't continued to stand at the foot of the bed, arms folded and staring at me.

But when she helped me into the master bathroom and I saw a tub big enough to fit half a dozen people and maybe a small car, I was prepared to move past that. I sank into the hot water, there were flowers floating on the surface and some kind of oil that smelled amazing and made me feel almost human again. Afterward, the woman tried to dress me in some skimpy, flossy-looking lingerie, but I took it away from her.

"I can do this," I smiled, showing all my teeth and trying to look threatening. Megumi sniffed and stood back, shoving some irritating silky lounge pants and top at me and letting me dress before pushing me to sit in front of the mirror and brushing my hair dry. "Is there a sweater here?" I asked, "maybe some sweatpants?" She ignored me. Of course.

Maksim looked up with a dark little smile when I forced myself back into the room, watching the housekeeper instantly and silently absent herself. He swirled his drink, looking me up and down. "Well, *now* you look like that delicious girl I picked up in my club again.'

Oh, god, there was my mouth opening; "Well, you didn't exactly pick me up, you-"

He shut me up. Two lush lips fastened onto mine and it felt like he was sucking the life right out of me. His huge arms wrapped around me and lifted me up, feet dangling to move into the kiss. Well, Maksim didn't kiss me so much as attack my tongue, shoving his inside my mouth and tangling with mine, tracing inside my mouth and finally letting me breathe after taking my lower lip between his teeth and pulling it slightly past painful.

"Wh- what the hell are you *doing?* Get off me!" I sputtered, shoving at his shoulders and trying to move his face away from mine.

"I can't decide if I like your smart mouth or it makes me want to choke the life out of you," he mused, huge hand sliding up to cup my neck, his thumb stroking my rabbiting pulse. I was gingerly licking my lower lip, checking for blood after that kiss of his, and his gaze was making a leisurely tour of my barely-clad body.

"Well," I offered, "we could just have an evening of stimulating conversation and I could impress you with my wit-" Flying through the air and landing hard enough on the bed to bounce twice, I realized this beefy lunatic would not be going with that option.

"Darling, as much as I have enjoyed our little battle of the wits, I've put more time into wooing you to get my information than I have with any woman. Ever." I opened my mouth to laugh about the phrase "wooing," and he put up one thick finger. "I did not invite you to respond." Straddling me, he stroked my pulse again, his grip still light against my throat.

plokhaya devochka - bad girl

CHAPTER 5 - THE MILLION DOLLAR VODKA BOTTLE AND THE WORST PROPOSAL EVER

In which Maksim is infuriating.

Maksim...

"Let's begin again. What is your name?"

She was pinned underneath me, pale green eyes wide. "I told you at the club! Ella Givens."

"I must admit," I said, still stroking that lovely, long neck of hers, "that I wasn't paying attention at the time, because I was certain you were a former business associate of my Bratva who had stolen from me."

"The weapons stash, I'm guessing?"

"Correct."

"Maksim?"

I pulled my gaze from her breasts, beautifully showcased in the lacy lingerie. "Yes?"

"Could you maybe take your hand off my throat and let me sit up? It's really hard to concentrate when you're doing this."

I slid my hand from Ella's neck, down across the smooth skin of her chest, running my fingers over the slopes of her breasts. before moving off of her. I helped her sit up. "Let's continue. Would you like a drink? You might need one."

She immediately shook her head, and I chuckled as I poured myself one. Holding up the bottle, I appreciated how the firelight filtered through it. "This is a limited-edition Russo-Baltique. The vodka is filtered through diamonds, and it is the smoothest vodka I've ever had."

"Is that bottle really gold?" Ella's brows were drawn together, as if this was the most outrageous thing she'd ever seen.

I chuckled; this woman did have a way of making me laugh. "Yes, the flask is encased in 24-carat gold. The Russo-Baltique sells for a million dollars."

"Oh, my god!" Ella gasped, "That's just..." She paused, clearly thinking about her next words, which was quite an improvement.

"This is an example of the kind of lifestyle I lead. And the one you will share. Nearly everything you could possibly want will be yours, as long as you are dutiful and obedient to me." Her pretty pink mouth was opening and closing soundlessly in outrage. I put up my hand. "You will not speak. Yet. Our... acquaintance did not begin well, it's true. But I intend to remedy that by marrying you."

Ella's mouth opened and she growled out, "Oh, you have to be-" before apparently, the power of speech deserted her. This was progress.

Her face was concerningly pale, so my hand slid to the

back of her neck, making her look at me. "You're about to hyperventilate, take slow, deep breaths. Come on. Do it with me." I pulled in a slow inhale of air, watching her follow me, shaky but trying.

Finally, between her gritted teeth, "Could I have a bottle of water, please?"

Like the day before, she greedily gulped the whole thing down before squaring her shoulders and looking at me again.

"I'm a New York City girl, and chivalry in this town is so dead. So ironically, this is probably the most romantic proposal I've ever had, and that includes the one from my cheating ex-fiancé."

"Would you like me to kill him as a wedding present?"

"What? No!" Ella was horrified, "He's a cheating weasel of a man, but that's no reason to kill him! His punishment is that he has to be... *him* for the rest of his life. You can't just go around killing people!"

I shrugged, "I initially intended on killing you."

"You know, coming out with that offer - right after this deeply troubling proposal that I am certain is a joke - is disturbing, Maksim."

"I'm not joking about either thing, Ella." I enjoyed her appalled expression. Not exactly what a man pictures when he proposes, but this was unconventional, even for me.

She was moving backward on the bed, crab-like, attempting to ease away from me. I calmly grabbed her ankle, pulling her back. "You mistook me for someone else. I got roofied, kidnapped, chased through your forest, nearly drowned... Some people might call you a terrible host. But let's just... put this behind us and you send me home. I know just enough that obviously, running to the police would be ridiculous. Let me go home."

Sweet little Ella's voice trembled on the last word. I'd seen her weep tears of frustration and outright terror, but this sounded exhausted. It was endearing. It also would not work.

I strolled over to the desk, opened my laptop and brought it back to the bed, turning it to face her.

"Ella Givens, Ph.D. in pharmaceutical research, very impressive. Over a quarter million dollars in student loan debt. Parents are deceased… one older brother, Charles Sean Givens. It looks like your brother made off with your parent's entire inheritance. That must be painful, with such high debt." I looked up to see her lips pressed tightly together, furious and with those red cheeks, embarrassed.

"You ran a background check on me?"

"Of course, I need to know who I'm marrying, darling. Your closest friend is Tania Hernandez. It will comfort you to know that she was pounding on the club door the next morning after your disappearance, demanding to know what happened to you. You sent her a text this morning, telling her you're deeply infatuated with me."

"You have my phone?" Ella screeched.

My gaze rose from the computer screen, and she quieted immediately. Ah. More progress. "Of course I do, darling. And I've already sent your resignation in to Adalen Labs-"

"Who the hell do you think you are!" She leaped at me, knocking the laptop to the floor and slapping at my chest and arms.

Within seconds, I had her immobilized on the floor. "You do not touch me," I hissed.

"I don't care-" her voice was muffled, but she kicked and bucked with all her strength. "How dare you think you can destroy my life because it's convenient for you? How dare you-"

My tone was no longer genial. "You stupid girl. I am Maksim Morozov, Pakhan to my Bratva, and one of the most powerful men in organized crime in America... and Russia. This is not a choice. I require a bride. Immediately. You will suit the role quite well. We will marry next week with much pomp and circumstance." I pressed my mouth against her ear, "If you make any attempt to disobey me or disrupt my plans, I will kill your brother. And your best friend, Tania." Ella was no longer struggling, holding still in my grip, her chest heaving.

Rolling her over, I impassively watched her horrified expression. "Do you understand me, darling?"

It took her a couple of tries to get the words out. "Why? Why me?"

Settling more comfortably on top of her, I answered her honestly. "You fit my requirements. You've certainly proven your intelligence and will to survive since I drugged you with that Mojito. You're beautiful," I ran one of her glossy curls between my fingers. "And I want to fuck you." This enraged her enough to start struggling again, and I gripped her tighter. "I don't want to hurt you, Ella. But I will."

"You evil..." her fury sputtered to a halt, head dropping back on the floor in defeat.

I kissed her again, enjoying her flinch. "Good girl. We'll return to Manhattan tomorrow, and you'll meet with the wedding planner." She made a choked, furious sound but didn't move. "I've got some work to do. You will go to bed; we'll be leaving early."

The door had barely shut behind me before I heard her scream and something shattering against the wall. Shrugging, I continued to my study.

My staff was used to cleaning up broken glass.

CHAPTER 6 - MEET THE PAKHAN

In which Ella faces a supercilious supermodel secretary, a haughty housekeeper, and a murderous fiancé

Ella...

"This is insane!" I screamed at the top of my lungs, knocking the expensive-looking lamp off the desk. *This can't happen!* I thought wildly, *Someone can't just-just stroll in and decimate my entire life!*

Of course, that was exactly what this gigantic sociopath had been doing since the first second I'd laid eyes on him in his stupid, pretentious club. "I hate your boring, overpriced drinks!" I shouted at the door, knowing that I'd gone off the deep end but I was way past caring.

Married? He has to be joking. This has to be another one of his twisted head games, like chasing me through the forest, right? I'm going to wake up tomorrow and he'll drop me off at home. Really, I'm perfectly happy to ride back to Manhattan in the trunk, just to be away from him. I'm going to stop screaming, now. I'm going to calm down. I will never see him again.

By the time I stopped angrily pacing and mouthing obscenities, I was so exhausted from the drugging and the kidnapping, then more drugging and getting chased through the forest, that I almost instantly fell asleep.

"You need to get up now."

The tone was deeply disapproving, and as I opened my eyes, it belonged to a face pinched with disgust, like I was gum on the sidewalk and she'd just stepped on me.

"Yeah, thanks, Megumi. You're a ray of sunshine today." I rolled off the bed, making my way to the bathroom, shuffling like I was an 80-year-old.

I heard a loud, put-upon sigh behind me and a click as she hung something up on the hook in the bathroom.

"Well, you are a lot of trouble. Get dressed. You are leaving soon." Megumi marched out the door after glaring at me one last time.

I was struggling with the zipper on my dress when Maksim walked in. My eyes narrowed as they caught his in the mirror. He pushed my hands away, slowly pulling up the zipper. I could feel his curved index finger stroke my skin as he brought the zipper to the top of the dress, slowly fastening the tiny hook and eye. His hands slid to my shoulders, holding me there. I was acutely aware of their size; long fingers reaching down to the beginning slope of my breasts, calloused, and almost hot, searing my skin. I wanted to shrug free, but I didn't dare. His gaze was expressionless, but I still felt pinned.

"Are you ready to go home?" Maksim finally asked, and I nodded vigorously.

Maksim...

Walking away from her last night was harder than I'd

expected. I was certain she was suitably terrified. Telling her I'd kill her best friend and worthless brother guaranteed that. But her outraged tears... I almost wanted to sit and let her hit me for another hour or so.

Ella had handled everything I'd thrown at her, even when I thought she was the traitor I wanted I intended to kill. But the horror on her face when I informed her that we would marry- it was the most violent response I'd seen from her.

I was Pakhan. I did not feel guilt. But maybe, a little pity. She did deserve better. But I required her, and my needs would always take precedence.

Ella...

"Since you scoped out my entire life history, you probably have my home address," I tried to sound matter-of-fact as we headed into downtown a few hours later in a heavy, luxury SUV that I suspected was bulletproof. "But if you take-"

Maksim was still speaking into his headset, looking at some specs of something on his phone. My eyes widened as the driver turned onto West 33rd Street. I could see The Vessel - the huge sculpture that towered inside Hudson Yards come into view.

"Seriously, I'm the other way-" I tapped on the glass separating us from the driver. "Hey, you have to turn."

Finally hanging up from his call, Maksim watched me for a moment with that creepy, expressionless stare he had. "I told you, Ella, that we were going home today."

"Yes, Maksim, and my home is in the opposite direction, and-" A shadow seemed to move over his face, like a cloud over the sun. I did not recognize this man. I'd seen this lunatic Russian angry, furious, aroused, amused, even threatening last night, but this? This was terrifying, ice-cold Maksim.

"Would you like me to kill your brother first, or your best friend?"

He was not joking. It was quite clear he wasn't joking.

"Please, look- I can't do this, you've got the wrong girl, I can't-"

The SUV was turning into the driveway of a stupidly high, futuristic-looking limestone and glass tower. A smartly suited doorman stepped up to the car and stepped back just as fast as the giant bodyguard in front got out, opening Maksim's door. He didn't move, staring at me coldly.

"Make your choice, Ella."

He put out one big hand, and I stared at it. Did he hear anything I'd said since his twisted proposal? I felt like I was twittering frantically like a parakeet and he was tapping the bars of my cage like I was adorable.

"This is the only choice I will offer you. To say 'no,' and take the consequences, or say 'yes' and enjoy a life of luxurious excess." His hand was extended patiently, and feeling like I was stepping into an open elevator shaft, I took it.

Maksim...

My assistant Alina met me at my private elevator, already holding a pile of paperwork and files for me.

"Pakhan," she said respectfully, bowing her head, "welcome home. Will you have time to look over and sign some documents for me?"

As the elevator soared up to the 92nd story, I flipped through some of the most urgent documents. "I'll look these over. In the meantime, I would like you to take my fiancee on a brief tour of the penthouse and get her settled in one of the guest rooms."

"Of course, Pakhan," she said, nodding again and stepping aside as the door opened, knowing I always entered first. Behind me, Ella was completely silent, an astonishing thing in of itself.

Ella...

I watched the stranger that held me captive all weekend walk away without a second glance. I stood frozen in the entryway, sixteen-foot ceilings soaring up and over to an entire exterior wall of glass, overlooking the Hudson River. Some kind of black wood flooring glowed in the sunlight.

"Miss Givens? If you will come with me."

The crisp, no-nonsense tone of Maksim's assistant made me blink, looking over at her. She was beautiful, of course. Of course. Taller even than my 5"8 with long, blonde hair in a perfect high ponytail, full lips, and blue eyes like ice chips. Her tailored black suit likely cost more than my entire wardrobe. Oh, and gigantic breasts. Why wasn't that Russian gangster marrying this supermodel? She was right here, the whole time! By the way she was looking me up and down, I had a feeling she was thinking the same thing.

We left the entryway where two hulking guards in good suits that didn't quite cover a plethora of tattoos stood by the elevator. "Here is the great room..." she was walking and talking with her faint, Russian accent, gesturing right to left like a tour guide at the White House.

"The kitchen is here..." The wood and marble cabinetry and huge island mellowed out all the crisp stainless steel wall ovens, gigantic glass fridge, dishwashers... and a bunch of other appliance-like things that I didn't even recognize. Also, another guard stationed by a service elevator.

She made a crisp turn into the main hallway, which was bigger than my apartment. There was subtly-lit artwork on the walls; I paused next to one, head tilted. I could swear to god I'd seen this painting at the Metropolitan Museum of Art- a Renoir. Two sisters in summer hats with long, tangled hair; just like every little girl's hair gets. The oldest is reading to the younger sister and the world around them is dreamy, just swirls of summer color. I'd read a couple of years ago that it had been stolen from the museum. This couldn't be the same....

"Miss Givens?"

Oooo, I thought bitterly, *Alina the Vogue Cover Model is getting impatient.* Nonetheless, I followed her numbly down the long hallway as she pointed out several other rooms, pausing by one, and opening the door. Also, more guards. Guards everywhere.

"Here is your room." She sort of hovered behind me, herding me inside. Another expanse of shining wood floors, twelve feet high windows that looked out over the city, and a fireplace facing the sleek, modern bed. Everything was in grays, blacks, and creams and depressingly sterile.

"Your closet and dressing room…"

"Your bathroom…"

I was tuning her out by now because the whole reality of my morning was building to the point where I was about to crawl under the bed and start howling like a feral cat. Alina glided back to the door, "You will be called for lunch in-" she checked her Gucci watch, "ninety minutes. I will leave you to get settled."

"Wait, I-"

With a chilly, supercilious smile, Alina closed the door in my face.

CHAPTER 7 - "WHY IS HE MARRYING HER?"

In which Maksim shows off Ella. To a lot of angry women.

Ella...

I spent my quality alone time silently freaking out, putting a pillow to my face as I screamed, rocking back and forth. "This doesn't happen in real life," I keened, sitting on the toilet seat with the fan going and faucet blasting water to drown out the sound of my wailing. Sure, I'd done plenty of terrible things in my life. Every time my big mouth opened, I managed to screw things up. But seriously? How bad does someone have to be for Karma to visit upon them the deeply twisted weekend I just endured and now, the very real possibility that I have to marry him?

When I lost my parents in that accident, I tried to understand it for the longest time. Why them? They were such wonderful parents and kind to everyone. A therapist finally made me see that the adage, "Sometimes bad things happen to good people," may be trite, but it was also true. There's no rhyme or reason for why this is happening to me. It's not because I'm a bad person. It's just-

A loud knock on my bedroom door halted my feeble attempt at Zen and I turned off the water, slinking out of the bathroom as Alina opened the door.

"Perhaps you didn't hear me knocking, Miss Givens, but it is time for lunch and a meeting with your wedding planner." She stared at me impassively as I swayed a little.

"Thank you, Alina," I smiled wide, "I appreciate it."

When I used to complain to my mom as a child about mean girls at school, she'd always grin and told me to "Kill them with kindness. It will either win them over or confuse them. And either outcome is fun." I would kill Alina. Kill with kindness, I meant. With kindness.

Leaving my room, I looked down the hall to the imposing double doors at the end. I looked at Alina, who was hovering with a smile that was getting more forced by the second. "What's behind those doors?"

She drew herself up on those stiletto heels and looked down her nose at me. "That is the Pakhan's suite. No one is permitted to enter without his invitation."

Aaand, my big mouth opens again. "Oh, I see. At least until we get married next week. I'll probably institute a more open-door policy." I leave her standing there, her perfectly lip-sticked mouth open and walk into the dining room. And to my doom, because Maksim is standing there and it's clear he overheard us.

"I see you've had your tour around the penthouse," he said, looking unfairly handsome in an amazingly well-tailored blue suit that makes his eyes light up. I'd seen him in Smooth Operator mode at the club before he roofied me, but I didn't get a chance then to appreciate the whole package, how those long legs fit those pants so well, his jacket stretched perfectly across his broad shoulders. His hair is swept back and styled and you would have never known this was the same sociopath who'd been chasing me through the woods in the middle of the night.

"Yes, Maksim, Alina was so kind as to give me a tour."

"Excellent. I'm sure you're quite clear on how well you're guarded. No one can enter - or leave - without me knowing it."

"I see that, thank you." I'm right on the edge of sass and with witnesses to this interaction, it was probably time to shut up.

Staring down at me warningly, he says, "Karida, this is my fiancée, Ella Givens, Ella, this is our wedding planner, Karida Hassan. She's the most sought-after planner in New York City, but she's graciously agreed to step in at the last moment to help us."

Karida was also unreasonably attractive. Silky black hair swept up into a smooth chignon, beautiful, tawny skin, and liquid brown eyes. She was also - just like Alina - staring at me with an expression that meant she thought she would have been a better option for the position of Mrs. Maksim Morozov.

"Lovely to meet you," she said, with a distinct New Yawk accent that clashed hilariously with her exotic gorgeousness.

"And you," I tried to smile, but my cheeks were beginning to hurt with all the fake expressions I was forcing.

"Before you two sit down to lunch, I will have to say goodbye."

I must have looked like a complete dolt, my mouth hanging open and staring at Maksim, but he was so... charming? So incredibly charming. Not at all like the man who'd told me he was going to murder my only family and my best friend not two hours ago.

"But first, darling, I'd like to speak with you for a moment." Maksim smiled charmingly at me. Oh, so charming.

"Of course," I tried to look at him adoringly but based on his expression, it wasn't working.

His hand went to the small of my back and ushered me briskly into another room. How many rooms were there in this tribute to excess? The door was barely shut when his giant hand landed on my throat. It seemed to be a favorite move of his, and my watery knees still wanted to buckle in acute fear. Charming Maksim Morozov had left the building.

"Here is our backstory," he said sternly. "We met at my other club in-"

"You have another club?"

Dark brows drew together as he stared down at me, his thumb pressing slightly against my tap-dancing pulse. "The Chvrch."

"In the Meatpacking District?"

"Yes."

"Oh, I never go down there. All the skeevy guys from Wall Street hit the District to party, so-"

"Be quiet."

Maksim waited for me to nod before continuing. "We met at The Chvrch about six months ago and have been seeing each other quietly ever since. I proposed on a weekend trip at my beach house in St. John's. You have not been wearing your engagement ring because we had it resized to fit your finger. In fact-" He dropped his hand from my neck and reached into his jacket pocket and pulled out a velvet-covered ring box. Flipping it open, he pulled the ring free and had it on my finger before I could get a good look at it. "We are not confirming nor denying rumors that you might be pregnant-"

"Hey! Hey hey hey-" I shut up as his hand moved up to my neck again.

"But we moved up the wedding date rather quickly, so there will be speculation."

Heaving for breath, I stepped away from him. He was too close and I could smell his cologne and feel his body heat and it was all too much. I was aware that I could not have possibly done that if he hadn't let me, but I must have looked as terrified as I felt.

Putting his hands in his expensive suit pockets, my "beloved" fiancé watched me try to drag in enough air to avoid passing out.

"Ella."

This time, his tone was not as terrifying. "You have to control yourself. You have to look and behave as a happy bride-to-be would. This ensures the continued good health of the people you care about. I know you are quite capable of doing this."

My hand was on my stomach, mindlessly making sure the baby thing was fiction. He was so convincing that I almost believed it. "H- how do you know that?"

Now, he was Pakhan again. "Because you never could have survived the forest if you were not capable of courage and intelligence under pressure." His hand went under my chin and held me for a long, firm kiss. "Now leave your lipstick smudged and go out looking like the happy bride you're about to be."

My first good look at the ring was during the salad and entree courses at lunch. Who has five courses at lunch? At lunch? I was ignoring the pictures Karida was trying to show me on her tablet. Something about draping for the arch. What arch, I wasn't sure, but we'd been at this long enough to apparently delay the fifth course - dessert - which was the only thing I was living for at this point, because the wedding planner would not stop hammering this information into my skull.

"It was quite the miracle, but I did manage the secure the Grand Ballroom at the Plaza Hotel for the ceremony and reception, and I'm working the with NYC Fire Department for the fireworks permit; it looks very promising, and-"

"We're having fireworks?" I nearly bit a hole in my lip to keep from howling with laughter. Fireworks. Of course. Looking down, I caught a glimpse of the ring. The ring, not *my* ring, because this whole thing was a nightmare that I would wake up from soon.

It was really quite beautiful, though. An absurdly large - what - maybe five-carat emerald, square, in a platinum setting. There were more pale green emeralds flanking the larger stone, and it fit my finger perfectly.

"...So, when Maksim's mother and sisters fly in tomorrow, they'll join you for your dress selection. Is there anyone you want to invite?"

My breath left me in a huff. Maksim had a mother? He had family? He was ruthless and cruel, and it never occurred to me that he would be human enough to have actual siblings. I guess I'd been thinking he'd hatched from an egg of evil, or something. I looked up to see Alina staring at me, those ice-chip eyes of hers widened meaningfully.

"Oh, yes! I'm so excited to see them!" I gushed. "I'd... I'd like to have my best friend come; I'll give her a call."

"Fine." The tablet was pulled from my hands and Karida snapped her notebook shut. "Well! I feel like we got a lot done today," she smiled at me brightly, and I stretched my mouth into a facsimile of a grin in return. "I'll see you tomorrow at the shop."

Rising from the table, I walked with her to the front door. "Thank you, Karida. I appreciate all your hard work."

"That's just fine," she smiled kindly, looking at my stomach, "you have more important things to think about right now."

Remembering Maksim's casual comment about my "surprise

pregnancy," I nodded a little too fast. "Oh, yes, uh-huh. Well, thanks again."

I lingered in the entryway as the elevator door closed on her smiling face and the guard standing next to it gave me a look. I narrowed my eyes back and glared back until he bowed his head in respect. There was a brief flush of triumph until I realized Maksim must be standing behind me. I could feel that solid wall of heat his body seemed to radiate on my back.

"You're finished with the wedding planner?" He was still looking at some documents as he spoke. "Good, you'll need to get ready for an event tonight. The dress should have been delivered by now."

He turned and walked away from me, so I chased him down the hallway. "Wait! She said your mom and sisters are flying in?" Not that he slowed down, but I trotted alongside as fast as my Prada pumps would let me.

"Yes," he said absently, "from St. Petersburg. We will discuss how you address my mother tomorrow."

"Wh-"

Aaaand, he was gone again, the door to the study shut by a smirking Alina.

"There will be other significant families at the fundraiser tonight," Maksim was lecturing me as the limo headed closer to the Morgan Library and Museum for their annual fundraiser. I'd never been, of course. Even though libraries were almost sacred to me, $50,000 for a ticket was a bit beyond my budget.

"No one will expect you to know who they are, tonight. But Alina will have a dossier on the most important figures to memorize before the wedding." He was still checking something on his phone, so I was allowed to feast my eyes without him catching me. Because as much as it pained me to admit it, he looked amazing. I thought his expensive suits, perfectly tailored for him, would be the height of his hotness. I would be wrong.

Maksim Morozov in a tux is the death of women's undies everywhere, I thought resentfully. He's wearing a sleek, black tuxedo with none of the silly embellishments. And this man is *meant* for black tie. Black tie was invented for him. I hated that this man was so hot. I really hated that I might be one of those women whose undies were in danger of immediate destruction.

"A dossier. Okay. Um, I really need my phone."

Now he looked up, blue eyes as chilly as the Antarctic. "No, you don't."

"Maksim, please. I have to call Tania. She's not going to buy your fake texts for very long. She's my best friend, I won't-" My throat closed up; I was furious I had to ask for something as simple as my own phone. "I won't call my work, I won't tell anyone anything. I'd be insane to endanger anyone else."

"This is unwise." At least he wasn't saying no, his gorgeous face lighting briefly under the passing streetlights.

"I am assuming, that even Organized Crime spouses are allowed cell phones?" I was terrified for a minute that I'd gone too far as his eyes narrowed.

"Do you question, even for a second, that I will not kill everyone you love if you disobey me?"

"No," I managed between numb lips, "I do not."

The limo slowed as we pulled up to the library, bright with spotlights. He lifted my left hand, studying the play of light on the engagement ring. Kissing my knuckles, he nodded. "Be a good girl tonight and you'll have your phone when we go back to the penthouse." When the door opened, he leaned closer. "When I help you out, lower your eyes to the carpet. The lights will blind you for a moment. It will help you adjust."

Smiling shakily, I nodded. I appreciated the small kindness, but I wondered if there was similar advice for surviving life as a Bratva wife.

Still holding my hand in his warm grip, Maksim turned into Charming Mr. Morozov again as soon as the cameramen caught sight of him. Keeping my eyes down and a demure sort of smile on my face, I managed to get up the stairs without tripping on the skirt of my long dress.

"You look lovely tonight, darling." The deranged sociopath who had just discussed killing everyone I loved was kissing my left hand again, staring down into my eyes. I could hear a couple of women sigh behind me and wanted to gag. "Let's get you a glass of champagne."

I gulped down the first glass almost immediately, an action that made his brow rise, but Maksim got me another. "Sip this one, darling."

Simpering, I fluttered my heavily mascaraed lashes at him. "Of course, *sweetheart*." He gave me a warning look, but turned to accept the congratulations of an older couple, beautifully dressed and oozing the scent of money. I nodded and smiled at the correct intervals and tried to memorize names and faces as he led me deeper into the main hall.

"Brother! You finally showed up." We turned to find a man almost as tall as Maksim, with blond hair and a broader face, but clearly related. The man turned to me with a mischievous glint in his darker blue eyes. "And my dear sister-in-law!" He leaned in and gave me a lingering kiss on the cheek. Still hovering, he whispered, "I'm Yuri, Maksim's brother, and his *Sovietnik*. You two have been together for six months, I'm told, so of course, you and I know each other well. I am also quite sure that he hasn't actually told you anything about me."

My big mouth opens, "That's okay, he hasn't told me anything about anyone. Or anything, so this is on point for him."

Yuri threw back his head and laughed. *Wow,* I thought, *the Morozov genes are amazing and dripping with hotness.* He looked just as spectacular as Maksim in a tux and wore it like a man used to being a rich bastard.

"You're correct, my darling sister. In law," he added mischeviously. Taking my hand, he spun me around effortlessly. "You look beautiful tonight."

"Thank you, Yuri," I fluttered my eyelashes again.

This dress really was spectacular, it was form-fitting black with sheer panels of black chiffon over the dress, trailing behind me, with more chiffon for the sleeves and draping masterfully over my shoulders. I'd put on an aggressive night face full of makeup and my hair back into a low chignon. Maksim had not liked the chignon when I met up with him by the front door to leave.

"I prefer your hair down," he'd said, fingering one of the curls already springing loose from the updo. I had silently resolved to wear my hair up for the rest of my term of captivity.

Yuri's right eye closed in the most subtle of winks before turning his attention back to a frowning Maksim. "It's about time you introduce your *secret* love to the world, brother." Oh, yes. He was enjoying this.

Not so subtly pulling me away and sliding an arm around my waist, Maksim smiled thinly. "You know how I am about being unwilling to share, brother."

"I'm sure the gala will shine all the brighter since you've unchained your fiancee and allowed her out in public," Yuri goaded, still smiling pleasantly.

Maksim leaned into him and whispered something. All I caught was the phrase, "shit docks," which made no sense.

Swear to god, I thought, *this is more entertaining than anything on Netflix.*

As the night wore on, I was increasingly grateful for Yuri having my back as my dear fiancé introduced me to more people, several of whom he'd clearly slept with, because they were giving me the same look as I'd had from Alina all day; the *Why the hell is he marrying her?* look. More than one grabbed my left hand pretty harshly under the guise of admiring my engagement ring. Watching me subtly flex my hand after the last round of "congratulations," Yuri smiled down at me sympathetically.

"Are you ready for a break, sister dear? I'm sure I can find somewhere to sit down and something to eat." Eyeing Maksim, who was deep in conversation with someone who I'm pretty sure is the Lieutenant Governor of New York, I nodded gratefully.

Leading me over to the section displaying the Michelangelo drawings, Yuri pulled up two chairs. We eyed the drawings for a blissful moment or two of silence. Handing me another glass of champagne and a plate of hors d'oeuvres, he let me gulp down a couple of tiny bites of tuna tartare before speaking.

"You must feel very overwhelmed."

I stopped chewing to look at him. His handsome face was blandly pleasant. "Did Maksim tell you to be so..." I waved the miniature blintz I was holding, "so affable to me?"

Chuckling, Yuri folded his arms and slumped more comfortably into his seat. "We have not spoken about you, other than his lecture on the deeply romantic origins of your relationship."

I liked this guy. "Your English is more formal than Maksim's," I said, popping a mushroom cap with crab into my mouth, "did you move to the US at the same time?"

He shrugged, taking a lobster puff off my plate, an action I noted with some regret. "We did, but I spend a great deal of time in St. Petersburg, so the language shift isn't quite as effortless for me."

I watched him chew, the same square jaw as his brother's. I wasn't naive enough to trust him, but... "Do you agree with what Maksim is doing?"

His entire face seemed to freeze. "Don't make the mistake of thinking you can persuade me to do anything for you, sister dear. Maksim's mind is made up. Make it easier for yourself and just... go along."

I was dangerously close to tears. "He's taking my life away."

Shrugging, Yuri stood up. "You are not the only one pulled into a life you didn't anticipate. Some of us are born into our roles. There's no other way. I can be nice to you, Ella Givens, but I can't help you."

"It looks like the two of you are having quite the conversation."

My eyes closed. How did that gigantic Slavic thug move silently like that? It was creepy.

"Hello, brother," Yuri said pleasantly, "we were admiring the Michelangelo sketches."

Maksim grunted, "Marco Bianchi is here with his idiot son. Will you give him the specifics of the shipments for next month?"

"Of course, Pakhan," and Yuri was gone before I could ask him to get me more crab puffs.

Hands in his tux pockets, Maksim strolled around me in a

circle. "I knew you'd be beautiful in this dress." It reminded me of our surreal conversation about fashion when he'd been holding that red-hot poker at the lodge and I shuddered.

He frowned, "Are you cold?" Pulling off his jacket, he settled it around my shoulders. He cupped my head with his gigantic hands, fingers stroking my hair. "I think the only thing that could make you more beautiful..." he drawled, "would be to have your hair down."

Deftly, he removed my hair pins until the heavy weight of it cascaded over my shoulders. I gave a nearly silent sigh of relief as his fingers gently rubbed my scalp. This man... he could crush my skull between those monstrous mitts of his, but his fingertips were gentle, precise as he took away the strain from the hairstyle, and the evening.

"There," Maksim finished his massage, hands still holding my head, fingers deep into my hair. "Now, you are perfect."

I barely held in an unladylike snort. "That is not a word anyone has used to describe me. However, I do clean up rather nicely."

He did that elegant arching of the brow thing that looked so hot on him. "They're fools." His mouth was on mine before I could think of a retort, his hands moving my head where he wanted me for the kiss. Such a kiss... His tongue parted my lips, leisurely exploring my mouth, swallowing my little, surprised moans. Tilting my head up, he sucked my tongue into his mouth and I slumped against him.

No one this crazy should be such an amazing kisser, I thought, vaguely disgruntled. One hand was sliding down my back, over the curve of my ass, and pulling me against him, absently moving his hips against my stomach, back and forth, back and forth...

"I want to fuck your cunt with my tongue, the way I do in your mouth," Maksim said, his Russian accent getting thicker, like syrup pouring over me. His mouth closed over my chin, then my throat, the place where my neck met my shoulder, adding in a sharp little bite and chuckling when I yelped. "You're sweet, aren't you? I can almost smell you..."

There was a very noticeable bulge pressing against my abdomen and it was big enough for me to question whether it was his dick, or his gun. Maksim pushed his hips against me harder, whispering filth, and whatever it was only got harder.

"Oh!" said someone loudly, a woman's voice, "I hope I'm not interrupting anything."

Maksim gave a growl I felt clear down to my toenails and reluctantly pulled back, straightening the neckline of my dress. "Katya," he greeted ominously, "how are you?"

I turned to look at the intruder, my lipstick smeared and hair sticking out in all directions. And, she was gorgeous.

"Of course," I sighed, just under my breath.

Katya slinked closer, hips swaying in her fire engine red dress, her gorgeous auburn hair up in some elaborate style that I could never replicate, even with the help of six stylists and freedom from the laws of gravity. The lack of the laws of gravity also applied to her breasts, large and barely holding up her strapless gown.

"I heard the silliest thing," she tinkled in a voice like a fairy's, "that you were engaged? New York's most handsome, elusive bachelor..." Now her voice was getting deep and scary, "Engaged?"

Maksim squeezed me more tightly against him and lifted my left hand. "I am happy to say that's true. Ella darling, meet Katya Sokolov. Her father and I do business together."

She was rubbing her lips together furiously, not even glancing in my direction. "This is a joke, Maksim. You and my father are making the announcement of our engagement next week!"

He had the nerve to look genuinely shocked. "I'm sorry, I don't know what you mean. Your father and I have never discussed an engagement. And now, as you can see, I am taken."

Katya's flawless skin was turning the color of her dress, "But it was understood! My fath-"

Now, the Pakhan emerged, and his grip on my waist was approaching uncomfortable. "Your conversation is not appropriate, Katya." His cold voice should have given her frostbite. "If you'll excuse us, I'm taking my fiancée home."

There was a moment as we passed her, where I thought she was going to leap on me, and her hands tightened into fists. Maksim turned me slightly so that he shielded me during our exit and I was deeply grateful until a thought occurred to me as we waited for the limo to be brought up.

"You knew she was there, didn't you?" I looked up at him, his gaze still scanning the crowd. "When you were rubbing up on me and talking dirty?" He didn't answer me, only helping me into the car. I angrily scooted over as far as I could, looking out the other window.

He was taunting her by being halfway to having sex with me when she "caught" us. I'm going to be lucky if I live long enough to see my wedding dress, much less walk down the aisle in it.

CHAPTER 8 - SPEAK OF THE DEVIL AND HE SHALL APPEAR

In which Maksim's idea of conflict resolution is not the same as Ella's

Maksim...

My phone buzzed, and I sighed as I picked it up. This is the fifth call from the most entitled princess in the Bratva. Katya was also the most vicious. I put the phone on silent and after stripping off my tux, got into bed. My suite had a panoramic view of the harbor on one side, and downtown on the other.

I'd fucked more than one woman against the glass, looking down at my kingdom. The one my father had built and died for. The one I'd expanded, even though the older Bratva leaders thought they could control me. With the cool head of Yuri, we'd danced on the edge of all-out warfare, but there was an uneasy truce between the Bratva. And the Italians, and the Irish.

Instead of sleep, or strategizing, my mind kept drifting back to the temptation in the guest room just down the hall from me. Ella, equal parts infuriating and arousing. She'd be asleep by now, wearing some of that sexy lingerie my personal shopper picked for me from La Perla. My father would have mocked me for even knowing the name of a lingerie shop. But I enjoyed how scraps of silk and lace could frame a woman so beautifully. I was very specific about what I wanted for my new fiancée.

Groaning, I put one arm behind my head as the other hand drifted down to my cock, already painfully hard. Why was I waiting? She was mine. She was only a few steps away. But the vision of having her on our wedding night, the ring on her finger finally forcing her to realize there was no getting away from me... I wanted that.

My hand slicked up and down my cock, already wet with precome and the vision of her racing along the trail in that dark forest...

"Blyad'!" I groaned, squeezing harder. I could picture chasing her again, this time Ella knowing I would fuck her right where she fell if I caught her. She's too competitive to allow herself to be captured easily, I'd hear her furious gasps as she tried to outwit me. But eventually, I'd catch her. I would always catch her. And true to my threat, I'd fuck her right there, on the forest floor in the leaves and grass, pine sap sticking to us both and our breath coming out in a cloud of vapor as the only warm place would be inside her. I'd hold her head with one hand to keep her from the twigs and rocks, my other would be pulling her thigh high, pressing against her chest, and letting me pound into her deeper. My toes would dig into the dirt to push harder, and-

With a long groan, I came. I came harder than I had in months. Lying back for a moment, chest heaving, I grinned. If the thought of that woman made me come like this, the real thing might actually kill me.

Ella...

I look like the Stepford Wife version of myself.

Freaked out at meeting Maksim and Yuri's mother, I tried to dress in a way that showed I was a Responsible, Well-Educated Professional with Excellent Breeding. It seems the continued good health of everyone I love depended on it. I'd opened the doors to the dressing room this morning to find a rainbow of dresses, suits, coats, evening gowns, matching shoes and boots and...

Good god, this man is nuts. How confident can you be about successfully terrorizing your fiancée into marrying you? Apparently, confident enough to spend more than the gross national income of several small countries on a wardrobe for me.

I hate that everything fits perfectly. I hate that I love the clothes. Like, the green cashmere dress I'm wearing. I'd pulled my hair into a well-behaved ponytail. My nails and my lips were painted in a simple nude shade.

I felt like a complete fraud. But better a fraud than someone who had two funerals to attend.

I'm standing in the fancy little lounge area in the back of the bridal shop and it's just like in the movies; little white couches, a platform surrounded by mirrors, and champagne chilling in an ice bucket. This was *so* cheesy. I always pictured getting my wedding dress at Sak's annual sale, where fistfights regularly broke out over the best gowns.

"Damn girl I have missed you!" Tania came rushing in, hugging me from behind and I grabbed her arms tight. "Are you okay? What did that crazy Russian bastard do to you?"

Turning around for a proper hug, I whispered, "Shh, I'm not joking when I say this guy has ears everywhere. I'm so glad you're here!"

The high, excited pitch of teenage girls echoes through the quiet shop's dressing area before the owners of the voices show up, along with a tall, terrifyingly beautiful woman who is clearly the matriarch of the Morozov dynasty.

"Holy shit, I might pee myself if she looks at me," whispers Tania, hovering beside me protectively, but still looking like she was on the edge of a panic attack. Not that I could blame her, I was, too.

"Thank you again for being here," I whispered back, barely holding in a yelp as she pinched me.

"Yeah, we'll talk about that later," she hissed, "but for now, let's get through this. Where's your hot as balls fiancé?"

"You must be Tania."

She couldn't control her yelp and once again, how could I blame her? That lunatic Russian had slithered silently behind us.

"Oh, god," she smoothed the back of her hair, "and you must be-"

"The hot as balls fiancé, yes," Maksim interrupted smoothly. He shook her hand politely and I knew she was getting weak in the knees over his gorgeous black suit - Tom Ford, I happened to know - crisp white shirt and a blue silk tie that just matched his eyes. Damn him. He *knew* he was hot as balls.

He took me by the waist, pulling me against him, "Mother, may I introduce my fiancée? This is Ella Givens. Ella, this is my mother Inessa Alyona Belyaev Morozov." He spoke her name with a heavier Russian accent that was doing bad things to my body.

Holding out my hand, I tried to sound like a well-bred young lady. Which I was not, but there was no reason to let her know that. "Mrs. Morozov, it is a pleasure to meet you. Thank you for flying in on such short notice." The last was a dig to Maksim, which he let me know landed by squeezing my waist hard enough to make me smother another yelp.

Mrs. Morozov gave my hand the briefest of touches with an expression that indicated she was wishing for some hand sanitizer. "I hear a trace of a British accent. Midlands, I think?"

"Well- I-" spluttering for a moment, I forced a smile and nodded. "Yes, Birmingham." I could see Tania stiffening next to me, and Maksim's mother's sharp blue eyes caught the movement. She had his icy blue eyes, but the blond hair of Yuri.

She pinned me like a bug under her stare for a moment before turning to her daughters. "Girls, this is Maksim's intended, Ella Givens. Ella, this is my youngest, Mariya…"

"A pleasure," she gave me a slight wink and a smile, "welcome to the family, Ella."

Ooooo, I thought, *Mama didn't like that,* enjoying Mrs. Morozov's pinched expression. I like this girl; she looked about twelve or thirteen.

"And Ekaterina, just entering University this year."

She couldn't quite meet my eye, but Ekaterina still smiled, "Nice to make your acquaintance, Ella."

"Mariya and Ekaterina, so nice to meet you both." These two gave me hope. They looked like they might want to be friends, rather than murder me and dump me in a ditch, which I was pretty sure was their mother's first choice.

"Well then," Maksim smoothly broke the staring stalemate, "I must be off, I have a meeting in just a few minutes. Ladies, enjoy your afternoon. I trust you'll help my beautiful fiancée find the perfect dress?"

That man could not sound less interested, I thought. Not that I could blame him, this whole nightmare could not be further removed from any modest wedding plans I'd had with my swine of a fiancé.

My former fiancé. The one Maksim had oh, so thoughtfully offered to murder as a wedding gift. This train of thought was not helping.

"Thank you, Maksim," I smiled sweetly. Okay, it was more of a grimace but I was working on it.

He took my chin in his long fingers, kissing me slowly and then whispering, "Behave," in his darkest tone.

There was an awkward little silence before Karida, the wedding planner said brightly, "Well, let's begin! Would anyone like champagne while Ella tries on the first dress?"

"Um, not for me, thanks," I said, eyeing the long rack of dresses. "I'm a terrible day-drinker."

"I'm not!" Tania offers, and I head off to the dressing room as Mariya and Ekaterina start negotiating with their mother for a glass.

The first dress makes me look like a bridesmaid at a second-class hooker's wedding in Vegas. The deep V-neckline made my girls spill out immediately. *Hmmm,* I thought, *maybe Karida's not quite over the idea that she should be Mrs. Maksim Morozov.*

The second one is a mini dress. Like something a stoner chick in the sixties would wear with white knee-high boots. Or maybe a wedding at Burning Man.

Really? Now I knew Karida was screwing with me. Dress number three was a pale lilac dress clearly made for Scarlett O'Hara because I looked like an escapee from a torrid antebellum romance novel.

"Ella," Karida's voice is a little strained, "everyone's looking forward to seeing how you look."

I look like an idiot, that's how I look, I thought resentfully. Stomping out into the room, I step up on the platform, enjoying the appalled silence.

"Who selected these dresses?" Inessa Alyona Belyaev Morozov was not pleased.

"These were all based on Ella's tastes," Karida says quickly, throwing me under the bus.

There's a snort from Tania. "Ella wouldn't be caught dead in that dress. She'd rise up from her grave and haunt whoever put her in it for eternity."

Oddly, this seems to please Maksim's mother and she pulls my best friend out into the boutique to look at other dresses. I'm about to change out of the minidress when I hear a familiar voice.

"Look, I just need a minute!" It's Marla from work. She's one of the few women who work in my department. We're like a tiny island of estrogen in the raging sea of testosterone of our fellow lab rats, who aren't nearly as funny as they think they are by putting boxes of tampons on our desks with a note that reads, *'That time of the month?'* when we dare to disagree with their analysis.

"I'm sorry, ma'am, but the store is closed for a private fitting, you'll have to come back tomorrow-"

"My wedding is tomorrow!" she objected, "I just need the shoes that I ordered with my wedding dress, so please just- hey, Ella? Is that you? Oh, my god woman where have you *been?*" She ignores the clerk's objections and bustles over for a hug. "What happened to you? Farid said you just resigned out of nowhere? No warning?"

"I... I had to, I'm getting married too, and it was really sudden, and I just..."

Her open, honest face scrunches up. "But... you worked your ass off for that position, you were so excited."

I rub my forehead; I can feel a headache creeping up on me.

"I was, and I just-"

"Ma'am," it's that officious sales lady again, "I asked you to leave and come back tomorrow."

"Hey, uh..." I check her nametag, "*Teal?* I mean, uh, Teal? Please just give my friend her shoes and put them on my tab, okay?" *Teal?* I thought, *there's a classic stripper's name.*

But she sniffs haughtily and nods to Marla, who smiles at me hopefully. "So, you are coming to the wedding, right? You RSVP'd?"

My smile fades. "I'm so sorry, Marla, I just- everything's up in the air and my fiancé's family just flew in and..."

Always the sweetest woman in the lab, she leans forward and hugs me. "I understand. But let's have coffee soon and I'll tell you about the new pharmaceutical trial, it's amazing, the-"

"The L-36 Neurology CaP?" I said wistfully. I was supposed to be the lead on that trial.

"Yep," she said. "Well, I'll get my shoes, but you don't have to pay for them! See you soon."

I watch Marla and my professional future walk out the door. Just talking to her brought back all my ambitions, my dreams, and how important this pharmaceutical trial was going to be. Six years of graduate school, gone. My Ph.D.? Worthless. All because of this heartless Russian.

I put on dress after dress, nod, and smile mechanically and I have no idea what any of them look like. Tania finally slips into the dressing room after the tenth gown.

"What's going on? Mentally, you're not even here." Her worried face peers over my shoulder in the mirror's reflection and I slump onto the fancy little chair.

"Will you just... pick something and go out and tell them it's my favorite? I can't do this anymore."

Here's why she's my best friend; squeezing my hand, she whispers, "We will talk later, you sneaky little shit. But for now, let's get you out of here."

I get out of the lace monstrosity squeezing my ribs and stare at the girl in the mirror. It's not me. I don't know who she is.

Maksim...

"Mother. How was it?"

She swept majestically into my office without knocking, as usual. She seats herself on the sofa in front of the fireplace and looks at me meaningfully. Yuri, who was going over some shipping reports with me, coughs to cover his chuckle.

"Would you like a drink, Mother?" I am resigned to this taking as long as she decides it will.

"Why, thank you, darling. Vodka, neat, if you please. That swill they served for champagne is still trying to fight its way back up my throat."

With a silent groan, I thought of the work piled up and waiting for me, I made drinks for us all.

"Your bride-to-be, she's quite..." she pauses, delicately sipping her drink, and Yuri's amused gaze meets mine. "Quite unusual. Not your type, really, is she darling?"

"Ella is exactly my type when it comes to selecting a wife."

She's waiting, I can tell, for me to expand on my statement. But

I remain silent, smiling pleasantly.

"She seemed a little despondent toward the end of the fitting," Mother said, "it took her quite a while to come out of the dressing room."

"Where is she now?" I asked.

"In her room, I believe," she rose, straightening her skirt and sauntering toward the door. "Such a mystery, and that accent… I'm quite curious about her history."

"Mother…" I growled, "she is off limits."

"Of course, dear." And she's gone.

"What's this about an accent?" Yuri's interested. He was the one who ordered Ella's background search, there was nothing about a British connection in the report.

"You know how Mother is with accents. She heard a tinge of a British accent when she spoke with Ella, she even narrowed it down to the Midlands, if you can believe that. Ella didn't look happy about it, but she confirmed she was from Birmingham. I'd planned on having you contact The Creeper again to see how he missed that."

My personal cell phone rang, and I pinched the bridge of my nose with my thumb and forefinger. It was Sokolov.

"Do you want me to stay?" Yuri asked, though I could tell the little bastard was fighting a grin.

"Get out of here." I could hear him laughing down the hall. He'd pay for that. Clearing my throat, I answered. "Hello, Pavel."

"Maksim." His voice was gravelly, furious. "Katya came home in tears last night. She told me something that can't possibly be correct."

"I'm assuming she told you about my engagement." Something crashes in the background, broken glass, I believe.

"How dare you! Marrying some American cunt and spurning my Katya?"

"Be careful how you speak about my bride-to-be," I snarled. How dare this *Мудак* talk to me like this?

Sokolov is bright enough to back off, at least a bit. "The arrangement between you and Katya has been planned for decades."

"This is the first I've heard of it."

"Your father and I planned to unite our families when Katya and you were of age, we spoke of-"

"Again," I interrupted, "this is the first I've heard of it. You and I have never spoken of this and I have been seeing my fiancée for over six months."

"Then why this sudden wedding!" Sokolov shouted.

"It has been planned for some time," I grinned, pausing for a moment, "but we have news that requires us to move the date up to next week."

"She's pregnant?" I hear something else shatter. There must not be many breakables left in his lurid mansion.

"That's not something we're discussing, but you should be receiving your invitation today. I do hope you can join us. Goodbye, Pavel." I end the call quickly, cutting him off mid-shout. The old *svoloch'* was lying about creating an arrangement with my father- he hated the Sokolovs. In fact, more than one had died at his order without ever being traced back to us.

I think back on what my mother said about Ella getting upset. Maybe it's time to pay her a visit and remind her of what is at stake.

Ella...

It had been easier to pretend that this whole horror story since Maksim roofied and kidnapped me was just... some weird fever dream and that I'd eventually wake up and get ready for work, reminding myself to never drink tequila again because it gave me terrible nightmares.

But seeing Marla at the wedding boutique smacked me right in the face with a big dose of reality. I'd lost my job and likely, my career, thanks to this unconscionable swine. Everything I'd worked for. I'd held down three jobs during graduate school, and tolerated misogynistic professors and then co-workers. I succeeded by working harder than they did, I knew I was smarter. And if I don't magically wake up, this is real and my life is over. And I still didn't understand why Maksim decided on trapping me in this Bratva freak show. Why? Why me? It can't be to keep me quiet about the whole, "Sorry we kidnapped and threatened to kill you, it's a case of mistaken identity, oops!" I'd have to be suicidal to ever speak of this to anyone.

So, why me? Maksim was apparently Bratva royalty. I don't know how they determined that. Highest body count? How many kilos of cocaine sold?

"There you are."

Speak of the devil, and he shall appear, I thought sourly.

"Why are you sitting in your closet?" He's leaning against the door, arms crossed and looking infuriatingly casual in his perfect suit.

Standing, I rubbed my sweaty hands on my dress. "It's quiet."

Maksim arched an elegant brow. "This entire penthouse is soundproofed. It's the quietest spot in Manhattan." He put his hands in his pockets and strolled over to me. "You selected a dress?"

"Yes."

He tilted his head, looking at me curiously. "What does it look like?"

"It's…" I had no idea. Tania picked something and sold his family on its excellence, "…white?"

His head lowered, like a wolf scenting a prey animal, which in this case would be me, because he moves closer. "Darling, you don't seem excited. My mother, in fact, commented that you seemed upset and hid in the dressing room."

I'm circling around him and backing toward the bedroom, where there's more room to maneuver. "Please tell me one thing, Maksim."

"And what would that be, Ella?" We're in the middle of the bedroom and I'm contemplating making a break for the door or the bathroom.

"Why me, Maksim? Just tell me the truth. I'd have to be clinically insane to tell anyone about last weekend, so why? I mean, half the supermodels from New York Fashion Week would give up a Vogue cover to marry you."

A dark little smile moves over his stupid, gorgeous face and it's creeping me out. "Well, Ella, I needed someone beautiful, but I also needed an intelligent, well-educated wife who could handle the stress and intensity of being a Bratva bride. You check all those boxes. You have… hidden depths. So intriguing."

"There's no intrigue, Maksim, none here." Yeah, I'm taking my chance on an escape to the hallway.

An expensively suited arm slams the door shut before I can slip through. "Oh, Ella. Did I ever tell you what happens to people who lie to me?"

I'm squished between him and the door. "Another trip through the forest, Maksim?"

"Well, Ella," he drawls, throwing me over his expensively suited shoulder like I'm no heavier than one of the throw pillows that goes flying when he dumps me on the bed. "If you were a man, I'd shoot you in the head. Or, torture you first, depending on whether I needed to make an example of you. But in the Morozov Bratva, we have rules, standards. One is that we don't kill women unless their crime is unforgivable."

I shriek and start thrashing again as he yanks up the back of my dress. I'm wearing more of that flossy, fancy lingerie since I don't have any of my nice, sensible cotton undies. These, as I recall, were nearly transparent and the heat from his palm radiates right through them.

"But I think a good spanking is a start."

Remembering that the man's hand is the size of a dinner plate, I thrash harder under the first explosion of pain on my ass. "Stop it! I'm not a toddler and I'm not one of your- OW! Maksim, you cut this out!"

"That's ten more." This time I scream because his hand lands across both cheeks and directly over the flaming mark of his last slap.

"I hate you!" I scream as loud as I can. "I hate your stupid penthouse and your stupid wedding dresses and your stupid Bratva!"

He paused for a moment, I could feel his hand hovering over my blazingly painful ass, and then a low chuckle. "Oh, Ella. You're going to pay for that." I can feel him tear my poor, pathetic undies right off me and his hand slams down again. And again, and again. Every time I think I've fought my way off his lap, his leg or arm slams over me and I'm trapped again. I have no idea how long this lunatic Russian keeps spanking me, but my entire bottom half is finally numb.

I had *never* been spanked. Not even as a child, my parents were anti-corporal punishment and this was unspeakable. Women got off on this? Seriously? Because I'm as limp as a flounder and crying when he lays me out, face down on the bed. Then something cool is sliding over my fiery skin and my weeping subsides enough for a groan of relief to come through. Then another streak of cooling comfort, and another, and I realize he's stroking his tongue along the marks he made. I feel him slide a pillow under my hips, raising me up, and then-

"Wait! You just- you stop that!" But, he doesn't. Maksim pushed my legs apart, held open by his broad shoulders and his mouth is on me, his tongue sliding up and down my center, pausing to pull one of my rapidly swelling lips into his mouth for a bite that is just hard enough to make me screech again.

"Be quiet, *plokhaya devochka.*" He's talking, face buried against my pussy, I can feel his mouth moving as he scolds me. "I can make you hurt, and I can make you feel better, you'll be wise to remember that." His tongue gets back to work, sliding in and out of my passage, circling my clitoris as I angrily try to pull away from him.

"If you move again, I'm binding you to the headboard with my tie."

Before I can yell at him, Maksim's finger slides inside me as his lips fasten onto my swollen clit and he *pulls.* He pulls and I come, shrieking, kicking, shaking...

What the hell was that? I thought, dazed and pissed off. *How could I come that hard? I hate this man and want him to die!*

Abruptly, his weight is off me and he runs his knuckles up my spine. "Go take a shower. I'll leave some cream to rub on your bruised little ass. Unless you'd like me to put it on for you?"

I roll away from him and off of the bed with a thump. Right

on my butt. Which makes me strangle my scream. Maksim is straightening his tie in the mirror, looking completely unaffected. As I'm weaving unsteadily towards the bathroom, he calls out, "We're taking my family out to dinner. Be ready in an hour. Wear something green, I like you in that shade."

It was right then that I vowed I was going to kill this man. No matter what it took.

CHAPTER 9 - MY LITTLE SUN

In which Ella endures Satan's Spa Day, a murderous carpool buddy, and the wedding of everyone else's dreams.

Maksim...

I'm certain I can actually smell the hate that is radiating from my blushing bride.

I'd spanked Ella that afternoon because I could see that she was withdrawing, curling inside herself. I'd seen it before, captives or hostages who simply checked out. I already knew that she operated better from rage than fear.

Dinner at the exceptional Le Bernardin was desirable and expensive enough for my mother.

They had offered both Royal Osetra and Golden Imperial caviars, so I knew she was pleased. She was moodily nursing an after-dinner tea while watching Ella chat with my sisters. My fiancée started the meal coldly furious, wincing subtly every time she adjusted her position, but by the cheese course, she was giggling at a story Ekaterina was sharing about a disastrous college tour.

I ran my finger over my lower lip. I'd not seen my sisters this animated and chatty for a long time, and it was clear Ella drew it out of them. This, of course, was lowering her even further in my mother's view. Yuri leaned across the table, watching the exchange and then winking at me.

"There are times I doubt you, brother," he murmured low enough to escape our mother's notice. "But she is clearly one of your better ideas." He watched as she flinched slightly, as she moved her chair a bit closer to Ekaterina's. She glanced over at us as she did, eyes narrowed and alight like the fires of hell. Yuri hurriedly picked up his drink, chuckling behind it. "Weren't you supposed to be winning her over with your charm?"

"What makes you think I'm not?" I haughtily defended myself.

This time, Yuri nearly choked on the mouthful of vodka he was trying to swallow. "You don't think I've seen your ex-girlfriends hobbling around after one of your spankings?" He smiled at me innocently, the little bastard. "When will you learn, brother, that violence is never the answer?"

"You're angling to handle that next shipment by the shit docks."

It was my favorite way to humble an arrogant lieutenant or irresponsible soldier. Some of our most sensitive cargo came in next to the dock that handled all the offloaded sewage from the biggest ships and cruise liners. You could not remove the smell from your pores, even if you burned your clothes and showered in vinegar.

Yuri mockingly held up one hand and turned to speak with Mother. My gaze moved to Ella, who winced slightly as she turned to include Mariya in the conversation.

I finished my drink. She needed a more effective way to cope, I couldn't spank her every time she started pulling away, especially since it was an activity that could be far more satisfying in other circumstances. What I needed was another Bratva wife from an arranged marriage. A happy one.

Ella...

"Okay, you better start talking." Tania was not screwing around.

I groaned, taking off my sky-high heels and sitting on my nice, cushioned window seat, angling on my right hip to keep my weight off my painfully sore butt. I'd spitefully refused to use the tube of cream that Maksim left on my bedside table. Knowing him, it was probably laced with paprika or stinging nettles or something.

"Sorry, I just got back from dinner with his family."

"Seriously? With his mom staring at you the whole time? I swear that woman is an emissary of Satan."

"The girls are nice, though. I think his mom has to be terrifying as the Ominous Bratva Matriarch."

"You're mentally putting her title in capital letters, aren't you?"

"Stop it," I laughed, and it felt good. I hadn't laughed for a long time.

Tania's laughter died off. "Tell me. Everything."

"Way to kill my happy buzz," I sighed. "I'm guessing you've already done some research because I know you. So, we won't discuss specifics."

"Yeah, you just got your phone back, right?" Tania snorted inelegantly, "I don't know anyone with worse luck than you. So, here's what I pulled up on Wikipedia:

Maksim Aleksander Morozov is the Russian-American CEO of numerous shipping and export companies, along with ties into banking, investment firms, real estate, nightclubs, and more. He took the helm of running the Morozov empire after the death of his father, Yevgeniy Maksim Morozov, in a hunting accident five years ago. His net worth is estimated to be over four billion dollars.

Morozov is well-known in the social scene in Manhattan and has dated several high-profile models and socialites. He is notoriously private and rarely allows interviews. He's a generous donor to several charities and sits on the board of directors for Safe Passage, a global non-profit that battles human trafficking.

"Okay, that's what I know," Tania says, "so tell me what the hell happened and why you're getting married to this dude that every publication refuses to call a gangster even though everyone knows it?"

"Yeah..." I give the safest version I can, in case that weaselly Russian put some kind of bug in my phone. "...and that's, apparently, why I'm getting married in three days."

"What do you get at Christmastime for the girl that has everything," she says in a TV-ish announcer voice, "how about a forced wedding to a man of dubious origins?" She draws out the word 'dubious' with her spiteful brand of glee. "Oh, god," she groans, "are you getting one of those godawful Christmas-themed weddings?"

"I don't think so..." my stomach sinks, knowing I paid absolutely no attention to any of the details Karida has been badgering me with every time we're within fifty feet of each other. "But now that I think of how she threw me under the bus with those hideous dresses... It's like *Gone With the Wind* threw up on every porn film ever made and they had a bastard fashion child."

"You should definitely buy your own lingerie for the wedding night," Tania says wisely, "she's probably going to try to wedge you into a full-body leatherette bodysuit with chains under the wedding dress. Of course, Maksim's seen you naked, so why bother? Just get the dress off and have at it. He's blessed in that area, isn't he? I'll bet he's huge. Maksim's totally got that BDE going on."

"Maybe you should be marrying him," I snarl, "at least you're seeing an upside here. And I wouldn't know. About his junk."

"You haven't had sex with him yet?" Tania exploded, "You're kidding!"

"No," I'm thinking about how odd that is. "His mom's here now, and his little sisters, so maybe that's kind of creepy to him. But at the lodge, you would've thought he would ... I don't know, seal the deal on this insane marriage thing."

"Just as well," she's apparently attempting to be comforting, "it's not like you have much experience, Miss Vanilla, and Maksim's probably like some **world-renowned anal master.**"

"Thanks, bestie," my tone might have been a little chilly.

"Sorry." She wasn't. "But you know... it's not like your ex could have ever found your G-spot, even if you gave him a map and a flashlight. You know that Maksim can probably go for-"

"I'm hanging up, Tania."

"Seriously! I bet he carbo-loads so he can just aggressively service you 'till-"

"Goodnight Tania."

Throwing my phone on the bed, I run my hands through my hair and groan. Tania really wasn't perving after my sociopathic soon-to-be spouse, she's just some kind of tangent bloodhound. Once she thinks of some random offshoot in the conversation, she'll just keep yapping about it until I leave the room or hang up.

Sex. With that lunatic? He's probably one of those freaks who has tried everything once, and all the really weird stuff twice. A billionaire mob boss and an unmitigated villain. He's the type who has memberships to horrifying sex clubs and probably has a dungeon behind some mysterious sliding wall. Like a panic room. But for sex so bizarre and unnatural, he has to lock the room down on a timer so his victims can't escape.

"This isn't helping your state of mind." Great. I'm talking to myself. "So what?" I say, "There's no one else to lecture me, so I'll just have to do it." That realization was even more depressing. I had friends, good office buddies, and most importantly a best friend who would do anything for me, and I for her. In this new and extremely unwelcome world, I had no one.

"Go to bed," I sighed, pulling off the expensive dress and deliberately leaving it scrunched on the floor. Hissing as the cool sheets touched my sore and heated ass, I eyed the cream

Maksim left me suspiciously. I put some on my fingertips, it was cooling, and I rubbed some on my right cheek. "Oh, mygodthatissomuchbetter," I mumbled. I finished half the tube but with my poor rear finally not feeling blistering hot, I fell asleep.

Two days to the wedding. And then one.

I remember the playground at my elementary school, the old, rusting iron roundabout that was popular back when school districts didn't really care if you lost an arm or got tetanus. My friends and I would spin it and then race around and around, trying to grab one of the metal handles and jumping on. I was always the last one to come aboard, the handles slipping out of my grasp just as I thought I'd managed to climb on. This feels like that; everything moving faster and faster and no way for me to hold on.

"Time for your spa day!" Kardia trills, and I just want to crack her over the head with her ever-present tablet.

"You know, I really don't need it," I plead.

"Don't you want to be *pampered?*" She seems genuinely shocked and all the other girls are clustered by the elevator in Maksim's penthouse and I force a weak smile. Surely, I can't be the only woman in North America who doesn't like 'spa day.' I always have things to do. Important stuff. Things I would be thinking about while getting my toes done or enduring a massage that I know I will come out of even more stressed than when I went in.

But... I get my toes and nails done in a soft neutral polish. My feet are viciously attacked to scrape away callouses and the three top layers of skin. There are things rubbed on me and scraped off of me. I am given a massage that's pretty good until I feel something warm spread over my pelvis. I have cucumber slices on my eyes and they go flying as I sit up with a scream.

"What the hell did- *Ow!* What is wrong with you!"

This woman looks a lot like someone who would play the Stern German Dominatrix in a porn film. "You're being a big baby," she scolds, "you were the one who ordered a Brazilian."

"No!" I shouted, cupping my stinging lady garden protectively, "I did not!"

"It's right here on your chart." She's rolling her eyes. Yep, sure enough, a "full Brazilian" is cheerfully circled. Twice. In red ink.

Karida. That spiteful cow. And now the Stern German Dominatrix has to finish the job because I have this godawful bare strip.

I threaten the hair stylist with death when he picks up his scissors. "You are not cutting my hair. Not a single quarter inch."

He gasps, clutching his non-existent pearls. "It's very clear on your chart that-"

Yep, I'm going to push Karida in front of a bus the minute we step out of this hell-spa. "I don't care what the chart says. I didn't order it. You people have already ripped out every hair follicle below my neck. You're not getting anything on top. Is that clear?"

He looks frightened and agrees, doing some conditioning thing with a "nourishing mask" and a "gloss protectant" like I'm the paint on Maksim's Maserati.

Thank god he's not the Stern German Dominatrix who xeriscaped my girl parts. I'm pretty sure she would have just stabbed me with the scissors and kept cutting.

"Wasn't that great?" Karida chirped adorably, making me examine the street for a vehicle big enough to push her under. Some really heavy. Like a tank.

Mariya, who is as tiny and precious as a fairy princess, does a dainty little pirouette. "It was! I feel so relaxed."

Maksim's mother is eyeing me. "You don't look as refreshed as I'd expected, dear."

I offer a huge and uncomfortably fake smile. "Oh, I'm just absorbing it all."

Checking her watch, Satan's Wedding Planner says, "Oh! We have to get going! We need to get you all to the Four Seasons to get ready."

Groaning, I realize I must have left my messenger bag by the hair stylist's station. "I have run back in and grab my bag-"

"No problem," Karida bundles the female contingent of the Morozov clan in one of Maksim's ubiquitous black SUVs. That car heads off and she points to the one drawing up to the curb. "I'm going to make sure the bill is settled. Do you want to grab your purse and meet me back here?"

"No need."

The dark, gravelly voice behind me makes us both turn and look. It's Lurch. That's what I've named him since he's never spoken a word in my presence. Lurch is a bundle of muscle slowly turning to fat with a nose that has clearly been broken sixty times or so. Scarred knuckles and a mean little face, he's got to be a former boxer, I'm thinking. He's usually in Maksim's security contingent.

He nods at Karida, "Go." Fixing his gaze on me, he points to the open door of the SUV. "You wait."

My cold, narrow-eyed glare clearly will not cow him, so I spin on my heel and head for the SUV, thumping ungracefully into the back seat and slamming the door shut.

"This is how you look after a spa day? I would demand my money back."

This cannot be happening. It's Katya, that crazy Russian girl who lost her mind when Maksim told her we were engaged.

"What are you doing here?" Yeah, not my most clever response.

Katya gives a high, tinkling laugh. It's adorable. She's wearing a bodysuit made of the delicate skins of unicorns or something and it fits her perfectly. Not a single lump or bulge.

"You remember me, don't you."

I'm eyeing the door, and as my hand reaches for the handle, the automatic locks click closed.

"You're not leaving until I give you permission, *сука.*"

I am unreasonably pleased because I know this word, thanks to our old lab supervisor, a misogynistic prick and also, a Russian.

"I think you calling me a bitch is a bit out of line, kitten. I'm not the one you should be mad at." Aaand, there's my big mouth again.

I almost immediately regret this statement, because as she leans closer, I can see the crazy stewing in her dilated pupils. She and Maksim really *are* made for each other.

"You, *сука,* are in my way. Ordinarily, I would simply have you kidnapped and placed in one of the Sokolov whorehouses." She checks her Cartier watch. "Unfortunately, I have to hurry home to change for Maksim's *wedding.*" Now, she's hissing like a viper and it's really freaking me out. "You won't be there."

"I won't? I'm pretty sure I'm on the guest list."

My big mouth has no preservation instinct.

She pulls a gun out of her Birken bag and points it at me. I hear the click of the safety releasing as she says, "You have two choices. Take this bag of money-" she thrusts the Birken bag at me, "-and get the fuck out of this city. Disappear and I'll let you live."

"What's the other choice? You have no idea how cranky Maksim gets when I'm not on time." I know I'm pushing my luck, but I'm hoping to drag this out and give Lurch time to come back with my purse and save me. Unless... is Lurch actually helping this lunatic?

Her right eye is twitching and I know I'm about to die. This somehow feels even worse than when Maksim kept threatening me with murder and ruin.

"The other option is I shoot you, right now. Not to kill. Just to sever your first cervical vertebrae, which will make you a quadriplegic for the rest of your life. And then..." she smiles dreamily, like she's discussing her best orgasm ever, "I will come to visit you in whatever disgusting care facility you are placed in. I will have terrible things done to you."

My lungs are compressing under my ribcage and I can't draw a full breath. There is a huge 'thud!' against my door and the window shatters, Lurch's giant paw reaching in to tear the door open while his other holds a Desert Eagle, pointed at... the empty space the psychopath had occupied seconds earlier.

"Are you hurt?"

I screech and jump, knocking my elbow painfully against the partition between the front and back seats. "I'm o- okay. She was going to shoot me, or- or- or put me in a family whorehouse which doesn't sound right but-"

"Move over." Lurch shoves in next to me and slams his gun on the partition, yelling at the chauffeur. "Drive!"

"What do you mean you didn't see her!"

We're parked in front of the Four Seasons and I'm still yelling at Lurch. "How could you possibly not see her? She had a gun pointed at my face, dude!" The hotel doorman is resplendent in his fancy suit, moving uncomfortably from foot to foot but hanging on to my car door, politely ignoring the broken window.

"I did not see Miss Sokolov. The door was locked and you would not let me in."

A cab pulls up behind us and Karida storms out of it and she is *pissed.* "Why did you leave me? Do you know how behind schedule we are?"

That hulking Slavic douche just folds his arms and leans against the car, smirking, and then it hits me. I never gave him the demented chick's name.

"You are *such* a liar!" I shout over my shoulder as the lobby's golden revolving doors swallow me up.

"Well, it's official. I'm completely screwed."

I'm staring at myself in the monstrously large mirror, all dolled up and looking regal and untouchable and totally not like myself.

"Yeah, you are," Tania agrees, hovering behind me. "At least you're gorgeous."

"Well, the dress is…" I look down, absently smoothing the full skirt, a cream chiffon overlay, and the pale, strapless silk underneath. It reaches mid-calf and it actually is something I would have picked myself.

If I was getting married to someone I loved. By choice.

"At least they didn't trowel the makeup on," Tania was still trying to cheer me up, in her Tania-like way, "just enough to make you look like a much hotter version of your actual self." She'd shoved everyone out of the dressing room for a moment, telling them we needed "a heart-to-heart."

"Uh, huh..." I could feel the tears rising and I struggled to stop myself. I was dead if I messed up this makeup job. "I'm not getting out of this, am I?" I could see her sympathetic gaze over my shoulder and the finality was painful. "No climbing out the window. No carjacking the limo."

"Yeah, I don't see that happening," she said, trying to straighten my veil. "Look. You're getting married to a rich, hot, bastard. That's the dream of like seventy-eight percent of the female population of Manhattan. He's letting you keep *me*, which is a massive bonus. I think Maksim sees me as your emotional support animal, or something."

I gave a watery chuckle. "Yeah..."

"Oh! I almost forgot..." Tania hands me a little box. "Your blue."

Maksim's mother gave me the 'borrowed,' an alarmingly large teardrop diamond necklace, and the 'old,' the family's diamond earrings that matched the necklace, which was currently hanging off me like a noose. I opened the box and found her half of our friendship bracelets.

"Remember? We got these at the mall when we were fourteen?" Tania prodded, "You have the half of the heart that's red, my half is blue." She's putting the little chain around my wrist and straightening it. "You can do this. Sure, you're kind of fucked, but you might end up liking that big-dicked mob boss, right?"

Naturally, Maksim's mother steps back into the room at the

end of Tania's pep talk. "Are you ready?" Her tone is glacial.

Maksim...

It's likely my mother will never forgive me for not having the ceremony at the St. Nicholas Russian Orthodox Cathedral in Manhattan, but there are people even my considerable fortune and persuasive abilities cannot sway and the Archbishop is one of them. He did, however, deign to marry us here, and he is standing behind me, Yuri at my side, as we wait for Ella to enter the ballroom.

The doors opened and the guests rose, turning en masse to watch my bride walk toward me.

o Gospodi... she is exquisite. I've seen this woman filthy and dragged from a river. I've seen her looking demure and proper to meet my mother. I've seen just how sexy she can be in the right dress. But here? My bride is elegant, regal. She sails down the aisle in a dress that clings to her breasts and waist and flares out at her hips. She's wearing the Morozov diamonds. They belong on her. They belong *to* her.

And she belongs to me.

Her hands are shaking when I take them in mine, and I squeeze them lightly. "No fears, *solnyshko,*" I whisper, and she nods, just a bit too fast, but we turn to the waiting Archbishop, and he begins. I hold her gaze with mine as he blesses us three times, I hold her hands for the *обручение*, and guide her on to the *рушник* to make our vows. Yuri and her irritating friend Tania hold the golden crowns over our heads and I look into her translucent green eyes, keeping her with me, here, in the now. I can't let her drift away from me.

When the Archbishop proclaims us married, I cradle her beautiful, fragile face in my hands and kiss her. I devour her. Ella's lips are soft, and she allows my tongue in easily and it twines with hers. Her chest is heaving against mine and I can feel her soft breasts. I ignore the cheering crowd and the Archbishop who clears his throat repeatedly, and I keep kissing her until her first, helpless little moan and she sags against me.

When we turn to greet the guests as husband and wife, I'm stunned. I had never, never expected to feel this solemnity, the power, and seriousness of the words and rituals. Ella was mine, completely and utterly.

I would show her that tonight when I finally had her alone, in my bed.

CHAPTER 10 - WHERE'S THE LEMUR SANCTUARY?

In which Ella and Maksim's union is consummated. A lot.

Ella...

At least the wedding wasn't Christmas-themed.

The massive ballroom was transformed into a glittering snowscape, with silvery white trees, strings of lights that glistened like stars, and bountiful arrangements of flowers in every shade of white. Ribbons and embellishments were all navy blue, and it might have looked overly masculine if it hadn't been for the whole fairy tale forest feel.

At least that spiteful cow Karida got that part right, even though my girl parts still stung and throbbed from my waxing attack. But as for walking down that aisle... Mrs. Morozov had suggested they grab a male relative at random and have him walk me, but I turned them down, it was one of the few battles I won. I was coming into this with no one, aside from Tania, who had my back literally and symbolically, being just behind me as my steps slowed the closer I got to the arch where the dude wearing a huge gold and white crown thingie was waiting with... *him.*

I *hated* Maksim, and I hated him more and more with each step. I finally felt a punch in the region of my kidneys as my best friend whispered, "Get moving!" I realized I'd stopped at some point and the guests were beginning to murmur.

I couldn't feel my arms or legs, everything felt numb; except the heat from Maksim's hands as he squeezed mine. As much as I hated his guts he grounded me, anchored me enough to attempt repeating what I was told to say. My teeth chattered against the goblet of wine he drank from, then offered to me, so Maksim held it steady, his hands wrapped over mine.

Tania and Yuri stepped up behind us, holding heavy golden crowns. They hovered them just over our heads, and I could see Tania's skinny little arms shake. It didn't stop her from winking at Yuri, who gave her a quick grin in return.

The woman really had no shame. At all.

Maksim took my left hand, sliding my "engagement" ring - *can it really be an engagement ring if there's no actual engagement?* I thought, and then my wedding ring. To my horror, a slight chuckle erupted from me from the same line of thought, is it really a wedding ring if...? Maksim is staring at me, eyebrow lifted and I realize the guy in the huge hat - the Archbishop? - is staring, too. Tania nudges me, handing me a ring. I've never seen it before, but it suits Maksim, a simple, thick, platinum ring. He's lifting his left hand, squeezing my right hand with his, urging me on.

I'm not religious. However, there was something about these ancient rites, spoken in a language I don't understand that's terrifying me. This is a serious thing. It feels bigger than me and the man who's squeezing the hell out of my hand. It feels like something I'm never getting out of.

My dilemma is solved when Maksim pushes his hand forward, slipping the ring onto his finger without my help. He has a death grip on my right hand as he leads me in a circle, three times, following the Archbishop.

When we're back in place, the Archbishop recites scripture to Maksim, who nods respectfully, and then turns to me. "And thou, O bride, be thou magnified as Sarah, and glad as Rebecca, and do thou increase like unto Rachael, rejoicing in thine own husband, fulfilling the conditions of the law; for so it is well pleasing unto God."

I realize he's changed my blessing to English, and I hold back a sniffle. It's a moment of kindness on this horrible day that I didn't expect, so I smile gratefully and nod, too.

It's like these last words set off a starting pistol, because my new husband takes my face in his giant hands and latches on. It's less a kiss and more a mauling, especially at first, his lips sucking at mine and his tongue sliding in without permission. I would think this is in bad taste during a religious ceremony, but the longer he's attacking my mouth, the louder the cheers get. At some point, I'm sagging against him, and Maksim wraps an arm around my waist and keeps going, his other hand spanning my jaw and keeping me steady.

Is he...? Is this conniving, perverted gangster trying to make me kiss him back?

His smooth lips are softer, his tongue gently toying with mine and urging me to slide it into his mouth. The wedding guests are cheering loud enough that this is sounding more like a rugby match than a wedding.

And then, I blow it.

Just one whimper. Just one girly noise and he finally pulls back, his beautiful face still scarily intent and focused, but at least I can draw a full breath again. He turns, leading me back up the aisle, nodding and smiling in his most patented charming way. I'm praying this mess wasn't filmed because I'm sure I look like a cross between a lunatic and a simpleton, mouth hanging open and a wide-eyed stare.

Because this Russian mobster owns me. Legally. And in the eyes of God, if there is one. But worst, in the eyes of the Bratva.

"Holy shit, I think I just found that iceberg that sank the Titanic!" Tania's moving my hand under the light, enjoying my wedding ring. "Seriously, are you walking with your right shoulder higher than your left yet?"

Yuri, who's been keeping suspiciously close to her, chuckles indulgently. "My brother never does anything by half-measures."

Satan's Wedding Planner bustles up and starts yanking me away. "We need to get in position for the receiving line."

"Please let go of me," I'm trying to come up with a complete string of words that will convince this red-lipsticked harpy to get her hand off of me before I bite it. Karida ignores me, of course, until Tania steps in front of her.

"Hey! Let go of her," she says sharply. "You're going to bruise her arm and that will not look good in the wedding videos." Karida releases me like I just set her hand on fire and I smile at Tania, mouthing, "Thank you."

"I have to go to the ladies' room." I was already backing toward the exit and Karida glared. "Five minutes."

One of Maksim's thugs is following us, but at this point, I don't care. It's not like I can manage a quick getaway in a $25,000 Vera Wang wedding dress. We pass a small corridor leading to the hotel's kitchens and lo and behold, Lurch is getting a blowjob from one of the banquet servers, he's leaning up against the wall, looking very pleased with himself.

"Aren't you on the clock?" I snarled. He looks up with his mean, slitted eyes, but he's trying to finish and get his pants zipped at the same time, so I don't think he's a master at multitasking.

Once in the ladies' room with the door locked, I slump against the velvet fainting couch, grateful for the first time that we women get furniture in our fancy bathrooms and the men don't.

"You don't really have to pee, huh? Are we hiding from someone?" Tania's rubbing my back and checking her hair in the mirror.

"Aside from the obvious reasons that would make me prefer cutting off my arm to standing in a reception line to shake hands with made men and mobsters, there's a girl here…"

"One of Maksim's exes? Because you know with that huge jackhammer dick, that man has left a lot of ladies wanting more-"

"Please, Tania," I moaned, "no more dick talk, okay? When we came out of the spa today-"

"They made you have a spa day?" Her sympathy was genuine, she knew my stance on anything spa-related.

"Don't make me relive it, but when we came out of the spa, Lurch made me get into the SUV alone while he got my purse."

"Who's Lurch?" She looked confused but she was kind of enjoying my nickname for that Slavic douche.

"The guy we just passed in the hallway-"

"The giant boxer-type dude getting a blowski?" Tania laughed heartily until she saw my expression.

"When I got in the SUV, there was a woman sitting there. We met at the Morgan Library fundraiser last week. Maksim was making out with me to piss her off and spark a confrontation so he could make it clear he was off the market. Her name's

Cat... uh, Katya, that's right, Katya Sokolov. She seemed to think she was getting engaged to Maksim and lost her shit when he flaunted my ring. Anyway, she locked down the car and flashed a gun at me. Telling me to get out of town or she was going to shoot me and paralyze me or put me in her family's whorehouse or- it's all getting mixed up in my head. But she's here, Tania! She's here and I'm supposed to, what? Shake her hand and thank her for coming to the wedding?"

I was desperately blinking back tears because I could not picture what Karida would do if I smeared my eyeliner.

Tania apparently had the same idea, eyes widening and frantically plucking tissues out of the fancy gold dispenser. "Oh, shit, oh shit don't cry!"

"Even when Maksim kidnapped me and sent me on that insane run through the woods, or threatened to kill all my loved ones? Even he never held me at gunpoint. She's my first held at gunpoint experience and I didn't handle it well."

"Oh, honey..." her arms were around me and I thrashed loose.

"Don't! Don't be nice to me or I am so screwed!" My voice was high and a little hysterical but I felt it was not unreasonable. "If you're nice to me I'm going to cry!"

"Okay, okay," Tania placated, waving her hands around a little. "Okay, listen here, little missy! You just suck it up, do you hear me!" I burst into laughter as she knew I would. Her mother was a stern woman who tended to yell that out when things got all emotional. She quelled many of our budding hysterics when we were teens.

"Look, fuck her. She can't hurt you here. Aside from Ass Face Lurch and his blowjob adventures, Maksim's got security clogging this whole venue. In fact, I can't believe your bodyguard outside isn't blasting through the door with his gun out, since we've been in here like six minutes." As if on cue, there's a sharp rapping on the door.

"Mrs. Morozov, they are calling for you."

"She'll be out in a minute!" Tania shouts, "So look, get through this shitshow, eat some cake - oh, and make sure you take a giant chunk home because that looks delicious - and then tell Maksim-"

"Mrs. Morozov you will come out now."

"In a minute!" Tania and I shout together.

"Tell Maksim though, I'm sure he knows how to handle the Sokolovs who are clearly seriously fucked up. Okay?"

The door slams open and there is the extremely large man who followed us here, his gun out.

"Will everyone stop pulling their guns out for just one afternoon!" I'm shouting and I sound crazy and at this point, I don't care. "I'm coming, okay?"

Stowing his gun back into his jacket, the man sniffs and lets me pass before more or less herding me back to where Maksim and his family await.

Maksim...

My blushing bride is, looking a bit pale and has clearly pasted an insincere smile on her lovely face. Sliding my arm around her waist, I lean close, smelling her sweet vanilla scent. "I know this is not easy, but you are doing well. Just smile and remember the names from your dossier, and we will be done soon and you can relax."

Ella's smile is definitely forced, but she nods and the stream of politicians, local celebrities and most of the kings of organized crime began to flow past us. Several of the Bratva families don't bother to switch to English when they greet her, until I refuse to speak Russian to them. I'm questioning Alina's guest list, which includes several of the women I've slept with; models and socialites who were only after a good time. I'm displeased by how unhappy they seem to be when greeting my new wife. But I'm feeling proud of Ella, she's greeting the most important Bratva families by name, nodding and smiling with a poise I hadn't expected.

Until the Sokolovs are in front of us. She takes a step back and another closer to me, and her smile is looking a little frayed around the edges. I put my arm around her and narrow my eyes at them. "Pavel, we are so pleased your family could join us today and share in our happiness." I sound less than pleased and they look less than happy that I'm warning them that there will be no tantrums from Katya here.

Ella handles Pavel and his wife perfectly, but Katya gives an odd, high-pitched squeal and leans in to hug her. My wife's elbow comes in to block her, but Katya still manages to hiss something in her ear before I step in front of her.

"Katya," my voice is colder than the ice sculpture at the buffet table, "my lovely bride and I are so pleased you could share in our happiness." Her glaring father drags her off and I kiss Ella's cheek. "Just a few more people. You are doing fine."

Ella...

I just want this to be over. At this point, I don't even care what Maksim does to me as long as it's somewhere other than here. I'm ready to weep with gratitude when he leans in to whisper that it's time to go.

"You're leaving already, son?" It's Maksim's mother, gliding up like a dark wraith of doom.

I close my eyes in defeat. We were so close.

Maksim turns with the slightest of sighs. "Yes, mother. It's time. I know you'll be a wonderful hostess for our guests, yes?"

She huffs slightly, but I can tell she's delighted to be the Morozov Matriarch in action. Maksim's sisters say goodbye, and Ekaterina even gives me a hug. "I'm glad you're going to be our sister," she whispers, "it won't feel so lonely now."

A straight punch right to the heart, I thought, and hug her back.

There's another couple leaving, too, and I remember them even in my haze of misery. Alexi and Lucya Turgenev.

"Ah, you escaped!" Lucya says with a smile. "I remember it took hours to remove ourselves from our own wedding festivities." She's lovely, with dark hair and pale blue eyes. She's Russian but her English is perfect and accent-less, so I suspect she was born here. She was the first one to smile at me sincerely, not with speculation or actual malice. "I must congratulate you on that kiss. That had to have beat the world record for the longest kiss in a Russian Orthodox wedding."

"That's a thing?" I blurt.

Lucya laughs delightedly, and even her laugh is perfect. Like a bell, or something. "It is. It's a Russian wedding tradition, to make the kiss at the altar last as long as humanly possible." She tilted her head, "No one told you about that?"

I feel unutterably stupid. "I... no. I wish I had been better prepared."

She nodded wisely, "I heard the wedding had to be moved up." She gave me a little wink and turned as her husband took her arm. "Oh, are we ready to leave, darling?"

Alexi is as blond as she is dark, gigantic, like Maksim but with a scar that crosses his left cheek and ends on his jawline. He's terrifying, but he's staring down at Lucya like she is something precious, and beautiful. "Da, *ангел*. The car is out front."

These two are also bristling with bodyguards, which makes it clear that Alexi and Maksim are not just your standard business associates.

Lucya takes my hand, squeezing gently. "Call me when you're back from your honeymoon, I'll take you to lunch and we'll catch up on all these things."

I feel a swell of relief, "That would be lovely, thank you."

Maksim helps me into the back of a black Escalade, carefully stuffing the voluminous fabric of my skirt in with me before the door shuts.

We're silent as the car pulls away, heading into traffic. For once, he's not staring at his phone, but worse, he's staring at me.

"You handled the ceremony very well," he said, running his finger over his full lips and reminding me of that kiss at the altar.

"Thank you?"

The momentary warmth is gone. "What did Katya say to you?"

I thought about evading the question, but I was too tired and strung out to care. "She said you were going to tear me in half, and when you were tired of me, you'd give me to her father for their whorehouses. And she'd make me watch her have sex with you before she had me raped by all their soldiers." Looking up, I was instantly sorry for being honest. Maksim's face was shaped into a mask of cold fury. Naturally, my big mouth had to open again. "The family whorehouse is definitely a thing with her. Though the word family would make you think something more wholesome than whorehouse would follow."

"What do you mean," his words were precisely shaped and

furious, "it is a 'thing' with her?"

I'm about to rub my eyes before remembering all the mascara caked on my lashes. "She was in the SUV today when I got out of Hellspa - I mean, spa day. Lurch put me in there and left to get my purse."

"Lurch?"

"I don't know his real name, the giant bald dude with a tattoo of a snake on his neck? She locked the doors and pulled a gun on me. She started off with the whole 'I usually put people I don't like in our whorehouse,' and finished off with trying to make me take a bag of cash and get out of town, or she'd shoot me... and paralyze me, and- look, it doesn't matter. Lurch broke the window with his gun and yelled at me for locking the door, and when I turned around, she was gone." He had a muscle tic'ing in his cheek, teeth clenched. "Your ex-girlfriend's a trip. She didn't take our happy news very well, huh? Why didn't you marry her? You two seem like a perfect match." I knew I was provoking him and I just didn't care.

"I knew she was insane, but- she isn't my ex-girlfriend, I would never be with someone as unstable as Katya, I am... sorry. She will never get near you again." Maksim actually looked regretful, which was an expression I'd never expected to see on his face.

"Then why did she get so hysterical at the fundraiser that night?" I decided if he was going to be remorseful, I was taking advantage of that.

"Bratva families usually intermarry for business reasons, to strengthen ties between families, create an alliance. Women are raised with the expectation that they will be used to make an advantageous match. I knew her father was going to attempt to make an alliance between our families."

"You-" I had never been so angry. I thought I might have burst a blood vessel in my eye because I actually had a red haze over my vision. "You destroyed my life because I was in the wrong place at the right time for your use?"

Maksim raised an elegant brow. He looked composed now, and amazing in his perfect tux. The sheer... I was just...

"You need to breathe." He put one big, warm hand on my abdomen and I scooted back as far as the seat would let me.

"Don't touch me! You did this to me! I don't even have to worry about you killing Tania, or- or- or my brother. Because she's going to sink me in the Hudson River, and I..." Damn him, he was right, I put a hand on my chest, wheezing. This gown had a corset that they'd laced tight enough to make my ribs fold in like the legs on a card table. When I tried to suck in more air, the corset seemed to tighten.

"Ella, look at me, darling. You're hyperventilating, breathe in and out slowly, we've done this together before. Breathe in..." I could feel him push me forward and unzip my dress, pulling on the corset strings to unlace them. "Breathe out... I've got you. Breathe in..."

When I opened my eyes again, I was lying on a bed, it was a small room, with low lighting and the strong drone of an engine.

On a jet? The small windows showed nothing but dark sky and the red and yellow flashes from the wing lights. Sitting up groggily, I looked down to see I'd been changed into a soft jersey dress and my corset was thankfully gone. It was splayed on the floor, cut bits of the strings everywhere.

"You're awake." My vile new husband came in, towering over me.

"You have a bedroom on your jet?"

He was putting pillows behind my back like some caring, attentive person and it was unnatural. "Yes." He smoothed down the skirt of my dress. "You fainted. As much as I enjoyed your tiny waist in that wedding dress, that corset was too tight. I had to cut it off of you."

"Yeah, super unhelpful during a panic attack," I mumbled.

Maksim let that one go.

It occurs to me that I never asked where we were going. That's just sad. "Um... where are we going for this honeymoon?" I ventured.

His smile was actually genuine. "My home on St. John's in the Caribbean."

There was a polite knock on the bedroom door. "Mr. and Mrs. Morozov? We're about to land if you'd like to take your seats."

I'd never been to St. John's, and it was clear why Maksim had selected this island. There was no words to describe the white sands and the searingly brilliant azure waters. The briny sweep of the air after the stale cabin was exhilarating, and Maksim watched me breathe in deeply with a bit of a smile.

There was something that kept nagging at me as we raced down the road toward Maksim's - no doubt - palatial vacation home. He'd helped me into the Jeep, the top was off and the wind was tearing through my hair. That's when it hit me.

"We're in a Jeep with no bulletproof glass? Where are the bodyguards and tank-like vehicle?"

He turned to me, his dark Ray-Bans hiding his eyes and not giving anything away. He looked unreasonably attractive in a loose white linen shirt and khaki shorts.

"The lifestyle here is not as dire as it is in Manhattan."

The Jeep rounded a corner and I gasped. There was a massive white stone and wood house perched on a cliff. It was perfectly positioned for a panoramic view of the ocean, and there was a cluster of small guest houses behind it, along with a beautiful pool surrounded by trees and vines like it had been carved out of the jungle. A tennis court. I was starting to giggle. A lap pool. Two hot tubs, one near the main house and the other halfway down the stairs cut into the cliff, heading down to the bay. My shoulders were shaking, trying to suppress my laughter, but when I spotted the nine-hole golf course behind the compound, I couldn't hold it in.

Maksim pulled down his sunglasses, eyeing me.

"Wh- where's the riding stables? And the outdoor theatre?"

He frowned. "The stables are half a mile that way, by the helicopter pad. The theatre is behind the guest houses."

That's it. I could not stop howling with laughter. "What, no merry-go-round? Where's the roller coaster? And the Lemur Sanctuary?" My stomach was beginning to hurt but it felt so wonderfully cleansing that I could still find the absurd in life. Because this was so ridiculously over the top.

Settling his elbow on his car door, Maksim sat back and waited for my laughter to subside into wheezing. "Do you want me to build you a merry-go-round, darling?"

Aaand, that set me off again.

Maksim's chef had left us a sumptuous feast on a beautifully set table out on the terrace. He gracefully absented himself after putting out the platters of seafood, so it was just the two of us, watching the waves roll into the bay below. It was unnerving, having his full attention on me. I was used to him being absorbed in his work, or on his phone, and this level of scrutiny was reminding me of the hunting lodge. And the forest, and chasing me.

Not that my discomfort was stopping me from plowing through my second lobster. The spiny ones here in the Caribbean were unbelievably good - sweet and tender, and I didn't care what I looked like with butter dripping down my arm. I'd been too freaked out to eat breakfast and the wedding dinner looked and tasted like sawdust after the first bite. But this lobster....

But after a solid forty-five minutes of non-stop staring from my terrifying spouse, even spiny ocean crustaceans couldn't distract me anymore.

"Here." Maksim handed me another cloth napkin. "You're dripping butter on your dress."

Briefly, I wondered if I could disgust him by plowing through the rest of the meal like a tourist at an all-you-can-eat seafood bar at the Jersey Shore, but he seemed amused, rather than repelled. I could hear the soft steps of his bodyguards making the rounds, but no one was in the house, aside from us. Maksim was leaning back in his chair at the head of the table like a dark lord in hell, still studying me with that faint smile.

Even knowing this is a terrible mistake but not able to endure his stare any longer, I blurt, "What are you thinking?"

"I've been having an internal conflict since we got here," he said, his voice deeper and a bit of his accent creeping back in.

"O- oh?" Yeah, I sound super calm. "Which is...?"

"Which part of you I want to taste first." Now he leans forward, and those cold blue eyes of his are on fire, and I'm clutching my butter-stained napkin. "Although," he muses, "I'm now having visions of laying you back on the bed, putting your feet against my chest to open you wide, and having you play with yourself."

A dirty talker. Maksim is a dirty talker. I am so screwed. His expression never changes from his half-smile, his voice calm and even while he says the filthiest things to me like he's discussing the menu the chef has planned for the next day.

"You *reprobate*." I gulped.

His brow raised in that irritating, elegant way he had. "Reprobate?"

"Reprobate," I agreed absently, "a morally depraved person."

He stands, ambling over to my side of the table, the breeze off the ocean ruffling his dark hair. His face has a five o'clock shadow now, changing him from the suave, clean-cut groom of today to something darker.

"You look alarmed, *solnyshko*." He picks me up, seating me on the table, pushing his hips between my knees. "I've been very patient, have I not? But you are my wife. I'm your husband." Planting his hands on either side of my hips, he leans in closer, chuckling as I lean back. "You're nervous."

Even my smart mouth has deserted me and my lips are opening and closing uselessly like one of those fifty-cent goldfish. "No!" I scoffed; it could not have sounded any weaker than it did.

His face is against mine now, that stubble on his chin scraping my skin lightly as he kisses my cheekbone, then the curve of my jaw. Maksim puts my hand against the rapidly growing monster in his shorts, it's hot, and I can feel it actually getting bigger as I touch it.

"I won't tear you. I'll go slow, but one way or another I'm going to get all of me into you. Before we head back home, this cock is going to be inside you in every possible way."

His hand goes to my throat, pulling me closer, and he's kissing me. You'd think this I could handle, after all, the man gave me a lengthy introduction during the wedding ceremony. That had felt like... staking a claim. This kiss was harder in some way, but softer, too. His tongue thrust harshly between my lips, exploring me while his long fingers stroked the side of my neck. Then he'd pull back slightly and suck my lips between his, very gently nibbling before releasing my lower lip and doing the same to my upper lip. His other hand slid under my rear, pulling me closer to his erection, which had gone past impressive and was definitely moving into threatening territory.

Tania was right.

Maksim carried me into the master bedroom, which might have been romantic but I think it was really because he didn't want to drag me behind him as those endless legs of his loped up the long, curving stairway to the second story. My dress is gone, ripped up and over my head in the kitchen and my undies have disappeared. He's yanked me to the edge of the bed and cupped my ass in his hands, long fingers spreading my lips apart and he's staring at my center like it's the most fascinating phenomenon he's ever witnessed.

"Keep your feet on the edge of the bed." As always, it comes out like an order, even when the man is debauching me.

"Oh, my god!"

He is licking me so aggressively with his hot mouth that I start squirming immediately, moaning as his tongue circles my clitoris, then he rubs his stubbled chin at the entrance to my channel and my hips come off the bed. I've never felt anything like it- so rough that its prickly attack on my softest parts is painful but the way he digging his chin up and almost inside me is just... so outrageously good. My hands slide into his hair, lightly scratching his scalp and Maksim stops, moving his mouth maybe an inch away from me, because I can still feel the heat from his breath as he orders me. "Put your hands over your head. Don't move them again."

Um. Okay, I think, pulling my hands away and placing them where he told me to. When he attacks my center again, it's almost more than I can take, he's sucking and gently biting my lips, humming as he slides his tongue between my clitoris and the entrance to my channel and finally my squirming annoys him enough that Maksim seizes my hips, holding them down.

My ex used to go down on me like it was a chore. I eventually refused to let him anywhere south of my waist after he said, "Well, since it's your *birthday...*" Maksim, on the other hand, is going after me like he is starving. But what's making my legs shake and sending me over the edge are the noises.

Bratva Death King Morozov is not a noisy man. He issues orders in a crisp, authoritative voice, he delivers dirty talk in a deep purr. But this? He's *growling.* I can feel it vibrate inside me and it is.... He looks up at me, his blue eyes glowing in the moonlight and slides two fingers inside me, scissoring against my walls. He's rubbing his stubbled chin against all the soft, swollen parts of me and this is different from the post-spanking oral sex in my bedroom. That felt clinical, like he was simply finishing a procedure.

He was enjoying this.

His lips close tight on my clitoris and sucks it. Hard. Pulling it slightly and I scream. I have never come like this before, certainly not from a man's mouth on me and my heels are drumming mindlessly on his broad back but apparently, that's allowed because he only sucks a little harder.

I'd like to beg him to stop because it's possible that this orgasm has gone on long enough to cause brain damage, but the only thing coming out of me is a long, low moan.

Maksim stops when he is damn good and ready to, waiting

until my legs have stopped moving and my chest is heaving, trying to draw in enough air to avoid passing out, which I am certain would only please him.

Back to why Tania was right. Because by the time I'm capable of focusing again, my terrifying new husband is pulling off his clothes, and he is... gigantic. His cock is thick and wide enough that I'm certain it should be anywhere other than inside me.

His large body is sliding over me, the heat of him radiating over my chilled skin and his big hand is gently squeezing one breast while his mouth is on the other. He's rubbing my nipple with his tongue, then biting down sharply, making me yelp, and he switches to my other breast to try it again.

"Such pretty breasts, *prekrasnyy,*" Maksim pushes them together, rubbing his mouth and chin on my skin and leaving red marks and the beginnings of bruises. It feels incredible. My hands drift down to touch him and he pulls away. "You do not touch me without my permission. Am I going to have to tie you to the bed?" he said coldly, "Or can you obey?" He puts my hands above my head again, his long fingers easily holding my wrists together.

He's looming over me, and the shadows over his beautiful face filter away everything but his vivid eyes, still looking down at me. I'm not used to looking a man in the eye when we're doing something so intimate. Maksim suddenly smiles, and it's so startling that I have to choke back a squeal.

"I've wanted to be between your thighs from the first moment I saw you that night."

"In Hell?" I supply, meaning the name of his club but his brows draw together sternly.

At least I've managed to distract him with my pussy, because Maksim's gaze goes there as his fingers spread me open. "You're soaking, *солнышко.* Soaking wet and so pretty." His knees push under me, lifting my hips and oh, my *god*, that thing cannot be

110

real. He's pushing his cock in slowly, withdrawing and doing it again with a practiced swirl of his hips that tells me that at least he knows how to be careful. But it still feels like he's splitting me in half. "You're doing so well," he murmurs, eyes still focused on where we're joined together, and when he's finally flush against me, with nowhere else to go, he gives the slightest guttural chuckle. "I'm going to sculpt your perfect, tight cunt to fit me, only me. You are exquisite..."

The last word is drawn out as Maksim begins moving in and out of me. My fingers are gripping the sheet, trying to keep still because even though it's possible this might actually kill me, I do not want him to stop. Not ever. Nothing has ever felt like this and there's nothing left but the feel of him against me and inside me. My strange and beautiful husband is murmuring Russian in my ear, words that I'm pretty sure are utter filth and it takes an embarrassingly short amount of time for me to come, gripping his narrow hips with my thighs and gasping.

Maksim moves inside me, side to side to make more room for his cock, and he starts again, this time pushing down sharply with his pelvis when he thrusts into me and the springy curls at the base of his cock rub against my extremely overstimulated clitoris and by the time he finally grips my waist, painfully tight and comes inside me with a growl, I tip over the edge with him again.

He's panting, his sweaty chest rubbing against my breasts and I'm oddly pleased that at least this man isn't completely unaffected by me after he's blown everything I've ever known about sex clear out of the water.

It's the strangest thing.

An act that's supposed to be so intimate - well, to me, anyway, I was never good with just hooking up - and Maksim's managed to make this... What *did* he make this?

He's still inside me, his chest hair tickling my nipples and he's panting harshly from completely rearranging my insides. We're attached, skin to skin with every inch of us, but I feel like it all happened without ever touching him. My hands are still gripping the pillow behind my head.

He gives me a kiss on my forehead and pulls out, grinning at my gasp and walks to the bathroom, getting a warm cloth to clean me before sliding into bed and falling asleep, his back turned to me.

I stare up at the patterns on the ceiling, shadows from the movement of the waves under the moon. It was the most intense sexual experience of my life, but he never let me touch him.

Why?

CHAPTER 11 - THE "NO TOUCHIE" RULE

In which Ella discovers there are some things that Maksim will not tolerate: coked-up Made Men and her hands on his body

Maksim...

"...Tania was quite agitated when she described the situation to me."

I was staring out the window of my study, watching my bride hobble over to a lounge chair. "Really. And what did she say?"

My idiot brother couldn't stop laughing. "She called Oleg a... how did she put it? She said, 'And that punch-drunk fuckboy left my girl in the SUV with this psycho bitch and her gun issues.' I would be furious right now, but I'm still laughing." I watched Ella gasp as she sat down and tried to smother a grin, waiting for Yuri to control himself. "However," he continued, "as per your order last night that Oleg should spend some quality time in the warehouse with Bodgan, we took him this morning. Do you think he's involved with the Sokolovs or just stupid enough to take a bribe?"

Ella has been shifting from hip to hip, trying to find a comfortable perch on the lounge chair. I had some numbing cream that I should be rubbing onto her swollen, sweet parts if I wanted to be inside her again.

Just watching my bride limp over to the hot tub was making me hard again, even though I'd fucked her four times over the last twelve hours. Each time, she'd forgotten and tried to touch me, and I'd been forced to tie her wrists to the headboard to keep them there.

"Maksim? Are you still there?"

Clearing my throat, I turned my back to the sight of Ella sinking into the warm water with a pitiful groan I could hear through the open window. "Of course. Pick up Oleg's cousins, too. They're likely involved and are just as stupid as he is. We've had six missing shipments - like that stunt with the arms storage in the Marx bodega - where he was on the crew. Oleg was the most likely suspect we've found in months. Even if he's not..." my hand clenched on my phone and the screen cracked, "he allowed my wife to be placed in danger. He should have cleared the backseat and not left her alone. For that reason alone, the *Сука* will die. Make sure Bogdan doesn't get too enthusiastic with him before I return."

Yuri hummed thoughtfully, "I'm still amazed you're willing to be away from your kingdom for a full five days. I'll bet ten thousand dollars that you're back in the penthouse within forty-eight hours."

Ella is falling asleep in the hot tub, I can tell. Admittedly, I didn't let her get more than an hour or two of sleep before I woke and slid back into her. She was still wet and warm enough, and it was so good, stretching her open again... Ah, yes, she is asleep and about to sink under the bubbling water.

"I have to go, brother, but no. I won't be back until I have to be at the summit of the families. There's too much to occupy me here."

The little bastard laughed again. "Ella must be something extraordinary then. Congratulations."

"If you ever talk about my wife in any way relating to anything sexual, I'll cut your tongue out," I snarled.

"Very well, Pakhan," he said respectfully, but I knew my brother was still silently laughing.

"What about you and Tania?" I looked out the window again to make sure my bride's head was still above water. "You sounded too cozy for a simple conversation about my wife's safety."

He hummed noncommittally.

It was my turn to laugh. "Really? Did she appreciate your special enhancement?"

"By the fourth orgasm, I was fairly certain she appreciated it. By the seventh and as she lost consciousness, that seemed like a strong endorsement."

"As always, you'll ruin her for other men, but be careful. I don't want to see Ella upset because you've broken her best friend's heart."

"Me, Maksim?" Yuri always loved to sound like I'd wounded him deeply. This had merited several punishments as a child for "torturing" my brother. Torturing us, of course, was my father's job.

"Goodbye, Yuri. Keep me informed about anything you find from Oleg, and keep him alive. I want to kill him myself."

Sliding into the hot tub with my dozing bride, I pulled her onto my lap, facing me so that she could rest her head on my chest. I thought she was still asleep until her voice, a little hoarse, piped up.

"What are the stars for?" She raised one hand to point at the tattoos on my left shoulder.

"In the Bratva, ink tells a story," I adjusted her slightly, enjoying the softness of her breasts pushed against my chest. "The stars indicate my authority over my men."

"Hmmm…" Her gaze moved to my knee. "And what about these stars?"

My hand slipped into her bikini top, lightly caressing her breast. Leaning close, I whispered, "I kneel to no one."

Ella chuckled quietly. She was so sweet and soft, exhausted but content. I wanted to keep her this way all the time. Which meant I'd have to fuck her constantly, but I couldn't see a downside to this plan.

"Yeah, I can totally believe that." Her head lifted, those clever green eyes looking at me more closely. "And the cross on your chest?"

"The Thief's Code, it means we obey no authority other than the brotherhood."

Why was I telling her these things? I'd planned to keep Ella ignorant of all the Bratva doings, but if this kept her from flinching away, I was willing to give her a little background.

Now her long fingers were linked with mine, pulling my left hand closer. "And this crown on your hand?"

"It denotes my authority as Pakhan."

"Did it hurt?" Her thumb's stroking over my knuckles, "I mean, it's right on the bone, and your tendons."

"Not so much," I took her top off, letting it float away in the bubbling water, and took her nipple into my mouth.

Ella...

After the episode in the hot tub, but before Maksim molested me on the desk in his office, I got a voicemail from Tania.

"Hey, Els! Hope you're not walking funny but I'll bet with a cockmaster like your hubby that's pretty likely. Oh! And I have familial proof that Maksim must be shaped huge. I slept with Yuri after the wedding-"

"You what?" I screeched at my phone. "Are you nuts?"

The message continued; "...we were pretty drunk and you two never used your honeymoon suite at the Four Seasons, so you know, waste not, want not and anyway..." Tania started laughing, that hoarse, half-snorting laugh that meant this was about to get really, really interesting. "Anyway, Yuri's packing some serious action, I mean, the guy is *hung!* But that's not the best part-" by now, she was laughing so hard she was hiccupping and I hoped she wouldn't choke to death before the end of the message. "Yuri has pearls inserted in his dick!"

Tania was screeching with excitement and I cringed, praying that Maksim's office door was shut. "No shit, we were doing it and I kept feeling something rubbing up hard against my G-spot and I made him pull out and- holy shit, girl! He has a row of six pearls under his skin on the top of his dick! What the hell, right? I could not stop coming!" Her voice calmed, sounding more like a woman who is well sexed-up, "I even went down on him twice because with those little additions, it was like some kind of sex Disneyland and really, I was-"

"Tania had a good time, I see."

Maksim was leaning against the doorway, arms folded and legs casually crossed, looking impassive, one brow elegantly raised. I yelped and dropped the phone, which unfortunately hit the speaker button on the counter and my bestie's voice was blaring across the kitchen.

"SO DOES MAKSIM HAVE THOSE, TOO? PLEASE TELL ME YOUR HUSBAND HAS THOSE BIG PEARLS SEWN INTO HIS DICK BECAUSE THAT IS-"

"Oh, my *god!*" I was mortified, dropping the phone again as I stabbed at the mute button. *This can't be happening,* I thought feverishly, *please god, just strike me down. I'd rather be a patch of soot on the floor than have to face him right now.*

"As you have already discovered," Maksim casually moved next to me, plucking a grape off the tray on the counter, "I do not have the pearls sewn into my dick."

I had my hand over my eyes. I won't look at him. If I don't look at him, this entire conversation never happened.

Naturally, the heartless reprobate pulled my hand down. "Would you prefer I get the pearls? They're actually a sign of nobility. Russian royalty covered themselves in pearls for centuries, and their clothing, jewelry, furniture..." He put a hand on either side of me, trapping me against the fridge. "However, it's said that Tsar Alexis decided to go a step further and had the royal physician put them under the skin of his cock around 1635. He was called Tsar Alexis, the Quietest, but apparently, he let his embellishments do the talking. But if you want me to do the same thing..."

Of course, my big mouth immediately made it all so much worse. "Are you kidding? You're gigantic! I'm already buried six feet under your... you know! What more do you want?"

Maksim laughed, and it was mesmerizing from a man who rarely even smiled, to see him give such an open, unrestrained reaction. "I only want to please you, *solnyshko*," he claimed, with the most insincere attempt at innocence ever.

"Please, let's not talk about it anymore," I groaned, "let's just pretend this conversation never happened, okay?"

He studied me a moment longer, he was enjoying this, I could tell. "As you wish. I want to take you out to dinner. Let's go look through your dresses."

He took my hand and headed up to the bedroom and I knew perfectly well that I wouldn't be eating dinner for at least a couple of hours from now.

"This is exquisite," I sighed.

Maksim ignored the sommelier hovering by the table for a moment to watch me. The dress he'd picked out for me was forest green, fairly demure in front and dipping low enough to show the dimples just above my bottom in the back. The skirt was short enough that I'd spent most of the ride into town trying to find a way to sit that didn't show off my lace undies, which he also selected. He seemed to enjoy it more in the car, less so now that other men were sneaking glances at us until he gave them the Bratva Death Stare.

The sommelier was still waiting for our order, his smile

becoming a bit strained, so I nodded at the wine list to drag Maksim's sinister glare from other hapless diners and back to the uncomfortable employee.

"We're having the seafood degustation," Maksim said briskly, "so let's try the Markus Molitor Bernkasteler Doctor Riesling."

"Very good, sir," and the relieved man is off.

I couldn't help chuckling a little, "Why are fancy wines always the ones with the endless name? Why isn't anything ever named 'Joe's Riesling?' I'd buy it just out of spite."

I felt almost dangerously relaxed - given the recent tensions - but he seemed pretty chill, too. He'd tanned a deep golden brown over the last 48 hours here on the island, while my English skin had stubbornly retained its pasty white sheen. Of course, it's not like any sun could fight its way through the copious applications of sunscreen that Maksim insisted on rubbing on me at every opportunity.

He was speaking softly to one of the bodyguards he'd brought along on our 'date.' Ivan, I think? The other one at the table just behind us was Fedor. But his distraction meant I could stare at him for a moment without his stupid, handsome face breaking out into a knowing smirk. He looked gorgeous, which seemed very unreasonable, in white button-down shirt and dark trousers, the shirt sleeves rolled up to show his tanned, muscular forearms and his stainless steel Patek Phillippe glinting on his wrist.

He was gesturing with those big, capable-looking hands of his, and it reminded me of how many times he'd held my wrists together and over my head as he was defiling me. No matter how many times or how many ways he was inside me, Maksim would never let me touch him. I was a little delirious by the third time last night and he got angry, tying my hands to the headboard because "I couldn't control myself."

I crossed my legs, but I could feel too much fresh air blowing up my skirt, so with a sigh, I crossed them the other way. What *was* it with Hot Murder Daddy, as Tania called him? He made me marry him, and the fact that I couldn't sit down without gasping like a Victorian maiden from the ache everywhere south of my waistline seemed to indicate he was attracted to me. Why couldn't I touch him?

If I craned my neck a little, I could see two more of Maksim's men patrolling outside the restaurant. It was built on a dock extending out into the harbor; boats returning from a day of fishing would sell their catch right to the kitchen in the back. There were walls covered in blooming vines, growing from window boxes lining the waist-high walls, giving me the feeling of being in the middle of a garden... on the ocean. The lights strung haphazardly overhead lit up the sharp, beautiful lines of Maksim's high cheekbones. Gulping half of my wine, I tried to refocus. I would not sit and stare at him and inflate his already unreasonable self-esteem.

"Max! You bastard you didn't invite me to your wedding? I had to find out from my father, motherfucker!"

"Dante," Maksim was at his most unwelcoming, and it made me want to crawl under the table, but the creep in the super expensive suit is, I suspect, already too coked up to notice.

He shouts across the restaurant, "Hey Kimber, get your ass over here!"

A muscle tic'd in Maksim's cheek as everyone turned to stare. Expensive Suit Guy swaggered over to my side of the table and picked up my hand, attempting to kiss it. "Shit, that really *is* a wedding ring. You really did get hitched? I thought dad was fucking with me!" My hand was immediately removed from his sweaty one and held captive by Maksim instead.

A girl with the most explosive head of flaming magenta hair I'd ever seen had wrapped herself around Expensive Suit- around Dante, I mean - but she was smiling dreamily at Maksim. It was a look I was beginning to get used to since everyone with ovaries would stare at him like they were begging him to impregnate them right there and then.

Oh, *my god.* Maksim wasn't planning on knocking me up, right?

Right? This whole married thing was like walking right into a glue trap. Add a baby to that? There is *no* way. I realized I was sweating and started fanning my face with my napkin.

"Darling? Are you listening?"

Smiling prettily, I apologize, "I'm sorry, uh, sweetheart. The restaurant is a little loud. You were saying?"

Maksim was not pleased, I wasn't sure if it was directed more at me or the couple leaning heavily into our table, but I was breaking out in a sweat.

"Let me introduce you, Dante and Kimber, this is my beautiful bride, Ella Morozov."

Man, he drew that last name out like it was the most deeply satisfying thing he'd said all day.

"And this is Dante Toscano and Kimber... I didn't get your last name?"

"Just Kimber," she was twirling a lock of that violent magenta hair and giggling. Giggling at Maksim, who'd already turned back to Dante.

This guy was a trip. The aforementioned super expensive suit aside, he had slicked-back hair with a stubborn lock, heavily weighted with hair gel, flopping onto his forehead. He had mean, dark eyes, rings on every finger, and teeth so large and unnaturally white that it was clear he'd paid some dentist's kid's way through college with that shiny new grille. He was attempting to smile in a way that indicated that he didn't know how, but he was trying out the look because humans used it.

Maksim...

"Nice to see you, Dante."

The useless little troll never did have the common sense to know when to move on before he really enraged someone. His father, Mattia, had two other sons - Giovanni and Dario - who were intelligent and good leaders. Then, there was Dante. Set to inherit his father's empire just by the virtue of being the firstborn. Their family's only hope would be that he finally infuriated the wrong man enough to kill him before Mattia died. But while Dante was vicious and usually high, he had a native, animal cunning that kept him alive this far. "But, as you can see, I'm here with my bride and we're spending some alone time."

Even emphasizing *alone time* wasn't enough to deter him.

Kimber was already wiggling into the chair next to Ella, who was regarding her with some amusement since the girl was still staring at me.

"Yeah, well, I gotta buy you dinner to celebrate the wedding, huh? *Congratulazioni,* motherfucker! Besides, I wanted to talk to you before the summit next week."

"I don't talk business in public," I snarled. I'd toss this useless meat sack over the side of the restaurant if I didn't respect his father, but that could change.

"Just want to make sure we're on the same page before we walk into that meeting," Dante lit up another cigarette, his eyes slitted like a snake's. "Since you and Senator Memmott are such good buddies, I-"

"Shut your mouth." I leaned in close, "Get up and walk away from this table. Anything I have to say, I'll say to Mattia."

"You think you can talk to me like that?" He was shouting, standing up, and knocking his chair over. "I'm gonna be running the show soon and you're going to work with me or suck my-"

Pitched into the bay it is.

Grabbing him by the throat, I lifted him, still kicking and squealing, and dragged him to the edge of the platform, throwing him over. It's a fifteen-foot drop to the water, and he screamed all the way down.

"Uh... do you think he's going to be okay?" Ella's at my side, searching the water for Dante.

"No," I take her elbow and turn her around, "he'll always be an asshole."

It's our final day on St. John's, and I'm watching Ella sleep. She sleeps like the dead, motionless and with an arm or a leg drooping over the side of the bed. She continues to surprise me with her stamina; and her stubbornness.

Still... she deserves a reward.

"Wake up, *solnyshko*," I'm placing slow, sucking kisses along her neck, and her skin's warm and so soft, and I'm rethinking my plans. We could just spend the day here in bed.

One arm comes flailing out. "I'm sleeping..." Ella whines.

I laugh softly, "A pity. I intended to take you on a little sightseeing tour around the island."

One pale green eye opens. "Really? I'm up!" She dashes into the bathroom so quickly that I hardly get a chance to enjoy the sight of her bare ass under the short nightie she's wearing.

Still, it takes her less than ten minutes to be ready, which is highly unusual, based on my past experience with women. When I take her hand and start heading up the hill behind the house, Ella looks around. "I thought we were going sightseeing?"

"We are." Rounding the rock outcropping, the helicopter pad comes into view.

"Oh, that's so cool..." She follows me over while I start pre-flight prep. "Where's the pilot?"

Opening the door, I lift her onto the seat. "I am the pilot, darling."

Ella...

"Oh, my god this is amazing!"

St. John's sweeps ahead of us in a thousand shades of blue

and green. I might have been a little alarmed when Maksim announced that he would be flying us, but as with everything else, damn him, he's competent, and he's looking really cool in those aviator sunglasses. He steers us sharply left, nearly sideways along the cliff as I squeal. When I look down, I can see a squadron of manta rays sunning themselves on the surface of the water. I'm clapping my hands like a six-year-old, but they're so magical. One of the rays, as if showing off, turns and leaps up into the air, then lands with a resounding crash into the surf, and I screech with excitement.

"Oh, sorry!" Maksim is wincing and I realize my scream just reverberated through his headset. "I love manta rays. And the ones they have here are actually a third species of ray." I lean dangerously far out of the helicopter to watch the charcoal grey rays, their white tips gleaming under the sun. "Do you know *Mobula cf. birostris* live for forty years?"

I'm expecting him to laugh at my marine nerd-girl rapture, but Maksim merely smiles, pulling me safely back inside.

An hour later, he's landing the helicopter back on the pad so smoothly that I barely feel the 'thump!' as the gear hits the ground. I'm feeling dangerously soft, and this is never good. I impulsively give him a kiss, and he smiles down at me, taking off his headset.

"And what was that for, *solnyshko?*"

"Thank you, that was amazing. The vastness of the ocean is just heart-stopping when you see it from that height."

Like I'm no heavier than the aviators he's just taken off, Maksim lifts me onto his lap, straddling him. "I'm glad you enjoyed it." His big, warm hands are stroking up and down my thighs and it's really distracting.

"Uh…" God, his hands feel spectacular, "when did you learn to fly a helicopter?" The stroking on my thighs passes for a moment, which is really a shame.

"I was sixteen when I earned my license. I keep my skills up by flying a few times a year."

It's then that I realize that I don't even know how old my husband is. "So, how old are you?" I'm already cringing, but it's not like I've gotten a chance to do any homework on the man. I just got my phone back before the wedding. But I still feel like an idiot. He's kissing along my collarbone, and he pulls down the strap of my sundress as he answers me. "I'm thirty-one."

I'm about to ask something stupid, like 'what's your favorite color?' when he planted his lips on mine, and conversation time is over. Maksim leaned me back against the control column and sucked a bruise just under my nipple and I might have been grinding on him a bit. I gripped the back of his seat and tried to remember the 'no touchie' rule but... I wanted to grab those big shoulders of his, and feel the muscles move under my fingers. I really, *really* wanted to sink my fingers into his thick, dark hair. It's silkier than mine and there was so much of it.

Maksim lifted me again while I'd been thinking about his hair, he unzipped his jeans and just pulled my undies aside, sliding into me, he was much rougher than usual.

"Relax," he's doing that filthy whispering thing in my ear and it's working. "Let me in." He's moving my hips side to side, trying to loosen me up. "I can feel your underwear grazing the side of my cock." Maksim abruptly pulls my undies up at the back, tightening them against my clitoris, which is now rubbing against the lace in a really distracting way. I could hear the crash of the waves against the rocks below us, the heat of the sun on my back. Everything else was gone, just the feeling of his thick, heavy cock inside me and the gorgeous words of filth he keeps whispering in English and Russian in my ear.

I really have to learn Russian...

I didn't mean to do it. I wasn't being sneaky. But one of my hands found its way under Maksim's t-shirt, flattened against the warmth of his skin and my fingers slid over a long, rough patch of scarred skin. He pulls my hand loose and imprisons it with the other behind my back, bouncing me harder on his cock and yanking on my underwear until it rips free. The last, vicious tug of the fabric against my clitoris tips me over the edge and I tighten down hard enough on his cock to hold him immobile inside me for a moment until the spasms slow, and he's thrusting viciously to his own finish.

My hands are still held hostage by Maksim, though his sweaty forehead is against my shoulder. When we can finally breathe without panting, he lets go and pulls me carefully off his cock. I can still feel the heat and wet from us both slicking my inner thighs as I unsteadily climb out of the helicopter with him.

"Why won't you let me touch you?"

Damnit. That just burst out of me, I wasn't going to ask. Was it because of the scar I felt?

His eyes are cold again, examining me in that impersonal way he'd had when he thought I was the woman who'd stolen his arms stash.

"This isn't love, Ella." If Maksim's voice had been a touch, he would have given me frostbite. "This is fucking. You're not allowed to touch me as if you have any right to." He abruptly moved me away from him, and zipped up his jeans.

Maksim walked down the pathway back to the house. I was left standing on the pad, my thighs wet, and wanting to set fire to his big, fancy helicopter.

CHAPTER 12 - ICE SKATING AND PEPPERMINT SCHNAPPS

In which there are heart-to-heart discussions and the slightest bit of redemption for heartless bastards.

Ella...

I stood at the head of the exquisitely set table. It's stretched clear across the vast dining room, set for, what? Forty people? It looks like something from an ultra, super uber-amazing Christmas Pinterest board. A snowscape, right down to the chilly, silver-white place settings. The back of each chair has a square boxwood wreath with an elegant name card in beautiful calligraphy.

It's perfect. And cold. And I'm freezing.

I see the reflection in the massive windows from the three artistically arranged Christmas trees. White and silver. And cold. Then I catch my reflection and I walk closer. I'm in a white cashmere dress to match the table, and the diamonds I'd worn for our wedding. Knee-high boots. The stylist came by today-on Christmas Day, what the hell! Who makes a hairstylist work on Christmas Day? I made sure he'd given her a gigantic tip.

I wanted to be angry. I always worked better from a place of rage than sorrow. But I just felt... tired, I guess. What's the point? Maksim despised me, even though he'd taken *my* life away from me.

Tania told me more than once that she'd "go on the run" with me, which is sweet but impossible. The vision of him chasing me through the forest keeps looping through my consciousness every time I consider trying to slip away. I've come up with a thousand escape scenarios and scrapped them all because, in the end, I know it's impossible.

My only hope is to make him tired of me and maybe he'll just let me go when he decides a bitter shell of a wife isn't that interesting.

The first move was obvious. Maksim hasn't touched me since we returned from St. John's, because apparently even he has a line he won't cross, which is me finding him completely repellant.

Four days ago...

When we returned from the silent flight back, I headed for the guest room.

"Your clothes have already been moved to the master bedroom," Maksim's voice stopped me. He was idly sorting through some important mail Alina left for him. "Your personal items from your apartment arrive tomorrow. I'll have them put in storage downstairs until you decide what to do with them."

He's waiting for me to flip out, I thought, *not happening.* Wordlessly, I headed for the massive doors guarding his bedroom. Our bedroom, I guess. Throwing them open and strolling inside I expected... something. Like a medieval castle guard with an axe intoning, "None shall pass!" But no blade swung down to cleave my skull wide open, so I headed for what I assumed was the closet. The master was similar in layout to the guest bedroom, just much, much larger.

The doors leading to what I thought was the closet here opened to a dressing room the size of the living room and kitchen combined in my old apartment; rows upon rows of beautiful, hand-made suits, drawers filled with watches that cost more than the average house, leather belts, stupidly expensive silk ties all displayed behind glass fronts. Slide-out shoe racks, huge mirrors, and even a seating area with glamorous lighting by another floor-to-ceiling window.

You know, in case your standard billionaire wanted to curl up in their closet and enjoy the scenery and their clothes at the same time.

Actually, I would really love to do that.

Walking past "my" side of the closet was less exciting. The clothes were beautifully displayed, everything from evening gowns to workout wear, just nothing I'd picked out. No soft and over-stretched sweatshirts with my college logo or ridiculously fuzzy socks. None of it was mine.

Nothing here was mine.

"Okay," I sighed, "self-pity time is over."

The master suite was imposing. There was a huge fireplace, masculine leather furniture, and - like every other room in the penthouse - a spectacular view of the city. And then, there was the bed. A giant sleigh bed made of elaborately carved walnut. Given that Maksim was 6"6 and broadly muscled, this was logical. But its vast expanse meant I could be on one side and he'd have to put on his running shoes just to make it over from the other end of the bed. I would never make it easy to touch me ever again, much less convince me to have sex.

Seating myself gingerly on the lovely thick mattress, I looked around. Black and white again, how creative. There were accents of forest green in the long curtains and the bedspread, but that was it. I could tell which side of the bed was his; there was an untidy stack of books on the bedside table.

So he read. Maksim was still a bastard.

Flopping back and staring at the white ceiling, I thought about his genuinely appalling statement on the helicopter pad. I'd bet my apartment - if I still had one - that it was related to the scarring on his back. He was never shy about stripping down, but I'd never spotted the scar before. Were there more? Who gave them to him? Or... maybe he was just a controlling, intimacy-deficient scalawag.

"Scalawag: a cruel and morally corrupt person," I mumbled. It didn't matter because he'd taken the last part of me I'd ever allow. Because I'd rather have him kill me than touch me again.

Maksim...

Ella was lingering by the dining room, running her fingertips over the backs of the chairs, reading the name cards. My Christmas Day brunch was a long-running tradition, hosted first by my father for all the key Russian families in Manhattan. I know my parties were more eagerly attended than his because no one was ever shot during brunch. I preferred to separate celebration from punishment, something my father could never seem to manage.

The only time I'd seen my bride since we returned was when she was asleep, huddled so far on her side of the bed that she was always in danger of falling off. She kept well away from my reach at any other time. I might be many things, but I was not a rapist. She could sulk all she liked; but as a Bratva wife, she would be hearing far more terrible words than what I'd said to her.

"Did you study your dossier on the families attending today?"

Ella turned her head slightly, not looking at me. "Yes."

The soft chime of the elevator opening with our first guests saved her from enduring further conversation with me. The penthouse filled with our partygoers, elegantly dressed parents, and their children scrubbed into their best clothes, but almost immediately losing their shyness and sliding down the long expanse of the marble flooring in their stocking feet.

Lucya Turgenev nudged me lightly with her elbow. "You know, it's next to impossible for us to make our children behave when Yuri is encouraging naughty behavior."

She was smiling at the sight of her daughter and two sons laughing uncontrollably as my idiot brother helped them get a running start.

"He is irredeemable," I shook my head, chuckling at his gleeful expression. "Yuri so rarely allows himself to let go of his responsibilities as *Sovietnik.* I think he's regressed twenty years."

"So? How was your honeymoon with your lovely new wife?" Lucya nudged me again. This must be her third or fourth glass of champagne.

"I'd like to ask your help, *moy drug.* She's not from our circle."

"Mhmm," she agreed, "I was surprised when you married a civilian."

"She needs guidance."

She opened her eyes wide, ready to taunt me. "Oh, didn't your mother tell her everything she needed to know?"

"You are so very fortunate that I like you, Lucya," I sighed.

"And also, that you are wisely and reasonably prudent regarding my husband," she added.

I chose to ignore her, though it was true that Alexi was one of the few men in the Bratva that earned my highest respect. And caution. "Would you help her? I know you and Alexi had your own challenges at the beginning of your marriage." This was an understatement. Lucya had been promised to marry Alexi's older brother, a vicious and abusive monster. Much blood was shed before her marriage arrangement was made with Alexi instead.

"That is the understatement of the century," she agreed, shuddering slightly.

"I didn't mean to bring up ugly memories, мой друг. My apologies."

Ella had lost her shyness and was laughing as she watched the children - and Yuri - sailing down the marble expanse. Her cheeks were flushed and she was wearing the first smile I'd seen since we left St. John's.

"Of course I will, Maksim. Only because I like her more than you already, and she'll need some survival skills to tolerate you."

"So cruel. And here I have always worshiped at your feet."

Before we could entertain each other with further insults, her husband stepped up behind her, kissing her cheek.

"Your children are very badly behaved," Lucya informed him.

"Oh, no milyy, when they are bad, they are definitely yours," Alexi said, with a soft expression I'd never seen, aside from when it was directed at her. Some arranged marriages did turn out to be love matches, even in the Bratva.

Sitting at the head of the table, I swirled my wine as I watched everyone take pleasure in the meal; traditional Russian fare like Oliver Salad, Pirozhki- tender buns stuffed with savory beef or mushrooms, flaky Kulebyaka with a perfect salmon center. Ella tried the Pirozhki, and reached out for three more.

I'd always thought gatherings like these were unthinkable for people such as us; blood-drenched with dark souls and black hearts. But these same families came every year to celebrate at my table. I'd made sure Lucya was seated next to Ella at the other end, and my friend had her laughing through the entire meal. By the time the Kyiv cake and pampushky were served for dessert, Lucya's youngest had planted herself firmly on Ella's lap and she was absently stroking his hair while she talked with his mother.

Groups of people began forming little islands of conversation post-dinner, settling into the long couches in the living room, or venturing out onto the heated terrace to look over the city. My wife had disappeared, but I knew her hiding spot. Walking soundlessly near the open doors of our dressing room. I could just see her curled up on the window seat with Lucya.

"No! That really happened?" Lucya couldn't stop laughing, "Look, you have to try this. This vodka is the best of the best, darling. It's so smooth that you'll never associate it with the swill I'm sure you've had in the past." I shook my head as they both downed a shot of my DIVA Premium Vodka.

"Okay," Ella allowed, "that wasn't bad. So how expensive is this best vodka?"

I heard a clink of the shot glasses as Lucya refilled them. "Oh, this bottle retails for half a million or so."

A spray of vodka came out of Ella's mouth. "What the- damn it woman! You can't just drop something like that when I'm mid-swallow!" She brushed around $50,000 worth of spilled vodka off her dress as Lucya poured her another one.

"Eh, cares? It's Christmas! Also, I took this from Maksim's liquor cabinet."

Silence, and then they burst into raucous laughter.

"So," even Lucya's words were slurring a little. "What would you be doing on Christmas if you weren't married to the most annoying Russian in Manhattan?"

"Oh…" the laughter died from Ella's words. "My folks are gone, but we used to go ice skating at Rockefeller Center and then have dinner at Grand Central's Oyster Bar. It probably sounds pretty touristy, but-"

"I think it sounds wonderful," Lucya interrupted. "Where are your folks now?"

"They passed away in a car accident a few years ago."

"I'm so sorry."

Lucya was the most soft-hearted of women, particularly in the Bratva world.

"Yeah, so my friend Tania and I keep the tradition going every year…" Ella's voice was flat again. "Well, we did."

"Marriage is always a time of great transition," Lucya said with empathy, "but even though you are going to have some huge changes in your life - there's no way around that - you should still hold onto some of the things that matter to you. You can't lose yourself to Maksim, the man is terribly overwhelming as it is." She started laughing again. "My god, Ella, you should see your face! That bad already, huh?"

Enough of this, I thought sourly, clearing my throat to alert them before I walked into the dressing room.

"Hey, Maksim!" Lucya was red-faced and valiantly trying to suppress her laughter while swiftly putting the vodka bottle behind her. "We were just talking about you!"

"I see that," I drawled, eyeing their empty glasses. "I believe Alexi is buried under your offspring and calling for you to save him."

Ella had quickly and silently exited the room while Lucya was still trying to hide the desecrated remains of their half-million-dollar vodka binge.

Ella...

As exhausting as this was, I was very sad when the last guests bid us goodbye, holding sleepy children on their shoulders and toting gift bags.

Lucya hugged me as she left. "Let's get together here before I see you in St. Petersburg."

"I'm... going to St. Petersburg?"

She glared at Maksim over my shoulder. "I think your new husband needs to work on his communication skills. Most of the Bratva families also celebrate the Russian Christmas holiday in St. Petersburg, on January seventh."

"It sounds fun," I'm forcing my smile, and it seems she's not buying it because she gives Maksim the stink-eye again before leaving with her kids and her hot, scary husband.

I might have clung to Yuri just a little, the last one to leave. He had something planned. By his expression, I suspected it involved a woman and it had better not be Tania. I was going to have a very stern talk with her. I don't care how many pearls Yuri has sewed into his- *oh, my god, I'm thinking about my brother-in-law's junk. That just killed my buzz.*

The silence of the empty penthouse was jarring after the cheerful afternoon, with only me and Maksim left. Lights were winking on in the city as dusk fell, there was something magical about watching the city pulse and change with the day turning into night. I could see why Maksim loved it. Standing here, surveying his kingdom.

The soft click of his shoes meant I'd gotten distracted. I'd been getting so good at slipping away when he was in the same room, darn it! He stepped next to me, hands in the pockets of his coal-black suit, a red tie as his 'festive' note to the Christmas brunch. I turned to leave.

"Wait."

I could feel his breath on my cheek, he was that close, staring down at me like- I don't know. But I don't care.

"Go change, put on something warm and comfortable. We have somewhere to be."

Maksim...

I regarded Ella's defensive posture with some amusement. She was plastered against the opposite door of the town car, staring out her window. She'd put on leggings and a thick, cream cable-knit sweater, looking just as lovely as she had dressed up in her diamonds and cashmere dress earlier today. The little line between her eyebrows that she appeared when confused appeared as we drove further downtown.

As the car pulled up to the rink at Rockefeller Center, Ella gasped, staring at the massive Christmas Tree and the laughing, stumbling skaters. She finally looked at me as Vlad opened her door.

I gestured at the rink. "Shall we?"

She looked away, not taking off her seatbelt.

Ah. "Are you afraid skating with me will tarnish the memory?"

Silence.

I got out, moving around to her side and crouching down. I tried to think back to how I would negotiate with my sisters when they dug in their heels with me. "We will have no expectations, yes? We'll just skate a little, and have some hot chocolate. I brought peppermint schnapps for the drinks, of course." Ella was looking down at her hands clasped together in her lap. "You know," I looked away, watching the skaters, "I learned to skate along the Neva River as a child in St. Petersburg. The river would freeze very early, since the city is only 800 kilometers away from the Arctic Circle. But I haven't skated in…" *When did I last put on ice skates?* "In a long while. So, your chances of tripping me are excellent."

There was a little grin.

"Join me, Ella." I tried to make it not sound like a command, but I was rusty at simply asking for something. We waited; I, still crouched by her door, Vlad, looking a little puzzled by the fact I was not simply dragging her out of the car, and my other guards silently hovering nearby.

With a long sigh, she finally got out of the car. I handed her some bright red cashmere mittens and pulled on my gloves. She laced up her skates, her fingers quick and precise. Stepping onto the ice, I held out my hand. Ella stared at it, not moving.

"No expectations," I reminded her, "and your hand is safely covered, your skin will not even touch mine." Yes, there was an eye roll, quickly concealed from me. Reluctantly, she took my hand and we were off.

It had been a long time, I could feel my thighs move in the old, familiar way, getting used to the overly groomed, smooth feel of the rink, instead of the rough hazards of the ice on the Neva River. Ella moved strongly alongside me, skating well with sharp strokes of the blade along the ice. Only two of my men knew how to skate well enough to follow us, so the others stationed themselves around the rink.

"I remember that it took Mariya years to learn to skate. She'd stand on the banks and cry, so I'd put her on my shoulders to skate with me. She was nearly ten by the time I realized she didn't bother learning how to, as long as she had me to carry her around, the little princess."

Ella chuckled, "She has those huge, innocent blue eyes. I'm sure she knew how to use them to devastating effect."

It was her first sentence to me in five days. Surprising me, how good it was to hear her. "She was shameless," I agreed. "The youngest, the smallest of us. I don't think she learned to walk until she was two because someone always wanted to carry her around."

She took a small, sideways glance at me. "You have a good memory for little details like that."

"Our sisters are precious to Yuri and me." We were skating faster, the lights circling the rink blurring just a bit. "My father planned to marry them both off to form useful alliances. He attempted to marry off Ekaterina at only thirteen to a vile old Pakhan in Moscow. I could never allow that."

"I'm glad," was all Ella said. But I knew she wanted to know more about the use of women as marital commodities in the Bratva. She'd used that phrase during a phone call with Tania. It was grim and clever at the same time.

But tonight was not the time. Giving my wife another reason to be enraged on Christmas seemed unnecessary.

She looked behind us and put a mittened hand over her mouth, trying not to laugh. "I think your boys are wearing out." It was true, both men were panting and red-faced, but still keeping to our backs.

Pulling her to the side of the rink near a fire barrel, I nodded. "Let's give them a break. Americans... no stamina. In St. Petersburg, they'd never last the winter."

I found myself counting each smile, each laugh Ella gave me as we skated and talked until she took pity on my men and suggested we end the evening, pretending that it was because she was cold. But I didn't miss her sympathetic looks at them.

When we returned to the penthouse, she faced me. "Thank you, Maksim. That was wonderful. I appreciate your thoughtfulness. I'm tired." She nodded firmly. "Goodnight."

Searching her determined face, I nodded. I could seduce her. I knew the ice skating had thawed her considerably. But... this had been a good day. "Very well." Raising her hand, I kissed her knuckles. "Goodnight, *solnyshko.*"

CHAPTER 13 – GO OUT WITH A BANG

In which there is schmoozing, splendor, and bullets.

Maksim...

New Year's Eve Day

Oleg might be many things, but weak was not one of them.

He'd been hanging in the warehouse under Bogdan's not-tender mercies for several days before I walked into the room, lined with concrete and sheet metal. He was still a giant, even chained up with cuts all over his chest, back, and arms. He was missing some teeth, his right eye swollen shut, and nearly every finger broken.

"Pakhan," Bogdan greeted me cheerfully. "It's been too long."

I would be inclined to disagree. Bogdan Đorđević was a recruit from the Serbian mob, dissatisfied with his place there. I consider luring him away as a major coup, though spending any amount of time in his company was not desirable. His skills in torture were unparalleled. Unlike my father, I did not enjoy torture, though I participated when necessary. But the genuine pleasure he took in his work... I admired the man for his work ethic, but his gentle smile at the best of times was unsettling.

"Bogdan," I shook his outstretched hand, ignoring the blood

that smeared on my shirt cuff. "I see Oleg is still alive and resistant. What about his cousins?"

He lowered his voice. "One succumbed almost immediately to his injuries, very disappointing." He frowned thoughtfully, "But we got enough from him for your *Sovietnik* to authorize further questioning."

I shoved down the fury threatening to take me over. "These men have been in our family's Bratva since my father's time. Were they plants from Sokolov?"

Bogdan was meticulously cleaning one of his scalpels, eyeing the handle to make sure it was spotless. "What I have so far from the other cousin is that Oleg was seduced by one of the women in Sokolov's household. The fool." he shook his head disapprovingly. "She's been passing along money and instructions from Pavel Sokolov, and the girl strings him along, telling Oleg that he can leave us soon to join their family and marry her."

"What a sweet story," I took off my jacket, rolling up my sleeves. "I knew he wasn't my brightest soldier, but that has to be the oldest con in organized crime."

Strolling closer to his bloody hulk, I nod, and Bogdan yanks on Oleg's hair, yanking his head up to look at me. His good eye opens and he growls at me. *"Idi k chertu!"*

I incline my head courteously, "What was that? Your speech is a bit mushy. That will happen when you lose half your teeth." He tries to spit at me, but it dribbles down his chest. "I would admire your stamina, soldier, but now you are wasting my time. What was the plan for my wife?"

He chuckles, and the sound is thick with clotted blood. "You won't have a wife soon. Or an empire."

"Hmm," I select a KA-BAR knife, enjoying how the dull light glimmers along the blade. "Then we have much to talk about."

My mood was not improved by a phone call from Yuri on the way back from the warehouse.

"We have a problem."

I pinched the brow of my nose between my thumb and forefinger. "Go on."

"The shipment of ammunition meant for the O'Sullivan clan was taken last night."

"*Blyad'!*"

"It gets worse, Pakhan." Oh, it definitely must be worse if Yuri is using my formal title. "They killed Sergei. He was overseeing the shipment directly because of the recent theft."

"Who? Who is behind this?"

"We've got nothing. The crew scheduled to arrive this morning found Sergei and the four others, all dead. No signs of forced entry, nothing on the security cameras. They were disabled around midnight."

I took a deep breath, trying to shove down the fury so I could think. "Set up a swearing-in ceremony for Patrick. He's the right man for *Obshchak.*"

"Pakhan."

Again with the formal titles, Yuri? I pinch the bridge of my nose. "Go ahead."

"There's going to be discontent because he's not Russian. You know this already."

"This isn't a democracy." I snapped, "He's earned this. I'll be happy to ask if anyone objects during the ceremony. Have him be the one to reach out to the Irish to tell them their shipment will be a couple of days late. Contact Joe Trazados in Miami and get a rush shipment. Bribe him if necessary."

"I'm not your *Obshchaka*," Yuri said carefully, "but I know he will remind you of the colossal loss here. Not only the original shipment but the cost of bringing in the next one."

"We're not showing weakness in front of the Irish. Get it done."

"Very well, Pakhan," Yuri said with just the barest amount of deference. Just enough to keep me from punching his face the next time I saw him, while still telegraphing his disapproval.

I headed for the master bathroom as soon as I arrived back at the penthouse. The first rule, always. Never carry blood home to the family.

A torrent of hot water was always an excellent tool to reset the sourest mood, and feeling less like I was ready to tear someone in half, I strolled into the dressing room, toweling my hair.

"Oh my god!"

I grin under the cover of the towel. Apparently, Ella was in her favorite hiding spot on the window seat. Moving the towel to dry my chest, I smiled at her lazily. She's trying to angle around the other side of the center dressers in the room to escape.

"Hello, darling. Are you uncomfortable? It's not like you haven't seen me naked before." She's clutching her phone to her chest, wide-eyed. Her pale skin makes it easy to see her painful blush.

"I'm not uncomfortable," she's defensive, trying to look haughty. "I just… have some stuff I have to do, so-"

"What are you reading that's so fascinating?" I gesture to her phone. The dressing room is as large as most bedrooms, but it's still easy to pin her against the wall. She's wearing a soft green sweater dress, and my hands are itching, wanting to feel her breasts under all that cashmere to discover if she's wearing a bra.

"Oh," Ella turns the phone to face me. "I was just looking up some of the traditions around a Russian Christmas." She doesn't finish the implication here.

"I haven't been very informative about upcoming plans, have I?" She folds her arms and her expression says it all and I can't take offense. "I have some work to finish." *Visiting Sergei's widow, swearing in Patrick as Obshchak, sending at least another two million dollars down to Miami for the new shipment...* "But before we get dressed for tonight's party, we'll sit down and I'll talk to you about what happens next in St. Petersburg. Does that please you?"

It was a small smile from Ella, but a smile nonetheless. "Yes, thank you. I would like that."

Ella...

New Year's Eve

While Monique, the stylist, cured my hair into big, glamorous waves, I was still thinking about this afternoon and getting comfortable in Maksim's study while he pulled up photos on his laptop and explained some of the customs and traditions for a Russian Christmas.

"Why do you celebrate on January Seventh?" I'd asked.

"The Russian Orthodox Church uses the old 'Julian' calendar for religious celebration days, rather than following the Gregorian calendar that is in use today. Christmas was banned during the days of the Soviet Union," Maksim said, "after the fall in 1991, the people began celebrating openly again."

"I see," I pondered, "How do I say 'Merry Christmas' in Russian?"

"Счастливого рождества." Maksim had a smile curving one corner of his lip as I tried to repeat it.

"Um, skah...stlee...vah...vuh... Wait, say it again?"

He chuckled, "Russian is a difficult language to learn. Say it like this; 'S-schah-st-lee-vah-vah rah-zh dee-st-vah.'"

I'd tried it a few more times before it didn't sound like I was trying to offend anyone by wishing them Merry Christmas, and we parted to get ready for the New Year's Eve party.

"All done!" Monique chirped, making me look up at the mirror.

"You did an amazing job," I said sincerely, "thank you." And she had; the dress was far too glamorous for me, but here I was, cinched into the pale green silk corset top with draped cups covering less than I would have preferred of my breasts, and a silk skirt that fell to my ankles.

There was a low whistle from behind me, and I could see Maksim in the mirror behind me. "You're beautiful, *solnyshko.* Stunning." Without taking his eyes off me, he said, "Thank you, Monique. Good evening."

The woman was no fool, she nodded, smiled, and made herself scarce as we continued our stare-down in the mirror until his gaze dropped to make a leisurely circuit up and down my body, then returning to my face. "It is missing something, darling."

I looked down, spreading out the skirt a bit. "I hope not, because there's no room left in this dress for anything."

He tilted his head, considering me. As always, Maksim wore a tux like a boss. His cufflinks were silver, set with pale green emeralds.

"We match."

"How so, darling?"

"Oh, I just meant- your cufflinks-" I gestured awkwardly, "the emeralds match my wedding ring."

"Ah," Maksim's voice lowered to a purr, which usually meant he was pleased with himself, or turned on. I really hoped it was the former because it was hard enough keeping up my very own little "no touchie" rule.

"Those are not emeralds. They are green diamonds."

"Green diamonds?" I held up my ring, "I didn't know there was such a thing as green diamonds."

"They're very rare and very difficult to source," he agreed, "but I told my jeweler I wanted something that matched your eyes for your wedding ring."

That was... such an oddly romantic notion that I didn't know what to say. "Well, they're beautiful," I finally offered, "so thank you."

"But back to your dress," he was looking at the corset top with a critical eye. "It needs a bit more embellishment." Maksim took a flat, velvet-covered box from his suit jacket. He opened it and I stifled a gasp.

It was a beautifully crafted pin, with swirls of diamonds set in platinum and at the bottom, a teardrop-shaped green diamond. It was huge, it was magical. It glowed with some kind of light not drawn from the room.

"What... how old is this pin? Brooch?"

"This is the Dresden Green. The green diamond is forty-one carats, presented to Frederick the Great of Prussia, who had it made into a hat pin." His gaze went from the pin to me. "May I?"

"Uh, sure?"

Two warm fingers slipped inside the dress between my breasts, and I sucked in a gasp. He pinned the diamond there, and stepped back, turning me to face the mirror. "Now, you are complete."

Carefully brushing my fingers across the pin, I shook my head. "Maksim- this is- I can't wear this, it's too much responsibility. Who does it even belong to?"

"Sadly, it belongs to the country of Germany, and the government does not seem inclined to sell it. It has resided in the Dresden Green Vault for three hundred years, though my countrymen managed to take it briefly during World War Two before returning it to Germany. I requested to borrow the jewel from an associate to adorn you with for one night. It is priceless. And so, Mrs. Morozov, are you."

"Am I priceless because I'm... me, or because I'm your wife?" I was tossing away what could be seen as a rather beautiful moment, but I had to know if he saw me as anything other than what he wanted to create.

Slipping two fingers under my chin, Maksim lifted my head so I had to look at him. "You are priceless because you are both."

Okay, then.

"So, how do you know Alexander King?" I'm leaning over to look out at the glittering high rise in front of us, ablaze with lights and limousines queuing up to drop their expensive cargo at the massive entryway.

"Through primarily legitimate means," Maksim was focused on his phone, but there was a tiny smile on those full lips.

"Primarily, huh."

He hummed noncommittally and I laughed. While clearly, I'd

never traveled in these exalted circles before, even I knew that Alexander King, billionaire, tech genius, and sort of a dick, threw *the* New Year's Eve for New York City's elite. In fact, Prince William and Princess Kate attended last year and Tania and I spent hours online, discussing who looked better, Kate or Amal, who attended her still insanely hot husband George Clooney.

And now me...

Maksim...

I was used to media attention, though I tend to go out of my way to avoid it. But there was no flying under the radar tonight, and to my amusement, this time most of the cameras and shouted questions were focused on Ella.

"Ella! How's married life?"

"Who are you wearing tonight, Mrs. Morozov?"

"Are the rumors of your pregnancy true?"

"Uh, this is so creepy," Ella murmured to me, "does this happen all the time?"

"It does at a King event," I kissed her hand. "Just smile and don't look directly at the cameras, *solnyshko.*"

"Ella, honey!" Tania galloped up the red carpet to grab my bride in a hug. "Can you believe this shit?"

"I see why you kept your date a secret," I narrowed my eyes at Yuri, who grinned innocently. "I told you I would kill you if you broke that woman's heart and caused friction between me and my wife because of it."

"Relax, brother," he chuckled heartily for the cameras, patting my back with a heavy hand, "my love life is not the cause of the friction between you and Ella. It's almost palpable. How did you enrage my sister-in-law?"

"Shut up or I swear I will punch your pretty face," I keep smiling at the photographers while I threaten his life.

King had taken over the entire top floor of his building to create this year's New Year's Eve party, and he was striding towards us as we stepped off the elevator.

"Maksim and Yuri Morozov, my favorite Russians!"

"Alexander," we shook hands, and he turned to Ella.

"And this is your beautiful wife?" He gave his best smoldering stare at an amused Ella and I gave a rather clipped introduction.

"Ella, darling, this is Alexander King, our host, a bit of a flirtatious bastard, and clearly a man who does not value his life. Alex, my lovely bride Ella Givens Morozov."

"Charmed," he crooned, kissing her hand as his gaze dropped to her cleavage. "You're right, Maksim, the Dresden Green could never be more beautifully displayed."

"Had I known you'd use it as an excuse to stare at my wife in an inappropriate manner all night, I would have declined the honor," I said dryly.

Ella glanced at me before turning back to our host. "Oh, you lent the pin to Maksim for tonight? Thank you so much, but… this has to be one of the most priceless jewels in the world, I'm feeling some pressure here, you know?"

He laughed, "It is worth the risk, sweetheart because you look amazing. Also, between your husband's security and mine, you're more protected than the President of the United States right now."

"Well, thank you," Ella said sweetly. So sweetly that I wanted to rearrange King's face and that new nose job.

"Yes, thank you, Alex. And don't call my wife sweetheart again."

He was already charming Tania; "Oh, and you are not yet taken, darling. Perhaps there's hope for me? Look at Yuri's face! He's aging terribly. How old are you, Yuri? Fifty?"

My brother chuckled pleasantly, "Ten years younger than you, Alex, and not yet needing plastic surgery." He pointedly eyed our host's nose.

"This place is insane!" Tania gloated to Ella. They walked a bit ahead of us as they took in the winterscape, with oddly animated snow men and women who offered drinks and canapes as snow fell from the twenty-five-foot-high ceiling, the false flakes melting before touching the guests.

Tania's voice carried, "Oh, holy fuck is that Beyonce?"

Yuri grinned at her, ignoring my glare. "She's got spirit. I'm sick of the models and rich girls who are incapable of admiring anything or anyone. Tania's refreshing."

"Refreshing indeed," I agreed dourly. "Keep an eye out for Thomas Williams, I know he's here tonight."

"From the London branch of The Corporation? Their reputation is brutal in Europe, they drove the Irish Mafia out of England, but I think they're mainly focused on securities fraud and money laundering now. I remember that we were talking about him the night you decided to…" he eyed my stern gaze with a barely concealed smile. "Well, that night. Didn't he cut the Solntsevskaya Bratva completely out of the European trade? I hear Mogilevich still spits on the ground whenever his name is mentioned."

"He does," I smile politely as the mayor passes by. "But that makes it easier to strike a deal with The Corporation as the only Bratva partner they'll have."

The head of Ella's security touches his earpiece and nods, and I see the other four men subtly alter their positions as she is pulled in a new direction by Tania. Yuri watches the movement and grins. "I'll go calm her down before she accidentally drags Ella off a balcony. How did you get your hands on the Dresden Green jewel?"

We were standing by an elaborately carved dragon ice fountain that poured out chilled vodka, clear and pure, and after the first swallow, excellent quality.

"Excellent," Yuri sighed in approval. "You should have one of these made for the penthouse, brother. But back to the jewel?"

I shrugged, switching between keeping an eye on Ella's progress and searching for the CEO from The Corporation. "I thought it would suit her eyes."

"That is a long walk for matching jewelry," he shrugged, "but she looks like a princess."

I spoke without thinking, "No, my wife looks like a queen."

For a moment, it looked like there was about to be a standoff between our security and Jay-Z's, but Beyonce turned to admire the jewel on Ella's dress and everyone's hands moved away from their gun holsters. I glared at Yuri. "Go."

"Of course, Pakhan," he smiled pleasantly, making his way through the crowd.

I took another drink, watching the guests thoughtfully. The Sokolovs weren't here, which was surprising. They would have cut off any limb of King's choice to secure an invitation to his annual party. Don Toscano had his arm around the waist of his wife and was speaking to his younger sons, Giovanni and Dario. Perhaps Dante was not in as much favor with his father as I'd assumed, or maybe his bodyguards didn't fish him out of the harbor fast enough.

Shrugging, I turned to greet my wife, still surrounded by our guards. "Are you enjoying the party, *солнышко?*"

"It's impressive to a degree that defies description," she laughed, "but these guys, it's like walking in my own self-contained electric fence."

"Perhaps we can carve out enough space for a dance," I said, putting my hand on her back to guide her to the glittering silver dance floor in the center of the cavernous room. I took her right hand, placing it on my shoulder and I clasped her left hand, linking our fingers. I could only tolerate someone else's hands on me if I placed them there.

Ella...

Maksim danced? Of course, he did. And probably like a god. He turned me to face him, and I stepped back. This was the closest I'd been to him since our Christmas ice skating episode, and I was acutely aware of the heat of his hand, radiating through the silk bodice and onto my skin.

Pulling me tighter, he leaned in to whisper, "Relax."

Even in heels, the top of my head only reached his chin, but he must have a lot of experience with shorter partners because he molded me against him in a way that was much more intimate than I was ready for, and when he spun me, his thickly muscled thigh slid in between mine.

I sucked in a nervous breath and was immediately sorry. How dare he smell so good? Like expensive cologne, the stretched linen of his white shirt, pine, and something that was just... him. Something wild, and dark. Something barely tamed and it surrounded me, just like his long arms did.

"I can feel you pressed against me," Maksim whispered, "your perfect breasts."

"It- it's the corset," I babbled, "it's like the fashion definition of catfishing because I look way bigger in this than a C cup." My eyes closed in mortification. *Smooth, Ella. Really smooth, there.*

"Hmm." I could feel his broad chest shake slightly, knowing he was laughing. "I know that they fit perfectly in my hands. How your stiff nipples peek between my fingers and I tug on them..." Maksim released a sigh that was more like a groan.

There is something about the sheer bulk of this man against me, solid, hard muscle and I'm sagging against him a little more than I should. *Remember what he said to me,* I scolded myself, *forget all the other stuff, remember how he spoke to me! I'm not falling to my knees and-*

He's looking down at me, beneath those thick lashes of his, given unfairly to a man who will never fully appreciate them. There's intent. Intent to kiss me, and I want to. I really want to, just let him submerge me in his bottomless pool of erotic mojo. Because damn...

Oh, thank god the song is ending and I pull away just a bit, clapping politely with everyone else as the band takes a break. Maksim seems unwilling to release me until I hear a low, cultured British accent behind us.

"Maksim Morozov, a pleasure to see you."

We both turn and I'm looking at another tall man, leaner than the Russian next to me but just as superbly dressed. Like my husband, he had dark hair and icy blue eyes, but he had a polite smile.

"Thomas Williams, how are you?" They're shaking hands.

"Let me introduce my bride, Ella Givens Morozov. Darling, this is Thomas and Lauren Williams."

I'm smiling at Lauren, who is also tall, blonde, and very pretty. She's smiling back at me, with a bit of curiosity. "Many wishes for a happy marriage, Ella." She shakes my hand, not waiting for the men to handle niceties. "I don't know Maksim well, but every rumor pointed to a man who was stubbornly planning to die single."

Oh, I *like* her. I can tell Lauren is pretty much in the same position I am. "No one is more surprised than me," I agree sweetly, and I can see Maksim's eyebrow rise threateningly.

Thomas is shaking my hand next, speaking with an impeccably cultured English accent. "A pleasure, Ella. Where did you two meet?"

He's incredibly good-looking, this guy, and has charisma to burn. He must be dangerous, too. I'll be he's... what is it in England? British Mafia? I don't know, but I realize he's still waiting for my answer and I can't remember the name of Maksim's other club so I settled on, "At Maksim's nightclub. He bought me a drink and the rest is history."

"That's so nice," Lauren chimes in. "What made you fall for him?"

I can't say 'roofies,' so I go with, "We both like to run," smiling sweetly up at the Russian who's squeezing my side, just slightly painfully.

"Oh, so do we!" She lights up and we chat about running paths through Central Park while the men have a low conversation. Thomas doesn't look completely invested in whatever Maksim is saying, but he's still listening.

"Hello, Beautiful People!" It's Alexander King, up on stage and shouting cheerfully. "Everyone grab your favorite person - date or otherwise - and get ready for the countdown."

"It's midnight already?" Lauren looks up at the giant clock

display.

"Time flies when you're having fun, huh?" Not my most brilliant response, but now then we're counting down with the rest of the guests.

"Five!"

"Four!"

"Three!"

"Two!"

"ONE! HAPPY NEW YEAR!"

"Auld Lang Syne" begins to play and I'm lifted into Maksim's arms, feet dangling and the wily villain is kissing me with a level of thoroughness that leaves no room for anything but opening my mouth when he slides his tongue in and I'm gripping his big shoulders as the "pop! pop!" of fireworks is going off, and-

He pulls away from my lips. "Those aren't fireworks, GET DOWN!"

Now, there's screaming, I can recognize the terrifying rattle that means there are automatic weapons going off and there's a mad stampede for the door.

"Oh, my god, where's Tania!" I'm trying to find her while I'm being yanked down behind a big table, Lauren on one side of me, and our guards and some well-dressed men that I suspect might be theirs acting as a barricade, already firing guns that appeared from their jackets.

"Head down, darling." Thomas sounds as urbane as ever, and Lauren mutters something under her breath but does as he tells her.

My hand presses against that priceless diamond pinned to my cleavage. Was this a robbery? No, not with automatic weapons.

My stomach gives a lurch as I realize that no, the shooters want to kill people. Lots of them. And probably, specifically us.

CHAPTER 14 – BAD NEWS AND MORE BAD NEWS

In which Maksim is capable of kindness for a full ten minutes before he jumps right back into Asshole Pakhan status

Ella...

I was frantically searching for Tania through the bullets and shattered glass when I felt something poke my breast, I looked down and remembered the priceless diamond. I tucked it deeper into my bodice, trying to hide it. Maksim grabbed my arm, "There is a side door to the kitchen corridor behind you to the left," he shouted over the gunfire, "Fedor and Ivan are covering you and Lauren."

"Wait!" I'm grabbing his arm as he's lifting his gun again, "Who's with you?"

He actually looks surprised, enough that his gun hand drops a little. "I'm fine."

"But Tania! I can't leave without-"

He interrupts me, "I'll find her, but I can promise you that she could not be better protected, Yuri will keep her safe."

"We have a window of opportunity in ten seconds," Thomas is

speaking in the same tone you'd use to ask for cream in your coffee. He's shooting with one hand and helping Lauren gather up her long skirt with the other. I do the same thing and grab her hand.

"Ready?" She nods, and with a push from Maksim, we're off, scrambling gracelessly across the floor toward the slight opening ahead of us. Thomas must have thrown in some bodyguards, too, because there's five men around us. The shooting behind us is dying down, and I'm not sure if that's a good or bad thing. Lauren and I are both slowing down, looking behind us and Ivan grabs me by the waist and hauls me through the door like a sack of flour.

There's a clutter of shaken-up guests ahead of us, stumbling through the kitchen, but I guess it's too soon for the police to have responded because the only people with guns seem to be a couple of security guards, and our guys.

"Ella! What the fuck!" Tania's sprinting toward me, followed by Yuri, still keeping his gun up, sweeping the area.

"Are you okay?" I'm hugging her hard enough to nearly knock us over until Fedor pulls us upright.

She won't let go of me, "How could this happen? Where are the police? This is-" Tania hates to cry, so when tears stream down her face, I hug her tighter.

I glanced over at Yuri, and there was blood on his tuxedo shirt, nauseatingly vivid on the starched white. "Are you okay?"

He did that mysterious Slavic shrug. "Most of it isn't mine." Never one to waste an opportunity, he nodded to Lauren, "Lovely to see you again, I ran into you and your husband in London at Wimbledon last year?"

"Oh, yeah." She pushed her hair out of her face, "I remember! You're Maksim's brother."

Tania sensibly interrupted, "Look, I don't want to break up the reunion, but shouldn't we try to get out of here?"

"Not without Thomas," Lauren says instantly. Whatever argument she might have had after that is cut off when one of her bodyguards pulls her down to the floor. I feel wind rushing past my cheek and I'm suddenly face down, too. *Someone's shooting at us,* I realize, *and that was a bullet that just passed within half an inch of my head.* Blood is splashing across the pale silk of my dress and it's from Fedor, who grunts in pain but still shoots back.

Oh, come *on.*

There must be at least twenty of them, wearing tuxedos and waiter uniforms, and they're heading toward us. The rapid staccato of bullets knocks three of our men off their feet. Yuri shoves Tania behind one of the steel prep tables and Lauren and I follow. There's a grunt and a thud, and I see Ivan bleeding in terrifying spurts.

"Help me grab him!" I shout at Tania, but she's frozen, staring at the blood. It's Lauren that comes to my aid and we struggle to drag the beefy Russian behind the table. "Craaap," I'm mumbling, trying to make my stupid brain work. "It's the femoral artery, Lauren hold it here-" I grabbed a dishcloth and pressed it against the bullet wound. She held it down firmly; her lips were white but she's calm. The cloth was almost instantly saturated with blood while I struggled to pull off my stockings. There was a wooden spoon lying on the floor close to us and I grabbed it, getting the stocking around his leg, twisting it into a tourniquet with the spoon. Ivan looked up at me, his big, square face was pale, his skin greyish, like his short-cropped hair.

"Go behind the... counter," he wheezed, trying to look stern.

"We're good here, just concentrate on breathing slow," I urged him, "breathing fast pushes up your blood pressure and you'll bleed more. Slow breaths."

"The bleeding's slowing down," Lauren shouts into my ear. Not that it matters, my ears are already ringing from the gunfire and we if actually live through this thing, I'm going to be deaf anyway. It could be my imagination, but it sounded like all the shooting stopped and there was the unmistakable thud of three, or four more bodies hitting the floor.

God, I hope they're not our guys. I paused, *when did they become "our" guys?"*

Silence. Did this mean it was over?

An explosion ripped through the ballroom, blowing the doors open and there's screaming everywhere, followed by a thunderous crash that sounded like three hundred windows are being smashed at the same time.

Tania is crouching, hands over her ears, rocking back and forth. "Sweetie? Hey, Tan, it's-" was I really going to say it was going to be okay?

The fire alarm is blaring and it's not helping the ringing in my ears. But I don't smell smoke, so I keep one arm around Tania and the other on the tourniquet on Ivan. We wait. I don't know for what, but I'm not moving.

"Lauren!"

She leaps up, sobbing in relief. "Thomas? Oh, I was so afraid you'd-"

He's hugging her, kissing her hair tenderly. "I will always come back to you; you know I will."

My eyes fill with tears for their happiness, and then it hits me that he's alone. "Wait. Where's Maksim?"

They part and he smiles at me. His face is covered in soot and his expensive tuxedo jacket is ripped. "It's all right. He's in the ballroom. I'll take you back, where's his brother?"

"He's..." I look around, rising up on my knees, trying to find him. I finally spot him around the corner by the pantry. Yuri's doing chest compressions on one of his men, his face set and determined. It's obvious the poor guy is gone, he was hit in the neck, and it's a terrible-looking, jagged wound.

"Yuri?" I clumsily get to my feet. I want to kick off these stupid high heels but there's broken glass everywhere. "Hey..." I kneel down next to him, but he ignores me, continuing his precise CPR on a man who's gone. "Hey, he's-" I try to put my hand on his, stopping him, but he brushes me off, continuing the chest compressions. "Yuri? Sweetie, why don't you let the paramedics take over? They're here now." He still ignores me, so I sit next to him, finding a napkin and putting it over the poor man's neck.

Maksim found us after having pried himself loose from a hysterical Alexander King. He apparently saved his life by taking out one of the shooters who had his gun to King's head. There are police crawling everywhere and none of them seem cool with us leaving without extensive questioning, but he gives a short statement and brushes them off by coldly reminding them that some of the men lost were his. Yuri finally stops his mechanical CPR when his brother crouches next to him, murmuring in his ear.

I lean in and whisper to Maksim, "Do you want me to take Tania home?" She's still sitting with Lauren, who kindly refused to leave her until we could find the rest of our group.

He looks up at me, blue eyes pale and blank. "No, we'll all go together." He and Thomas do that manly thing where they grip

161

each other's shoulder while they're shaking hands to indicate extra emotion.

Lauren and I just hug. Pretty tightly because I'm learning fast that nothing bonds a new friendship more quickly than imminent death. "Let's talk soon," she whispers, "I have some experience, so maybe we can process this together."

"You have experience with shootouts?" I whisper back.

She sighs, "You have no idea."

Looking down, I groan. "Oh, my dress. I'm sorry." It's ripped in a dozen places and decorated with some nauseating splashes of blood. For some reason, there's gravy covering most of my left side.

Maksim shakes his head. "It's only a dress. You're not hurt." He looks down and frowns. "I'll send in a couple of men to search for the Dresden Green. It might still be by the table where we took shelter."

"Oh-" I plunge my fingers into my corset top and fish around for a moment. "Here it is, I stuck it in there for safekeeping."

His brow rose, and one corner of his mouth. "In the middle of a firefight? Impressive."

Maksim and his bodyguards shepherd us through the ballroom, trying to hustle us past the dead bodies. The ear-searing crash we'd heard was the two massive chandeliers falling from the ceiling and crushing ten or so of the gunmen under a ton or so of rubble. "Did you do that?" I ask as he's hustling me past the piles of shattered crystal.

"Possibly."

"What, what does that mean, possibly? Like, how did you-" Even I know to shut up when we're joined by other people, including two police officers.

By the time we're exiting the elevator and sweeping into the limo, there's a barrage of reporters and hundreds of New Yorkers with their phones out. Yuri takes his jacket off and holds it around Tania to block her from view. He seems to have put himself back together after losing his... friend? Employee? Family member? I don't know how they're all put together but I've heard a lot of family-based terminology in the Morozov Bratva. But Tania sits next to me, and I hug her tightly.

"My place is the other way," she finally mumbles.

"I know." I put my head on her shoulder knowing Yuri is watching us, his expression blank. "But you should spend the night with us, okay?" I haven't asked Maksim, but he nods at her, too.

Later...

"How is Tania?" Maksim looks as rough as I feel, still wearing his bloody tuxedo shirt. A doctor had showed up at the penthouse just as we made it back, to clean and stitch up a bullet wound in his arm.

"She's asleep," I sit on our bed and groan with relief, taking off those horrible high heels. "I got her in the shower and she took two of the Xanax the doctor left. How's Yuri?"

He sighed, running his hand through that silky, dark hair I wasn't allowed to touch. "The same, though his medication of choice was half a bottle of vodka."

"Who was the guy he was trying to revive?" I wondered if he would actually tell me.

"One of our first cousins. He served under Yuri. He'd just transferred him to our organization here from our St. Petersburg one."

"Oh, man..." Yuri must be heartbroken. "What was his name?"

"Stanislav."

"I'm so sorry about Stanislav. Are you okay?"

He won't look at me, his jaw clenched. "Of course."

Rubbing my neck, I'm aware that there's blood drying on my skin and flaking onto the beautiful green bedspread. "Oh, I'm sorry- I'm messing up the bed- I'm-" The floodgates open and the whole, horrible night collapses in on me, big, heaving ugly tears and I can't stop.

Maksim...

Ella's stoicism - very Russian - had been admirable. I knew she had no experience with violence, certainly nothing like this night. But she saved Ivan's life by stopping the bleeding, cared for Yuri, for her friend, and still expressed concern for me.

She was magnificent.

But when the inevitable collapse comes, I'm ready. Carrying her into the master bathroom, I seated her on the long granite counter, turning on the shower. I have never used the silly essential oil diffusers that were built into the controls, but I know she likes them. I unzipped her dress as the smell of lavender drifted through the room.

"Raise your arms, *solnyshko*." She obeyed me silently, still crying. I pulled off my bloody tuxedo, lifting her to bring her into the shower.

"Your bandage," Ella's voice was small, like a child's and she was still crying. "You're not supposed to get that wet."

"It's all right," I soothed her, piling her long hair up to work the shampoo through it. She has not let me near her for weeks

- aside from the moments at Rockefeller Center - but now, she simply stood still and let me move her arms and legs, washing the blood and dirt away. I found a cut on one knee that needed bandaging before wrapping her in one of my robes and putting her into bed. Sliding in behind her, I put my arm around her, drawing her against me. Her damp hair smelled sweet, and her skin was so warm from the shower. I waited to see if she would try to pull away from me, but Ella snuggled a little closer.

"Maksim?"

"Hmm?"

"What does *solnyshko* mean?"

I pressed my lips to her forehead. "It means 'little sun'."

"Oh..." Ella's almost asleep. "That's nice."

I watched the moon make its way across the sky. Five dead yesterday in the ammunition theft. Another three guards were shot to death tonight, and two more were wounded. We had widows to visit, and funerals to plan.

And vengeance. I would rip apart anyone who brought this down on my family. We weren't the only ones who suffered losses tonight. I'll be making phone calls to the others - Thomas Williams, the Toscano mafia and everyone else who'd have a score to settle. Whoever did this - and my money was on that worm Sokolov - made a fatal mistake by angering this many crime families in one colossally stupid attack.

Shifting, I put my arm over my head, staring at the ceiling. But that raised the question. Sokolov's clan was greedy and vicious, but stupid? Pavel hadn't survived this long as Pakhan through recklessness. There were pieces missing here.

After lying in bed for another two hours, I got up and headed for the gym, pounding into one of the punching bags until my knuckles were bloody. I'm still on the weight machines when Yuri walked in. But he paused in the middle of taping his hands, just staring blankly out the window.

"Brother," I sighed, "come spot me." I'm hoping he's still with it enough to keep me from strangling on my own barbell.

After six repetitions, he speaks up. "Tania left early this morning. She asked me not to call her again." He shrugs, returning the weight to the stand. "But Stanislav... I must contact his mother." He drops his head. "I'm the one who arranged to bring him here."

Sitting next to him, I say, "He wanted to come here. You know this."

Running his hands down his face, Yuri stares out the window. "It was my responsibility."

"In the end, it is my responsibility. Stanislav was young, but he's been Bratva since he was fifteen. He made the choice, even knowing the risks." I nudged him with my shoulder. "We'll go see his mother together." Standing with a groan, I haul him up with me. "But before we leave for St. Petersburg, we have men to bury, funerals to attend."

"And above all else," he added, "who would dare attack five crime families at once? You haven't slept at all, have you?"

"Later," I shrug.

The bad news kept coming. Toscano succumbed to his injuries after the news that his wife died during the firefight. Did that mean idiot Dante was now head of the family?

I'm still trying to count the number of organizations affected by the attack. The Yakuza was there at the party, I knew they'd lost people. I called Thomas.

"How are you and Lauren?"

"We're fine." I heard her voice and his soft answer before he shut the door. "I lost another man to his injuries last night." His fury bled through his composed tone.

"Please tell your wife I am indebted to her for her help in saving Ivan's life. She was very calm under such pressure."

I heard the faintest shade of amusement in his tone. "It was not her first gun battle," Thomas said. "I can agree to a meeting to discuss your financial proposal, but I think you'll agree that discovering who was responsible for last night should be a priority. That level of disrespect cannot be tolerated."

A strange way to develop a business relationship with The Corporation, but I'll take what I can get, I think, before agreeing with him. "We're not the only ones from last night bent on vengeance," I add. "We might find allies in the search."

Ella...

For the first time, I wake up not teetering right on the edge of the bed, just about to fall off. I was smack dab center and not only was this thing the size of a cruise liner, it was unfathomably comfortable. The pillows were fluffier. The bedspread was thick and velvety and luxurious. I could have petted it like a kitten. I've missed out, sleeping on the edge.

The pillow next to me had a Maksim-shaped indent, so he did sleep next to me.

Sitting up, I rubbed my face. How did I feel about that, my gangster spouse, right next to me? Washing the blood off of me in the shower?

Of course, my snarky inner voice adds, *the man's had plenty of experience doing* that. But still, there was kindness there. He almost looked like he'd been waiting for me to lose it. Is there some sort of order on how you process being in the middle of a shoot-out at your New Year's Eve party? But then the vision of poor Ivan's spurting leg came back in technicolor and I have to run for the bathroom.

Of course, Maksim had to walk into the bathroom while I'm vigorously brushing my teeth.

"Are you all right?" He frowned, not even slowing down on shedding his clothes, which he had no problem doing in front of me at any time.

I put my thumb up, hoping he'd leave me alone, but he lingered, wearing shorts from working out and nothing else. God, that chest… sculpted pectorals and just exactly the perfect amount of dark chest hair. He handed me a towel.

"Um, thank you." Wiping my face, I looked at him in the mirror. "How's Ivan?"

"He's conscious and swearing his lifelong loyalty to you." Maksim was smiling as he said this, so I assumed that doesn't break any Bratva laws.

"I'm glad." I was. Ivan wears a perpetually dour expression, but he always waited for me to walk on my own without trying to hustle me along like I was a wayward toddler. "I'm going to go check on Tania."

He looked over his shoulder as he pulls off his shorts. "She's already gone."

"What? Was she okay?" Oh, damn it now Maksim has turned around and I'm trying to keep my eyes above his waist and it's really difficult because his dick is already half-hard. Does he just walk around perpetually tumescent?

"She told Yuri she didn't want to see him anymore and left early." He still wore that smug little grin, where one corner of his mouth curls up and his entire being is radiating with a self-satisfied knowledge that he is aware every woman wants him, and I'm sure he thinks I'm one of them, but he can-

"Wait. Tania left and she blew off Yuri?" This is bad on two fronts. Tania couldn't get out of bed before ten, even if you set her mattress on fire. And she was crazy about Yuri... at least his dick, which was all she'd been talking about.

"Apparently."

"I should..." His body was wreathed in steam from the shower, and soap suds traveled down his sculpted back. *What? I should what... oh!* "G- go call her. Yeah."

But for the first time that I could remember, Tania sent me to voicemail.

Maksim was gone for most of the day, not returning until I was fast asleep and leaving early the next morning. I wondered if he slept at all. I'd called Tania fifteen times and left various threatening texts. The bodyguards swarming the penthouse refused to let me leave.

"Mr. Morozov requested that you stay here for your safety."

Yeah, and Mr. I'm Such A Dick Morozov didn't answer my calls, either. I was seconds away from caving and asking Alina if she'd call him for me when Maksim came home.

"Hey, can you have one of the guys take me over to Tania? I really need to check on her-"

He walked past me. "Not today. If everything goes smoothly, you can check on her tomorrow before we leave for St. Petersburg."

"Maksim, I need to go today, she's not taking my calls and this is completely un-Tania-like, and-"

Finally, he stops but it's only to look sternly down at me. "I need you for a Bratva function today. This is part of your role as a Pakhan's wife." He's guiding me into his study. Oh, the inner sanctum.

"What is this function?" I sit in the wonderfully big, squishy leather chair that I've noticed he prefers. So, he leans against his desk, folding his arms.

"A funeral. For eight of my men."

Now I feel like a complete scumbag for being so cranky.

"Oh, no. You lost that many guards at the party?"

He shook his head. "Five others were killed the day before."

"Wha-" my hands are waving helplessly, "I'm so sorry, that's-that's really awful. How did they-"

"It doesn't matter," Maksim waved my question away imperiously, "but our role here is to show respect and comfort, should the families wish it."

Oh, this is so bad. "Do many of them have wives? Kids?"

"Yes."

The funeral was held at St. Nicholas Russian Orthodox Cathedral in downtown Manhattan. There were eight coffins, and we circled each one as I carefully put a flower on the bodies. One man was in such terrible shape that the burial shroud was already covering him. But Maksim leaned in and kissed the forehead of each one, his face stoic. I snuck sideways glances at the families, at the other people who work for him. I'd tried to smile and offer my condolences, but none of them were interested, and I backed away quickly. I got it. I was the outsider, some of their husbands probably died guarding us on New Year's Eve. Alina was there, too, looking chic in a black Chanel suit and the crying women were hugging her instead.

She looked at me over the shaking shoulders of one new widow with a little smile only I could see.

Maksim sent me home after the service. Alone for the rest of the night, I kept trying to reach Tania.

"Hey, honey. Please pick up. I know what happened was... just. I know. I don't know what to say. I feel like it's my fault because you never would have been there if you hadn't been sticking with me like a true friend. Please..." *Please don't hate me.* "If you need time, I understand but will you please tell me..." *Please tell me that you're okay. Please tell me you'll speak to me again.* "Just, let me know you're okay? I love you."

CHAPTER 15 – SKATING THE NEVA RIVER

In which Ella gets some much-needed Girlfriend Wisdom, dinner out, and the most impressive mansion in St. Petersburg

Ella...

Surprise, surprise. Maksim doesn't come home that night.

The next day, I'm told to pack for the trip by the ever-(not)helpful Alina, and it takes everything in me not to scream, "You do not tell me what to do!" I pack, of course, but as god as my witness, I'm not leaving this city until they let me see Tania.

On my fifth rotation through the penthouse, ignoring the stares of Maksim's guards and wishing death and murder and horrible acne on all of them, I hear a voice in the other room. A new voice, made apparent by the fact that his accent isn't Russian, it's Irish.

"Hi, who are you?" *Okay, a little abrupt, Ella.*

He has a nice smile, looks later twenties, your standard Irish ginger, and he's talking to a couple of Maksim's senior guards. "Ah, you're the new Mrs. Morozov, and looking lovely today, may I say."

He's cheeky, I like this guy. "You probably shouldn't say that if you want your head still attached to your shoulders, sadly. And call me Ella."

"I'll be calling you Mrs. Morozov because I do wish to keep my head. I'm Patrick Walsh, the Pakhan's *Obshchak*."

I happen to know what that means, thanks to my Wikipedia study. "The head of his security? You've certainly got your work cut out for you, huh?"

He laughs, and it's a nice laugh, too. Really, he seems too cheerful for a killer. "Your husband definitely keeps us hopping, but it's an honor."

This Patrick is nice, I think, *he has some authority. I'll bet that demented, conniving swine answers his Obshchak's phone calls.*

"Patrick, can I ask a favor?"

An hour later, I'm pounding on Tania's door.

"Look, woman! Just answer the door because I know you're in there! You're burning that horrible holiday candle your mom always sends that smells like a reindeer pooped out a pine tree! I'm not going away until you-"

The door opens, but she still has the security chain on. No silly fight or pissy moment we've had as best friends hurt as much as this does. "Hey."

"Oh, sweetie..." I'm trying not to cry. Tania looks exhausted and a little drunk. "How are you... Look, please just tell me you're processing this. Can we talk?"

"You look nice," she drinks directly from a wine bottle and I wince.

"We're flying out today. St. Petersburg for the Russian

Christmas. I don't want to go; I want to stay here with you. I know..." I pause for a moment, trying to find the right words. "It was really bad. It was my first... well, all of it. Just like you. Yuri says you don't want to see him anymore. I don't blame you."

She chuckles mirthlessly, "Yeah, if only we could get you cut loose too, huh?"

My hopes rise at the use of the word "we" again. "Honey, no one could be a better friend than you have been. I just..."

"You know what?" Tania interrupts me, "If I hadn't insisted on going to his pretentious club that night, he never would have roofied and kidnapped you. If you think about it, this is my fault."

"No," I shake my head firmly, "No, Tan, you can't say that. No one could predict this totally screwed-up Karma train that barreled over both of us. It just did. Please, will you let me in?"

Patrick, damn him, has been lingering a polite distance away, letting me talk, but now he steps over to me. "Mrs. Morozov," he says in a super polite, deferential way that is really irritating, "I apologize for the interruption. Mr. Morozov has arrived at the jet and is requesting that you join him immediately."

"It's *his* jet!" I hiss, "It's not like we're missing a flight. Can you ask him to-"

His smile's getting a little strained. "Ma'am, I have instructions to pick you up and carry you if I must."

I whirl back to the door. "Sweetie, will you please take my calls? Please? We don't have to talk about any of this, we can just..." I do not want to cry in front of Maksim's *Obshchak.* I don't want him telling that heartless prick that I cried.

Tania seems to soften, just a little. "Girl, get on the jet. Steal all the little soaps and towels in the bathroom for me." She pulls me in for a hug and I sag a little with relief. "I just... I have to figure this out. We'll just. You know."

I don't know, but I put my hand on her cheek. "I love you. I'll call you later, okay?"

"Okay, I love you right back," she gives me a wobbly smile, "I just need to put this all together. I've been so busy trying to cheer you up and pretending that this was normal, that... I'm an idiot. I guess it never hit me until all those bullets started flying that..." Her chin trembles and I want to hug her but I know she'll kill me. Tania hates it when people see her cry, even me. "I'll work it out, Els. Go. Have some fun. I'll text you every day, I promise. Don't worry about me."

"I'm sorry," Patrick said on the way down to the entrance, "I tried to give you as much time as I could."

I can't be mad at him, he at least got Maksim to agree to let me see Tania by taking over my security personally. "I know. Thank you."

The jet is full of gigantic Russians. And me. Maksim is deep in discussion with Patrick, Yuri, and two other men I recognize from his senior staff. And Alina.

Seriously? I'm raging silently, *Take your Russian wifey with you and let me stay here, you-*

"Alina," Maksim is talking, "I'm keeping you here in Manhattan. You'll need to keep track of the new building's permits and codes with the city."

Her eyes are wide and crazy-looking, but she says, "Yes, of course, Pakhan." She says Pakhan in a tone that really means 'My King,' but I do not care. It's one less person to make my life hell for the next two weeks.

175

Finding a comfortable seat in the far corner, I put in my earbuds and try to pretend I'm somewhere else for a few blessed moments.

I wake up when the jet hits some turbulence, bouncing up and down again in a way that reminds me I'm in a little steel tube 25,000 feet up in the air. As I convince my stomach to go back down my throat, I look around. The cabin's lights are dimmed, and several of the Russians are sleeping, some of the others are playing cards and cursing at each other in low voices.

Maksim is still working. His suit jacket is off and his shirt's cuffs are rolled up his tanned forearms. That look *does* something to me, damn him. Yuri's next to him, shuffling through some papers, handing a few to his brother every now and then with a comment. Trying to stand, I nearly trip over something tangled with my feet, it's a cashmere blanket, soft as a baby's bottom and a deep green. Maksim looks up.

"Ah, you're awake. Are you hungry?"

A quick check of my phone shows I've been asleep for six hours. "No, I'm fine, thank you. Maybe you should get some sleep?"

Yuri is smiling at me, kind as always, but his brother shakes his head and goes back to their discussion. I sigh. *Score one point for putting the blanket on me,* I thought, *aaand, knock that score right back to zero for being a dismissive swine.*

After a couple more hours, it's clear Maksim's fallen asleep, his dark head drooping over his laptop. Yuri carefully pulls it away and closes it, turning off the light over their chairs. Making his way over, he drops into the seat opposite me with a sigh.

"How are you doing, sister dear?"

I smile, shaking my head. "How can you possibly be so likable, Yuri? It certainly doesn't run in the fam- I mean, really. You are."

His chest shook, he was laughing at me silently, but I didn't mind. There was a consistent sort of kindness with Yuri that clearly wasn't a genetic trait, since his brother would rather be eaten by a shark than show such a soft emotion.

"Expectations for me were different than the ones Maksim endured," he said, cracking his neck and rubbing it.

"Endured is an interesting choice of words," I ventured.

He looked around us, I suspect by habit. Anyone nearby was asleep, but he lowered his voice. "Being born into a Bratva family removes any chance of a normal life. Maksim says he's told you of the expectations for women. Groomed and traded off for a better alliance."

"I keep trying to remind myself it's the twenty-first century when I hear about the power structure," I shook my head, still mildly nauseated about their father's plans for Ekaterina and Mariya.

"For the men?" He chuckled joylessly. Yuri's square, handsome face was cold again, his blue eyes hollow. "Maksim was groomed to take over as Pakhan since birth."

"When you say groomed, you mean like…" I wasn't sure what to ask, but I didn't think he meant reading contracts and taking leadership courses.

He leaned back, watching me with his index finger tracing his lower lip. It was a very Maksim-like gesture. Yuri was his brother's height, but bulkier somehow. The same big hands, scarred fingers that I'm sure inflicted damage on dozens of victims. Or bad guys. I don't know anymore.

"I was fourteen, the first time my father put a gun in my hand and told me to shoot a business rival." He examined my expression, "Maksim was even younger."

Moistening my suddenly dry lips, I asked, "Did you do it?"

"Of course."

Exhaling, I racked my brain, trying to think of anything to say that wasn't along the lines of: *Are you kidding me right now?*

"That's… unspeakable. What did he do if you refused to do something?"

Yuri laughed. Not his usual pleasant chuckle, this was bitter. "There was none of that. If I made a mistake, he'd torture Maksim. If he made an error…" He shuddered. "My father nearly beat me to death one day after Maksim made an error collecting a pickup from one of our casinos."

"Wh- what happened?" He didn't answer me, he was staring over my shoulder, his eyes blank and pale. Leaning forward, I hesitantly touched his hand. "Yuri? What happened?"

Blinking, he seemed to come back online, it was the only way to describe it. "Maksim stopped him."

I bit the inside of my cheek, concentrating on the pain so I wouldn't cry. Yuri would hate that; he deserved better than pity from me. "I'm glad he's gone," I offered, "and I don't know how you've managed to remain as kind as you are after growing up under…" Can I call his father an evil fuck? A complete bastard? Is that considered rude even with what he just told me?

"Take whatever I endured and times it by ten and you have Maksim's childhood." Yuri squeezed my hand and stood up. "I'm going to try to get some sleep. Just ring for the flight attendant if you're hungry."

Like I could sleep after that story.

By the time the pilot announced our descent, I was pressed

against the window like a tourist staring down at the diamond-spangled carpet of white covering the landscape. There was a massive, black body of water, Lake Ladoga, I think. The jet circled, and the glittering blue of the water swooped out before us.

"The Gulf of Finland." Maksim was leaning over me, looking out at the view. "It leads out to the Baltic Sea."

As the jet descended, I asked, "Where's your home? What general direction?"

He pointed to a thickly forested area. "The estate is there, and we have a house in the city, in a section called the Golden Triangle." I'm trying to remember my research. "It's where the nobility lived before the revolution in 1917, right?" He looked down at me, brow raised as if surprised I would actually know anything about the city's history.

"Correct," he looked up at the flight attendant's pleading stare and seated himself next to me. "Put your seatbelt on, darling."

Maksim...

Every time I returned home, I'd take a huge breath as I left the jet. The faint, salty tang of the sea, the scent of pine that always swirled through the city under the haze of smoke and car exhaust. And the strangest thing, the smell of old parchment. That one couldn't be real, but St. Petersburg was always the center for academics and artists since the 1800's. Our greatest literary works and our most magnificent music were created here. I looked up from a discussion with Yuri to see Ella moving from one side of the seat to the other, trying to see everything at once.

"I am guessing this is your first visit to St. Petersburg?" Yuri inquires in his most falsely solicitous tone.

"Very funny, Yuri," she laughed at him, "I don't care that I look like a tourist, everything's so beautiful! Oh, that's the Hermitage Museum, right? It's so regal!"

He chuckled, leaning closer to point out the Smolny Cathedral, explaining, "The convent was originally built to house Elizabeth, the daughter of Peter the Great. Even after she accepted the offer of the Russian throne, the construction continued, but it's actually used as a cathedral."

Ella eagerly asked questions, completely at ease with my irritating brother, grabbing his arm to point at something else. Smiling and talking in a comfortable way she's never used with me. I was filled with a desire to open the door and throw him out onto the street, but I controlled myself. Taking in a deep breath and letting it out, I reminded myself to behave like the Pakhan I'm expected to be.

When the Mercedes stopped, I allowed myself to enjoy my bride's expression.

"Is this a hotel?" Ella asks, eyes wide, "It's so imposing."

It is imposing. The Morozov mansion is situated on a curve in the Neva River, a four-story stone building with copper fixtures and a statue of a copper eagle on the crest of the roof, weathered green against the pale stone. Helping her out of the car, I enjoyed her awe, her pleasure in the architecture.

"No, this is our home." I put my hand on the small of her back, guiding her through the gate, nodding at the men guarding the front.

"Are your mom and sisters here?"

"Not until tomorrow," I squeezed her hip, "are you relieved?"

"No!" She seemed almost offended. "I adore your sisters." Realizing she didn't include my mother, Ella rushes to add, "And your mother is..." Smothering a laugh, I watched her flail around for something to say.

"My mother is intimidating. But you'll learn to like her."

The entry hall has always been a magnificent greeting to me, two stories high with a twenty-five-foot-high Christmas tree dominating the space between the grand staircase.

"I am heading over to my wing," Yuri said, kissing Ella on the cheek. "I will see you later."

"Wait, you have a *wing?*" she called after him.

"My brother and I both prefer our privacy," I said, and for a moment, there was a stillness in the hall, and I can tell it was making her uneasy. "You're not uncomfortable being alone with me, are you?" My voice was deeper and I'm hard almost instantly, hearing her breathing quicken, and her cheeks flush.

"Pakhan, it is an honor to have you home again."

The moment is spoiled as our housekeeper greets us with a big smile. Stifling a sigh, I introduced them, "Darling, this is Anya, she has been with the Morozov family for over forty years. Anya, this is my bride, Ella Givens Morozov."

"A pleasure," Ella says warmly, holding out her hand.

Our housekeeper stared at her, then gingerly shook her hand. It was not too long ago that my father insisted that the staff bow deeply and avert their eyes out of "respect" for his role. The old bastard would have been much happier two centuries ago when he could have outright owned his servants.

"Anya, let's save the tour of the house for tomorrow. Could you send up something light? We'll be going out tonight." The grand staircase sweeps up to the second floor on both sides of the entry hall, one heading to Yuri's wing, the other to mine.

"Your own wing," Ella murmured, shaking her head. The master suite looks out over the Neva River, frozen solid and dotted with skaters. The marble floors are cold in winter, and I've had them covered in priceless oriental rugs in deep reds and blues. The stone fireplace dominates one wall of the bedroom, and the ancient four-poster bed sits grandly on the wall opposite, with an antique tapestry for the canopy.

Running her hand over the graceful swoop of the couch in front of the fireplace, she asked, "How old is this furniture? This all looks hand-carved."

I pull my tie loose, unbuttoning my dress shirt. "Probably 250 years old, or so. The nobility back then demanded extremely ornate, heavy furnishings, but as you can see, they were crafted to last for centuries."

"Amazing," she whispered, tracing the detail on the carved marble fireplace mantel with a fingertip.

"Why don't you change and come back into the sitting room, Anya will bring you something to eat, and I want you to try to sleep for a few hours, it will help with the jet lag. We're having dinner with Alexi and Lucya tonight."

Ella...

It's not like I didn't know that Maksim Morozov was filthy rich. But it takes walking into a mansion like this to realize he was shamelessly, wantonly, disgustingly filthy rich. These rooms... this house. I was so overwhelmed by all the opulence in the suite that I pulled a chair over to curl up by one of the enormous windows and watch the white lights that seemed to outline every building slowly turn on in the twilight. The days were very short, this far north. But the city seemed to push back against the early night. There was so much to look at, I didn't think I could possibly sleep.

"Wake up, *solnyshko.*"

I'm in the giant bed, and the fireplace is blazing, turning the room golden. Maksim is leaning over me, one hand next to my waist, the other braced on the headboard. His unreasonably handsome face is close to mine, close enough to see the gold flecks in the blue of his eyes. Why does he have to be so good-looking? Why does he have to be so warm? Why can't I just stop noticing these things?

"I'm up," I mumble, trying to scoot away so I can sit against the headboard. "Um... did you sleep?"

He shrugged. "I don't need much sleep."

He was lying, he looked exhausted, I doubted he'd slept more than the few hours of rest he caught on the jet since the shootout. Maksim may be a heartless dick, but he takes his responsibility for the men in his organization very seriously.

"I can't imagine how hard this is for you," I ventured, "I can see how important your people are to you."

He looked up, as if surprised that I would say anything. *Crap,* I thought, *was that bad? Was I not allowed to talk about it?*

"When I find the people responsible," he said casually, "their suffering will go on for days. Well beyond when they're begging for death."

Was that supposed to be comforting? I thought, *Or a little jump into the sociopathic thought process of the Morozov Pakhan?* I nodded. There was nothing to say.

Maksim took me out into the St. Petersburg winter night and it was... magical. So perfect that I could forgive him for the last maybe... seventy-two hours or so. Every house and building were lined with white lights, which were also draped across the streets, creating an unbroken line that beckoned us down along the river, watching the impromptu hockey games, and vendors alongside selling hot drinks and sweets.

If it had been anyone else, I would have taken their hand, maybe swinging our linked hands as we walked. Not Maksim, who looked spectacular in his black cashmere coat. I was bundled in something nearly identical, but my coat was bright red, with silk-lined black leather gloves. People turned to look at us, but I suspect it was not due to my possible hotness but first to the fact that we were circled by black-suited men - Maksim really had a thing about suits on his employees - and also, because he was gorgeous. I could admit this, even when hating him.

But now? He walked with his hand on the small of my back, occasionally circling my waist to help me over an icy spot. It was warming up the shriveled, coal-black lump in my chest.

"Ella, darling! *Dobro pozhalovat' v Rossiyu!*" Lucya Turgenev kissed me on both cheeks and we joined them at their table at Terrassa, on the restaurant's rooftop with views spanning St. Petersburg. Alexi was shaking Maksim's hand with a rare smile on both faces.

"*Spasibo,* Lucya," I said shyly. I would die rather than admit to Maksim that I'd been studying Russian every spare second where I could be alone and no one could hear my painfully awkward pronunciation. "The view here, this is just spectacular."

"You will love the food here at Terrassa," she promised, smiling warmly up at her husband as he held her chair for her. The menu, of course, was in Russian, and I pointed at the only thing I recognized.

"Can we get some pirozhki?" I asked Maksim, "I don't care what else you order."

He leaned in close, "I do remember you seemed quite fond of them at the Christmas brunch," he whispered before kissing my cheek.

Lucya did not lie, the meal was some of the best bits of food I'd ever put in my mouth, the delicate shavings of raw fish in the Stroganina dish with slices of orange, rye bread and onions. It should not work all together, but I could have eaten another three platters.

During a lull between courses while the men were discussing the merits of one wine or another with the sommelier, Lucya edged her chair closer.

"How are you doing, really?" She looked so beautiful, chic red lipstick and a cream-colored wool dress. And sincere.

"I'm..." I debated what to say. Do I lie? "New Year's Eve was horrible." It burst out of me, my big mouth back in charge. "Who has a black tie party where the waiters are trying to take out half the guests? I..."

Still, Lucya looked so kind. She squeezed my clenched hand. "There is no way to ever be prepared for that. And you're new to this life. In the real world, no one is expected to be ready to hike up their evening gown and dodge bullets." She laughed, her perfect white teeth glinting in the candlelight. "Though I heard you did an amazing job of doing just that and hiding one of the most priceless jewels in the world in your bra. That's impressive."

"Oh please, there was no way I was going to lose the Dresden Green. Are you kidding me right now? Sweet baby Jesus, I'm sure Alexander King would have shot me himself if I lost it!" We're giggling, whispering together and my chest unclenched. Just a little.

"I am not stupid," Lucya was almost whispering at this point, head tilted away so no one could read her lips. "I know this was not..." she floundered a little, "something you agreed to." I sucked in a breath so fast that I started coughing, and she patted my back handing me a glass of water. "I've known

Maksim most of my life, and he can be so charming. But he is also a charming, controlling bastard." I made a humming noise, eyes darting to Maksim and Alexi. "But…" she put her hand on mine again, "there is potential, even in the worst possible circumstances, to find that you love the man you married, even in the Bratva. One day - probably when I'm much drunker than now - I'll tell you my story. What I'm trying to say, I guess, is give yourself a little room to see if Maksim is more than he seems."

"An autocratic cad?" I whisper.

Lucya laughs so loudly that Alexi looks at her, brow raised in concern. She kisses him and shakes her head, still laughing.

"Cad?"

"Cad," I nod sourly, "a man who acts with deliberate disregard for another's feelings or rights."

Yes, that tracks," she admits. 'He can be an idiot. He's a man raised to give others orders. But I have faith that Maksim can learn to be a better man for you."

The men turned to look at us, and she squeezed my hand, launching back into conversation with them without a hitch. *So smooth,* I thought in admiration, *I could never be like that.*

With the vodka, the good food and conversation, and the jet lag, I fell asleep on the way back to the Morozov mansion.

"*Solnyshko…*"

"Mmmm?" I tried to force my eyes open.

"We're back home," Maksim's hand was cupping my cheek, and I realized I was halfway on his lap, my face buried in his neck. "Would you like me to carry you in?"

"Oh," I awkwardly struggled upright. "No, I'm fine, thank you."

Still, he wrapped his arm around my waist, supporting me on

the trek up the stairs and to the master suite. I was dozing off again, so I didn't move when he pulled my dress off, and my shoes, leaving me in my underwear and tucking me in. "Sleep well. We're going ice skating tomorrow."

Maksim...

She was so beautiful, sleeping in my ancestral bed, the size of it making Ella look smaller, and her glorious, black hair spread over the white sheets. The lingerie I'd selected for her was outlining her body so sweetly, displaying her lovely breasts...

Blyad'! This woman was going to be the death of me. But I would not force her to have sex with me. Still... holding her as she sprawled casually over my chest, nose buried between my pectorals as she slept was... good. I could never allow this when she was awake, but I was not that stupidly rigid to not enjoy it now, feeling the soft exhale of her breath on my skin. Sighing, I carefully adjusted my legs. I would sleep tonight. I was holding my bride and, in my bed, the bed I'd earned by killing my father. I could sleep.

"Dress warmly today," I warned Ella, "ice skating here is a much colder experience."

"Everything here is a colder experience," she laughed, "how far away from the Arctic Circle are we again?"

"We'll warm your thin American blood yet," I promise her, wrapping a silky green scarf over her turtleneck and her jacket.

We're meeting Alexi and Lucya again today, along with their children. This time together with the head of the Turgenev Bratva is crucial. Whatever's coming, alliances will be crucial.

"Ella!" Lucya descends on my bride, kissing both cheeks, she grins tauntingly at me. "Maksim."

"Hello, Lucya," I say dryly, hiding my amusement. Their daughters and youngest son huddle beside her, but Konstantin, their sixteen-year-old, walks up boldly, shaking my hand.

"Hello, Sir," he says seriously, "it's good to see you again."

Alexi ruffles his son's hair fondly. "Kon's been accepted to the Ares Academy."

"Congratulations," I'm impressed. The private school he's speaking of is populated almost completely by the children of families in organized crime. It is notoriously difficult to get into.

"Are we skating or talking!" Lucya shouts, and everyone piles onto the ice.

"I guess your bodyguards here in Russia are better skaters, huh?"

Ella's skating alongside me, but I didn't take her hand this time. My standing as Pakhan was different here. My reputation is crueler, harsher here in St. Petersburg, it has to be. A romantic, silly thing like holding hands is not something I can do here.

"They are," I nod to a loose circle of men around us, and two more on the suspension bridge above us, keeping watch.

"We're skating under a freaking bridge," she marvels, craning her head back to see the cables and steel cross beams as we pass under it. On the other side, the river widens, and there's fewer people skating along.

Yana, their fourteen-year-old, skates parallel with us, looking hopefully at Ella, who notices immediately. "Hey, girlie, you want to do some tricks with me?" She nods vigorously, and they're off, laughing and skating in circles around each other. Yana is nearly as tall as Ella, and I watch my wife exclaim over the girl's lack of a scarf and pull off the green one I'd given her, wrapping it around her neck.

"Your new bride is good with little ones," Alexi skates alongside me, "do you plan on building your own dynasty of strong, terrifying children soon?"

Chuckling, I shook my head. "I don't know if I am ready for children, particularly if they take after Ella." She and Yana are both wearing white jackets and holding hands, they almost look like sisters.

Alexi gestures for two of his guards to move closer to them as their circles grow larger and larger. But the guards are still too far away when the first gunshot sends a vicious crack into the ice and the second hits Yana in the side, spinning her around and falling through the crack in the ice into the black water of the Neva River.

Dobro pozhalovat' v Rossiyu - welcome to Russia

CHAPTER 16 – THROUGH THE ICE

In which there's nothing like impending death to make Maksim realize he's capable of feeling actual, human emotion.

Maksim...

I have to trust that my bodyguards are already taking down the sniper as I sprint toward the open water. I hear a hail of bullets striking along the riverbank, and some distant screams but all I can see is the child slipping into the water and Ella throwing herself on her stomach and grabbing her coat, yanking on her with all her strength. Ella slips and her head goes underwater, but her skates dig in and she pulls herself out, and Yana too, getting her halfway onto the ice before it cracks again, the fissure weakened and unstable against their weight.

"Ella!" I'm shouting, on my knees, and trying to gauge the ice's stability.

She doesn't look away from the terrified Yana, her skin already blueish-white. "Th- th- the ice keeps cr- cracking- I can't pull her-!" She's already shuddering violently and Yana's grip is loosening where she's clinging to her. Falling to the ice, I starfish as wide as I can to spread out the weight. I know Alexi is behind me, and he throws me a hastily improvised rope of scarves with a loop at the end.

"I've got you," he rasps, "how close can you get?"

I'm already doing a slow army crawl, edging toward them, ignoring the ominous creak and sing of the frozen surface underneath me. "Ella!" I'm shouting, trying to get her to look at me, not the desperate little girl. "Grab this!" Snaking the scarf rope along the ice, it lands on her arm. This time, she looks away to find it and shakes her head. Dread is clogging my throat because I know she's thinking the same thing I am, it's not strong enough.

"Where is the goddamn rope!" Alexi is roaring at the others, but there's not going to be enough time.

"Ella..." I'm selfish, I'm so selfish but I want her to save herself. She's already risked letting go of one of Yana's arms to get the loop around her, sobbing in frustration as the scarf rope keeps slipping. Her tears are freezing in silver tracks on her face. "Ella! Just hold on to the scarves, we'll pull you both in!"

A thick sheet of ice under her chest cracks, and their combined weight dips them both in the water and I can hear Lucya wail behind me.

When Ella surfaces, she spits out river water and screams, "Pull!" Alexi and I frantically haul the stretched line out of the water, it's holding Yana, and we're dragging her across Ella's back, which sends the ice she's balancing on underwater again. Seven minutes it's been at least seven minutes... a cold voice in my head is reciting the signs of cold incapacitation, which will kill Ella well before hypothermia will. *The victim will lose meaningful movement in hands and feet, then arms and legs between five and fifteen minutes...* She is smaller and slight, my wife, and the frigid water of the Neva will take her sooner. If she can't hold on, she will slip under the ice.

The fissure in the ice is widening, and I can feel the water surging across my chest and legs, and grunting, I dig the blades of my skates deeper, pulling as fast as I can. Yana is no longer using Ella's body as a makeshift bridge and is sliding across to us, her head is lolling and she's half-conscious, and we pull faster as the weak, improvised scarf rope begins to unravel. Lucya seizes her daughter and runs for shore.

"Here's the rope! The rope- Maksim!" It's Yuri shouting at me and I grab the thick line, sending the loop over the ice. Alexi's hands are digging into my ankles. He's pushing me to inch forward, even though he must be covered in the water by now, too.

"Ella!" I say sharply, "You need to listen to me. Grab the rope, put it under your arms."

"I ca... n't... mov my..." Her eyes are struggling to stay open and she's shuddering so hard that her grip is slipping.

"Grab the rope!" I shout over my shoulder, "pull as soon as I have her!" I'm crab-walking sideways, circling to a thicker patch of ice to support my weight, but as my wife starts slipping back into the water, I loop the rope around my arm and leap for her. I land in a crash of ice, chunks flying past me as my face dunks underwater but I have a death grip on Ella's jacket and we both slide back onto the ice, which keeps cracking under our combined weight, but less and less as the others pull us faster until we're free of the open section.

"Over here-" Yuri's directing the others, "there's a rescue sled ready, get them on-" Eager hands haul us onto the sled, yanking off our sodden coats and piling heated blankets onto us. I look up, squinting in the sunlight to see an anxious crowd, other skaters had raced over to help our men rescue us, and a huge, burly man is piling hot coals from his hot drinks stand into a fireproof bag and putting them on our feet.

Looking down at Ella I see she's lost consciousness, and I begin rescue breaths. There are *feldshers* here by now and one tries to speak with me.

"Sir, I can take over-" I shove him aside and continue as we're lifted into the ambulance.

Ella...

I'm having the best dream, Maksim is on top of me, kissing me and it's really great until someone starts sticking pins into my feet. They sting and it's pissing me off and I keep shaking my feet, trying to make them let go of me...

Then my eyes open, and they're stinging, too. I can't quite figure out where I am until Maksim leans over me, kissing my forehead. "There you are, *solnyshko.* How do you feel?" We're both in his massive bed and wearing next to nothing.

Now I remember. "How's Yana?"

"She's all right. The bullet that sent her into the water only caught her jacket, she wasn't wounded. She's got a mild case of frostbite on her ears and fingers, but Alexi says she's already chattering incessantly and demanding soup."

I can't help laughing, "I like that girl." Sobering a bit, I squeeze his hand. "Thank you for saving us."

His face darkens, and I wonder if I offended him. "You saved Yana, and neither of you would have been in danger if my men had been doing their job."

Oh, god. Maksim's getting pissed off and that usually means someone dies horribly, I thought.

"Hey, you know what? I think we suck at having a good time. We get shot at every time we try." I'm hoping he'll laugh, no luck but at least there's a hint of a smile.

"Are you feeling any pain?" Maksim's hand smooths over the heavy blankets piled on top of us.

"Not too bad," I'm struggling, trying to sit up. He helps me, putting pillows behind my back and pulling the blankets up to cover me. I notice his gaze drops to my breasts for a moment or two but under the circumstances... "I do feel like someone's jabbing needles into the sides of my feet, but given the alternative I'm good."

"You have some minor nerve damage from being wet for so long, your skates did nothing to protect you. The pins and needles are your nerves coming back online, so to speak." His big hand is cupping my cheek, and it's so warm. "What you did was very brave. Alexi and Lucya say they are forever in your debt for saving their little girl."

Rubbing at my stinging eyes, I disagree. "If I hadn't put my scarf on her, they wouldn't have shot at her. They were targeting me, weren't they? Man, your ex-girlfriends can hold a grudge."

Maksim does not find my attempt at humor worthy of a grin, but the man is stressed, I can respect that.

"Yuri and two of our men caught the shooter. They're questioning him now."

I have a pretty good idea of what "questioning" really means, and I can't help shuddering. Misunderstanding, Maksim tugs the blankets higher and pulls me onto his chest, rolling to his back, so every inch of me is pressed against his wonderfully heated body. "I have to admit, I'm a little surprised," I venture, resting my chin on his sculpted pectoral muscle.

"How so?" Maksim put his arm behind his head, looking down at me.

Shifting uneasily, I can feel that crisp mat of chest hair tickle my breasts, barely covered in a thin tank top. "You're the bloodthirsty, hands-on Pakhan, I would think you'd be... uh, wherever they're 'questioning' the guy you caught. Unless..." a new thought occurs to me. "Oh, crap, you're not hurt, are you? You got wet too, but did they shoot you, or-"

He smiles strangely, smoothing my hair out of my face. "I'm fine, *solnyshko.* I had something... more important to do. Yuri and Fedor are very talented in this arena."

"Is torture considered an arena?" Aaand, my big mouth just cannot keep me out of trouble, can it?

This time he laughs, shaking me slightly on top of him. "I am here because you very nearly died. Why didn't you take hold of the scarves so we could pull you both to safety?"

"You know it wasn't strong enough for both of us," I said flatly.

His big hand is still stroking my hair, and it's oddly comforting. "I'm selfish, I know this," Maksim says, "but when the ice was collapsing under you, I wanted you to save yourself. I wanted you to live at all costs." His eyebrows are drawn together like it's physically painful to say the words.

Now I'm sitting up, straddling his narrow hips, "You know I couldn't leave Yana. I couldn't do that. Besides," I smile, trying to lighten the mood, "I knew you'd save us."

Pulling himself to a sitting position too, Maksim says, "I would like to kiss you."

I'm waiting to see if there's a question in there, until I realize this is as good as it's going to get. But since I would like to kiss him, too, I lean closer. "Can I touch you with my hands?" Oh, here comes the existential dilemma, I can see it. But he leans even closer, close enough that when he speaks, it's against my lips.

"My shoulders and arms."

Now it's my turn to whisper as my hands slide up his arms, my fingers trailing along his biceps. "Shoulders and arms," I agree, "for now."

Sex with Maksim at his St. John's palace had been explosive. Incendiary. Something so good that I was reduced to single words, then mainly just noises by the time he'd finish with me. But while sex there was a tidal wave, here in this bed, it was like plunging into a hot spring, where the heat of him flowed over me, making my muscles relax, my legs loosen and it set aside so much of my anger, my resentment of what Maksim did to me.

His dark head was between my breasts, giant hands playing with my breasts, squeezing them, pulling on my nipples. He pushed them together, humming with pleasure and it shot a line of fire down to my center. I was stroking my hands over his wide shoulders, enjoying their smooth, sculpted musculature. Maksim's cock was hard, pressing hot and heavy against my leg, so I rubbed against it.

Groaning, he looked up at me, those vivid blue eyes narrowed. "It's been a while, darling. If you want me to last long enough to give you an orgasm, stop rubbing me." He went back to my breasts, giving each nipple a long suck and a sharp bite before continuing down my stomach.

His words stuck with me. "You mean... you haven't had sex since St. John's?"

Maksim went up on his elbows, frowning at me for disrupting his debauching of my body. "No, of course not."

"Oh, good!" It burst out of me in a flood of relief, I didn't know what his plan was. Did Bratva men cheat on their wives? Would he cheat on me?

He had my ankles on either shoulder and he was running his tongue up the sensitive skin of my inner thigh. "This is the longest I've been without a woman since I was sixteen."

I paused for a hopeful moment as his hot breath moved over my center, but he tortuously moved to my other thigh, sucking a bruise into the thin skin. "You mean..." it was really hard to concentrate when he was using his mouth like that, "it's been what, two and a half weeks. That's the longest you've gone without sex since you were a teenager?"

Maksim looks up from where his tongue is caressing the crease between my thigh and my lady garden. "Yes," he says as if this is obvious and also unprecedented. "Now be quiet, I have work to do here."

My giggles are cut off by his voracious mouth landing on me, and he sucks and tongues me like he is starving. Like he hasn't eaten for weeks, and all I can do is cling to his shoulders and keep thinking, *don't touch his hair, don't touch his hair, oh god this is amazing...* He is relentless, sucking on my clitoris, flicking it with his tongue, slamming his arm across my hips when I try to wiggle away from the sheer, overwhelming intensity of it. Just as his thick finger slides inside me, I can't stop the explosion that sets my lower half on fire. My thighs are pressed against his head, and I put my hands in my hair and pull to keep from touching his. I'm yanking hard enough to make my scalp sting, and the pain grounds me a bit. I don't want to forget his rules and lose this moment.

"That's one..." he murmurs, sliding his finger from me and painting a number one on my thigh with my own slick. It is so filthy that I nearly come again. This time, he's using his tongue like a piston inside of me, and the movement has the tip of his patrician nose rubbing against my wildly sensitive clit. He pushes his whole face into me and I come again, legs stiff, toes pointed, shuddering and I cannot pull myself together. Maksim draws himself up on one elbow, painting a two next to the one and watching my slick and swollen center with interest, sliding two fingers inside me and his thumb sliding up and down between my lips and the feeling is so outrageous and his fingers are so high up inside me that I come. Again. This one is weaker but no less overwhelming.

"That's three," he murmured, painting another number with a finger wet from being inside of me. "Hmmm," he hums thoughtfully, running his tongue up and down, "there's nothing sexier than watching you come like this." His words vibrate almost painfully through my nerve endings there and sizzle up my spine like electrical shocks. "I can feel you," he groans, "you come so hard."

"Enough," I'm whining but I don't care, "please Maksim, enough.

I can't take anymore."

This seems to galvanize him into transforming into some kind of terrifying Slavic Incubus because he rises to his knees, sliding my ass up on his thighs and running his thumbs along the marks he's made on me. Maksim is radiating a wild sexual energy that makes me feel like my skin is on fire. In the deepest, most wildly arousing tone he's ever used with me, he says, "I'll tell you when you've had enough."

His eyes move to my hands, which have the pillow in a death grip. He cups me with one hand, not moving, just letting me feel the heat of his palm on my slick center. His hand is huge and it covers me completely, just holding me there. It is so unreasonably erotic that I almost come again, shivering with excitement.

Maybe he misinterprets it because Maksim frowns, his fingers on me flexing just slightly, his palm pressed firmly against me still. "Are you certain you're well enough, солнышко? We can wait."

"Don't you dare," I wheeze, "don't you dare stop right now."

His frown clears and his unfairly beautiful face is lit up with an unholy arousal. "I won't, I assure you." The heel of his heated palm is rotating very slowly on my clitoris, sort of pressing it down and making me want to arch up against him. His muscular thighs spread, and it pushes mine wider, too. It takes Maksim's impressive strength to pull me up against his chest.

"Put your hands on my shoulders."

I've got them on him in a second, stroking his skin, tracing his biceps and the veins on his forearms, marveling at just how beautifully sculpted this man is. I feel the tip of his cock stroking up and down, gently nudging my sensitive, overstimulated nerves and sliding down to circle the entrance to my channel. My eyes are drooping until he slaps my center sharply with his cock. "Aaaah!"

The debauched fiend grins. "I want you to watch me push up inside you. The feel of you pulling me in... there's nothing like it."

So, I do. The sight of Maksim, his spread knees pushing my legs apart, his taut stomach flexing as he slides into me slowly... It's too much and not enough at the same time. *Oh, wow, it has been a while,* I think, flinching a little at the stinging spread of my walls, but I suspect it's always going to be like that when Maksim first enters me. His cock makes it feel like there's no room for anything inside me but him and the heat surrounding me with his body on mine. Strange, for a man so cold and from such a frigid climate to be a human furnace.

My supremely smug spouse leans back on his heels, enjoying the sight of being buried inside me. *"Blyad'!"* Maksim groaned, "You're gripping my cock, I can feel you squeeze me from the tip all the way down to the base. You're silk inside, *solnyshko*, you're gripping me like warm, wet silk wrapped around me." He looks up at me, blue eyes flashing. "I'm going to fuck you until being empty, without me inside you will feel uncomfortable, you'll always want my cock back inside you."

I want to laugh harshly and tell him that he can't. That he's not filling the empty spaces inside me. I want to. But I can't, because everything he's saying is wildly arousing, and my skin feels hot and tight and when he slides his hand up my heaving abdomen, between my breasts, and settles lightly on my throat, I reach up and press his hand down harder. It shocks me, but he doesn't wait for me to gather my senses, tightening his fingers just a bit, pulling out of me and taking a long, lewd slide back inside me with a thrust of his hips.

Maksim's other hand lands on my back, pulling me up to rub my excruciatingly sensitive nipples against his chest hair, then moving my hips side to side, just keeping himself buried inside me. He has the audacity to lick his thumb and bring it down, spreading my lips to rub it against my clitoris in the same easy motion he's using to fuck me.

"I would imagine," he murmurs, "that I could make you come like this, hmm? Just holding deep up inside you, feeling you squeeze around me."

"Uh…" yeah, such an articulate response, but nothing is shaping into an actual sentence, because he may be outrageously conceited, but he is correct. He's throbbing inside me, and I'm stretched so wide that I can feel every minute movement his cock makes inside me. The memory of his offer to insert pearls into his dick makes me shudder and grip his shoulders tighter.

There was no more room. No more room for anything and certainly not for those. His lips take mine, and he squeezes my throat just a bit more. Not enough to scare me or to hurt, just a strange, pleasant buzz that's amplified by the feel of him taking over my insides. His skin is sweaty, rubbing wet trails against my nipples and I'm moaning, I have no idea when I started getting so noisy but he's enjoying it, arching his pelvis against mine to get every bit of him buried inside me.

"Are you close? I think you are..." his breath is hot as he whispers against my mouth, my lips feeling the words as he speaks them. Maksim slides his hand behind my neck and arches me back against the mattress, my spine at an impossible angle and my shoulders just touching the pillows as he angles a bit higher and then I am done. His cock is pushing and stroking against so many sensitive places inside me and he's looming over me, skin golden in the firelight and there has surely never been anyone more beautiful. Or bigger. And I'm coming, my hands flailing to hold onto his arms and Maksim gives a deep growl and comes with me, both of us pushing against the other to hold that perfect position that makes me come again as I feel him flood me with more warmth.

He's wrong to call me Little Sun. Maksim is the sun; he's fire and heat and everything else falls to shade when he's blazing this brightly.

"*Solnyshko,* wake up, it's Christmas Eve..." Maksim is leaning over me, dressed in a crisp, charcoal grey suit, a cream-colored dress shirt, and a green paisley tie. He looks scrumptious. I am flailing like a turtle flipped over on its back, hair snarled and with a mouth so dry that I can barely talk.

"I might need to call in sick, I think you broke me with your cock."

His laugh, of course, is loud and hearty and I want to smother him with one of his high-quality goose-down pillows.

Maksim...

My sisters were horrified to hear about Ella and Yana's near-drowning and even my mother held off from suggesting I wake my wife until it was nearly time for Christmas Eve mass.

"Perhaps she'd like to give thanks to the Lord for her rescue," she says, but Ekaterina snorts inelegantly.

"Mama, Maksim saved Ella, not the Lord."

Putting up my hand to stop any argument, I say, "Ella saved Yana, nearly at the cost of her own life. I'll go wake her; we should be ready to leave soon."

Passing Yuri in the hallway, I pull him aside. "Did you find the man who helped us with the rope, and the hot coals?"

He nodded, "He sells hot chocolate and sausages on the bank of the Neva. He told me he always keeps a rope in his stand for occasions like these."

"Buy him a house and deposit 64,875,000 rubles in a bank account for him and his family."

Yuri nods and smiles, "I had a feeling you'd want to do this; I already contacted the bank."

Ella was just a lump in the bed, topped with a pile of tangled black hair. She'd slept for twelve hours after we'd finished together.

"*Solnyshko*, wake up, it's Christmas Eve…"

She opens one pale green eye, not looking enthused about getting out of bed. "I might need to call in sick, I think you broke me with your cock."

I'm surprised into laughter, loud and oddly freeing. I didn't laugh much. In my position, it was either a polite chuckle or a dirty snicker.

"I mean it," she whines, flailing weakly and looking rather pitiful.

"I'm sorry darling," I soothe, "but my mother and sisters are here. Christmas Eve mass begins in less than an hour."

"You're going to church?" Ella seems shocked and then seems to realize this was perhaps not the best way to express this. "I mean, um, we're going to church?"

"Yes darling," I smile darkly as I help her out of bed, "Even my black and sin-stained soul goes to mass on Christmas Eve, though it is possible that I will go up in flames as I enter the church."

"Sorry," she mumbles, "it just didn't seem like it was a big interest of yours. What does one wear to mass on Christmas Eve here?"

Sorting through her dresses quickly, I hold up a long-sleeved, black dress with a modest neckline. "Covering me up like a nun, are we?"

"Oh, *solnyshko,*" I purr, "only so I can take you out of it later."

Eyes wide, she seizes the dress from me and escapes into the bathroom.

Ella is ready within the half-hour deadline and even manages to greet my sisters warmly with hugs, and smiles pleasantly at my mother; not attempting to embrace her and knowing quite well that the matriarch of the Morozov clan will not offer one, either.

"This is where your family attends church?" She's staring, fascinated by the multiple pillars of cream-colored stone and the massive bronze doors.

Yuri has decided to offer himself as tour guide again, I note sourly. "Yes, the cathedral is dedicated to Our Lady of Kazan, the most sacred icon in Russia. The architect wanted to model the cathedral after some of the most important churches in Rome."

"It's so beautiful..." She marvels over the design as I help her out of the Mercedes.

My mother hands her a folded square of black silk. "It is customary to wear a headscarf to mass here." She shows Ella how to wear it and drapes the ends for her. It is the first sign of a thaw, and I'm unreasonably pleased that it is happening so quickly.

Despite the church being full, we walk to the second row, held empty for us and the family files in, with our bodyguards in the row behind. "They keep special seating for you?" Ella whispers, her eyes lit up with mischief, "Just how generous are you with the donations, hmm?"

"Hush," I whisper, taking her hand and resting it on my thigh. Though no one else can see it, my mother gives me a slitted-eyed glare, which I pleasantly ignore.

The service is grand; soaring music, song, and messages of love and forgiveness. As a child, it was hard for me to understand how these things could possibly relate to my life. Love is difficult, forgiveness is impossible. But while this cathedral is the grandest of all the churches in St. Petersburg, there is humility here tonight. The warmth of the candles and the songs sung by hundreds of voices joined together make me feel that there is the slightest possibility for the concept of love. I love my family fiercely, and I would protect and care for them to my dying breath. But for my wife, with her foul mouth and stubbornness, her undying loyalty to her friends, and her courage to save another life before her own? On a night like this, all things seem possible.

"That was beautiful," Ella sighed, taking my offered arm. "I have never been to a Christmas mass. It definitely makes this day have more meaning, doesn't it?"
"It is the only time I attend church, but it is time well spent," I agree. I nod politely to various acquaintances and the members of other Bratva families here. There is a permanent truce in the cathedral, which is a crucial time to renew partnerships and establish bonds.
"Oh, there you are, Maksim!"
My spine stiffens at the girlish trill. I know exactly who this is. How dare she approach us? "Merry Christmas, Mrs. Morozov," Katya says sweetly to my mother, ignoring my sisters and my wife, who is frozen in place at my side. Of course, the little bitch dares, the truce here means I am required to be civil, and her spiteful grin shows she knows it.
"Katya," I acknowledge coldly, "where are your parents?"
"Oh," she shrugs, "they chose to spend the holidays at their estate in Costa Rica, but I had to come home for a special engagement. Mine, in fact!" She thrusts out her left hand with nails as long and sharp as a polar bear's, an engagement ring catching the candlelight as Katya flutters her fingers.
"Congratulations," my mother says coolly, she has always despised the Sokolovs, "and who is the lucky man?"
Katya dramatically points to the man next to her. He's not

looking at us, clearly bored. My jaw tightens as I recognize him.
"Vasily Shevchenko," Katya gloats, "this is Maksim Morozov, a *dear*, old friend." He grunts at me, and I nod in return. "We'll be sending invitations soon," she adds, "you must join us to celebrate!"
I know without looking that my sisters are rolling their eyes, but Ella stands perfectly still, holding my arm. When I notice Shevchenko staring at her, I move into his field of vision. "Congratulations, of course," I say impassively, "we must be going."

Safely back in the car, Mariya bursts out, "Does that poor man have any idea what kind of a leech Katya is?"
"He was so big," Ekaterina said, "he looks like a bear who learned to walk on his hind legs."
"Enough," Mother interrupts them, "no more criticism on Christmas Eve, this is the time for love for your fellow man."
Yuri and I exchange glances. There would be no love lost between those two families and ours, and their union is not good news.
Yuri follows Ella and me up to our private sitting room. "This reeks of disaster," he says sourly, loosening his tie.
"You must admit they are perfect for each other," I said, "both narcissistic sociopaths."
"Who was that guy?" Ella asked, taking off her high heels with a relieved sigh, "he looked like he'd just discovered indoor plumbing."
Yuri laughs, but I shake my head at him. "Vasily Shevchenko is an enforcer for his uncle's Bratva in Kazakhstan, they are the most vicious organized crime outfit in the entire country. They're responsible for thousands of murders, and sex-trafficking victims from Eastern Europe to brothels all over the world."
"Interesting, though, that Katya would be paired with him," Yuri mused, helping himself to my vodka. "He's not high up in the organization. He's an enforcer, not even a *Sovietnik*. I'm not sure I see the value of the union to her father."
"She was definitely excited to introduce you to her beloved fiancé," Ella contributed, "but it was more of a 'look at my new toy' vibe." She paused for a moment, "Or a warning? Like, look at

what's coming your way?"

Running my finger over my lower lip, I considered her appraisal.

"She picked the right place for it," Yuri added, "she knew you couldn't menace her, not at the Christmas Eve mass. I'm going to check in with a few people and see if she was introducing Shevchenko around, any details she might have dropped."

"Thank you, brother." I gripped his arm. "Ella, are you ready to go downstairs for dinner and the fortune-telling?"

Her face brightened. "Fortune-telling? This sounds interesting."

As I guided her to the dining room, it occurred to me that for the first time as Pakhan, I had discussed business in front of a female member of our family. She'd contributed to the conversation. And it seemed perfectly natural to have Ella there.

CHAPTER 17 – TROUBLING FORTUNES TOLD

In which troubling fortunes are told, lots of stuff gets blown up, and Ella gets a reality check from Lucya. Because life is like that with the Bratva.

Ella…

To say that I'm ridiculously excited about tonight is an understatement. I just want thirty-five minutes where no one is shooting at us or trying to drown me. The memory of being pressed underneath the ice in the current of the Neva River halts me for a moment on the stairs, making Maksim look at me in concern.

"Are you all right?"

I look at him, blue eyes so vivid and intent on me, watching my expressions, his thumb stroking my wrist and checking my pulse, his arm holding me carefully. Who *is* this man?

"I'm fine," I nod firmly like that's going to totally sell it. "This is going to be fun. We can both use some uncomplicated fun right now. So, explain the history with the fortune telling?"

"It's a custom that evolved pre-Christianity, and it's not approved of by the Russian Orthodox Church, but everyone still participates." Maksim puts his hand on the small of my back, leading me in another direction I haven't explored yet. How big is this place?

"So, is there a psychic who comes to the house, or…?"

One corner of his mouth turned up, not quite a smile but showing he found something amusing. "The early traditions were a little outrageous. Imagine unmarried, young women in, say, the 1500s meeting in a bathhouse in their nightgowns, their hair down and loose, to read fortunes."

I have no problem with laughing, "Seriously? That's so sketchy, and their parents were okay with that?"

Maksim shrugged, "Well, the other tradition involved these young, unmarried women stepping out of their house on Christmas morning and asking the first man they saw what his name was. Supposedly, that would be the name of the man they married."

I slowed down a bit, enjoying the talk and not wanting to lose him to the rest of the family yet. "Now that we're no longer tossing young women in their nightgowns into sticky situations, how does it work?"

"Sofia Ivanova is a well-known psychic in St. Petersburg," Maksim says, turning left into yet another hall, "she'll read our fortunes with her Tarot cards."

"Has she been accurate in the past?" I meant it teasingly, but his face grows dark, like a shadow over the sun.

"Christmas Eve dinner is always best when it's after midnight and it's already Christmas," Mariya said with satisfaction, sucking her thumb after a pickled mushroom dripped on the way to her mouth.

Pickled everything... I thought, *lucky that I like this stuff.* There was toast with sauerkraut, cute little gherkins, and pickled apples. And so many little pies! Tasty pastries stuffed with meat, veggies, or fish. I put the fish one down after a bite. *Mushy...* I looked for something to drink to kill the taste.

"This is *сбитень*," Maksim poured a golden liquid into a glass mug, garnishing the edge with sugar.

"ZBEEtyn'?" I attempted.

"Quite close," he nodded. "It's a honey drink with cinnamon, coriander, cloves, and our chef's special ingredient, bay leaves."

Nodding, I took a sip, it was mellow, warming my throat as it went down. I shivered for a moment. I would never forget to be grateful for moments of warmth after falling through the ice. My feet prickled as if agreeing with me.

"Is everyone ready to retire to the library? Sofia is arriving any minute." Mrs. Morozov waved her manicured hands gracefully.

Retiiiire to the Libraaary, my inner snark was giggling. I stopped being snarky when I walked into said library. *I'm going to live here,* I thought, *I don't care what I have to do. Drop in a mini fridge for snacks and I'm never coming out.*

This elegant paradise was two stories high, two of the walls were lined with beautiful oak shelving, and each one was crammed with books. Two tall rolling ladders reached up as high as the ceiling so a lucky soul could grasp any book they wanted. A third wall faced out onto the garden, where the snow was falling softly, and on the fourth, a huge fireplace faced with beautifully carved stone with a thick wood mantlepiece. The gigantic fire busily roaring away could have roasted six oxen. There were multiple nooks furnished with comfortable chairs, little tables, and reading lamps. In front of the fire, Maksim had clustered two huge leather couches and a long, low table.

Leaning down, he murmured, "I had them light the fire, I thought you might be getting cold in this giant, drafty house."

Sighing, I stared back up. "That is the most romantic thing you have ever said to me." He laughed, and the sound made his family all look up and stare at him.

Nope, I thought, *the man never laughed. Now if I can just keep tricking him into laughing more.*

"Ah, happiness and merriment, what a wonderful way to begin." Yuri was ushering in an elderly woman in a black caftan, an alarmingly large fur coat, and silver hair flowing down her back. Essentially, who you'd send in for a Central Casting call for an "enigmatic psychic."

"Ella, this is the wise and beautiful Sofia Ivanova," he said, laying it on a little thick but it was clear she was enjoying it. "And lovely one, this is Maksim's new wife, Ella Givens Morozov."

"Lovely," she said, plopping herself down right next to me. "Yuri, be a darling and take my coat?" Well, damn... Her eyes were black, her pupil and iris both, an endless sea of darkness and a little scary. And they were focused on me. "Fresh blood. This family could use some vigorous American energy to offset their centuries of endless stoicism."

My cringe was a reflex, just waiting for Maksim to strike her down for such outrageous comments. But to my shock, he gave the Gracious Morozov Pakhan chuckle, "Already with the taunting, Sofia? You haven't even begun the readings and already, the insolence?"

She waved an age-spotted hand, "I have so much stored up for you, young man. Now, who is first?"

"Me!" piped up Ekaterina, and with the expertise of a Las Vegas croupier, Sofia spread the tarot cards in a graceful flourish.

Maksim...
After pouring a drink for Yuri and myself, I seated myself next to Ella, who was watching Sofia work with fascination.

"Have you never had a reading?" I ask, enjoying the little spray of goosebumps along the thin skin of her neck as I whisper to her.

"Nope," she murmured, careful to keep her voice low, "I'm a science-based person, I never believed in it. But it looks interesting, all the same." I can tell she's a little startled when I put my arm around her but in the privacy of my family home, it feels comfortable. For once, I don't have to be concerned if it makes me look soft. My father beat any softness out of Yuri and me, but he is dead and I am Pakhan now. And since I nearly lost Ella to the river, I find myself touching her constantly, always ascertaining that she's well and safe.

Yuri is watching us with a subtle grin that I want to smack off his face, but it fades after a moment.

"Hey, Yuri, come over here." Ella pats the couch next to her. "I have some questions about the library, and..." They're chatting within moments, and I wonder if my wife had seen the same loneliness on his face that I did.

"Are you ready for your reading, Pakhan?" Sofia says it with a little smirk, but after decades of reading our family's future, she is allowed.

She spreads her cards, and Ella leans in with interest to watch. "Hmm... well, Maksim, this is an interesting year ahead." Sofia turns over The Emperor. "Your power as Pakhan is strong. Your people respect you and your authority." Next, the Five of Swords. "There is victory through deceit, not yours, it is a betrayal, a double cross within your own system. And the Wheel of Fortune, change is coming, an inevitable fate." The room is quiet, aside from the soft shuffle of the cards and the crackling fire. "Ah, the Queen of Swords reversed. There is someone vicious, bitter, and cruel in your path. She will not be turned away. The Tower..." she hesitates here, fingers caressing the card that shows cataclysmic loss and death. "Upheaval. Foolish pride will cost you, Pakhan, disaster, if you hold your control too tightly. And the Queen of Wands. There is strength, courage, and determination waiting for you to see it."

Sofia's hands go to her lap as she waits for questions. I never have any. I do not ask for clarification. But The Tower card... upheaval? Destruction? The foolish pride is not something I wish to examine.

"Thank you," I nod in appreciation. "And now my wife?" Despite her claims as "a woman of science," I'm amused to see Ella lean forward eagerly.

The first card turned over for Ella's reading is The Fool. Laughing, she says, "Well, that's an auspicious start."

"Ah, but the meaning of The Fool is not what you think," Sofia corrects her, "The Fool signifies innocence, new beginnings, a free spirit. This card introduced into a stuffy, rigid hierarchy can be a very good thing." She has the nerve to cast her eyes pointedly in my direction. The Seven of Wands is next, and reversed. "You have many obstacles ahead of you, my dear. This card warns of giving up, feeling overwhelmed, and confidence destroyed. You have to prepare yourself to make sure these challenges don't defeat you by taking away your belief in yourself. And your next card... The Seven of Cups. You are searching for your purpose in your new life. You have choices, even though you may not see them yet."

I'm watching Ella's expression as each card is introduced. Her skepticism is fading, and she's listening carefully to what Sofia is telling her.

"The Magician reversed here means that someone close is watching you with greed, eager to manipulate you. It is someone you want to believe in, but you know - if you're willing to see it - that they do not have your best interests at heart. It's important to understand that the past always comes for us. You cannot hide from it." The psychic's hands rest on the final two cards, both are still face down and the wrinkles on her elegant face deepen. "These next two, my dear, seem to contradict each other. There are two paths ahead of you. Your decisions affect more than just you." She turns over the first card. It's The Hanged Man. "There is a sacrifice ahead. Only you can decide to offer it."

Ella's frowning and I put my hand on her thigh, squeezing lightly. "Hasn't she already offered the sacrifice?" I'm asking a little aggressively, but Sofia is indifferent to it.

"No. It is ahead. But here is your last card, dear. The Sun. In one of the two paths ahead, happiness awaits you. The Sun is a powerful portent, and it can shine a light on the path you're meant to take." Ella's looking up at me with an odd expression, and for the first time, I'm not certain what she's thinking.

We're the last two to have their cards read, so Sofia is stuffed with cakes and sweets, and some of the best wine from my cellar. Around two in the morning, she stretches and checks her watch. "It is time to rest. Thank you all for your hospitality."

Walking her to the door, I help her with her coat and press a thick envelope of rubles into her hand. "Thank you, as always, for spending your time with us tonight."

Her head is tilted curiously, and she's watching me with her ebony crow's eyes. "You have a question, Pakhan?"

"Not for myself..."

"I think you are more attached to your bride than you're willing to admit," she's grinning with a level of impertinence I do not allow, but even my most thunderous scowl doesn't quell her.

"With this sacrifice you warned her about... does it mean death?"

I can barely get the words out. Where is my self-control? *You're weak...* the ugly voice of my father slithers through my thoughts. *Pathetic. You disgust me.*

Sofia is no comfort. "The sacrifice that will be asked of her? Death is quite possible. But trying to keep her from making this choice could destroy you both." She smiles, shaking her head as she watches me. "Love and union can't be controlled like you do your empire, Pakhan. One of you can make a choice that could destroy you both. And that warning is meant for you, too."

I escort her out to one of our cars where the driver is waiting to take her home. "Goodnight, and Merry Christmas."

"Merry Christmas." She reaches up and pats my cheek gently, I have to fight the urge to snap her fingers for daring such a thing. "You have selected an excellent wife. I have faith that you can change enough to keep making the right choice for you and your little family."

Little family? My brow creases as I watch the car turn the corner. A little family meaning my wife, and...? I can't think any longer of what the old witch meant. She loved taunting me, knowing she was one of the very few who could. It meant nothing.

Ella...

January 8th was a gloomy day. Christmas in Russia was glorious, and I was sad it was over. Seriously, it's the best holiday I've had since my parents died.

Maksim was called away from lunch for an important phone call and returned with a face white with fury. Yuri rose instantly and left the room as Maksim leaned over to kiss my cheek. "There's some urgent business, I must leave, I don't know when I'll be back. I know my sisters are seeing friends this afternoon. If that doesn't interest you, why don't you call Lucya? She's been wanting to see you again."

I nodded, rising to walk with him to the door. "It's something bad, I'm guessing. Will you two be safe?" My husband never lost his look of rage, but Yuri, at least, gave me a nod and a reassuring smile as they left. Standing alone in that massive hallway where every step echoed on the marble flooring, I decided an afternoon with Lucya was an excellent idea.

"Yeah, he was furious. Whatever it is, it's not good."
I took another sip of the excellent mimosa Lucya's butler served us. I'd teased her about having a butler. A butler! But once we were settled in her wonderfully warm and expansive great room, two mimosas down and one in hand, I felt safe asking some questions about this life. "He got a call, and he and Yuri were out the door in half a second."
Lucya sighed, "Unfortunately, nothing ever slows down. Christmas? Please! Nothing to these guys." She made a rude sound and drank half her glass in one swallow.
"I'm so used to seeing Maksim all... urbane, you know? Nothing impacts him enough to actually show emotion. I wouldn't have known how serious today was until Yuri leaped up and went with him."
"Your organization - and ours - are always under attack," she said, "you have to expect that your man will disappear at any time and you may never know why."
"Alexi doesn't talk to you about his business doings?" I asked delicately, not sure if I was stepping over some invisible line.
"Sometimes, he has to, if it's a serious threat to the kids and me. I used to be so angry at him for disappearing without explaining anything, not telling me when he'd be back. Not telling me if he was in danger..." Lucya looked out the window, her beautiful face was so solemn, I could feel the pain the memories caused her. "When I was pregnant with our first child - Konstantin - I nearly lost him from all the stress and the constant terror that Alexi was risking his life; as if our life together meant nothing."
Smiling at me, she said, "He stood by my hospital bed and cried. That gigantic oaf wept like a baby. He promised me that he would be honest with me, as much as he could." Rolling her eyes, Lucya, snarled, "And I made him promise to stop taking so many stupid risks. I told him I wouldn't live the rest of my life as a widow. I told him..." she's laughing and it makes me laugh, "I told him I would pick up the hottest, youngest *Sovietnik* I could find and make him the new Pakhan. You should have seen his face!"

I'm laughing and also a little horrified. "I... just cannot picture that. Seriously, that's just too much to contemplate." Taking another nervous gulp of my drink, I drag together all the bits and pieces of my courage.

"I am so, so sorry that Yana's life was in danger because of me. I couldn't imagine... I didn't even think giving her my scarf would put a target on her, I just..." My little speech cuts off in a weepy gulp. I'm crying and that is the worst way to deliver a sincere apology.

Leaning over, Lucya grabs my hands. "Don't, Ella. Don't be. It's not your fault. You saved my child's life and I owe you mine in return. A million different reasons could have centered that sniper on her that day. It's part of our life with these men. But when Alexi and Maksim find out who did this, they will rain down hell upon them, believe me. It's an old Russian saying, "If someone hits you, hit them back. And keep hitting them until they don't stand up again.""

"Wow... that's uh, that's really intense, Lucya." Right now, she looks just as scary as our men do.

Then she smiles sweetly, and my new friend is back. "Let's have some cake and fruit to go with these drinks, hmm?"

Maksim...

"They hit both warehouses at once, here in St. Petersburg and in Queens. Anything they couldn't steal, they torched along with the structures. There were enough explosions that the police launched an investigation in the US. Here, of course, there's no further official inquiry, but..."

I rubbed the back of my neck. No news Yuri delivered after a pause like that was going to be anything less than disastrous. "Go on."

"They found fifteen bodies charred in the fire at the Queens location. We were luckier here since it was Christmas and everyone had the day off, but we still lost four guards."

"We lost eight men on New Year's Eve, another nineteen last night," I could feel the headache thundering into my skull. "The coordinated attack here and there seems to make it more likely this is a rival Bratva. The Sokolovs still make the most sense, but as brutal as Pavel is, this seems suicidal."

"We managed to pull two of the survivors from the New Year's Eve attack from police custody and question them," Yuri poured us both a generous drink, the chilled vodka slopping over the sides of the glass, "the most Bogdan could get from them - and you know how talented the man is with torture - was that they were mercenaries. They didn't know who hired them, money was sent in untraceable Bitcoin."

"And the same with the sniper here," I sighed.

"You know I employed everything in my skill set to drag more information out of him, Pakhan," he apologized, "though it was nothing compared to what Alexi did when he showed up." Yuri took a healthy gulp of vodka.

"I don't think I've ever seen you so shaken by a torture session." He glared at me. "You didn't see this one."

Irritably tugging my tie loose and taking off my jacket, I resumed pacing. "How much inventory did we lose?"

"Both warehouses were a complete loss. Over thirty million dollars' worth. What makes this worse is the loss of the structures. They were our main sites for arms storage and movement. We can't supply most of our clients for orders they've already placed."

The vodka spread like fire down my throat, but it didn't warm me the way it usually did. "How much money do we have to return?"

Yuri sighed, "Even if we find new warehouses we can run that are away from other Bratva territories in the city and free from police scrutiny, the very least we have to return is around one hundred million dollars. That doesn't include buying new inventory and bribes to end the police investigation in New York."

I'm staring out the window of my office, trying to come to terms with what I've heard. An incalculable amount of manpower and money was wiped out in one night. "Get in touch with your sources on the dark web. No one can hire this many mercenaries without leaving tracks somewhere. And call Farid in Morocco, he can arrange a new route for weapons."

"You said you would never work with him after he started sex trafficking, you said-"

"I know what I said, *Sovietnik!* We're running out of weapons sources and we have orders to fill," I'm shouting, but it doesn't crush the queasy feeling of disgust from even mentioning that *svin'ya.* "We're not buying women, we're buying guns."

"Women and children," Yuri said coldly.

"You have the audacity to speak to me like that?" This day... the loss, the destruction, and my own brother defying me?

"If you buy from one side of the business, you're still supporting the other." He stands and straightens his jacket. "I will get started immediately."

"I'll call Farid since the thought is so repellant to you," I snarl. To be honest, if only with myself, the man is a pig. I would not expose my brother to him, it's my duty.

"And have the jet prepped and word sent to Ella to pack," I add. "We'll need to leave within two hours."

Ella...

I'm sitting back in my little corner on the jet, and it feels just as bleak flying home from St. Petersburg as it did going there. Maksim, Yuri, and three of his senior advisors are sitting with their heads close together, speaking in urgent, low tones. I know something terrible has happened, it was clear when I boarded the jet and they were in this exact position. Maksim didn't even look up to acknowledge I was on the jet.

Ivan, my new personal bodyguard after I put that tourniquet on his leg during the New Year's Eve Shootout, is my biggest fan in the Morozov Bratva. He's the one who set me up in my cushy leather seat, fetched my "special" blanket, and ordered snacks. The man even remembered the charge cord for my phone which is nice, since I had approximately thirty seconds to pack before I was hustled into a car and brought to the private airstrip.

I didn't even get to say goodbye to Ekaterina and Mariya.

Putting my earbuds in with a sigh, I tried to relax. Another fourteen hours to go.

Halfway through my book *(Indian Arranged Marriages: A Social*

Psychological Perspective), Maksim sits across from me, where Yuri sat on our way to St. Petersburg and shared a bit about the horrors of their childhood. The lines of tension radiating out from his eyes look even deeper than they had when he left the house this morning.

"How are you?" He's rubbing his forehead.

"I'm fine," I said. I know I should leave it there. But no, my big mouth cannot stop. "But you're... things are pretty bad, huh?"

Oh, there we go. He haughtily stares at me, his blue eyes chilly. "It's none-"

"-of my concern, I know." I'm being pissy and I'm sure I'll pay for it. But for a few moments yesterday when we were analyzing the creepy appearance of that lunatic Katya and her ginormous Kazakhstani, I felt like I had something to offer. It felt like he might have valued my opinion. It made the fall back to American Mail Order Bride that much more painful. He's so beautiful, this heartless Russian. I can't look at him anymore without wanting to cry, so I stand, gathering all of my travel rubble. "I'm just going to sleep in the bedroom, all right?"

He pauses long enough that I'm forced to look at him. "Very well. Get some rest."

No crying, you big baby, I thought angrily. *No crying here.*

Maksim...

Yuri and I had gone over any crumbs of information garnered from the dark web about the hiring of so many mercenaries. While we still couldn't narrow down who was behind it, there was more concerning news, it looked like even more soldiers of fortune were being hired daily.

"I've already got some program searches running on some of the biggest Swiss banks and offshore accounts," he said, rubbing his eyes. "The money trail will lead us to them sooner, or later."

"Here is hoping for sooner," Ilya said, rubbing his eyes. He was a big man, arms covered in ink. His hair had only just turned silver, even though he'd served as a key advisor under my father as well. Ilya was one of the few I'd retained from his inside circle. He was steady and had a calming influence when the discussions got heated. "We have two locations ready for you to approve to replace the warehouse in St. Petersburg. Stateside? We are still searching."

Standing, I rolled my shoulders feeling the muscles creak. "Thank you for your hard work, gentlemen. Why don't you all try to get some rest? We have a challenging week ahead of us." Yuri is looking at me with mild surprise, and I tilt my head, inviting him to walk with me. "Why the expression?"

He grinned, impertinent *malen'kaya zadnitsa.* "I haven't heard you thank your advisory council in... I can't remember you ever thanking your advisory council, in fact."

Glaring at him, I pour another drink before rubbing the back of my neck. "I can still send you to the shit dock warehouse to work."

Yuri burst out laughing. "No surprise that no one is willing to get near that warehouse, not even to torch it."

"Hmm," I glance at the closed bedroom door.

"Why don't you get some rest as well?" He nods at the door, then back at me. He's bright enough to not add any impertinent remarks this time.

The bedroom is cool and quiet. No clouds of cigar smoke, no men needing answers. Just my bride, who is curled up into a little ball in the center of the bed. Taking off my shoes, I get in behind her, putting my arm around her waist, and pulling her closer. With a relieved groan, I bury my face in her mass of sweet-smelling hair, and breathing in deeply, I manage to fall asleep.

No bad dreams tonight.

malen'kaya zadnitsa - little ass

svin'ya - pig

CHAPTER 18 – TICKLE TORTURE AND THE REAL THING

In which the hits just keep on coming. Also, so does Ella.

Ella…

There's a change in the engines, a shift that wakes me up. Am I really experienced enough now in fancy jet travel that I can tell these things? I guess so, because a peek out the window shows the ocean beneath us, and a bank of bright lights ahead of us spreading as far as I can see. That has to be New York.

The second thing I notice is that Maksim is wrapped around me like the best body pillow ever. My back is toasty warm from this human blast furnace and not for the first time, I wonder how such a cold, composed man from the most glacial spot on the globe can be so gloriously hot to the touch. His hand slipped under my shirt at some point and his long fingers were spread, pressing against my stomach. He's still asleep, but his fingers flex slightly against me and I wonder why they're so rough, calloused. You'd think that a billionaire crime lord like Maksim would have soft, pampered hands. He was too high up in his organization to do any dirty work. I tentatively rest my hand on top of his. Knowing what I do about him by now though, there's no question he enjoys getting his hands dirty. But maybe it's a good leadership position, the whole, "I won't ask you to do something I won't do myself," style of management.

The thought makes me chuckle silently, but the movement was

enough to wake him.

"What's making you laugh?" Maksim asked, not moving. His face was buried in my hair and I can feel his hot breath against my skin.

Answering with, "Your management style," seemed to invite more questions than needed, so I shrugged. "Your fingers are a little ticklish."

Those long, elegant fingers of his twitched on my stomach. "These fingers?"

I squirmed, trying to move away.

Maksim tickled me along my horribly sensitive ribs. "These fingers, *solnyshko?*"

I press my lips together, trying not to laugh, even though his tickling has escalated to the point where I'm writhing like a demented eel.

"Or do you mean *these* fingers?" He's kneeling over me now, using both hands and attacking my soft midsection. Pausing the torture for a moment, Maksim looms over me with an evil little grin. "You do know where you are the most susceptible to ticklish torment?"

"No?" I wheeze, trying to catch my breath.

"Here!" The heartless reprobate attacks my inner thighs which are indeed horribly ticklish and I'm screaming with laughter within seconds. Damn him, there's no holding out and I'm kicking and laughing hard enough to make my stomach hurt, trying to bat him away with my flailing hands.

Thank god, the man stops torturing me just before I'm about to wet myself, and my hysterical laughter tapers down to some gurgling as we watch each other. We're pressed together, my heaving chest is rubbing against his beautifully sculpted pectorals. Maksim's pale eyes were actually warm, not cold, and calculating as always.

"I'm pretty sure tickle torture was outlawed by the Geneva Convention, Maksim." I manage, still trying to catch my breath.

His full lips twitched. "I do hope you won't report me to the High Court in Belgium, Ella."

"Well, Maksim, I'm sure you can see this is a serious offense," I countered, a little excited and freaked out. Was this grim Russian monolith actually being *playful* with me?

His gaze went up and down the front of me, and Maksim gave me an evil little smile. "Hmmm, Ella, perhaps I can offer some kind of compensation for your pain and suffering?"

My suddenly dry throat made a clicky noise when I swallowed hard. "What, um… What did you have in mind, Maksim?"

He paused as if considering his options, his unreasonably handsome face fighting a bit of a smile. "Hmm… this, possibly?" Leaning down, he kissed a soft line down my throat. "Or, this." His mouth moved to my collarbone, the tip of his tongue sliding out to trace the bone.

Now, Maksim was back in full Hot Murder Daddy mode, eyes glinting as his hands tightened on my hips.

"Or, Ella darling, *this…*"

Maksim…

Why could I not keep my hands off this woman?

Ella was staring up at me, eyes wide but not afraid, which was a refreshing change. I slid down, running my mouth over the soft slope of her breasts after pushing her shirt up.

"Definitely this," I groaned, pulling her skirt over her hips, then down and off, throwing the fabric over my shoulder. I could feel her jolt with silent laughter again and nipped the silky flesh of her inner thigh, where I'd just tickled her. Her alarmed squeal told me she was still sensitive. Wedging my shoulders between her legs, I spread her legs wide, enjoying the sight of her thin, white panties showing her arousal. I put my mouth against the silk, puffing a breath of hot air against her center.

"Still arms and shoulders?"

Distracted, I looked up.

"Can I still touch your arms and shoulders," Ella clarified, looking anxious, but based on how her legs were tightening against me, she was still decisively invested in this moment.

Running a knuckle along the delicate crease between her thigh and her pussy, I nodded.

"Your hair?" Ella persisted, "Can I touch your hair?"

"Just don't pull it." The words flew out of my mouth and I buried my face against her to stop this odd moment of weakness. I'd never admit that no one was allowed to touch my hair - aside from my barber - because my father used to get a vicious grip on my hair, dragging me down to the basement for another "conditioning session," where he'd torture me until I passed out or begged for mercy. That latter moment of weakness always guaranteed another "session" the following day.

I lunged, angry but craving the taste of my wife. Nudging her clit with my nose, I circled her opening with my tongue, feeling her flinch slightly as my stubble rasped against her thighs. Tightening my grip, I rubbed my face against her greedily. Her heat, the silky feel of her center, her taste... *O Gospodi,* nothing was sweeter. Ella came, her back arching and moaning and I grinned against her swollen lips.

"So pretty when you come, *solnyshko,*" I murmured, enjoying how her breasts heaved as she gasped for air. I kissed each taut nipple on my way back up to brace my arms on either side of her head.

Ella's black hair - blacker than black and glossy - spread out around her on the pillow, and I twisted a silky lock between my fingers. I'd wrapped her long tail of hair around my fist before, pulled her head back to kiss her while I fucked her from behind. But this wasn't the time for that. The only time I could stop thinking, plotting, and planning was when I was inside my wife, as deep inside as I could get.

I guided one of her legs to wrap around me, and the other followed, locking her heels together at the small of my back. "Sliding my cock inside you challenges my restraint, every time," I said, sucking in a harsh gasp of air from the heat and pressure of her inside. "Look at me, don't close your eyes."

It took Ella a certain amount of courage to meet my gaze when I was inside her. "So lovely, with your flushed skin, your mouth is wet and open..." I pushed my feet against the mattress, driving in my cock, feeling her walls still rippling from her orgasm. Changing the angle of my thrusts, I watched her pretty eyes widen and she gasped. Pressing the heel of my hand against her abdomen, I grinned. "Do you feel that? That's me. I can feel my cock pushing from inside you. Your tasty pussy is just full of surprises."

Sliding my hand under the small of her back, I arched Ella up, stroking in and out of her in slow, easy movements that took all my self-control.

"You're deeper," she gasped, "you're pushing so high that I've..." Her hands were slipping on my shoulders, fingers tightening to hold onto me.

"Tell me, *solnyshko,*" I bite her earlobe, "tell me what you feel."

"How can there be a place inside me that I never knew was there? Because you're nudging me- it's different- I-" My bride came again, so intensely that she froze, internal muscles locked tightly and holding me immobile inside her. Groaning, I came too, feeling her squeeze me from the base to the tip of my cock.

Dropping my head onto her chest, I panted harshly, trying to regain my breath.

Ella's hands slid to my shoulders, and one very carefully, lightly, stroked my hair. It wasn't repellant, the way I'd expected and as something to be tolerated. Her delicate touch was good, and gentle in a way I'd always despised.

Until now.

Ella...

"This is quite the development."

That's Yuri, I thought, *the master of understatement.* Because this is a huge "what the actual hell is this?" moment.

We were both standing in Maksim's office in the penthouse, staring down at an elegant, cream-colored card.

Dear Friends,

Due to the tragedy of recent events I, Katya Sokolov, the only child of Pavel Sokolov, entered into marriage with Vasily Shevchenko, son of Trofin Shevchenko on January 10th.

It was not appropriate to have a large celebration after the terrible loss of my parents. Thank you for your sympathy and condolences for my family, and congratulations and well-wishes for our marriage.

"Did you know that the Sokolovs died?" I asked Maksim.

"We heard the news when we arrived back from Russia, they were both killed in a fire on January seventh while Katya was showing off her engagement ring in St. Petersburg. The blaze was said to be so intense that everything - and everyone - inside the house was incinerated almost immediately."

"That's horrible," I said. I had barely met them at our wedding, and I know they certainly didn't like me, but what a terrible way to die.

"It's suspicious that any home of theirs would not have a state-of-the-art security and fire system," Maksim said, still frowning at the announcement.

"So, she managed to work through her mourning period in, what? Twenty-four hours?" I asked.

"Now, now, Ella," admonished Yuri with a barely concealed smirk, "I am sure Katya was completely inconsolable for at least eight or nine minutes."

"Enough joking, you two," Maksim said sternly, tapping the card against his desk. "The timing here is too perfect. She has to be behind the death of her parents; a blaze so vicious that it consumed the mansion in moments? There are very few accelerants that can create that level of destruction in that amount of time."

"And none that are available in your standard household products," I added. "What?" They were both staring at me with speculation. "I'm in pharmaceutical research but you'd be surprised how many chemical compositions cross over from one use to another. But wouldn't fire investigators in... where were they? Costa Rica? Wouldn't they be thinking the same thing?"

Maksim shrugged. "Not if they're bribed well enough, or educated to the fact of how quickly their lives could end if they brought attention to it."

Yuri seated himself next to me on the long, comfortable office couch. "Katya could not have taken over her father's organization without a man to actually lead it. So how quickly did she pivot to Shevchenko when she couldn't sink her talons into you, brother?"

"It was known that Pavel used the Shevchenko Bratva for his dirty work in Eastern Europe every now and then," Maksim said, "picking a lower-level enforcer to marry may have been what she thought was insurance that she would be the one leading her family's organization."

I'm sitting there, a fire blazing cheerfully in the fireplace and snow falling delicately outside, and in a state of disbelief that not only were we talking about such bloody business - but even more outrageous - that Maksim and Yuri were discussing it with me instead of kicking me out of the study.

So, since I was there...

"Do you think Katya hired the mercenaries who shot up King's New Year's Eve party like it was the OK Corral?" I asked.

Both men turned to stare at me, and I was struck with how much they looked alike- not just the familial resemblance, but the cold, focused expression that was unmoved by violence and more interested in how to retaliate.

"She has the means and the motive," Yuri speculated, "she could have been making a head start on eliminating other major families and opening up their territory."

"The attack at the party, the raids on our warehouses, the attempt on Ella's life," Maksim shook his head. "That would cost an incalculable amount of money, plus a percentage for whoever brokered the deals."

A light knock on the door interrupted my next question, and Alina simpered her way in after Maksim called, "Enter!"

"I have some forms for you to sign, Pakhan," she said, fluttering her eyelashes like deranged lunar moths. He nodded, holding out his hand for the paperwork without looking at her.

I was just childish enough to smother a grin as she flounced back out of the room. Then it hit me. "Wait, what raids on your warehouses?"

My heart sank as I watched his face sculpt back into the cold, emotionless expression he wore so well.

"This was a mistake. Ella, if you'll excuse us?"

I knew better than to look at Yuri for help. Without a word, I stalked out of the room, repressing the urge to throw something.

"Hey, Tania. I'm not giving up until you talk to me. You know I'm annoying like that. Please, girlie... I know you need time to process everything and I respect that. But it's been two weeks. I have not gone more than a day or two without talking to you since we were in middle school! Just... will you please let me know that you're okay? Please? Anyway. Talk to you soon."

Hanging up from my fruitless daily call to Tania, I rubbed my eyes with a sigh. Though she was sending me the agreed-upon "proof of life" text every day, not speaking to Tania in person was utter misery.

Yet another terrible thing had happened, not that I'd known because Maksim hadn't forgiven either of us; he for letting that first little nugget about the warehouse raids slip, and me for asking about it. That was three days ago, but he'd gotten a call around two this morning and exited the bed like he'd been shot out of a cannon and I hadn't seen him since.

"Ugh!" I paced our bedroom, looking out the windows at the glittering view of Manhattan. Everything looked very glamorous and exotic from here, this was how the rich protected themselves from the darker corners of the city. Of course, I know that for the Bratva King, Maksim Morozov, the scary, dingy parts were his playground. Was he out there now?

Maksim...

The dull "thunk!" of a fist meeting flesh sounded behind me with metronomic accuracy. First, breaking the nose. Loosening some teeth on the next punch. Moving down the body. My phone rang, and I stepped away to take the call.

"Am I interrupting something?" Thomas sounded amused.

"Nothing particularly useful," I admitted, rubbing the back of my neck. "And you? Does The Corporation have anything to offer?"

There was a distinct chill in his cultured British accent. "Nothing definitive. But there's something off here."

I stepped out into the dingy hallway, closing the door on Bogdan's efforts on our latest captive. "In what way?"

"We've both been getting the same information, mercenaries, hired from the dark web, nothing traceable. Until today."

"You found the broker, didn't you?" My fist clenched, imagining the bastard's face collapsing as I pounded him into the concrete.

"Not exactly," his tone never deviated from his usual urbane presentation, but I could feel his frustration. "Not the broker who handled the recruitment for the New Year's Eve attack. But all this activity stirred up some new chatter. There's another interested party. They're keeping an extremely low profile, but I recognize their patterns."

"Another group?" I frowned, "It makes sense. I don't see how one organization could handle this much devastation."

"You got hit again?" Thomas' voice sharpened.

"They went after my *Obshchaka*," I snarled, "a crew of ten broke into his residence, they tortured one of his sons to tell them the location of our financial ledgers."

"Did they find the ledgers?"

"No." I gritted my teeth. "My *Obshchaka* locked himself into his safe room with the books. He watched them torture his son, but he didn't come out. We got there in time to save Dmitri's life, but…"

There was a respectful silence before Thomas offered, "Loyalty to the Family over all things."

The thought of Dmitri's broken face made me take a moment before I could agree with Thomas. "Tell me…" I tried to gather my thoughts. I hadn't slept for two days, the attacks were coming right and left, coordinated strikes that meant we had more than one traitor in my organization. "Tell me about this interested party."

"There's no conclusive proof," he said slowly, "but I believe it's the Irish. The O'Connell's. They run the West End Gang in Toronto and Montreal and they've spread like a fungus here in London." Now, his accent sharpened. "We'd kept them out of this part of England, but they find a new way in every time we think we've crushed them."

Frowning, I went over the information. "The Irish who control the East Coast have no connection to the O'Connells."

"The Murphy's," Thomas agreed. "I can't imagine they'd welcome a push from the West End Gang. But I'm certain it's them. The O'Connells have been bringing in more and more men, and I know they're behind hiring men out of the Black Watch Organization."

"The Black Watch? More mercenaries, and even more vicious," I agreed. *Blyad'!* Can this get worse?

"They're looking for something," Thomas warned me. "I'm not clear on what, but shore up your defenses."

"Thank you, my friend." My headache is ratcheting up again. "I'll pass on anything I hear from this side of the pond."

"As will I," agreed Thomas. "Ah, Lauren wanted me to pass her greetings along to your Ella. She would like to speak to her when it's convenient."

"I will give my wife the message," I promised. "Be safe."

Ending the call, I listened to the groans from behind the metal door. We're being attacked from every direction. This isn't just one enemy, and every time we kill their men, more pop up like toadstools.

CHAPTER 19 – WARM MOMENTS AND CHILLY REJECTIONS

In which there are more funerals, more disasters and a tender moment when Ella calls a toddler "the world's most adorable barnacle."

Ella...

"My sisters are coming to visit," Maksim says one afternoon, straightening his tie.

"Oh? It would be wonderful to see them again." I looked up from the row of black dresses on my side of the dressing room. Who knew these little fellas would get such a workout? Along with three more Beautiful People parties; we'd unfortunately also attended two more group funerals since coming home from St. Petersburg, and my frenzied work with Duolingo helped me overhear some of the mutterings from the families. Everyone was scared by how the Morozov empire was under attack, seemingly from all directions.

Warehouses - like the ones Maksim and Yuri mentioned - were torched. Another group went after Maksim's bookkeeper and I'm guessing that man has all the knowledge of the Morozov empire's financial doings. To add insult to injury, some spunky group of gang members went around to businesses under his

Bratva's "oversight" and collected the protection money before Maksim's men shut that down.

While his Brigadiers were chasing these douchebags, whoever was behind this broke into his new club *Gehenna*, where he and I had our "meet cute" - as Tania insisted on calling it - and tried to set it on fire, too. There was something about the activity under the club that was actually in danger, but the conversation broke off as Alina - still playing Bratva Queen Bee - waltzed over with cookies and commiseration for the widows.

There's been muttering that all the other Bratva families are in on it, wanting to destroy Maksim and divide up his territory. The Morozov empire is bigger than the other Russians' and according to Yuri, bigger than the territories held by the Italians and the Irish, too. So, it stood to reason that every rat wants a nibble. I couldn't believe that Lucya and Alexi were involved, they were too honorable, even if Alexi was as cold as Maksim.

I was pondering the enormity of the problem as I struggled to zip up my dress, and I felt Maksim's warm fingers gently push mine away and finish the job. His hands slid up to my shoulders, and we looked at each other in the huge mirror.

"You look really nice," I offer, and he does. However, the lines of strain around his mouth and the dark circles from his utter lack of sleep are telling a different story.

"Thank you," he said, pinching the bridge of his nose between his thumb and forefinger. "As do you. This is an unfortunate way to measure progress, but I saw several of the children and a few of the widows speak with you at the last funeral. They are beginning to accept you in your position."

I felt a wave of sympathy for this man. I knew how seriously Maksim took his responsibility for the people in his empire. The wholesale destruction of his properties was bad, but losing people loyal to him? It was eating him up, I knew it.

"You're right," I agreed, "that is a terrible way to measure progress." I watched him tilt his head to one side, obviously stiff. "We have a couple of minutes, if you want to sit down, I could rub your neck?" He looked at me, one elegant brow raised and I threw up my hands. "Not your spine! Not even your shoulder blades! But if you add your neck to the list of acceptable places to touch, I could work out those kinks." I smiled, trying to lighten the words, and Maksim sighed, nodding and seating himself on the ottoman. The tendons in his neck were strung tighter than a violin string.

His low, relieved exhale made me oddly happy. At least it was something I could do to help. So small as to be almost insignificant, but... it was still something. I could spot the tip of one of his tattoos peeking out from the collar of his expensive dress shirt and another thick scar I'd not seen before. *Of course,* I thought sardonically, *since I'm not allowed to touch 85% of his body, I'm sure there's dozens of scars I've yet to map.* But... my fingers worked without me as I pondered this. If Maksim was a regular human, one with insecurities and childhood trauma...

His dad.

I remembered Yuri's stories about the 'tender, loving care' their father inflicted on them as children. I'd thought the scars and burn marks scattered over his spectacular body were just byproducts of his life as the Bratva Death King. But there was something about how I was only allowed to touch certain parts of him, and even as carefully and lightly as I'd stroked his hair, his muscles initially went rigid, like he was prepared to endure it.

I knew his father was evil. But what did he do to Maksim? How horrible was it that he couldn't tolerate anyone touching him?

The funeral was oddly lovely, the beauty of the cathedral, the practices, and traditions that were becoming so familiar to me, even the gentle kiss Maksim placed on the brow of every man he'd lost. I placed a flower inside the casket of each of the men, and noticed a little girl, three, maybe four, lingering by one.

"Hello," I tried to look like a Pakhan's wife, one who would know everyone and understand what they needed. "I'm Ella, what's your name?"

Aaand there was the chin wobble. Her eyes were already filling with tears and I asked, "Is that your...?"

The little one didn't answer, but she pointed at my flowers.

Oh. "Would you like to put a flower on the..." I offered the blooms, letting her pick one. How do you ask a toddler if they wanted to place a flower in their father's coffin? Looking around at all these families again, it hurt, the young men's stoic exterior, the weariness of the newly widowed, the confusion of children. How many funerals could these people attend without losing everything that held them together? Meanwhile, my flower girl was on tiptoes, trying to reach the casket. I looked around helplessly for her mother, for Maksim, hell; even for Alina but I was on my own.

"Would you like me to lift you up?" Nodding, she reached up and wrapped her arms around my neck once I had her perched on my hip. *God, I hope this is the right thing to do,* I moaned silently, *am I traumatizing this child for life?*

But I had seen family members lift the smaller kiddos before to look at their loved ones and say goodbye, so... Adjusting her again, I leaned over the coffin, her father in a dark suit and almost looking asleep, if you kept some distance. "Do you want to put the flower on your papa's jacket?" I asked, "I think it will look very nice."

How was this child not crying? How? How could even the

smallest members of this community be so stoic? She reached out and put the blossom on his chest, straightening it a bit. "I'll bet your papa is so proud of you," I whispered into her hair, her little body smelling of warm skin and lavender.

"Luda!"

A young woman raced up, exhaustion and anxiety on her face. She's wearing a shapeless black dress with a spit-up stain on her shoulder, likely from the baby propped on her other shoulder.

"Privet, tvoya doch' takaya milaya," I say haltingly, and she looks up at me in surprise. Clearing my throat, *"YA ochen' sozhaleyu o vashey...* um... *potere."* I think what I said was, "Hello, your daughter is so sweet. I'm so sorry for your loss." God, I hope that's what I said.

"Spasibo?" Her awkward thanks is interrupted by Luda and a flood of Russian that I cannot keep up with.

"Mila, prikhodi i posidi s nami." Maksim is behind us and puts a gentle hand on her shoulder, urging her to sit in the front row with us. I'm following, still holding on to Luda, who is clinging fiercely to me like the world's cutest barnacle.

Yeah, super maternal, Ella, I thought. I didn't have much experience with kids, so sue me. I tried to look dignified while carrying her, following behind them. *Even Mila looks more like she fits with Maksim than I do.*

But he helps her settle with another one of the widows, baby in her lap and when the other woman reaches for Luda, she stubbornly buries her face in my neck. I point to her, and then me, and nod encouragingly at Mila, who smiles in relief, nodding back.

I can't blame her. Two kids under three?

Maksim...

Ella sits next to me, somehow still looking graceful and lovely while holding the squirming little girl. When she starts playing with my wife's opal necklace, Ella simply takes it off and gives it to her. I'd bought the opals, interspersed with diamonds, for $42,000. The little one immediately puts them in her mouth, snuggling deeper onto my bride's lap. I sing, bow my head when appropriate, and hand my pocket square to Mila to blot her tears, but I can't stop watching this woman, dragged into my world kicking and screaming but attending her sixth funeral, comforting a widow, playing with her child... Behaving like a queen.

At the small reception afterward, Ella offers to hold the baby when Luda needs a clothing change from spilling her dessert down her best dress. Absently rocking back and forth to calm the baby, she's talking to two of the other women, laughing with them over some discussion. I'm looking at her perfect, shapely ass in that tight dress - an excellent choice - and how it flexes as she moves. Her legs are strong, looking long in her high, high heels. My wife wears them anytime we are appearing together, I suspect so that it brings her height much closer to mine, wanting to look more authoritative. If only she knew that it was her warmth and sincerity that was finally winning over my people.

Two children, a boy and a girl scamper across the room to me. "Sir, do you want to hear my audition piece?" Oksana tries to keep her voice down, aware of the seriousness of the moment, but those around us still turn to look. "It's next week! Mr. Hesse says he's very confident about my chances!" I stifle a chuckle; I'd forgotten how she always spoke as if every sentence must end with an exclamation point.

"No!" Vadim interrupts her, "My selection is much more challenging, the Pakhan will want to hear mine!"

"I am proud of both of you," I assure them, "but this is not the time or place. Do ask your mother to notify Alina of the audition date and time. I will attend if I can." Vadim and Oksana were the children of Sergei, my former *Obshchak.* The twelve-year-old twins were extraordinarily gifted. I promised their mother that if they were accepted into the Juilliard Junior Program, I would pay their tuition. Their father was always so proud of them. I looked up to see one of the women whisper into Ella's ear, and she was looking at me with a soft smile. I wasn't happy with the women telling tales to my wife.

Patrick steps up to me urgently. "Pakhan, there's another attack. At the Chvrch. They're trying to fight their way down to the lower levels."

Gritting my teeth, I nodded, but not letting my fury show on my face. Not at a place of mourning for our fallen soldiers. "Pull everyone who's not running security here."

Patrick has made an excellent *Obshchak* in the last few weeks, even if he hasn't slept more than five minutes at a time. He simply nods and heads off as quickly as he can without drawing attention.

Ella spots me heading for the door and hurries over. *So close to a clean getaway,* I thought wryly.

"You're leaving?" She says it softly, already experienced enough to not draw attention.

"I have an issue. Ivan will drive you home."

Brow furrowed, she nods. "Be safe."

I'm already turning away, but the words stop me for a moment. Has anyone ever said that to me before? Leaning down, I kiss her cheek. "I'll see you back at the penthouse."

There's something about a firefight that makes time slow down and then speed up in random bursts. My eyes narrow in on movement, the trajectory of a bullet showing me where the shooter is hiding. The positions of my men to the enemy's. This is the second nightclub of mine that these scum have shot up in the last ten days and none of them are going to survive this.

"Why did you have this club designed with so many hiding spots!" Yuri shouts to me.

Closing one eye, I focus on the idiot spraying bullets from an AP4 semi-automatic and take him out with a headshot. "Check the perimeter alert. Have they accessed the elevator?" Our key gambling facility is under the Chvrch in a three-floor underground club that's twice as large as the one hiding it.

One of my soldiers is sprinting toward the hidden entry to the underground location, and I see the two men he's shooting at. One is taping an explosive device to the steel panel. I rise high enough to take out three of the men shooting at him, and it leaves me open long enough to feel a punch to my chest as a bullet tears through me. My soldier is able to take out both men and is still alive. The rattle of bullets hitting everything on the main dance floor is slowing, and we take out another six of their men. These are not as expert, not as experienced as the mercenaries we've fought before. Does this mean whoever is behind this is running out of money to hire the more elite, experienced men? Or could these be their organization's own soldiers?

"Yuri! Patrick!" I shout, "Take one of them alive, I don't care how!"

There is a groan from my men as the distant sound of sirens grows closer and I know we have mere minutes before the NYPD is breaking through my doors. The shooting from the enemy stops almost instantly, the police are a complication no one wants.

"Patrick! Dismantle the explosives, get them out of here. Dmitri and Timur, help the wounded. Someone find me a survivor!" The sirens are rapidly growing louder and Yuri stops me. He has a cut over his forehead, bleeding red onto the collar of his white dress shirt.

"Pakhan, you must leave. You can't be here. Our guns are gone - aside from the legal ones. I'll handle this."

I hesitate, even as I hear car doors slam open.

Yuri pushes my wounded shoulder, grinning as I groan. "Go!"

A few men stay behind with my brother, and I help haul out the most severely wounded, throwing one young soldier over my uninjured shoulder. "Call Dr. Malyshev, and have him meet us at the safe house." Dmitri nods and puts the two worst wounded in the back of his car and speeds off.

The 'safe house' is actually a large apartment in one of the buildings I own under a different corporate entity and is untraceable to me. Sixteen men were wounded, and six of them are in critical condition. I hold a towel over my bleeding shoulder and listen to the lieutenants' reports as I wait to make sure the men are out of danger.

"You should let him look at your shoulder," Patrick says. He's nodding toward the elderly doctor and his assistant, who are both swaying with exhaustion.

"I'll take care of it at home," I said, heading for the door now that I know all my men will live, "the bullet went through so there's nothing to dig out." Patrick eyes my makeshift bandage, sopping wet with blood but says nothing.

Resting my head against the car seat, I'm glad Dmitri is not injured and that he's driving me back to the penthouse. It's possible I might have lost more blood than I'd thought. But even so, perhaps tonight has turned the tides, we didn't lose anyone, and the only thing the NYPD will find is my brother, outraged at a violent attempt to rob our best club and our legal firearms, used with permits by the club's "security guards." No one could buy the services of this many mercenaries without finally leaving a trail. It was just a matter of time.

"Pakhan?" Dimitri's calm, solid voice wakes me. "We are here."

"Maksim?"

Ella had waited up for me, an action I viewed with some regret. I'd wanted to patch myself up quietly and rest. She had changed from her serious black dress into leggings and a big sweatshirt I didn't recognize.

She must have finally unpacked her belongings we put in storage, I thought, *she's settling in.* The thought pleased me more than it should. *It's just the blood loss,* I lied to myself.

"What happened to you?" she gasped, fluttering her hands anxiously but not daring to touch my bloody shirt.

"I'm fine," I said dismissively, "I'll just-"

"I know where that giant first aid kit is," she interrupted, "will you come into the bathroom? It'll be easier to work there."

It was proof of my excessive blood loss that I allowed her to interrupt me and take my hand to draw me down the hall.

"I'm pretty sure you could perform open heart surgery with this medical kit," Ella said, only slightly sarcastic.

"Hmm…" I leaned my head back against the bathroom wall, keeping my eyes open with some effort. "Are you sure this won't make you ill?"

"No, I'm kind of enjoying this," she said with a poorly concealed grin.

"Making me suffer?"

"Yes."

No shame, my bride. No shame at all.

She held up the shears. "It'll be less painful cutting your shirt off if you're okay with that."

The thought that I would ever allow anyone near my person with such a sharp object seemed impossible, but I nodded, letting Ella carefully slice through my bloody shirt, pulling the pieces away from my torso.

"Are there any other injuries aside from this bullet hole?"

Now I was certain she was being sarcastic. "You must be under the impression, Ella, that I can't spank you in this condition for your tone."

She had the nerve to hide her smirk by pawing through my carefully assembled medical kit. "Well, Maksim, it would take a fair amount of effort on your part, but..." Leaning me forward gently, she looked at the exit wound on my shoulder. "Good, the bullet went right through. I'm not seeing any debris. I'm going to irrigate the wound, okay?"

Watching her sure, swift hands open the cleaning solution, my curiosity - and some suspicion - rose. "You seem quite confident with your medical treatment, Ella. Now, why would a Ph.D. in pharmaceutical research give you such insight about this side of the field?"

"Well, Maksim," she sassed, drenching both bullet holes until satisfied they were clean and snapping on some gloves, "I initially wanted to be a surgeon. I went to four years of medical school before deciding it wasn't for me. Also..." she hesitated, carefully threading the needle, "I didn't think I could possibly get a loan for the rest of the tuition money. With all the expenses, it would have been around half a million. It just... it wasn't in the cards, I guess."

I thought about the five million dollars in assets that her brother had stolen when her parents were killed. Yuri's report was quite specific. Perhaps I would just kill him anyway. They weren't in contact; how would she know? When she pulled out the Lidocaine, I shook my head. "That won't be necessary for something this small."

Frowning, she put it back. "If you say so..." Carefully pinching the wound together on the front of my shoulder, she continued, "I'm guessing the presence of this very large kit with so many excellent medical instruments means that you are used to patching yourself up?"

I shrugged and she pulled the thread a little too hard. "Ack! Please don't move, okay? I haven't stitched a wound in three years!"

I chuckled, "I assure you; your worst will still be a better job than my best."

Carefully tying off the thread, she looked it over before turning me to start on the exit wound. "I'm assuming this is a result of whatever had you bolting from the after-funeral gathering?"

Jaw clenched, I simply nodded.

"Is everyone okay?" Ella persisted, "What about Yuri?"

Rubbing my eyes with a thumb and forefinger, I sighed, "He's alive, he has a minor cut on his forehead."

"No!" She gave out a soft, overly dramatic wail, "Not his face! Yuri's face is the moneymaker! This is terrible!"

Opening my eyes, I gave her a slow, filthy smile. "Yuri's pretty face is quite definitely not the reason for his popularity with the ladies. His pearl-enhanced co-"

"Don't! Don't say it!" Ella gave a mortified groan. "Please don't talk about my brother-in-law's junk, that's so gross! It's bad enough that I have to hear it from-"

I watched the humor and animation drain from her lovely face as she made another precise stitch in my skin. "Tania is still not returning your calls?"

Silently shaking her head and looking terribly sad, Ella finished her needlework, cleaning and bandaging the wounds. "You need a transfusion. You're really pale. I'm not sure you can even stand up on your own."

Giving a sneer, I stood, but just barely. Rolling her eyes, my bride ran a warm washcloth over my chest, removing the rest of the blood and fetching some sleep pants so I could get out of the rest of my ruined suit.

Getting into bed felt so good that I let out a groan, and Ella smiled as she arranged the pillows behind me. "Clean sheets and a good mattress are the best things in life, am I right? Can you drink some water?" She handed me an antibiotic tablet and watched me drink it down with half the bottle of water.

Lying close to me, but not touching, just near enough to feel her body heat, she murmured, "Goodnight Maksim. I'm glad you're safe."

I wanted to say goodnight to her, but I fell asleep with the words on my lips.

Ella...

Ekaterina, Mariya, and their four (four!) bodyguards stepped out of the penthouse elevator, staring at the activity. To the untrained eye, it looked a lot like the time I knocked my brother's ant farm off of his dresser. Bratva soldiers walked back and forth, conferring with each other in hushed whispers and Maksim's higher-ups issuing orders on iPhones wedged to their ears. Alina tip-tapped her way down the marble hall in her five-inch heels, carrying files and coffee to his office.

"Did we arrive at an awkward time?" Mariya asked, an unholy grin on her face.

I leaned in, whispering her mother's favorite admonition to her; "Always the troublemaker, aren't you?" We giggled childishly while the bodyguards looked uncomfortable.

"Hello, sister," Ekaterina said, hiding a smile, "so nice to be back."

Hugging them both, I guided them into the warm alcove by the living room. That room was gigantic and high-ceilinged and everything echoed there. The alcove was intimate, with another little fireplace and room only for two delightfully squishy couches and a table between them. A jewel-colored Persian rug - the colors faded over time - was warm under bare feet. I hated wearing shoes in the house.

"Sit down," I suggested, "I've got snacks coming."

The bodyguards looked into the space dubiously, and Mariya fluttered her eyelashes. "No boys are allowed in our secret club, why don't you take a moment to yourselves?"

The housekeeper for the penthouse marched in, setting down a tray filled with Cheetos, home made corn chips and a thick, chunky salsa from Los Tacos No. 1, with banana pudding and doughnuts from Magnolia Bakery.

Ekaterina clapped her hands, bouncing with excitement. "You remembered all of our favorite treats?"

"A girl's gotta relax," I said, grabbing a doughnut with lavender frosting, "no stress about calories either, hear me?" I point a stern finger at both of them, "You're on vacation." I'd seen how calorie-restrictive their diets were at home, even though they were both very slim. And based on their brother's physiques, it's not like their family had trouble with keeping their weight down.

There was a serious amount of damage done to the snacks before the housekeeper, Ludmilla, returned with drinks, a look of pinched disapproval on her square face. Of course, she always reeked of disapproval when she looked at me. It made me almost miss Megumi back at the hunting lodge.

"Things seem very unsettled," ventured Ekaterina. Mariya paused chewing, her banana pudding, still wedged in her cheeks like she was a chipmunk storing it up for winter.

I smiled, trying not to look too bitter. "As a wife, you know I'm not privy to this kind of information."

Mariya's brow furrowed. "Privy?"

"Meaning not allowed to know anything about anything," I smiled sardonically. Helping myself to a Cheeto, I said, "I used to date this Southern guy? Totally hot. But when I'd ask him anything complicated, he'd say, 'Aw, darlin' don't you worry your pretty little head about that.' We didn't date very long."

Both of them laughed, Mariya choking a little as she tried to swallow the rest of her pudding.

"Three beautiful women in one place? I sense trouble." Maksim was leaning against the doorway, arms folded and smiling amiably. "But darling, do continue about this... Southern boy?"

"I have never dated anyone before you, my dear husband," I offer, blinking up at him adorably.

At least I get one corner of his mouth to curve up in a half smile before he kisses both of his sisters. *"Sestra,"* he says fondly to Ekaterina, before squeezing Mariya into a hug, *"malen'kaya ugroza."*

Little menace? I think with a grin, *Looks like I might have a partner in crime here.*

Yuri is behind him and the greetings begin again as I watch with a smile. It's wonderful to see these two hardened men go all soft and kind when it comes to their little sisters. They're all so lucky to have each other. Ekaterina links her arm with mine, squeezing me a little.

"Our sister has been giving us snacks," she announces proudly, and both men look down at the rubble of carbohydrates while I dust the Cheeto powder off my skirt.

"So I see," Maksim says dryly, "and here I was planning a dinner at the Russian Vodka Room, should I cancel, or...?"

"No!" Ekaterina wails.

"Please, brother!" Mariya, clinging to his hand.

"Oh, this is so dramatic," I roll my eyes, leaning over to Yuri, who is laughing quietly.

"They... what is the phrase?" he says, "they own Maksim, and they know it."

"No doubt," I shake my head, grinning at the three of them.

I'm delighted to see that Alexi and Lucya are already at the table when we arrive, their girls squabbling over the place settings and Konstantin sitting stiffly, with perfect posture and ignoring the childish antics of his sisters.

"When did you get back from St. Petersburg?" I ask, kissing Lucya three times, left cheek, right cheek, left cheek... I was actually remembering all the Russian customs without studying up before we went anywhere! *Progress*, I thought, *at least in some part of this life.* Maksim orders Kasha with mushrooms and assorted Pirozhki to start as I look around the room. It's white and elegant, but I see the tables are filled with mostly families and everyone is speaking in Russian.

"Maksim brings us here every time we visit," confided Ekaterina, "we like it better than the fancy French stuff Mother loves."

"Everything looks amazing," I say, going for a Pirozhki, "you'll have to recommend something for an entree." Looking over at Lucya as I try not to stuff the entire bun in my mouth, I notice she's watching Alexi and Maksim speak softly, her eyes narrowed. When Ekaterina turns to talk to Yana, I lean in.

"Is everything okay?"

Her gaze drifts to me, and Lucya smiles. A social sort of smile. Not a real one. "It could be worse," she says cryptically. "I am just reminded that no matter how much our world progresses, how stubbornly some things stay the same."

"Care to enlighten me?"

With a sigh, she taps her wine glass against mine. "Not here. Another time when we can talk. How long are the girls here?" We launch into standard table chatter, but I see her glare at our husbands when she thinks no one is watching.

After settling Mariya and Ekaterina in the guest rooms, I meander down the hall to Maksim's study. The door is closed, and it's so well-soundproofed that I can barely hear the quiet drone of voices inside.

What the hell, I think, and knocked firmly.

"Enter."

The men look up as I come in, both holding glasses with a rather generous helping of Maksim's more expensive vodka.

"Oooo, the Russo-Baltique?" I tease, "What's the special occasion?"

"Just relaxing," lies my husband, standing up. The bullet wound in his shoulder is barely making a dent in his movements, still fluid as if nothing could possibly damage The Pakhan. "Would you like a drink?"

"Do you have anything to mix that with?" I asked, knowing that Yuri would choke on his vodka in horror. He does, and I smother a laugh.

"Sister, dear," he says, grinning, "would you like me to fetch you some fruit punch and rubbing alcohol? I think it would suit your palate nicely."

"Hah, ha, *brother*," I sneer credibly, taking a glass of white wine from an amused Maksim, "at least I'm a cheap date."

"This is true," he chuckles, moving over to make room for me. It's becoming a familiar triangle; Yuri and I sitting on this comfortable leather couch, Maksim sitting behind his shining mahogany desk.

"You okay, pretty boy?" Yuri's wearing a discreet bandage on his forehead over some stitches.

"Better than that poor soul," he says, nodding at his brother.

"You know, he wouldn't even let me numb the wound before I stitched him up?" I say conversationally, "Seriously, what is the point of that?"

They exchange glances, and I can feel the well of pain between them, a deep well from years and years of misery poured into it.

"Are you quite finished taunting me, Ella?" Maksim forces a mood switch, smiling at me.

"Never, Maksim," I say sweetly. Taking a deep breath, I plunge in. "I know things are bad. Can we talk about it? Maybe I can have some value in problem-solving, maybe I can't, but..."

Floundering a little, "Why not give it a try?"

It's silent for a moment, just the gentle crackle of the wood in the fireplace, and I stare hopefully at the man who made me marry him. When he shakes his head, I know it's useless. I'm apparently useless.

"Nothing to worry about, darling. We're taking care of it," Maksim says.

"Just don't worry my pretty little head?" I finish my glass of wine and place it carefully on the sideboard, fingers trembling with the urge to throw it at him. "I'll leave you two to get back to business."

Yuri's mouth opens, I know he wants to say something. But looking at the Russian monolith behind the fancy desk, he closes it again, lifting his drink as a farewell.

Don't slam the door, Ella. You're better than that, I think, wanting desperately to storm back in and sweep all the expensive crystal on his sideboard off in a deeply satisfying crash.

But I don't.

Before I go to bed, I'm about to make my fruitless daily call to Tania when I see four missed ones from her.

"Tania?" I whisper the minute she picks up. "Are you okay?"

"I will be," she sighs. "Girl, I'm so sorry for just disappearing. I'm sorry I left you on your own."

"It doesn't matter," I'm shaking my head, even though of course she can't see me. "As long as we're still friends."

She laughs, her hoarse chortle that always makes me laugh, too. "Are you kidding? Babe, I'm your emotional support animal, remember? You're not getting rid of me so easily."

We talk for hours, I'm curled up in the comfy spot in our fancy dressing room. About the New Year's Eve party. About gunfire and dead bodies. How everything can change in a second in our lives and we are helpless to do anything about it. And then, about the latest stupid thing her boss said, about my weird fortune told in St. Petersburg, but not falling through the ice because she's not ready to hear about it and I'm not ready to tell it.

By the time we hang up with mutual and multiple "Goodbye, I love you's," it's four am. And the bed is empty, except for me.

CHAPTER 20 – CLUB BAD JUJU

In which Ella finds family, betrayal, and danger. In that order.

Maksim...

"You'll have to tell her eventually."

"Exactly who do you work for, brother?" I growl, not in the mood for Yuri's prodding and still seeing Ella's expression as she left the office.

"You're just going to wait until it's time to stuff Mariya into a wedding dress?"

"This is a good match," I snap, pouring another drink. Rotating my shoulders, my mouth tightens at the stab of pain. "Mariya will finish school, the Turgenevs are quite liberal under Alexi's control, she might even attend college before they marry."

"We always said we would never be like our father," he persisted, and I gritted my teeth.

"Our father," I spat, "wanted to give Ekaterina at the age of thirteen to Torshin, that disgusting old drunk in the Moscow Bratva. I am gaining an ally with another powerful Bratva by making a mutually advantageous union between our families."

Yuri is looking down, hands gripped together. "I know," he sighed, "I know. Alexi's contacts in the police commissioner's office will be very helpful. When the police were at the club, they were already talking about getting a search warrant, even though we were the injured party."

"We'll get that effort crushed immediately," I said, "any news from the man we caught at the club?"

Yuri grinned, "Well, Bogdan wished me to tell you that he's exhausted from interrogating prisoners and is requesting a raise."

"Please," I scoffed, "he would pay us for the chance to play with all these captives."

"In any case, while the man hasn't cracked yet, his tattoos are helpful. He's spent a lot of time in a Russian prison. He has dots on his forehead."

This means he's sided with prison guards against his fellow inmates before, I thought, *interesting.*

"He's not strong enough to hold out under questioning if he's changed sides so easily before," I said, "what else?"

"No family tattoos," Yuri says regretfully, "but a forced one on his knuckles; *ssuchenye.*"

"A dishonored thief? Then they are scraping the bottom of the barrel." Taking another swallow of the excellent vodka, I say, "Give Bogdan another couple of hours of fun, then offer the prisoner a chunk of money to talk, and we'll let him live."

Yuri laughs, "The man is going to talk, no matter what."

"True," I walk over to the window, staring out at Manhattan. It is still mine, and those bastards are about to realize it. "But we need intel before another attack." Turning, I catch him wearily rubbing his eyes. "You need rest. Why don't you sleep in one of the guest bedrooms?"

He groaned, standing up and stretching. "I'll go home. Our sisters will be waking you up with their shrieking soon enough."

What he isn't saying is that he doesn't want to look at Mariya's sweet face, knowing we've promised her hand in marriage to Konstantin Turgenev.

Ella...

I enlisted Tania's help to plan a trip around the city. The girls wanted to sight-see like "the tourists do," and we'd promised them some off-the-beaten-track adventures. Ivan overheard me making some reservations on the phone and looked concerned. "Relax, it's not like I'm bringing them to an opium den," I assured him.

"I know where one is, though," Tania volunteered helpfully as my poor bodyguard's face turns white.

"First stop, Battery Park!" I wanted to start with something for Mariya since I suspect she doesn't get enough whimsical moments in her life.

"The Seaglass Carousel?" She's smiling eagerly as we get closer. "This place rocks!" Tania promises, "The fish are LED lit and once you get on, they twirl and swirl around the building, which is nautilus shaped. I did this once when I'd taken a couple of mushrooms and Ella had to pry me off the seahorse one, which was-"

"-Not suitable for mixed company," I finish. Mariya's likely heard worse but I don't want the bodyguards tattling back to Maksim, or worse, to their mother.

"We're heading down to Chinatown, bitches!" Tania is crazed about the adorable lattes at Sweet Moment and when I hear Mariya give out a high-pitched squeal when she sees the adorable little bear face laced delicately into the surface of her pink drink, I know this was a good choice. We stop by the Harry Potter store for Mariya - who am I kidding, Tania buys two Ravenclaw robes because, "You need one for classes and one for Quidditch, duh!"

Ivan is beginning to make noises about returning home when Ekaterina screams with excitement, making the driver stomp on the brakes in alarm and at least two of our guys pull their guns. "Look! The Meow Parlour Cat Cafe!"

Tania and I exchange glances, cat cafes were so 2016, but if she wants it... "You want to stop for a cup of tea and a cuddle?" I offer.

Ekaterina may have just entered college, but she has her nose pressed against the car window like Tiny Tim at the grocer on Christmas morning.

"I always wanted a cat," she said wistfully, "but Mother is allergic to cats."

"Like, deathly allergic, or sniffles and red eyes?" I ask.

"The second one," Ekaterina clarifies.

"Maksim is, too," Mariya added.

Tania and I lock glances.

"Well, we have to go in," she says.

"For Ekaterina's sake," I add sweetly.

Seeing her face light up when a fluffy Persian cat seats himself on her lap is worth the lecture I'm going to get when we go home. We drink tea, tell stories about our pets - the Morozov sisters never had pets, unless you counted their guard dogs, which is horrifying - and play with a basket of kittens until the sun's about to set.

"Are you tired?" I ask, "Are you up for one last place?"

"What are you thinking?" Tania asks, she's still wearing her Quidditch robes. Of course, so is Mariya.

"The Dream House?"

Her expression softens. "Yeah, we should do that."

"The Dream House was first created in 1993 by composer La Monte Young and Marian Zazeela, they're a visual artist," I'm narrating as we climb the three stories to the art exhibition. Ivan is stomping ahead of us, "clearing the perimeter," I'm sure. "Here- take off your shoes and jacket," I'm so weirdly excited to share this; also, it's hilarious asking four Bratva tough guys to take off their shoes. "So, when you go inside, everything is a wild, neon pink, and there's endlessly changing sound waves that flow over you; you'll never hear anything like them again."

Everyone glides through the pink light like it's ocean water and

I can feel my entire body vibrate.

"Why are you crying?" Ekaterina's whispering to me and I quickly glance around to see if anyone else caught me, but even the giant Russians are swaying slightly.

"Oh, um… The last time I was here, my brother Charles knew I was tired and cranky. Mom and Dad brought us because she was a musician, and she wanted us to 'feel' the music." She's listening, a slight smile on her face. "I was getting mad because I couldn't feel it, the way she'd promised I would. So, Charles held my hand and told me that the music would vibrate through him and into me and it would be like I was getting the sound from inside out, sort of. So, we held hands and I could feel the vibration travel up my spine, just like he said, and it was like we were making music together." I'm smiling and trying to wipe my wet cheeks. "We weren't very close, you know? I don't have many good memories with him. So, this place is precious to me."

Ekaterina takes my hand and squeezes it, and I'm filled with the sound and vibration and the warmth of her hand.

Maksim…

"I am sorry, but you can see why your offer is not enough."

I'm Facetiming Farid in Morocco, and the slimy bastard is grinning at me, which shows his absolute lack of desire to live. He can't imagine I will let this stand. "My offer for your guns is nearly twice what you can obtain anywhere else," I say coldly.

"True, Morozov, true. But what I need is a safe travel route into America for my livestock." He's leaning back, confident and grinning and if he were here, I would slit his throat for his audacity.

"I am not in the business of human trafficking," I hiss.

"Understood, of course. Understood. But I am, and I assure you, you need not ever see the cargo. I just need a location to ship it to."

He means women. Not cargo, not livestock. He means children.

"I will not agree to that," I am coldly furious, and he would be insane to say no to me.

"Very well," Farid sighs, as if disappointed. "I understand. But there are other bidders, so, good luck to you, my friend. Let me know if you change your mind."

I want to shoot him in the face. I want to beat him to death. Not even for the foolishness, the audacity of refusing our generous offer, but for thinking I would sink so low as to help him bring women and children here for a short, horrific life of misery and pain. But instead, I disconnect the call and then throw my glass against the wall, watching it shatter in a spray of crystal. We are being attacked on every side. I am running out of time, guns, and men. And I still can't find who's attempting to destroy our family. I cannot do this without more manpower to protect what is ours. And unlike the scum who is hiring mercenaries to destroy us, I must have men I can trust. Allies I can count on.

Checking the time, I see it's 10:15 am in Milan. Placing my hands flat on the glossy surface of my desk, I stare at them. I've killed with these hands, caused pain. Sometimes, given pleasure. But it's not enough. I place the call. "Giovanni. It's Maksim Morozov."

The next day...

The door to the study slams open and I look up, ready to tear the intruder apart.

"How could you do this to Mariya!" Ella is furious, flushed, and stalking toward me with her fists clenched.

Leaning back, I put my fingers together, watching her calmly. "I take it you had lunch with Lucya today?"

"When were you going to tell me? Wait!" Ella spluttered, "Wait, what is far more important here is when the hell were you going to tell your fourteen-year-old sister you just traded her off in an arranged marriage! Who are you? You told me that you hated your dad for nearly giving Ekaterina to that creepy

Moscow Pakhan and now you're doing the same thing?"

If it weren't for the fact that Ella looks ready to stab me, I would be hard right now. She's magnificent, her pale green eyes blazing and her long hair flying everywhere.

"This doesn't concern you." I expect her to stalk around my office in circles, still furious and shouting, but she surprises me. She sweeps all the expensive contents of my bar onto the hardwood floor in a resounding crash. There's broken shards of crystal shooting across the floor mixed with ice from the silver bucket and my last bottle of vodka soaking into the nearby antique Persian rug.

"Don't you ever say that to me again!" Ella screams. She's unhinged now and topples over a table lamp to add to the rubble on the floor. "You were a complete monster to me! You forced me to marry you! But oh," she chuckled nastily, "even then I could still see your redeeming qualities. You would never allow human trafficking in your Bratva. You at least loved your sisters. Oh yeah, right up to the point where you're pimping them out!"

Looking for something else to break, she headed for a sculpture on a stand by the window. But this was a crystal dragon piece from the Ming Dynasty and I could not let her destroy it.

"Stop!" I wasn't shouting but my voice cut across her shrill one as I seized her wrists, crossing them over her chest and immobilizing her against me.

The door opens and Fedor and Ivan tumble in, guns drawn. They're shocked at the sight; I'm holding a thrashing, cursing Ella and my study is in shambles. A wide-eyed Alina is trying to get a look over their shoulders.

"You may leave," I say coldly.

They both instantly turn and leave the room, though I note Ivan sends a worried glance over his shoulder at my shrieking bride. I hold her against me until her struggling weakens and her attempts to kick me stop.

"Can you be calm long enough to listen to me?" I growl into her ear.

Her ass has been rubbing against me this entire time and I'm getting hard. If she doesn't stop fighting me, there's going to be a bigger problem than her screaming fit.

"You are a disgusting human being," Ella hisses, with a quiver at the end that tells me she's about to cry.

"Sit down and we'll talk." She angrily pulls away from me the second I loosen my grip, but she does sit down, eyes blazing with hate in a way I haven't seen in a while.

Leaning against my desk, I folded my arms and waited for her harsh breaths to slow.

"How could you do this to Mariya?" Her eyes are wet as she glares at me.

"I told you that I did not allow my father to give a thirteen-year-old Ekaterina in marriage to that vile old pervert for his alliance. I did not say that I would not arrange good unions for my sisters. This is the way it has always been."

"This is the twenty-first century," she hissed, "women aren't cattle. This is your little sister, she's fourteen, did you forget that?"

"She and Konstantin are not getting married tomorrow," I scoffed, "Mariya will go to school, and have a normal teenage life - at least as close to a normal upbringing as Mother and I can manage. You've met Kon, he's strong and smart. He'll be a good man just like his father. My job as their brother is to make sure they are married to men who will treat them well, and with respect. Alexi and Lucya are the only other Bratva family I trust. This alliance is crucial, Ella. We are being attacked on all sides and I cannot hold without this alliance. We are no closer to finding who is behind this - or how many - but they intend to destroy the Morozov Bratva. And our family. Do you understand what could happen to my sisters if Yuri and I are killed? What could happen to you?"

This doesn't scare her. "Don't throw *me* into your magnificent protection plan," she snarls, "none of this is about, or *for* me. Won't Alexi and Lucya help you because of your friendship? Because they're good people?"

I shake my head at her naivete. "They are good, as good as people can be in this world. But no family risks their own safety without something in return. This alliance strengthens us both."

Ella's rubbing her face, I can see she's trying to calm down. "Does Mariya know that this was always the future you had planned for her?"

"Every Bratva princess knows this is her future," I say flatly.

"Don't call them that," she hisses, "they're not dolls. They're young women, with dreams and goals. Not that you care. What if she says no?"

I'm grinding my teeth, holding onto my temper by my fingertips. "She won't."

Standing up, she stares at me, her fury tempered down now to a chilly rage. "Promise me you'll tell her. Right now. Promise me you'll at least ask her what she thinks."

Irritated by her audacity, her rudeness, I step closer, looking down at her and her defiant little stance. "What makes you think I owe you any promises?"

This time, she doesn't scream at me. "Because no matter why you married me, I'm still Mrs. Maksim Morozov. I still have a place in the hierarchy of this family. And because your life will be so much more pleasant if you stop treating me like a simpleton who's only good for dressing up and fucking."

Putting up her hand to stop me, she continued, "Oh, I know all the stories. You can kill me like some of those other gangster scum, or beat the hell out of me to make me compliant. Why don't you decide what you can tolerate in a wife? Because I'm not giving up unless you get rid of me." Her chin quivers. "Promise me."

So defiant, this woman, standing in my way and refusing to step back, even though I know she wants to cry, to hide in our dressing room and not come back out.

"I give you my word, I will tell her. I will ask her how she feels about it."

"You'll tell her now?" Ella persists.

Taking in a deep breath and letting it out, I nod. "I will tell her now."

Opening the door, I escort her from my ruined study, sneezing twice. "Are you catching a cold?" Ella asks.

"No," I sneezed again, "it's nothing. Seasonal allergies, perhaps." She turns to head toward our bedroom but not before I catch her spiteful little smile. Rubbing my stinging eyes, I knock on Mariya's door.

Ella...

"This is bullshit!" Tania is shouting, "Are you fucking with me right now?"

I laugh bitterly, "Oh, no. This antiquated crap is for real."

We're sitting on her bed, passing a wine bottle between us. "You know the infuriating part?" I continued, "Mariya wasn't even surprised. She even told me that she thought 'Kon was cute.' What the hell, Tania! That's what you say about the guy who just asked you to prom, not a lifelong ball and chain to a mobster!"

"This whole Bratva thing was fucked up, but this is a special brand of assholeishness." Tania says sourly.

Taking the bottle away, I have a gulp before passing it back. "I don't know what makes me the most upset, that Maksim did this, or that the girls just assume this is their future!"

"Well," she shrugs, "do they know the true love story of you and Hot Murder Daddy? They probably think this shit is normal."

"Don't call him that," I sigh, finishing the bottle. "You know what I hate the most? Over these weeks, I think I'm getting to understand him a little better. Like... maybe there is some common ground. And then, there's days like this, where he seems so alien to me. Where everything he believes in is just unthinkable." Finishing off the bottle, I hand it to Tania. "You got any more of this stuff?"

"Yeah," she snickers, "this is from the crate Yuri sent over from

Maksim's wine cellar."

I'm silent, watching her process this for a moment as her expression goes from gleeful to sad. "For the record, I really like Yuri," I offer, "but I agree with your decision to step back from this world. Are you doing okay with..." I wave my hands uselessly, "...this?"

She's heading back into the kitchen, so I lean against the doorway, watching her sort through her wine fridge. "I could have loved him, you know? That dick, I mean..."

"No!" I'm cringing, "no dick talk!"

Tania laughs, but it's more like a polite chuckle. "I could have. Yuri's smart, suave as hell, and really sweet when he's not playing Bratva *Sovietnik*. But... I can't handle this, Els. I just- it's too much. I can't be shot at every day. I'll be your emotional support animal for life, and you'll be mine. But I can't be a Bratva wife."

I put my arm around her and we moved outside to the fire escape, swapping the bottle and watching nighttime in New York City happen on the street beneath us.

"The girls have been here for three weeks? No way!"

Tania's getting into the SUV with us for the "after party," as she calls it, we're taking Ekaterina out for a drink at *Gehenna.* We had to agree to take her to one of Maksim's clubs before he'd allow her to go out. She's wearing one of my more modest dresses, but since she's taller and more blessed in bra cup size, it looks unfairly hot on her. These Morozovs and their spectacular gene pool...

A vision of Maksim lifting up a dark-haired, blue-eyed child suddenly appears in technicolor glory and I shake my head vigorously. Where the hell did that come from?

Tania's been talking; "So Ekaterina, what's going on with school? What's your major?" I'm listening to them and watching my sister-in-law light up when she talks about her major in Special Education.

"There are so many advancements in teaching approaches for... for instance, children on the autism spectrum." Her lovely face is lighting up, her blue eyes - blue like Maksim's - are sparkling. The difference between her open, happy gaze and his constant look of polite speculation makes me sad. "...for some little ones, their environment is the worst problem..." She's on a roll now, and her enthusiasm for teaching is so obvious.

"You need to teach," Tania says emphatically, "it's so obvious that you are meant to do this. Those kids need you."

Narrowing my eyes at her, I shake my head slightly. I know what she's doing. This isn't the time to spark Ekaterina up. Maksim already stated that she's going to finish college and get her teaching degree. It's what happens after, that's making my stomach churn. But he promised that he would ask her about the match, that he would pick a good man. I had to hope that would be enough.

"Let's go be the Beautiful People," I interrupt, "Tania's the one that perfected that nightclub strut."

"The Beautiful People nightclub strut?" Ekaterina is laughing helplessly. I squeeze her hand. She's already one of the beautiful people.

Maybe it's because nightclubs are just bad juju for me now. Maybe it's this particular nightclub that has it out for us. Because it starts out the same. *Gehenna's* on fire tonight; I see a couple of A-list actors in the VIP section - where we promised to stay as another concession so that Maksim would let us take Ekaterina out - and every dance floor is a sea of glittery, swaying people. The three of us dance with each other, our bodyguards a humorless triangle around us to keep any hopefuls from oozing into our little circle within them.

We dance until we're laughing and sweaty and tumble back into our cozy little couch section in the VIP lounge. There's already a bottle of Shipwrecked Champagne chilling and waiting for us. Because, Maksim.

"Wait, I remember this!" Tania gasps, "Isn't this the stuff a bunch of divers found in the Baltic Sea like ten years ago?"

"Yep," I nod to the bottle, "look how old it is! All these cases went down with the ship almost 200 years ago, and the cold water apparently kept the champagne intact and in good condition."

"To sisters and friends, there can never be enough of either!" Ekaterina toasts us, and we clink glasses and take a sip.

"Amazing," Tania sighs, "how much is this stuff?"

"About $14,000 a bottle," I answer, and she chokes on her mouthful.

"Are you shitting me?" she wheezes, and I can't stop laughing.

"This is my brother's idea, isn't it?" Ekaterina is giggling, too. "He is such a... what is it called? He is such a wine snob."

"This is true," I'm still laughing at the expression on Tania's face.

"Well, who do we have here?"

Oh, you have to be kidding me. It's that skeevy Dante.

"Hey, honey. We meet again. And look at your hot friends! I was watching you all on the dance floor. There's not a man in this club that's not sporting wood right now." He's eyeing Ekaterina and Tania, who clearly have the same visceral reaction to him that I did. "Now that I'm the Don, I wanna establish closer ties to your family."

Yeah, I thought, *like a grizzly bear wants to establish closer ties to a salmon.*

"Ladies, this is one of Maksim and Yuri's *work associates,*" I say repressively, "Dante Toscano." Forcing a smile, I add, "Dante, this is my friend Tania and my sister-in-law Ekaterina."

This vile weasel is about to kiss a cringing Ekaterina's hand when he pauses, looking from me to her with a huge grin. "You're the Bratva *princessa*?" Our bodyguards stiffen at the "B" word and I want to slap my hand over his big, stupid mouth. His overstyled head dips again to her hand, his greasy mouth kind of slobbering on her.

"Hey, Dante!" I said sharply, "Can you please let go of her hand? I'd hate to see my husband throw you over yet another railing." That gets his mouth off of her skin, and I see Ekaterina wipe it on her dress out of the corner of my eye.

Leaning in close, Dante tells me, "You're gonna want to be nicer to me. I'm the Don of one of the most powerful Mafia families in the world. So why don't you shut that smart mouth and just... look pretty?"

I see Ivan stepping up with some alacrity, his hand going to his jacket where I know he's got a gun in a shoulder holster. I also see four other men, Italian, by the looks of them, moving in to cover their boss.

Standing up between him and Ekaterina and Tania, I smile with all my teeth on display, like I want to tear his throat out with them. "Why, thanks for such a lovely talk, *Don* Toscano. I'll be sure to pass your good wishes on to my husband."

He sneers, but it evolves back into a weird smile as he looks at Ekaterina again. "You do that, honey." He swaggers off with his little entourage of scoundrels.

Ivan shakes his head mournfully, grumbling in his thick accent, "I wish he would give excuse to shoot him."

"Not funny, Ivan," I sigh, "No shooting Mafia creeps. I like all of your organs on the inside of your body where they belong. That man's such a douchebag that he'll get himself shot soon enough, I'm sure of it."

Dante turns around and gives that weird grin again, the one that makes him look like he has no idea what it means but he's aware that it's an expression humans use and he's giving it a try. But on him, it's horrible. And he's not looking at me. His gaze is fixed on Ekaterina.

CHAPTER 21 – THE RECKONING

In which there is disillusionment, heartbreak, and hot Italian guys.

Ella...

"Hey, you know what I noticed tonight?" Tania grinned at the sight of a dozing Ekaterina, her head already on my shoulder.

"What did you notice tonight, my bestie?"

"Well," Tania stretched, giving her ribs a scratch, "I noticed that this is the first time you have ever called Maksim 'my husband.' Not only that, you said it twice."

"Really?" I frowned, "I did?"

"Oh, yes you did." Grinning at me meaningfully, Tania used her most arch, inquiring tone. "You went all Bratva Queen on that weasel. 'You better get out of here before my husband throws you over another railing,' in that super intense tone."

"Well," I adjusted my shoulder carefully, trying not to disturb my dozing sister-in-law, "that guy was a spectacular ninnyhammer when I met him on our honeymoon-"

"Ninnyhammer?" Tania interrupts

"Ninnyhammer – ninny, simpleton or fool," I answered absently. "But tonight?" My voice dropped to a whisper, "I don't like how he was looking at Ekaterina."

"I remember you pointing out his folks at the New Year's Eve party," Tania said, "he wasn't there, but didn't he have two hot brothers?"

"Yeah..." I tried to remember, "uh, Giovanni and Dario."

"Hot as balls?" Tania interrupted, "Really tall and built? That olive skin and dark hair that Italians have that is just-" She made a chef's kiss gesture.

I laughed, shaking my head. "They looked hot from a distance. We never met them, Maksim just pointed them out to me, saying it was a tragedy the oldest brother got none of the brains in the family."

"Well," she shrugged, "I'm pretty sure you scared him off."

Looking out at the elaborate streetlights lining the avenues in Hudson Yard, I hoped she was right.

The next day...

After seeing my sisters-in-law off at the airport together, Maksim returned home with me and promptly closed himself off in his study with Yuri and a couple of his senior advisors. So, I made my way to the gym for a long session of bitter yoga. While heading back, I noticed Alina hastily leaving the office with an empty drink tray and ice bucket. I still felt a surge of deeply satisfying spite that Maksim's fancy-dancy booze was on a rush order from Moscow and that they'd had some issues getting the limited-edition Waterford crystal ice bucket and glasses he was so fond of. It almost made up for the fact that he was no longer sneezing from his covert exposure to cat dander. But the interesting thing? She left the door cracked. She was always so careful to close the study door firmly, blocking the sound from within.

Stepping closer, I leaned against a little alcove in the wainscoting that held a beautiful Fabergé egg on a stand. This kept me out of the line of sight of the men inside the study, but I could hear pretty well. "...the man was not quite himself by then, but his explanation was clear enough. This mysterious enemy uses an odorless gas, piped into the location and rendering those inside helpless long enough to take them down. The gas also has an effect similar to Rohypnol, affecting the victim's memory and making identification of the enemy near impossible. Quite an elegant thing, actually."

I didn't recognize the voice, but he sounded quite impressed with this magical gas that was responsible for the deaths of so many of Maksim's people.

Speak of the devil. "Thank you, Bogdan. A gas. Knowing you, Yuri, I'm certain you've already sent someone in to find a sample in the latest warehouse shooting?"

"Yes, Pakhan."

I smiled in spite of myself. My dear brother-in-law always balanced that fine line of respect for his Bratva chief and totally laughing at his brother at the same time.

This time, he was definitely erring on the side of respect. "We found nothing. The chemist I hired speculated it was a quick-dissolving compound, but there was no residue he could find to test."

My brow furrowed. Even with the scraps of information I'd parsed together, there was nothing about a gas used during the attacks before. I'm assuming the intel came from one of the poor souls they'd managed to capture.

"Anything else?" Maksim's voice was sharp.

Another long sigh from someone likely flown in from the home country, based on the thick accent. "The Yilmas cartel has canceled their standing order with us. This is a loss of around sixty million dollars annually. There is concern that they have found a new supplier through Kazakhstan."

"That would point back to the new Sokolov hellhound," Yuri said.

Maksim made a rumbling noise in his chest that I recognized as his effort to keep from smashing the room to bits. "We have new reinforcements coming in tonight from the Turgenev Bratva. Patrick, make sure the Brigadiers are there to get them assigned to their units."

"Yes, Pakhan."

I grinned; I'd know that Irish brogue anywhere. Footsteps just about to turn the corner from the kitchen into the main hall jolted me out of my hidey-hole and into walking briskly down the hall, toweling the sweat off my forehead for extra effect. Ludmilla nearly ran into me with the drinks tray, scowling as we dodged each other.

"Good afternoon, Ludmilla." I always greeted her, every day. More of that killing-with-kindness approach that still wasn't working with Alina, most likely because I kept thinking about the killing part.

The housekeeper managed the barest of nods as I passed her.

Maksim...

With another exhausting, infuriating meeting done, I yanked off my tie, heading down to our bedroom to change and go beat a punching bag to death. Ella was sitting in the big wingback chair by the lit fireplace, her laptop open. She was completely focused on whatever she was reading and gave a little yelp when I closed the door.

"What are you reading?" I'm pulling off my dress shirt and enjoying the fact that her gaze keeps coming back to my bare chest every time she tried to drag it away.

"Uh..." My wife's eyes are drifting down, following my hands as I unzip my pants and drop them. "I..."

With a grin, I hooked my thumb in the waistband of my boxer briefs and she shut the laptop abruptly.

"Just boring stuff," she stammers, her gaze fixed on me. "What's um... what's your plan today?"

I lean down, my hands on the armrests of her chair and caging her in. "Well, I was planning to work out my aggression on my boxing equipment in the gym."

Ella's head tilts slightly, her chest rising and falling. Is she scenting me? "Well, that seems unkind," she drawls, "to attack a perfectly innocent punching bag."

I'm enjoying this, my wife not flinching away, her pupils flaring wide and her breathing slowing down. "Did you have another suggestion, *solnyshko?*"

"I'm sure a big, strong man like you can come up with

something," she says primly and I pounce on her.

She's laughing as I haul her up in my arms, her hands flailing to steady herself but she still remembers to hold on to only my shoulders. My mouth finds hers and I want to chew those full lips of hers, so pretty and pink. I restrain myself and her tongue comes out to coil with mine, lazily teasing me while her hands rub up and down my arms, squeezing my biceps and stroking along my skin.

"You're far too overdressed, *Missis Morozov*," I murmur between slow, sucking kisses as I pull off her dress.

"How kind of you to assist me in this process, *Мистер Morozov*," she whispers before biting my earlobe. My wife has very sharp teeth, but at the moment, I don't mind. I throw the ruins of her dress and bra over my shoulder, and she giggles.

Ella giggles. I've never heard it from her and it's charming, like her, lighting up her face and making her green eyes glow. She's on her back on our bed, arms thrown up above her head, and her black, black hair spreads across the white pillowcase like a spill of ink. I'm straddling her, running my hands up and down from her waist, along her ribs, cupping those perfect, silky breasts and my rough fingertips sliding along her collarbones. She's breathing fast and it's making her stomach press against my painfully hard cock. Then, she has the audacity to push up her hips, trying to angle me where she wants me.

"Do you want my cock, *solnyshko?*" I flex my shaft, pushing it lower against her pearl. *Blyad'*, it is pretty, already swollen and glistening between her lower lips. Ella nods and pushes her hips up again. "You can't have it yet," I shake my head, sliding lower, pressing my cock between her thighs and laughing when she groans irritably. "Not until you come on my tongue." I am not subtle, thrusting my tongue hard inside her, enjoying her muffled shriek and how her thighs tighten against me. I'm growling, enjoying the vibration and knowing it's affecting my bride as her hips twist back and forth. Rubbing my stubbled chin along her slick, tender center, I breathe her in. Sweet. Sharp. This soft, silky slit is swelling hopefully for me, like a flower and it's beautiful to watch. Being able to see her give herself with enthusiasm is wildly arousing. Not because I've seduced her into submitting with orgasms first, but watching her come greedily, pushing and sliding against my face and mouth and arching her back as the first one washes over her.

"Maksim, c'mon..." Ella says in a tone that might be characterized as whining, but I can't hold back, going back on my knees and hauling her onto my cock, admiring the long arch of her back and how it feels to be inside my wife, her pussy already clenching and contracting against me, forcing me to push harder to make my way up her channel. My thumbs are spreading her wide so that I can see my cock inside her.

"So slick, you're gripping me so tightly," I groan, "this perfect, tight *pizda* is mine, isn't it?"

Ella doesn't answer me so I push hard, burying inside her, so deep that every place inside my secretive bride is filled with me.

"Oh, god, Maksim," she's moaning pitifully, chest heaving and gasping for breath.

"This is mine, isn't it?" I cruelly rotate my hips, not pulling out in the slightest, pushing side to side to loosen her a bit. "Hmmm, *solnyshko?*"

She's licking her lips, and I suspect she's trying to string enough words together to tell me that indeed, this pretty pink cunt is mine. Laughing, I slide my hands under her shoulder blades and pull her up to me. This pushes me that much higher inside her and Ella screams, louder than I've ever heard her and so beautiful with her flushed face and open mouth.

"Yes, Maksim. Pakhan. *Da, eto tvoye.*" Her eyes open and she squeezes down on my shaft so tightly that I'm frozen inside her, and it's my turn to groan. Sliding her hand down, Ella smiles slyly. "May I touch your cock?"

I nod blankly, feeling myself harden impossibly more as she slides her fore and middle fingers down, scissoring me between them, squeezing through the wet and the heat of us together and I slide my hands over her ass, gripping her tightly with both and lifting her a bit. Her fingers move lower, her eyes never leaving mine. "May I touch your balls?"

Iisus Khristos, she's going to kill me.

"Da, you may," I'm barely breathing as her fingers, slick from us, began squeezing and toying with me. Hauling her up slightly, I drop her onto my cock again, enjoying her gasp. "I'm going to keep you impaled on my cock until I hear you scream again, *solnyshko.*"

It doesn't take long at all.

The next day...

We haven't left the bedroom, not since yesterday afternoon. I cannot seem to get enough of my wife and she seems perfectly happy to stay in bed with me, allowing me to worship her with my mouth, my fingers, and my cock. A sour-faced Ludmilla leaves trays of food on the table outside the doors of the master suite and I direct everything to Yuri's oversight. The chance to finally see this woman, relaxed and happy and enthusiastically involved with me and the things we do to each other is too rare to miss.

I repeated Ivan's story of meeting Dante Toscano at the club. "Ivan was very proud of you and how well you handled it."

"Ugh, that skeevy little cockalorum," Ella shuddered.

"Cocka... what?" I started laughing at her expression.

"You know, cockalorum," she repeated, "a boastful, self-important person, a strutting little fellow."

I pulled her on top of me, putting my arm behind my head. "Is this another one of your more creative insults? I've heard scoundrel used by you quite often, scalawag, you called that attorney a pettifogger..."

"Oh, well, the British have the best insults," Ella laughed at my expression. "Why use jerk, or scumbag when you can call someone a lickspittle, or a pillock, or a snollygoster?"

"Really..." I was intrigued now. "And what do you call me behind my back, *solnyahko?*"

"Hmm… You are definitely a scoundrel, a rapscallion, sometimes even a reprobate. I mean," she shrugs, "I *used* to call you those things. But not *now*."

Blyad'! My wife was delicious with that attempt at an innocent expression. "And what would I call an impudent vixen?" I murmured, kissing my way down her neck. She wiggled against me enticingly.

"I'm sure you couldn't be talking about me, *Мистер Morozov*," she smiled smugly.

"Oh no, of course not." My mouth closed over her breast and there was no more to be said.

"You look better today."

Ella's voice is muffled, her face is pressed into my chest and she's limp and exhausted after riding me to another orgasm. My cock is softening inside her, but she's so warm and snug; I don't want to leave her yet.

I look down. "Have I looked so terrible before this?"

"You looked exhausted," she answered, "all those stress lines around your mouth and on your forehead." My bride smiled up at me, "You look… hmmm. Less Pakhan and more Maksim, I guess."

She's beautiful, this woman I married. Strong, intelligent, kind. Of all the random, mistaken encounters in this universe; I had the one that gave me the perfect queen. But she's still an outsider. Her horrified fury after finding out about Mariya's match with Konstantin Turgenev is proof of that. But she stood up to Dante Toscano at the nightclub magnificently. Ivan was quite proud of her when he'd given me his report.

Twenty-four hours earlier…

"You would have been proud of her, Pakhan." Ivan was bragging about Ella's performance at *Gehenna*. "Toscano would not take hand off Miss Ekaterina's and Miss Ella got on his face and-"

"In," I clarify, "in his face. On his face means something else."
I'd been having Ivan speak to me in English to improve his skill.
I wanted him to be able to communicate easily with my wife as
her primary security.

His brow furrowed before his expression cleared and he
nodded vigorously. "Of course." He waited to see if I would lose
my temper and continued. "She told him to let go, she did not
wish to see her husband throw him over another railing."

I forced myself to not laugh, one must keep composure around
the men, but I wanted to. I could so easily picture Ella's
expression and how she'd aggressively point her finger in
someone's face.

"What did he do?"

Ivan frowned, "He left, but he turned around and stared at Miss
Ekaterina. He was very excited to know she was your sister."

Allowing them to take Ekaterina out was a very bad idea, I
thought, feeling another headache bloom. I knew this and I
still allowed it. This was a serious mistake.

Ella...

The next day...

Tapping furiously on my chemical schematics app was giving
me so much happiness right now. It felt like long-dormant
muscles were warming up again, stretching and expanding as
I scanned through the composition structure.

Something the mysterious Bogdan said the other day kept
nagging at me. Odorless gas, unconsciousness, and lapse in
memory afterward. No chemical trace left to sample... I'd
logged into Marla's account at Adalen Labs; she was notorious
for never changing her password and fortunately, that paid off.

"L-36 Neurology CaP can be administered in an odorless,
colorless gas for patients whose swallow reflex is inadequate
for tablet or liquid application," I'm murmuring as I read
through the research. I'd noticed when I read it the first time -

back when I worked at the lab and had an actual professional life - that the application element seemed odd. After all, you can use an IV to administer meds that can't be taken orally. And this research was far too expensive to have been created for patients with a needle phobia.

Looking through Marla's notes, I found what I was looking for. *Here's the missing piece from their original findings,* she wrote, *this gas is meant to be airborne and cover a larger area than would ever be needed for a medical application.*

I sit back in shock. They're testing a weapon, not a medicine.

"Which is illegal in so many ways," I mumble, scrolling through the application structure. This matches up against everything the report Bogdan had given in Maksim's study yesterday. Stretching my arms over my head, I looked around. I was back in the cozy alcove behind the living room and the sun coming through the window was warm on my face.

I read through the latest lab results again. This was a weapon in development and would not be utilized in a real-life setting before it passed through the testing process. Whether this was an actual medication, or the obvious weapon it is and likely something for the US government. But it wouldn't be the first time a new pharmaceutical development - or weapons-based, in this case - was stolen during the process, no matter how good security was.

"So..." I stood up, pacing over to the window. "This could be a coincidence, but it's unlikely. Drugs in development get stolen all the time, so there's no reason that a weaponized drug wouldn't be any different. The big problem here is how do you counteract the gas?"

I spent another hour pulling up everything I could on L-36, but apparently, the study hadn't gotten that far. "Typical," I sneered, "develop the drug without creating a counteragent."

I screen-capped everything I could and put the research in a documents folder before I logged out. The one thing the lab was good at was monitoring time spent on any research, though I suspected it was to justify hours, rather than any security concern.

My first thought was to scamper down the hall to Maksim's office to share what I'd learned.

"Well, crap. If I do that, I have to admit that I was spying on his meeting." My eyes narrowed. "I shouldn't have to be spying on him in the first place!"

Still, this could change everything. Maksim could stop the raids on his men and property and if I could re-create the gas outside of the lab, the Morozov Bratva could use it right back against whoever was doing this.

"It wouldn't be that hard to get the necessary chemicals," I'm talking to myself as I walk down the hall. My excitement deflates a bit when I find he's not in his study, but I know he hasn't left the penthouse. Walking into our master bedroom, I see the bathroom door is open.

Maksim's talking to someone on the phone, and he is furious. "You must be joking."

The acoustics of the tiled bathroom allowed me to hear a bit of the conversation from the other side. "When he found out about our initial agreement, he was indifferent to it, other than the value of your alliance. But he called me last night and told me that he was claiming the right to marry her as the head of the Toscano *famiglia*. Dante is still the Don, you know this."

"Then our agreement is void," Maksim's voice dripped ice. "I will not force Ekaterina to marry him."

"You know that would not be considered a reason to void this alliance," the other man argued, "But I will never-"

Just then, Maksim's eyes met mine in the mirror. "I will have to call you back." He slips his phone into his jacket pocket and looks at me, cold and calm. The Pakhan.

"Please tell me I'm wrong," I whispered, "tell me you're not giving the sweetest, kindest girl on this planet to that complete and utter pig. Please tell me that."

The Pakhan of the Morozov Bratva is known for his self-control. I know some of his lieutenants call him the 'Ice King' because he never displayed his emotions in public. But this time, Maksim snapped. Instantly and terrifyingly.

"I don't need to tell you anything," he said, his voice was cold but the fury radiating off of him felt blazingly hot against my skin. "Who do you think you are?" He walked toward me slowly, backing me into the bedroom, "You're not one of us. I married you as a convenience and your opinions are immaterial. You will not demand anything from me ever again."

The bed hit the back of my legs and I sat down abruptly; he towered above me. "You don't understand our world. You don't understand what I am doing. You don't even seem to understand that I have offered you the courtesy of explaining some of my actions to you when you deserve NOTHING!" Maksim thundered the last word and I jumped. Pushing with my heels, I scrambled to the other side of the mattress. I was going to stand in front of this enraged titan, not cower on the bed.

"Your place in this life is only where I put you!"

He was shouting now and I clenched my fists, trying to hide the fact that my hands were shaking. I wasn't shaking from the adrenaline and fear. It was from heartbreak. I was furious and heartbroken. This is who Maksim Morozov is. Not the man who had playful sex with me, who risked his life to save me from the ice, or who paid for music school tuition for little kids.

Nope, this is the coldhearted bastard I'd known from the first moment he kidnapped me. This had always been him. And I'd let myself forget it.

"You're not a leader," I finally said, "you're a curse. You destroy everything you touch." Maksim stared at me, his eyes blazing but the rest of him was frostbite. I turned around and left the room. I couldn't seem to feel my feet or hands, so I wasn't sure where my steps carried me but I found myself in my old guest room, so I shut the door and got into bed, falling asleep immediately.

Maksim...

I stayed where I was, barely breathing as I fought to control myself.

"You're not a leader, you're a curse..." Ella's emotionless tone. Her utter disillusionment. There was nothing I could do to change that. She cannot think she has a say in Bratva doings. We were at a tipping point and the news today could plunge us into war with yet another family. I can't risk her being in the line of fire. Let her hate me. As long as she stays put.

Still, I winced when I heard the guest room door shut.

"Brother?" Yuri was leaning against the doorway, looking concerned. "Are you all right?"

"I... didn't hear you," I said, rubbing the back of my neck.

"That's what I mean," he scoffed. "When have you ever let anyone creep up on you?"

Eyeing him, I straightened my jacket. "I know that expression. There's good news? You look too happy."

"Indeed, there is," he's grinning now, unaware that I just shouted at my wife, battered down her belief in her place in this family as hard as if I'd used my fist.

"Good," I sighed, "in the study."

It was dark by the time Giovanni and Dario Toscano met us at the warehouse. "It's good to see there are one or two of your warehouses that remain intact, Maksim," Dario said with a grin, shaking my hand.

"You are lucky that I find your sense of humor charming, instead of offensive," I replied, but the little *Жóna* laughed and slapped me on the shoulder affectionately. They're both tall men, with dark hair like mine and covered in scars. Like me.

"Good to see you again," Giovanni said, "you said you might have the answer to both of our problems?"

"Oh, I can solve one of those," Dario shrugged, walking through the warehouse, "I'll kill Dante. Long shot, back of the head."

"You're talking about our Don, and your brother," Giovanni said sharply, but his brother shrugged.

"You know what direction he's planning for our family business," Dario said, no longer grinning. "The question is why haven't you killed him already."

I took in a deep breath, oddly, it was a pleasure to watch another family argue among themselves for change, instead of it being mine at war with each other.

I touched my thumb to a discreetly placed scanner and an elevator door opened.

"Fancy," Dario commented.

"Some of our lower-tech facilities are out of service at the moment," I said drily.

The steel door opened into a concrete-lined bunker. Some enterprising soldier with a terrible sense of humor once painted the doorway with the sign "Bogdan's Playhouse." I made him remove the paint with a toothbrush and his own spit. The man in question turned to offer me a respectful nod. He had three men dangling on chains from the ceiling and a fourth tied to a marble slab. That particular prisoner was missing a few body parts.

"Ah, Pakhan." Bodgan said happily, "I am so pleased to have truly useful information to offer you. This gentleman-" he lifted the prone man's head and dropped it again with a bloody-sounding "thunk!" "This gentleman has something he would like to share with you."

"*Signor Toscano mi perdoni-*" the man's words were mushy, likely from missing teeth.

"*Fottuto traditore!*" Dario, always the hothead, surged forward to smash his fist into the man's face.

"Stop!" Giovanni yanked his brother back, "Let him talk and then you can kill him."

He questioned the man in English, for our benefit. I would never tell him, of course, that I spoke fluent Italian.

"Marcos. You were one of my father's most trusted lieutenants," he said coldly, "how did you sink so low?"

The man spat out some blood on the floor. "I am loyal to the family," he attempted to sneer, but the effect was spoiled when he began coughing. "After your father died, I knew Dante would lead us in a stronger direction. He would bring the Toscano *famiglia* to a level of power your father was too soft to achieve."

"By taking on the Red Trade," hissed Dario. "Perhaps we should sell your children and see if you're still as enthusiastic about the idea?"

More coughing, and Bogdan considerately wiped it off the man's face.

"My sins are my own," he wheezed, "I did not know about the plan to murder your parents. Dante brought me into his confidence after-"

"That *bastardo* killed our parents?" Dario took a step closer and Giovanni held out his arm, blocking him.

"Our brother is too stupid to plan this on his own," he said, still looking cold and composed. "Who is he working with? Who's buying up the mercenaries?"

"Dante handled the recruitment on the dark web," the man gasped, "but the more the Bratva have killed, the harder it has been to procure good fighters. I had to supervise this last mission because the stupid bastards couldn't follow directions without a leader."

"Who is Dante working with?" I interrupted; I was so close- I could end this now.

When the man tried to spit in my direction, Giovanni backhanded him. "Listen closely, Marcos, if you do not answer with everything you know, I will keep you alive to watch us sell your children into the Red Trade."

"The Toscano *famiglia* do not punish women and children," he garbled, "you would not-"

"Ah," Giovanni purred, "but you are no longer a member of our *famiglia,* you are an enemy. And Dante, your Don, happily tortures the innocent. Make your choice."

The last spark went out of the prisoner. "The Sokolov Bratva.

The daughter funded all of it. They intended to kill you and your brother as well, and the Morozov brothers. The Sokolovs and the Toscanos could step into the power vacuum and take over all the territory."

"Who else?" Giovanni said, "There's another family involved. Who?"

The man's body started shuddering violently and he grabbed him by the throat. "Who else, Marco? I will spare your family if you tell me."

"Ah, it is a seizure," Bogdan said in disappointment.

"Who!" Giovanni leaned down to hear the man's last words before they ended in a gurgle. When he straightened up, his mouth was a thin slash of fury. Taking out his pocket square, he wiped the man's blood off his face. "He tried to give me a name, but all I got was one word. Irish."

Thomas had tried to warn me about the Irish, I thought. *There's another traitor in my ranks.*

"Patrick," I hissed.

Back in the SUV, I dialed Yuri. "Find Patrick and take him. Quickly, no fuss. Don't let him get a word out to anyone."

"What are we dealing with?" Yuri asked.

"It is that *suka* Katya, she managed to bankroll the New Year's Eve attack and she's been paying for the mercenaries. Dante Toscano was recruiting them." My fist was tightening on the phone and I forced myself to relax it. "There's Irish involved; we don't have a name but Patrick could be our traitor."

"Patrick?" He sounded incredulous and I knew he'd worked alongside our *Obshchak* for nearly ten years.

"He has access to all of our movements, where everything is stored. It makes sense. Are you in my study?"

"Yes," I could hear him issuing rapid-fire orders to Fedor, "should I call Alexi and put him on alert?"

"I will, we need to put together a raid. Locate the most likely locations for Tanya and her lap dog to be hiding. Make sure that-"

A door slammed open on Yuri's end of the line and I heard

Ivan's urgent voice.

"You're sure?" Yuri said sharply, "Did you search the penthouse? Call Tania immediately and see if she knows where she is."

"What's going on? Who's missing? Is it-" A punch of fear hit me in the chest. "Is it Ella?"

I've done it, I thought, *I've finally broken her enough that she'd rather risk an escape than stay with me.*

Yuri came back on the line, "She left an envelope for me," he said, I could hear the dread in every word.

"What does it say!"

"Sladkiy Iisus, ona ne," he groaned. He was reading ahead as he talked to me. "She figured out the gas they've been using on the raids that has been taking out our guards. She left me instructions on how to compound it."

"How did she know about the- never mind, this is Ella we're talking about. What else?" I loosened my tie; my breath was short and I felt like it was choking me.

"Oh, Ella..." Now, Yuri sounded panicked. "Katya kidnapped Tania. She is going to give herself up in exchange."

Ella...

An hour earlier...

I was surprised to hear my phone ring. Now that I was married to a Bratva monster I didn't get many calls. The number came up as unknown and I stared at it for a moment. This was going to be bad. I somehow knew it but I answered anyway.

"Hello?"

"Ah, there she is." The voice was gleeful as if this was a call she'd waited a long time to make.

"Katya," I answered numbly, "I do hope you got our wedding present."

Her laugh was so sweet, tinkling like a bell. "It was shit. I threw it out. But on to business. I have something you'll want. I think we should get together, relax, and have a discussion."

Aaand here goes my big mouth, "Since I'm certain your idea of relaxation includes putting kittens into a food processor, I'm going to pass."

There was an irritable sigh, and then an image came up on my phone.

It was Tania, clearly in mid-scream and lunging at the camera, even though she was tied to a chair. There was a huge bruise blooming on her cheek.

"Don't you hurt her!" I hissed, "D- don't you put your fucking hands on her!"

There was that Tinkerbell-like laugh again. "Of course not. Just as long as you get to her before my dear husband gets bored."

Picturing that Kazakhstani musk ox she married, my throat closes up. "Where?"

An address pops up and I shake my head. One of the scariest sections of New Jersey, mainly warehouses and construction sites probably populated with dead bodies. Several, no doubt dumped by my dear spouse.

"You must be nuts. I show up and you just kill us both. A public place so I can see Tania walk away safely."

Who is this stone-cold bitch? I wonder. *Oh, me. Tania would be so proud.*

There's a scream that echoes through the receiver and I jam my fist in my mouth. "It's almost like you want your best friend to suffer," Katya giggles.

"Stop it," I hissed, "you want me, so stop wasting time. Public location."

Am I going to wet myself? I'm definitely going to wet myself.

Waiting for another scream, I sag with relief when Katya snaps, "The NJ Galleria. The food court. You have an hour."

"Got it," I managed. "Now leave her alone. Save your energy for me."

Would this woman ever stop laughing? "Oh, I am darling."

It takes me ten minutes to copy off the gas formula and

scribble a note to Yuri, who I know is in Maksim's study right now. Then, it takes less than sixty seconds to steal Ludmilla's key to the service elevator in the pantry next to the kitchen. There's supposed to be a guard there but I get lucky. Maybe he's on a potty break or something.

Managing to flag down a taxi was my biggest fear - this is New York, after all - but one swooped right up as if the Fates had decided it was absolutely time for me to die and were just helping things along. Ten minutes later, my phone started buzzing. First, Ivan. Then, Maksim and then Yuri and then Maksim again. I put the phone on silent and stared out the window.

CHAPTER 22 – THE RESCUE

In which Ella sees her Christmas Tarot reading come true. In all the worst ways.

Ella...

Walking through the mall made me chuckle. Apparently, I'd lost track of time because the Valentine's Day swag was up and stores were aggressively promoting all the crap you should buy your sweetheart if you really, *really* loved them.

Well, Tania wasn't my sweetheart but she was the only person I really, really loved and she was in this position because of me. Sure, Maksim is really responsible for this cavalcade of complete crap. But in the end, Tania wouldn't be terrified and hurt if it wasn't for me. *God, I hope I can get her out of this alive,* I thought. *One of us should live through this.* Because I'm pretty sure it won't be me.

Tania was sitting at one of the grimy tables in front of the Chick-fil-A and my knees nearly buckled. She looked okay. They'd made her arrange her hair to cover the bruise on her cheek, but my girl looked *pissed,* which was so much better than terrified.

Katya's husband Vasily was sitting next to her, looking vaguely hilarious with the chair straining under his massive bulk. Another two men were hovering, scanning the food court.

"Els!" Tania tried to burst out of her chair to hug me, and he grabbed her arm in his meaty fist, not gently, by the way she was flinching.

"I came alone, just like you demanded," I said, clutching my messenger bag, "so just let her go, all right? That was the deal."

His mean little eyes stared at me for a moment. They were pale blue, like a weak skim milk blue so it almost looked like he didn't have irises at all. Finally, he grunted, nodding his head at the men and releasing her.

Tania's hug almost knocked me over the neighboring table. "Let's run," she whispered in my ear, "just take off. They're not going to start firing in the middle of the Galleria, for fuck's sake!"

I looked around, there was a table of six teenagers, an exhausted mom barely holding on to two toddlers as she tried to eat her sandwich, a couple of businessmen scrolling through their phones…

"I can't, honey. This guy is as crazy as his demented wife." She tried to protest and I squeezed her tighter. "Look. Just go to the nearest exit. Call Yuri, he'll have bodyguards on you in a second."

"I don't have my phone," she groaned.

"Here-" I started rummaging in my bag and the two men crowded me, hands inside their jackets. Slowing down, I held one hand up. "I'm just getting my phone, okay? It's not like you're not going to take it from me anyway."

Did Vasily just smile? His mouth twisted like he'd just eaten a ghost pepper but he nodded to his men. "Give her your purse," he grunted, "you will not need it again."

"No, nononono NO!" Tania moaned, and I hugged her tighter.

"Honey, you have to go now, okay?" I whispered, "If you don't, they're just going to kill us both. Maybe… I'll bet Yuri can find me, okay? So work fast. You have to go, please!" Pushing her away, I nodded, a big, fake smile on my face.

She backed away, sobbing but I nodded my head like a broken marionette, hoping she would keep going.

The extremely strong smell of Hugo Boss nearly gagged me and

I realized Vasily was right up against me. He leaned down and I swear I could hear all his joints creak from having to move that pile of muscle and bone around. "You speak like you have experience with kidnapping."

The high, almost hysterical laughter was apparently coming from me, and I finally managed to say, "Oh, you have no idea."

In the car, he unceremoniously jammed a bag over my head and I tried to breathe calmly. Hyperventilating with a bag over your head seemed like a good way to die. Admittedly, it was probably much better than what that ferocious lunatic Katya had in mind for me. I kept trying not to think about that.

I was terrified of pain. The accident that took my parents' lives left me in the hospital for months. I remember crying in my bed so many times when they told me I'd had "plenty of pain meds" but everything still hurt so much. One of the doctors admitted to me later that there was some severe nerve damage they'd initially missed. Tania was furious, demanding that I sue the hospital but all I could remember was the pity and irritation when I'd asked for help.

That was the last time I'd ever seen Charles, in fact. I woke up one day and he was standing by my bed, hands in his suit pockets and staring at me.

"It's just us now, Charles," I'd croaked. They'd just taken the tube out of my throat the day before and it was all torn up.

"Yeah..." he'd mused, looking me over. "Sorry about that."

I put out my hand, but it was all taped up with an IV and he just stared down at it. "Are you going to stay in town for a while?"

"No, I can't," he shifted uncomfortably, "I've got to get back to work. You just... rest up, you know?"

I think I fell asleep then because when I woke up, he was gone.

I chuckled under the bag. My brother was not interested in ever seeing me again. My husband has clearly reminded me that I was "a convenience," and nothing else. And thanks to that heartless prick, I've endangered my best friend - the person I love more than anyone in the world - simply by association.

Better me than her.

"You're not crying, eh? Strange girl." I recognized Vasily's voice.

"What are you getting out of this?" I asked. "I'm sure Katya's hot and everything, but this whole revenge fantasy, what's in it for you?" Aaand, there goes my big mouth, "Don't you wear the pants in the family? I thought you Slavic gangsters were big on the male hierarchy."

My head bounced off the seat in front of me and my ears started ding-donging like the bells of Notre Dame as he slapped me on the back of the head again. "Shut up. Don't make this worse."

Really? I thought, *this guy was the voice of reason?*

Naturally, I cackled, a little hysterically. "Define worse."

We drove for another hour or so. I think. Vasily hauled me briskly out of the car and hustled me into a building, grunting in irritation every time I stumbled. He threw me down on a table and held me, thrashing angrily, while one of the others tied my hands and feet to the edges. When he ripped the bag off my head, there she was.

Katya looked amazing, of course. A perfect St. Laurent red suit, elegantly coiffed hair, and a sweet smile.

"Hello, *suka*. I'm going to have *so* much fun with you."

Maksim...

"There is a reason I have a tracker in my wife's phone!" I thundered, "Why is this taking so long?"

"We have location, Pakhan," Ivan assured me, reading his device, "the NJ Galleria."

I leaned over the seat. "Drive. Faster." I said between clenched teeth. Fedor slammed his foot on the gas pedal.

Yuri was rapidly texting our lieutenants. "There are six cars moving in now-" His breath drew in when his phone rang. "Ella?" There was a screech bursting out of his speaker that made everyone in the car wince.

"YOU BETTER FUCKING GET HERE IN A HURRY BECAUSE I SWEAR TO GOD IF THEY KILL ELLA I WILL CUT YOUR HOMEBOY'S BALLS OFF DO YOU HEAR ME YURI?"

"Tania?" Yuri cut through her hysteria, "Where are you now? Where's Ella?"

"She gave me her phone," she yelled, "Vasily laughed and said she wouldn't need it anymore. It's that crazy bitch Katya! She was so happy to get Ella!"

I broke in, "Tania, are you still in the mall? Is Ella there?"

"*You...*" her voice lowered to a hiss. "This is your fucking fault! You put a target on her back you are so fucking selfish I can't believe-"

"Tania!" I said sharply, even while her words felt like a punch to my chest, "All of this is true but right now, we have to find Ella! They may take her back to the same place they held you, can you retrace it?"

"No," she was weeping now, "they put a bag over my head, pulled me right off the street. I just know it was maybe an hour and a half from my place-"

"We see you," I interrupted, "we're in the black Porsche Cayenne, come out to the curb." I pulled another device out of my jacket.

"What is that?" Yuri asked.

"Another way to find Ella," I said, the rest of my explanation was cut off as he leaped from the car to hold Tania.

Tania and Yuri sat next to me, but I ignored her tears and his whispered reassurances. I couldn't look at her, I knew everything she'd said was true.

"How long will this take you to compound?" I was speaking with Yuri's chemist. He was apparently one of the best in his field, but not used to dealing with the Bratva.

"Uh, your people have been very good about fetching me the items needed," he stammered, "so maybe a day or two?"

"WHAT?" I roared, "I need this gas now! This is a matter of life or death! And by this, I mean yours."

"I'm sorry, sir, uh, Pakhan, I just- twenty-four hours is the least amount of time needed to compound this. I'm sorry, there is no way around this." Growling, I hung up on him and sent the men guarding him instructions to stand guard while he worked.

I placed another call to Giovanni Toscano. "Are you ready to join us?"

"We are," he answered, so much calmer than his brother, who I could hear shouting in the background. "How do you intend to play this, since your wife is a hostage?"

"We're sending in a stealth drone to track the heat signatures in the building. But if she's underground..." My throat closed up, and there was a respectful silence from Toscano. We both knew we'd have to blast through Katya's men if that was the case. The more time they had to recover from the surprise, the higher the chance that Ella would die.

"Well, then we'll have to move fast," he said firmly.

Ella...

The stainless-steel table was terribly cold, and it was leaching all the warmth from my skin. Of course, Katya had ordered one of her creeps to cut off my clothes, so my bra and panties weren't offering any help. He'd been pretty sloppy with that knife, and I had half a dozen little cuts bleeding all over me. I gritted my teeth, trying not to shiver.

So far, not so bad, I tried to comfort myself, *they sting more than anything, right?*

"So, my darling husband has quite the head for business," she was saying, kissing Vasily on his giant cheek. *Seriously*, I thought, *his face is half the size of a football field...*

Oh. She was still talking.

"He thought it was a waste of money for me to damage you enough that even those men with the lowest standards would be unwilling to fuck you."

"Oh, yeah." I croaked, "The family brothel again, huh?" A spurt of blood flew across my face as she slapped me, her wedding ring catching on my lip. It swelled quickly, sending a flash of heat across my face.

"What made you think," she hissed, "that you could ever keep a man like Maksim?" Looking over her shoulder, I see Vasily's potato-shaped face frown. "Did you really think I would allow you to survive after you ignored my warning to not go through with the wedding?"

There's another slap before I can answer her, this one making my eyes go out of focus for a second. Still, I opened my big mouth again. "Have you ever seen Maksim not get his way? How did you think I was going to pull that off?"

Now Katya's really angry and she punches me in the stomach. Her rings are cold- such a stupid thing to notice but they drive into me so hard. I lose my breath and wheeze, trying to inflate my lungs again as she's ranting. "How could you think an outsider like you could ever belong? You must think you're so clever to get pregnant and trap him!"

My brow furrows and I'm one second away from blurting, "Huh?" before I remember Maksim's cover story. "It takes two to tango, Katya." Annd, here comes my big mouth. "Do you have any Tylenol? It can be generic, I'm fine with that."

She's lighting up a cigarette and I don't think about it until the lit end comes down on the thin skin of my throat. There's a little sizzle, like when you put out a cigarette in an ashtray but this is on me. The pain sears, blooming across my neck and I can smell it; my burned skin and it smells like roast pork. I turn my face to the side and heave uncontrollably.

Maksim...

My gaze is directed solely on the device in my hand, the green blinking light showing me the path to my wife. The wife I don't deserve. I thought I could protect her, but of course, Ella would fling herself into the path of an oncoming bus if it meant saving Tania.

Her Tarot reading at Christmas came back with nauseating clarity; The Hanged Man card and Sofia's words, *"There is a sacrifice ahead and only you can decide to offer it."*

Ella didn't deserve this. If anyone's life should be sacrificed, it should be mine. I remembered when we were standing at the door, Sofia had also told me, *"One of you can make a choice that could destroy you both. And that warning is meant for you, too."* The choices I made when I shouted at her and told her she was an outsider. A chain of choices all the way back to forcing her to marry me because she fit my requirements, because I admired her spirit.

I'd been so used to being hard since I was old enough to throw my first punch. But in this moment, I felt a surge of self-disgust so intense that it threatened to choke me.

"Brother," Yuri spoke softly so the men could not hear us. "Are you ready for this?"

"What do you mean-" I snarled, but he cut me off.

"You need to be Pakhan right now, to save Ella and finish these bastards off. We're facing a considerable amount of firepower, much, most likely stolen from us." Yuri's expression was compassionate, but his warning was clear.

Taking in a deep breath, I let it out. "I'm ready. Where are we dropping her?"

"No!" She leans over him to grab my sleeve, something he regards with alarm. "I'm not leaving, I'm not leaving her this time!" Tania's crying and I sigh, removing her hand.

"We do not have time to protect you," I said sharply, "do you understand?"

"Yuri says this car is armor-plated," she said stubbornly. "I'll stay here. I won't move."

"Tania," Yuri takes her chin, forcing her to look at him. "I cannot see you hurt or taken by these scum."

"It's my choice," she argues. "Don't take that away."

He sighs, rubbing his forehead. "Do you know how to shoot?"

She brightens, "I do! My dad used to take me to the gun range."

My idiot brother pulls out his gun and shows her how to use it.

I put in my earpiece and hear my brigadiers sound off, then Giovanni chimes in with a count for the Toscano soldiers, and Alexi with his Turgenev group. Closing my eyes in relief, I dare to hope we can do this, save Ella and wipe out the pestilence of Katya Sokolov and whoever she has dragged into her sewer.

"I think Patrick should be here as your *Obshchak*," Yuri says quietly, "I have worked with him for ten years."

My jaw tightens, "We know we have a traitor on the inside of the organization. We know the Irish are somehow involved. We cannot risk it."

He shakes his head, but he knows better than to argue with me.

I listen to everyone count off their positions one last time and look at the heat signatures from the drone. "The largest group is centralized in the northeast corner of the building," I said, "there's five guards at least at each entrance, and another four on

289

the roof. We can see there's a lower level. Keep your gas masks close. If they deploy the gas, you'll have only a few seconds' notice." I pause, gritting my teeth against another stab of fear. "My wife is in there. Most likely with Katya, who will attempt to use her as a shield. My wife's survival is paramount."

Pulling on my bulletproof vest, I take Yuri's arm. "Be safe."

He grinned back impudently. "You have told me the same thing since I was ten years old. I am still alive, brother."

I give the signal, and I hear the rapid gunfire begin.

Ella...

I thought the pain I felt in the hospital was the worst pain any human could endure. I was wrong. Three of the fingers on my left hand won't move, crooked and limp on the table. I screamed as Katya watched Vasily break each one, smiling at me sweetly the whole time. My left side feels like there's nails being pounded into my chest when I try to breathe. Blood's pooling on the horrible stainless-steel table. I'm not sure where it's from.

It's hitting me all at once and when I try to catch my breath, she does something else and I'm screaming again.

But there's worse pain. Who knew? It's because of my brother.

My eyes are screwed up tight, trying to pretend I'm not in this place and so ashamed that I'm crying. I'm sure Maksim would be laughing in their faces right now.

"Every time I see you, you're all broken up and on your back." It's my brother Charles. He's dressed in an expensive blue suit and looking down at me with disgust.

Kayta is glowing with happiness, hovering behind him with an expressionless Vasily.

"Charles?" I'm sobbing and I feel so stupid but I can't seem to stop. For one second - just one - when he walked through the door, I thought he was here to save me.

"The O'Connell clan has a stake here," he's talking to Katya. Their voices fade in and out like a bad phone connection.

I don't want to breathe because it makes my ribs move and scrape against each other.

"This bitch is mine," she snarls.

My brother shrugs. He *shrugs*. "I don't care as long as she's alive and serving in the Red Trade as agreed. The video of the wife of the mighty Maksim Morozov in a whorehouse will shame the Morozov Bratva and weaken their position. There's no respect for a man who can't protect his wife. There needs to be an example set."

I stare up at the ceiling. It's concrete, and there's a crack with a water stain shaped like a turtle. I wish I had a hard shell like a turtle. Maybe it wouldn't feel like I was bleeding to death inside. I wish I was, but I'm pretty sure Katya knows how to make things hurt for a long time without letting me die. But I wish I could. Tania would move on with her life, away from people who would hurt her because of me. And there's nobody else who matters.

I thought Maksim might matter, for a while. That his family could be mine. Well, not his mother, but...

I stare at the ceiling while they discuss what they're going to do to me.

Maksim...

The night lights up in flares of red and orange and I'm listening to the chatter as I mow down two more soldiers. The defunct office building Katya is holed up in is surrounded by a big, empty parking lot, unfortunately making their visibility excellent. Two well-aimed grenades take out the men on the roof, and we gun the engine, accelerating toward the building, shooting out the windows of our car to take down as many as we can before we jump from the protection they offer and move into close combat.

"There are far more men here than the intel showed," Alexi shouts, "I see a dozen headed for the southwest corner, I'm guessing that's the entrance to the lower level."

Growling, I reverse course and head in that direction.

Katya won't kill her, I think, *she'll want to do it in front of me. I've got time. A little time to find her.*

The gunfire is slowing down as our soldiers take over more ground in and around the building. "Don't let anyone get out!" I'm shouting, desperate to make sure they can't take Ella away. The entryway to this corner of the building is in shreds, the broken doors riddled with bullets and hanging from their hinges. Ivan is keeping pace along with me, slightly ahead to take out any threats, but I want to shove him aside. I have to get to Ella.

A bullet hits me like a vicious punch to my ribs - one or two are likely broken - but the bulletproof vest does its job. I'm in the open as I'm heading for the lower level and another bullet tunnels through my shoulder. I remember Ella carefully bandaging the opposite shoulder the last time I was shot and grinned foolishly.

Ella...

There's shouting and I open my eyes to see Katya shoving at her husband, screaming, "She's not getting out of this! She is dead before I let that *svoloch* have her back!"

Charles is yelling back, "She's our human shield! He's not going to shoot us if we have a gun to her head!"

"You're such an asshole..." I mumble, "no wonder Mom and Dad loved me more."

I didn't even think he heard me but he whirls on me, his furious red face close enough that he's spitting on me while he screams at me. "You were supposed to die with them in that accident, why can't you ever do what you're supposed to!"

I laugh, tasting something metallic in my throat. "They still loved me more."

"Where are the gas canisters!" Vasily is roaring at Katya and she doesn't look so happy anymore.

"The formula takes at least twenty-four hours to create," she stammered.

I make an agreeing sort of noise. "I could have told you that."

There's a thunderous crash and part of the ceiling in the corner caves in. Katya is screaming and it's just killing my head. I'm pretty sure I'm hallucinating when I hear Maksim's voice.

"Take me! I will take my wife's place. I'm coming down, my hands are empty!"

There are footsteps, loud and chunks of concrete are clattering down the stairs, too.

Oh, sweetie, I think, *they're just going to kill you too, but thank you for coming to get me.*

Maksim's in full Pakhan mode, blood staining his shoulder, hands up, and looking cold and powerful. "I'm unarmed," he repeats, "let my wife go, I will take her place and guarantee you safe passage out of here." He's looking at Charles for a moment, brow furrowed in that *"do I know you?"* way.

"You have no bargaining power here!" Katya is screaming, trying to lunge at him but her husband is holding her back. He's the one with the survival instinct. "I'm going to kill this *suka* while you beg me to let you live!"

Maksim ignores her, looking at Vasily and then Charles. "Your only way out of here alive is with me. Take my wife off that table and she will leave first. Then you can put a gun to my head and get out of here."

I can see it before my husband does, this evil cow isn't letting me live. Kayta's hand is shaking, clutching a gun that sweeps between him and me, over and over with her finger absently tapping the trigger.

"No!" she's screaming, her fancy hair is down and snarled around her face, she has sweat stains under the arms of her fancy suit and stupidly, it just makes me so happy.

"The *suka* does not get to live! You do not get to live, Maksim!" She's backed away from her alarmed husband and my bro- no, from Charles, not my brother. "And you cowards will not stop me!" She's pointing the gun at me again and I watch her finger press the trigger. There's a weight on my chest and everything goes dark.

Night, night, I'm so grateful to go away.

CHAPTER 23 – PLEASE PRETEND, JUST FOR TONIGHT

In which a broken, vulnerable Ella asks Maksim to do something for her, even if he's just pretending.

Ella...

There's a beeping sound that wakes me up and for a horrible moment, I think I'm back in the hospital, all those years ago. I want to cry out for someone to get me out of here, but I can't make my lips move. I hear some kind of pathetic grunting noise and I realize it's from me.

"You're awake," it's Maksim leaning over me, one big hand on my cheek.

"You look really bad," I wheezed.

He laughs, "I'm sure I do," he agreed. He's got dark circles under his eyes, a bandage on his head and as my eyes drift down, there's several more on his chest and arms.

"Does this mean we won?"

"Yes, *solnyshko*," he said gently, "we did. Katya and her hellhound are finished, the Sokolov Bratva is ours for the taking."

"That's good," I agreed, and then I fell asleep again.

I woke again as the doctor was taking my pulse. Maksim is standing behind her and I can tell it's making the poor woman uncomfortable.

"Mrs. Morozov, how do you feel?"

"I'm fine." My voice sounded so blank but I couldn't think of anything to say. I was still thinking about my brother wanting me sent to a whorehouse. That I can never see Tania again to keep her safe.

"-want to be sure there's no sign of shock."

Oh, it's the doctor again. "I'm sorry. What?"

She's shining a light in my eyes, "I'm checking you for shock. Can you tell me what you're feeling right now?"

Empty. Pretty much empty.

"I'm really fine, I promise." I make an attempt at a reassuring smile, but she doesn't seem that impressed.

"We ran some x-rays, I was concerned that the full left side of your ribcage was broken, but you must take a lot of calcium supplements, only two were actually fractured," she says.

Oh, a little joke, I think, trying to concentrate. I smile again.

"It looks like from your x-rays that you've had multiple fractures in this region before?"

When I don't answer, Maksim says, "Ella was in a serious car accident a few years ago. She lost her parents and she was in the ICU for several weeks."

"That must have been brutal," she says sympathetically, "I've started you on a round of antibiotics for the..." her mouth thinned with anger, "for the cigarette burns and I've left an ointment here to apply..."

Her voice fades out and I fall asleep again.

It's dark when I open my eyes for the third time. Maksim is still here, lying on top of the covers with his eyes closed. His hand is resting on my arm. It's warm, and heavy. It feels comforting. I knew for the next little while at least, he would comfort me and I'd feel treasured and in the circle of family. An odd, violent dynasty, but still family and friends. And then something will happen to trigger him and Maksim will tear me apart with cruel words. Scornful. But if he's kind to me long enough before that happens, I will never be able to stop loving him.

Then, the next time he lashes out at me and reminds me that I'm merely convenient, it will kill me.

"Solnyshko," Maksim's speaking to me, "How do you feel?"

I think about it. "Can I have a bath?"

"Of course."

He insists on carrying me into the bathroom, filling the tub and helping me in. Drawing my legs up, I awkwardly cradle my hand with the broken fingers and ignore all the blazing bits of fire igniting from the burns and cuts. But nothing, *nothing* could be as brutal as what I felt on that horrible table so I can handle it.

So maybe I am tougher than I thought.

"Did you kill my brother?"

Maksim actually flinched. "Yes."

"Okay." I couldn't think of anything to say.

"He intended to use video of you imprisoned in a whorehouse to rise in rank to Captain. The O'Connell Mob are making a move into New York." He said the ugly words quickly, like they tasted bad in his mouth.

"I know," I agreed blankly. "He told me it would disgrace you."

He soaped up a sponge and ran it gently over my back, jaw tightening as he tried to avoid my bruises.

"Tania is very anxious to see you tomorrow," Maksim continued, looking at me with what I'm guessing is concern. It's not an expression I've seen from him before.

"That's not a good idea," I carefully shaped each word in my mouth, trying to make sure they made sense.

The sponge slowed. "Why?"

I angled my broken fingers higher, ignoring the burn. "Every bad thing that has happened to her is my fault. I don't think we should see each other anymore."

Maksim's big, rough hand cupped my cheek, very carefully. "You're beginning to worry me, *солнышко*."

I couldn't think of anything to say, so he helped me out of the tub, and I stood in the middle of the bathroom, refusing to look in the mirror while he carefully toweled me dry. Maksim picked me up again and carried me to the bed, kneeling in front of me.

"Tell me what you need," he urged, his icy blue gaze meeting mine, "what can I do for you, Ella?"

I leaned forward and kissed him. Maksim didn't move, his eyes were still open and watching me. "Would..." I cleared my throat, "Could you please make love to me? I know you don't love me, I know that. But could you pretend? Just for tonight?"

"Oh, *solnyshko*," he said sadly. But he placed kiss after kiss on my face, feather-light on the bruises Vasily's fists had made, and his tongue soothed the cut on my mouth from Katya's ring. "Shhh, my beautiful girl. My brave girl."

Maksim...

Of all the things I'd done to my wife, the heartless words, the careless stripping of her life away from her, the cruelest was that she didn't know that I loved her.

I did. I did love her. There was very little love left in my sin-stained heart, but she had created more somehow, and it was all for her.

Lifting her hair, I spread it out across the pillow, and carefully placed her hand with her poor, broken fingers in a comfortable spot by her head. I'd had my fingers broken. Several times, back when my father was "teaching me how to be a man." But to see her long, elegant fingers splinted hurt more than when my own were torn and fractured.

"Are you sure?" Ella nodded, her face was still troublingly blank, but I could tell she was at least focusing on me now, seeing me. "You must tell me immediately if I hurt you."

She nodded.

"Say the words, *solnyshko.*"

"I will," her voice was soft, but at least it sounded more like my Ella. Pulling off my clothes quickly, I looked up at her sharp inhale of breath. My torso was covered with bruises as well.

"I'm all right," I assured her, "I've had far worse." I was rewarded with a small, sweet smile and I bent to kiss her, running my lips lightly over hers. I'd never made love to anyone. I'd always laughed at the phrase. But for Ella, I'd try. I kissed her shoulders, gentle brushes of my mouth over her breasts, lightly sucking one nipple, then the other. She gave a small sigh of relief, and I understood. I'd often used sex for the dopamines to reduce the pain from injuries and wounds.

Parting her legs, I moved between them, keeping most of my weight off of her. "So pretty," I murmured, running the tip of my tongue slowly between her lower lips, watching them swell hopefully. "You're like a flower unfurling, did you know that?" Ella's eyes are closed, which is hard to see. She'd always loved watching me lick and suck her; it was wildly arousing.

I slow down, blowing lightly on her wet center and watch her shiver. Alternating long, slow swipes of my tongue with sucking one lip, then another into my mouth, I feel her hips start moving against me again. Circling her clitoris with my tongue, I make smaller and smaller circles, still not quite touching it until I see her uninjured hand lift.

Putting it on my head, I squeeze it gently, encouraging her to run her fingers through my hair.

I groan involuntarily, and my wife shivers again. "Are you cold, *solnyshko?*"

Her voice is shaky, like she might be crying, but Ella answers me. "No, I'm okay."

She's most definitely not okay, I thought bitterly, hating myself for letting this happen to her. *But I'll do everything I can to make her feel loved.*

More circles, round and round her swollen little bud until she pushes up into my mouth and I grin against her before sucking her clitoris into my mouth. My sweet bride comes almost instantly, and I slowly lick her, prolonging her orgasm as long as I can.

"You're beautiful when you come," I whisper in her ear, enjoying her little shudder. Bracing my forearms on either side of her head, I smile reassuringly down at her. It's not an expression I use often and I can only hope she feels my concern. "Are you still all right, *solnyshko?* Do you want me to stop?"

The tears in her eyes catch the dim light, making them almost supernaturally beautiful. "No, please don't stop."

"I won't," I promise, kissing her again. Ella has such a perfect mouth, her lush, full lips, and her sweet, timid tongue. Why haven't I kissed her more?

Sliding my cock between her swelling lips. I rocked back and forth, nudging her clit with the head of my shaft each time. I could tell by how her knees tightened against my hips that she was ready for more, but I wasn't in any hurry. My little sun deserved all of my attention; I would take my time.

Running my tongue up the undamaged side of her neck, I whispered bits of Russian poetry to her. I told her that I was sorry that I didn't get to her before she was hurt. I told her I was sorry that she had suffered because of me.

Her slick was silky against my cock and I moved against her so easily, our skin was wet and sliding smoothly together. Sucking gently on each nipple again, I blew lightly on them, watching the pink tips pucker so sweetly. Ella's leg came up to wrap around my hip and I reached down, putting my cock at the entrance to her channel, pushing as slowly as I could manage to avoid jolting her broken ribs.

o Gospodi, it was hard to not thrust up inside her. Being inside my wife was all-encompassing, the one place where everything else left my mind and the only thing I could focus on was her, the heat, her snug fit around me. My head dropped to her collarbone, breathing for a moment, trying to regain control. The relief of being inside her again, that Ella was alive, and safe... it was overwhelming.

Cradling the back of her head, I lifted it slightly to kiss her, slowly, like my hips moving into her, twining my tongue with hers, kissing her forehead, whispering how beautiful she was, how courageous. My poor Ella was weeping silently, and I kissed away each tear. When I could feel her thighs tighten even more, I knew she was close, and I whispered, "I do love you, *solnyshko,* I do."

Her uninjured arm wrapped around my neck and her channel gripped me as she came, and I groaned, filling her tight, heated center, coming harder than I'd ever come in my life.

If this was making love, I could do this. With Ella, always.

I watched her the rest of the night, she'd fallen back asleep with her head on my lap, and I wouldn't move. Finally, when the sun rising sent rays across her face Ella flinched, waking up and tensing until she realized where she was.

"How do you feel?" I brushed her hair off of her face.

"I'm okay," she whispered, trying to sit up. Lifting her, I settled her against the pillows and offered her some water.

"It's time for your pain meds, Dr. Connor left them along with your antibiotics."

Drinking until the glass was empty, Ella shook her head. "Not yet, I want a clear head to ask some questions."

Remembering the notes about how much she'd suffered in the hospital after her accident, pride rose in me. My *solnyshko was* strong. Taking a deep breath, I nodded. "Ask me."

"I remember..." her brow furrowed, "I remember Katya shooting at me before I passed out?"

"I was fortunate to get in front of you in time," I said, "it hit me in the chest, but I had a bulletproof chest on."

For the first time, Ella's gaze landed on my chest. "Oh my god!" Her hand rose up and then hesitated.

"It's fine," I took her hand and put it on my chest. Her warm fingers carefully hovered over the blooming mess of red and purple bruising over my heart and along my side.

"This must be so painful," she fussed, lightly pressing her palm next to the bruising."

"It's not bad. It's better than the alternative."

Ella looked up with the first smile I'd seen. "Why Maksim, was that... *humor?*"

I chuckled, then immediately regretted it as my ribs twinged angrily.

She looked down again at her hand resting on my chest. "Did you know who Charles was?"

"Not immediately, I was more concerned about you."

Her chest rises and falls slowly. "But you knew what he was."

"I knew you had a brother who'd stolen your inheritance. Since he took your mother's maiden name and used his middle name, I didn't connect him to the Irish mob until recently. The name Sean O'Connell is a very different matter. He used your parent's money to buy his way into the higher ranks. Did you..." I was used to saying the hard things, the truth, even when painful.

Ella looked up, her pale eyes, so green like the Dresden diamond, were wet. "Did I know Charles was involved in organized crime? No. We lived in Birmingham, not Ireland. But my mom never talked about her side of the family, she'd just tell me there was 'nothing to say about such people!'" I could hear the trace of the English accent my mother caught more strongly in her words now. "We uh... we moved here when I was eight. Charles was so angry. My parents insisted we needed a fresh start."

I took her hand, "Do you know that he caused the accident that killed your parents?" When I watched her lovely face crumple in agony, I wished I'd not said it. My wife was sweet. She must have held out hope for years that her useless brother would somehow become family again.

"I shouldn't be surprised, huh?" Ella said bitterly. "I'm sure he meant to have me die in the crash, too. Nice and tidy. He was standing there, watching Katya put her cigarette out on me... his expression never changed. He was telling her that, 'the O'Connell Mob had a stake here.' He wanted a video of me in..." she gagged a little and I helped her sit up, her poor, battered body heaving. "He wanted a video of me in the whorehouse because it would shame the Morozov Bratva and threaten your power." She smiled blankly, "I was too busy trying not to scream to tell him that it wouldn't have the desired effect since your people wanted nothing to do with me. I'm an *outsider*." She spat the last word, as if it tasted bad.

Another cruelty to lay at my feet, I thought, *another thing I've done to her.*

Ella wearily rubbed her eyes. "Mom had an inheritance from her family. She refused to access it; she called it dirty money. I remember hearing Charles screaming at her to 'give it back' when he turned eighteen. That had to be why he did it, why he would..." I slid my arms under her, gently lifting her on to my lap as she wept, kissing her forehead, smoothing her hair. Waiting for her storm to settle.

When she fell asleep again, I dressed and left the bedroom to find Yuri.

"Tania's calling me every fifteen minutes, demanding to speak to Ella," he sighed, rubbing his eyes tiredly.

"Tell her Ella's asleep, but I'll have her call later." I groaned, sitting down in my chair behind the desk.

"Don't tell me the great and powerful Pakhan is feeling like shit this morning," my idiot brother taunted me.

"The only reason I'm not stabbing you right now is that you

saved Ella's life last night."

"And yours," Yuri adds helpfully.

"That was some impressive shooting, by the way," I complimented him, "did you use the mirror trick to shoot around the corner of the stairway?"

"It worked like a charm," he agreed, "I took them both out while they were distracted with Katya shooting you - though Shevchenko took three bullets to go down, the man was part polar bear."

"I remember you disarming Katya, but I was focusing on getting the restraints off Ella and getting her out of there," I'm trying to remember. "What happened?"

Yuri's expression was frigid. "She was ranting, telling me that she knew we had 'exquisite tortures' planned for her, something about that she had won, because Ella was dead."

I tilted my head curiously. My brother could be an emotionless killer when necessary, but I don't think he had ever killed a woman. His eyes, darker than mine, lifted to look at me. "I told her that her first mistake was taking Tania, and the second was hurting Ella. I told her that she did not matter enough to make a fuss. I told her that we would burn her body with the others. And then I shot her."

It might have only been midmorning, but I poured us both a drink.

Ella...

Another visit from Dr. Connor finally got me out of bed. She checked my broken ribs and fingers and was pleased to see the swelling going down, though she assured me I'd be, "A mess of bruises for another couple of weeks."

Putting her stethoscope and other gear back in her bag, the doctor smiled at me. "Do you have any questions?"

I thought about it. "Will I regain full use of my hand?"

"Yes," she nodded firmly, "you're fortunate that there's no ligament damage."

Chuckling a little, I thought, *Yeah. Fortunate.*

Dr. Connor leaned forward, putting her hand carefully on my arm. "I do think that some time with a therapist would help you. I can send you a list of professionals I trust if you'd like it."

Shaking my head with a polite smile, I tried to picture exactly what I could tell a therapist. *Yeah, I got kidnapped by this Russian gangster and had to marry him and people keep trying to kill me, so...*

"Thank you for the suggestion, I'll let you know."

She nods and smiles, but she doesn't look convinced.

When the doctor finally leaves, I slowly get dressed and stop midway to take a pain pill. I don't need to be brave now, so why not?

The penthouse is startlingly quiet when I finally emerge, I'm used to the low-key buzz of advisors and security and Alina and her tip-tapping high heels. Other than the guards at the main elevator (and the service elevator now has two guards, I notice) it's quiet. Wandering into the kitchen, I notice Ludmilla is gone. Good. I haven't eaten for a day and a half and I'm starving. I stare into the overstuffed fridge, but I don't think I can keep anything down. Maksim finds me slowly eating crackers at the counter.

His steps halted for a moment, but then he's right next to me, looking me over.

"I could have had someone bring lunch to you," he said, eyeing my Saltines.

"This is fine," I shrug, taking another bite. "Where's Ludmilla?"

Maksim's face could have been carved in stone.

"Ludmilla was our traitor. She passed information to Katya Sokolov for months."

"What? I-" I shook my head, "she worships you."

Maksim...

Ella was wrong there. Ludmilla's hate and resentment apparently built for years before turning traitor to the Sokolov Bratva. Once I reviewed the surveillance tapes for the penthouse and figured out how Ella made her escape, it was clear. The footage showed my housekeeper leaving her elevator key out on the counter and asking the guard at the lift to help her with something. Her timing could only work if she knew when Ella would try to leave.

Earlier that day...

"Why would you do this?"

Ludmilla knelt on the floor of my study, bound securely. She looked up at me and for the first time, I can see the malice, her hatred. But I didn't know why.

"You had an honored position in my household. You have worked for my family for twenty years. You were paid well."

"You elevated that *postoronniy* to the housekeeper of your hunting lodge! I should have been next in line! I had to work as a common household maid for another two years before you appointed me to housekeeper here! That outsider worked for this family for hardly any time and you give her this honor over *me?* You disrespected me!"

Even Yuri looked a little stunned. "You betrayed this family because of some imagined slight?"

Patrick, my *Obshchak,* stood behind her, arms folded. He looked at me, waiting for my orders.

"We do not harm women or children in the Morozov Bratva," I said. "But you willingly turned traitor. You knew you were sending my wife to her death. You will pay for that with your own."

Patrick's men quickly hauled her out of the study, muffling her shrieks as they took her away. He stood in front of me, arms behind his back, awaiting orders.

"I misjudged you, *Obshchak.*" I said, "It was the wrong choice."

He smiled, knowing that is as close to an apology as he'll get from me. "I will never betray this family," he said earnestly, "I will guard your safety to my last breath. You brought me into this family when my own threw me out. I'll never forget that."

Yuri grinned broadly and rose to slap him on the shoulder. "That means I'll be seeing your ugly face for years to come, *ginger.*"

Patrick chuckled, darting a glance at me to make sure levity was appropriate. I unbent enough to return the smile and made a note to give him a hundred-thousand-dollar bonus.

Currently...

I explained as much as I could to Ella, who looked utterly astonished throughout the entire story. "She gave you up for an imagined insult? Well," she shook her head. "In the hierarchy she's created, the one that gives her life value and status, it was an insult. It's not something you could have predicted, but it was everything to her." She's crumbling her half-eaten cracker, not looking at me. "I guess I shouldn't ask what happened to her."

Frowning, I lift her chin, making her look at me. "Forty of my men died because of the information she gave to Katya Sokolov. Over seventy-five million dollars were lost from the theft of goods and destruction of my property. Even if I could overlook that, I would kill her for this one thing. She sent you to your death. She notified the enemy when you left and made it easy for you to escape. There are other Bratva organizations who would kill her entire family, from the oldest down to the youngest with no mercy. But I don't place the sins of one traitor on their family."

Ella lets out a sigh. "I understand. All those poor men..." she shook her head sadly, completely discounting the last thing I said.

It doesn't matter, I thought, *I have time now to show her what she means to me. What she means to all of us.*

Ella...

It's time to ask Maksim for what I want. My heart is pounding and it feels like it's ready to surge up my throat, but I have to do this. I know he didn't mean anything he said last night, I know it was just part of the moment. I'll treasure those moments for the rest of my life.

"I have something important to ask you."

"Oh?" Maksim nods toward his study.

That's his place of power. "Can we go into the bedroom and talk there?" I ask.

"Of course." He offers me his hand, helping me off the stool. When we reach the bedroom, I take one of the chairs by the fireplace and he joins me. "What's on your mind, *solnyshko?*"

I'm rubbing my hands over my skirt repeatedly until he reaches out a gentle hand to stop me. "The Sokolov Bratva, Dante, my..." I grit my teeth together for a moment, "my brother. They're no longer threats to your Bratva, correct?"

His head tilts curiously, he's trying to read me. "This is true, and thanks to you, if anyone else manages to obtain the formula for the gas, they won't be able to use it against us. It was brilliant work, by the way."

I nod nervously. *Getting off track here, Ella. Don't let him be nice to you.*

"I'm glad, but-" closing my eyes, I silently ask my parents for strength. "The reasons for marrying me no longer exist," I plow on. "I want you to let me go."

postoronniy - outsider

CHAPTER 24 – LET ME GO

In which Ella prepares for the most depressing Valentine's Day ever.

Ella...

"The reasons for marrying me no longer exist," I plow on. "I want you to let me leave."

"What are you saying, Ella?"

I steel myself and look him in the eye. The dark and dangerous Pakhan of the Morozov Bratva is stunned.

Never thought I'd see that.

"I'm not part of this world," I plow on, "I'm an outsider. You saw what happened with your housekeeper when you insulted her by promoting an outsider before her. It only reinforces what I know." I smile, thinking about the twins chattering to him about their music at the funeral, the exhausted mother, and her little girl. "Your people are very strong, they're stoic to a degree that I can't imagine. But... they know I don't belong here."

"I decide where you belong." Maksim interrupts me, "I know that the last few days have been terrifying, but it is done. I will keep you safe."

Staring at him in despair, I know I can't tell him the truth. I know last night wasn't real, but for one magical moment, I knew what it was like to feel loved. I know when he told me he loved me, he didn't mean it. I know Maksim is never going to love me. But now that I know how it feels, I can't stay here. I can't live with him day in and day out knowing that I love him and that he will never be capable of returning it.

"I want to leave, Maksim, I want you to let me go," I said, trying to sound determined instead of dissolving into a weeping mess that'll agree to anything he says. "I can't be close to anyone without putting a target on their back-"

"I already have a bodyguard for Tania," he interrupts, "I intend to buy her an apartment in a high-security building-"

"No. Look, just... I don't want to be here. I want you to marry some nice Russian girl who your people will accept. She'll give you..."

This is going to kill me.

"She'll give you Russian babies that will make your mother so happy. She'll... she'll fit. But I can't do any of those things, and I don't want to." I sharpen my tone, praying I can get through it. "I never wanted this life."

I chanced a quick look at him and he is utterly still, his eyes are glacier blue, pale, and blank.

"Maksim, please. Please give me this. If you care about me at all, please."

"Solnyshko-"

"I can't be here anymore! God, don't you hear me? Let me go!" Now I'm sobbing and he's leaning forward like he's going to try to comfort me and that cannot happen. I scramble off the chair and back away. "I'm just *convenient,* remember?"

"I was angry when I said that, and it was wrong," he growled, "it wasn't true. You are-"

"I deserve better," I said flatly, "let me go. Please." I can see the mask slip over his face like a cloud over the moon. Maksim rises, looking down at me from his considerable height. And leaves the room.

Maksim...

The next day...

I'm looking down at my kingdom, the lights glittering through Manhattan and the softer illumination of Vessel, each staircase connected to another and spiraling into a honeycomb shape in a glowing spiral.

The Sokolov Bratva is disbanded, their men pledging loyalty to me. The O'Connell Irish Mob has been driven out of New York before they could even gain a foothold. I have powerful allies with the Turgenev Bratva and the Toscano Mafia. And I'm standing here alone.

Yuri was stunned when I told him about my decision.

"This can't be- Maksim, you cannot be serious."

"I already had the top floor of The Cormorant cleared and furnished for her," I'm looking out the window, I don't want to see his expression. "Have all her things moved to the new apartment and set up a bank account for her. She's going to need round-the-clock security. In fact, I want it doubled. Contact the Vijayumar legal firm to start the divorce proceedings, be sure it is completely confidential. I don't want even a whisper about this until it is done and Ella is relocated to wherever she wants to be."

He moved in front of me, blocking the view. "Brother, you cannot want this. I know you don't. I never thought I would say this, but I know you love her. She cracked your cold, black heart wide open."

I turn my head and stare at the fireplace instead. "I do love her. And that's why I'm letting her go."

Ella...

"Why are you doing this?"

I look up from the bag I'm packing. Oh, great. It's Alina.

"Don't you have something for Maksim to sign?" I'm tired and it's hard to remember how to be polite.

She steps into the Inner Sanctum, her four-inch heels clacking on the hardwood. "Why would you leave?"

Zipping up the bag, I sigh deeply, straightening up even though she's towering over me in those heels. "Look, you should be thrilled. You can make a play for Maksim the minute I'm out of the picture."

Her perfect, smooth brow actually wrinkled a bit. "What?"

"C'mon, I know you've been crazy for him the minute I met you. Not that I'm blaming you. He's the perfect Russian package." The thought of the two of them together, the crowns held over their heads as he guides her on to the *рушник,* and the misery it causes makes me slump gracelessly onto the bed.

Alina cautiously moves closer to me, still clutching her customary tablet and file folders. "I worship him of course," she says matter-of-factly and I just want to grab her perfect, high ponytail and drag her out of here and down the hall. "But, the Pakhan was never meant for me." She's talking in the same tone you'd use to recite the lunch menu. "I knew this long ago, but when he married you? It was clear you two were meant to be."

Shaking my head, I stare at her. Is she drunk? Did she knock her head on something? "Are you feeling okay today?"

Her perfectly shaped brow rises. "Of course. I would never presume to know what the Pakhan thinks or feels, but... it is clear he cares for you. He has been kinder with you here, even in the middle of this upheaval."

Standing, I put the strap of my bag over my shoulder, realize it's landed on one of the burns and wince, moving it to the other shoulder.

"I wish you would not leave," Alina says. "The Pakhan will be very unhappy."

"I have to admit, that is the last thing I ever imagined hearing from you," I marvel. Impulsively, I hold out my hand and she cautiously shakes it. "Thank you, Alina, that... you know, that really means a lot to hear from you."

Walking down the marble hall, I smile, hearing her high heels clicking away for the last time. Yuri is waiting in the entry with Ivan, who looks like a pit bull with a bad cold.

"Sister..." Yuri puts his arms around me and for just a moment, I let myself sag into him. "Please do not do this," he whispers.

One pathetic sob escapes me before I pull it together. "I have to, Yuri. If I stay any longer, this is going to kill me."

He hugs me harder. "Maksim would protect you from anything."

"There's some things he can't protect me from." Pulling back from him, I smile. "I love you. I'm going to miss you so much. Though not the endless mentions of your... you know."

He gets that same shark grin that Maksim wears when he thinks he's The Man. "There are some things too impressive to remain without praise."

Pushing him away playfully, I gratefully laugh. "Yeah, okay, weirdo." Squeezing his hands, I risk a glance at the closed office door.

"He is..." Yuri hesitates, "he is not good company right now."

Forcing a smile, I nod. "Sure, just..." pausing, I try to think of what to say.

Goodbye? I love you? I wish you could love me back? Thank you for letting me go but I wish so much that you could feel the same way and want me to stay?

I settle for, "Just tell him goodbye. And thank you."

Ivan moves to get in the front of the car with the driver and I reach out, grabbing his sleeve. "Sit back here with me?"

He does, sitting straight with his hands placed on his knees.

I eye him, trying not to smile. "Are you stuck with me for the immediate future?"

Ivan sniffs indignantly. "I requested this position, of course. And the Pakhan trusts me to keep you safe at all costs."

"It won't be for that long," I assure him, forehead pressed against the car window. "Once there's an exit plan and I'm relocated somewhere."

There's a grunt or something and I turn to see a tear course down his square face before he hastily brushes it away. I pat him on the arm and we sit together in companionable silence.

The apartment is certainly magnificent, I think, walking around the place where Maksim has "relocated" me. Beautiful windows overlooking Madison Avenue and the usual high-end touches like the stainless-steel gourmet kitchen and an expansive deck off the master bedroom with comfortable wicker furniture and lots of plants.

Ivan and the other bodyguard have carried the last of my things into the bedroom and they've discreetly removed themselves to a small room by the entry. I sit down gingerly on the huge leather sectional and rub my hands together. *It's so quiet,* I thought, looking around, *where is everybody?* I'd gotten used to the hustle and bustle of the penthouse, I used to jokingly call it "Pakhan Central."

I'll just have to get used to it. I think. I can't work or really go out much until Maksim relocates me with a new identity.

A moment later, Ivan came into the room. "You have a visitor, Mrs. Morozov."

"C'mon Ivan, just call me Ella," I sigh. "Who is it?"

Faintly from the entry I hear, "Hey Els! Tell them to let me in!"

Dropping my head with a groan, I ask, "Yuri gave her my address, didn't he?"

Ivan shrugged uncomfortably, his grey suit bunching up a bit across his big shoulders.

"Okay, thanks, can you send her-"

Tania had apparently already side-stepped the other bodyguard and burst into the living room. Putting her hands on her hips, she said, "I want you to know I'm not holding this against you since I ghosted you for like two weeks."

Naturally, I burst into tears and she ran over to hug me. "Hey, Ivan, can you go grab us a bottle of wine and some snacks?"

He turned toward the kitchen, mumbling something about, "I am not the maid."

Settling back on the couch, Tania stubbornly hugged me until I stopped crying; primarily out of self-defense so she'd stop squeezing me.

"Okay, talk to me," she demanded.

"What is there to say?" I shrugged helplessly as I rubbed my eyes, which smeared any remaining mascara over the rest of my face. "Being friends with me has nearly gotten you killed twice. I'm a coward. I was hoping to just... vanish from here before you saw me again. I'd leave you a big long letter telling you that I love you too much to let you almost get killed again. But that idiot Yuri just cannot leave well enough alone, can he?"

She drew back, outraged. "You cannot seriously think I'd let you slink out of town, never to be seen again? Are you high? Because that shit is not happening." Tania paused to pour an overflowing glass of wine and handed it to me, then taking one for herself.

"Okay, let's go over what I know. First, you were hurt pretty bad and if that bitch Katya was still alive, I would kill her myself."

Her expression was a level of rage I'd never seen before, and I was sorry that I was the one who sparked it. "That's dark, Tania. But understandable."

"Second, you had A Moment with your husband. Yuri said that his brother was actually smiling and happy the entire morning. And that's while they were discussing who else they wanted to kill, or something."

I'm frozen, clutching my wine glass. Maksim smiled? He was *happy?*

"And then, third, you woke up and there was a big talk in your bedroom and then Maksim walked out like someone has just torn his heart out and then all of a sudden it was moving day. Have I missed anything yet?"

"No, that's pretty good," I agree, gloomily taking a sip of wine.

"So, are you going to tell me what happened?" Tania reaches out to squeeze my hand.

"I was... I don't know, I was weak, I guess. Everything hurt so much. Realizing what my own brother wanted to do to me made me realize that in the end, you are the only person I have, Tan. You're my most important person and because of me, you're always in danger. I..." taking another gulp of wine I plowed ahead, "I felt so weak and needy. I asked Maksim to make love to me. Like, pretend that he really did love me." I stomped down another urge to cry.

"So...?" Tania prodded me.

"He did," now I couldn't stop the tears. "It was beautiful. And he told me he loved me, he said that he was sorry he couldn't save me before I was hurt. I realized that I love this man. Never mind the most terrible 'meet cute' in history and everything that followed. I love him."

"Then why are you here?" Tania screeched, "You got it all!"

"No. No, I don't. I know what it *feels* like to be loved, and it was beautiful. It was perfect, and..." I took a deep breath, "it wasn't real. It will kill me to stay with him, loving him and knowing he will never love me."

She refilled our glasses and we drank silently for a while.

Tania fixed me with her sternest gaze. "So, here's my moment of wisdom, are you ready?"

"Yeah, okay," I sniffled.

"There's this thing guys do. When they finally love someone and they're not selfish bastards anymore, they get all *altruistic*." She spat the word like it was a gnat that flew into her mouth. "Men like Maksim may have been completely terrible people, but love makes them noble," Tania sneered. "And men when they're being noble are just so stupid. They start thinking the best thing they can do for the woman they love is to send them away because that man is no good for them. Ugh!"

She gulped down some more wine. "So, they will be miserable as shit and the woman they love will be miserable as shit, all because the man *loves* this poor woman and he's being *noble*."

She sighed irritably, "Men are so fucking stupid I swear to god. Look, Els; it's obvious Maksim loves you. And not just because you are so damn loveable - which you are - but for some reason, you cracked that icy Slavic heart wide open."

No, I thought, *that can't be right. He just said it that night because I asked him to. Not because he meant it.*

I'm shaking my head when Tania grabs my hand again. "Honey, think about it. What other possible reason could he have to let you go?"

"Because-" I floundered, "because he felt guilty."

She rolls her eyes and I can see now why it irritates Maksim so much when I do that. "The only reason that frigid, black-hearted ruff- what's the word?"

"Ruffian," I said automatically, "a brutal, cold-hearted villain."

"Right! This brutal, cold-hearted ruffian would only feel guilty if he loved you. Think about it, Ella!"

I'm shaking my head. She doesn't know. There's no way Maksim loves me. Thinking of his tenderness that night makes it all hurt worse.

"Honey, you have to hear this. Maksim is only letting you go because he loves you and he knows it's the right thing to do. You're leaving because you love him and it hurts too much to stay. So, you dumb shits will both suffer and it's for all the wrong reasons! Talk to him. Be honest with him. Make him be honest with you. Oh my god, I sound like one of those creepy advice columnists!"

At least that's good for a laugh and we settle down, finishing the bottle out on the deck and watching the rich and famous swan up and down Madison Avenue.

Valentine's Day...

"Please, Tania," I groan, "the last thing I want to do is go out tonight. You have to be kidding me."

"It's not like I'm asking to go clubbing and pick up a guy-"

"Yeah, because we know how that turned out," I interrupt.

"-I'm just asking you to take a shower, put on a nice dress and we'll go have dinner at that cool pop-up restaurant Noma's hosting in the warehouse district," she continues after pretending I didn't speak. I'm burying my face in my hands because the last thing I could ever want is to leave this apartment. I haven't gone out since I moved here. I spent most of my time crying and waiting for word from Yuri telling me that my new identity and relocation were ready to go.

"Babe, c'mon," Tania pleaded. "I don't get much more time with you. Please come and make a couple of good memories with me, okay?"

Damn her. She knows I can't turn her down. "All right."

"Excellent!" Tania's her usual happy self again. "And make sure you take a shower and at least attempt to look good, okay? Put in some effort."

"Thanks, bestie." My tone might have been a bit chilly.

"I'm just saying..." she was unrepentant, "when's the last time you bathed?"

My heart twists painfully. I remember. It was the night Maksim gently cared for me in our giant tub after rescuing me from the trio of people so evil that I refuse to even say their names.

"I'll clean up, I promise," it's a listless response, but she knows I'll do it.

"Okay, I'll pick you up at 7, okay? Be ready!"

I'm running late when Tania shows up because I've broken down into violent weeping twice and had to keep reapplying my makeup. I wonder if Maksim is going out tonight. Not that Valentine's Day is really his scene, but he has two nightclubs packed with women who'd give their right arm to sleep with him. The thought is so acutely painful that I have to sit down and breathe for a minute. The thought of losing Maksim cuts deep. *You never had him,* I remind myself, *and you have to keep moving or you'll drown in this.*

I finish my makeup, nod, and say goodbye to the happiness that was almost mine.

"You look great!" Tania cries when I finally step out onto the street, tailed by Ivan. I'm wearing a dress Maksim bought me, a silky dress that fits tightly until it flows into a big, swirly skirt at my hips. My hair's down and curled into big, glossy waves and I'm wearing a pale green diamond necklace he'd given me that matched my wedding ring. But I'd left my ring on his bedside table.

"Don't sound so surprised," I tried to smile, "what's this?"

Tania was practically dancing with excitement in front of a black Bentley. "You need to travel in the style to which you have become accustomed."

The door opens and Maksim steps out onto the sidewalk. He's wearing his black suit and the blue silk tie that matches his eyes. He is gorgeous. He's also smiling, but his gaze is wary. "You look beautiful," he says, kissing my bare left hand.

"What are you doing here?" I ask stupidly, but his smile is still kind.

"I would like to take you out on a date," this beautiful dark angel says, his Russian accent is thicker like he's... nervous? Maksim Morozov? No.

"Wh..." I can't even finish single-syllable words. Impressive.

"It occurs to me," he adds, "that I have never taken you out on a date. An outing that..." his mouth curves cynically, "an outing that you have agreed to. I would like to take you to dinner tonight, Ella."

"Maksim, I just..." I want to go. God, I want to, so much. But it's just going to hurt worse to say goodbye again.

"Please say yes," he murmurs, "just for tonight."

I look at his outstretched hand. Can I do this?

"Yes. I'd love to."

"Have a good night, you two!" Tania helpfully slams the door shut the minute we're inside. "Don't do anything I wouldn't do! Make good choices!"

"I'm not sure what we could do that Tania has not already done," Maksim says wryly, and I burst into laughter.

"That's truer than you know."

The limo is approaching *Gehenna* and my smile's a bit more forced. How are we having a quiet dinner in Maksim's nightclub? But the car turns the corner where the line is snaking toward the entrance and heads in back, where there's a private elevator that takes us up to the top of the building.

"This has been here all this time?" I gasped. The roof of the building's enchanted. Seriously. There are twinkle lights strung everywhere, outdoor heaters to keep the space warm and a table set with white linen, flowers, and china place settings. "The view- look at this!" I'm walking from one edge to the next, admiring the lights of the city. I glance over and

Maksim is leaning against a brick pillar, looking at me.

"I chose this location because I wanted to give you another - what did Tania call it? Another 'meet cute' story that will sound better retelling it than the first time we met here." He hands me a flute of champagne and taps his glass to mine. "To a better beginning."

Laughing, I take a sip, "Hear, hear!" The phrase "meet cute" coming out of Maksim's mouth is hilarious.

The dinner menu was all of my favorites; mussels in white wine sauce, lobster with saffron rice, and I laughed again when I saw a plate piled high with Pirozhki buns.

"How is everyone?" I finally worked up the courage to ask.

"Yuri's well," Maksim leans back, holding his wine glass. "I suspect he and Tania are seeing each other again."

"That scapegrace!" I gasp, and Maksim chuckles.

"Which means?"

"Scapegrace," I reply absently, "a reckless person, an incorrigible rascal."

"It fits," he allows. "Mariya is doing well in school, but she's already campaigning to attend college here in America. It's possible that she might exhaust Mother enough by then to allow it."

"And Ekaterina?" I know this is dangerous territory, but I have to know.

Maksim leans back, running his finger over his upper lip. "She was consulted about an alliance between our family and the Toscano *famiglia* by marriage to Giovanni. He flew to St. Petersburg to meet her."

"Really?" I shocked. "I've learned enough about alliance marriages now to know most couples don't meet until the engagement party.

"She agreed to the marriage," he continued, "they were quite taken with each other."

Now, the hardest question. "Would you have married her to Dante?" It's hard to look at him, the rage I'd seen that day on his face...

Maksim waits until I can finally look up. "I would have never allowed that marriage, even if it plunged us into open warfare with the Toscano Mafia. But his brothers knew he wanted to steer their organization into the Red Trade. They already knew they would have to remove him. But..." he huffed, I don't know if it's in irony or humor, but he continued, "Giovanni, the next eldest, is a principled man. He insisted on giving Dante every opportunity to change his mind before he took the necessary step."

Aaand there goes my big mouth. "Is that what we're calling murdering your terrible brother these days?"

But he only shakes his head at me. *"Solnyshko."*

The waiter delivers a domed plate for our dessert and backs away hastily. The rooftop around us is quiet, though I'm sure there's bodyguards all around us.

Maksim lifts the cover to display a perfectly created marzipan cake with beautifully crafted flowers and... my wedding ring. It sits in the middle of the cake, gleaming under the fairy lights and casting its own glow.

He's elegantly hitching his trousers and kneels (he *kneels*) in front of me. "You are the only person I have - or ever will - kneel to. I know you believe that I told you that I loved you as part of the night you asked for, but..." Maksim's brow furrows. "I did not think I had any love left to give to anyone, aside from my family. But being with you has somehow created more love than I deserve to offer. But let me say it again, clearly. I do love you, Ella. Truthfully. Completely. More than I could have imagined possible. I have much to atone for, for how I treated you. But I would ask you to give me the chance. If you think that you might one day return my feelings, I would like to ask you to marry me. Properly."

He's holding up the ring and it takes me three tries to blurt out, "I would love to. Yes. Thank you. That's good."

There's a cinematic moment.

It doesn't matter, Maksim is grinning and he slides my ring back on my finger and kisses it. "Thank you, *solnyshko.* I love you, I do."

CHAPTER 25 – SO MUCH SWEETER THE SECOND TIME AROUND

In which Ella and Maksim discover there is such a thing as second chances.

Ella...

Well, when Maksim makes a move, the man *moves.*

"Where would you like to be married?" he asks, "We'll fly there tomorrow."

"What- are you serious?"

"Yes, Ella, I am." He's seated me on his lap and he's feeding me marzipan cake. Because my husband knows that the only thing that can improve this beautiful moment is cake.

"Well, Maksim..." I think about it for a moment and burst into laughter.

"What are you thinking, Ella?" He's looking mildly concerned.

"You've recreated our meet cute into something lovely, right? And it is," I give him a quick kiss, smearing vanilla cream on his lip. "Thank you, it is. So... what do you think about recreating our experience at your hunting lodge?"

His brow rose. "That, I did not expect."

"Well, think about it," I'm wiggling a little because this is exciting. "To be honest, when you weren't trying to kill me, you were the most... weirdly playful at the lodge that I've ever seen you. How about renewing our vows there - maybe just Tania and Yuri - and spending the weekend there alone?"

"Really?" Maksim asks, looking amused and a bit distracted, but I think that is because my wiggling has made him hard.

"Really. If we're remaking our memories, that's the next move. One thing?"

Yeah, he's really distracted now. "Yes, *solnyshko?*"

"Are you attached to all those dead animal heads?"

Maksim abruptly lifts me to straddle him, rubbing me against his swollen cock. "No, you can have them all removed. They are my father's. I don't hunt animals."

I pause, leaning back to stare at him. "You only hunt humans?"

Oh my god, here is Wicked Maksim. One dark brow rises and he could not look more devilish. "As you well know, darling."

Maksim...

She's beautiful.

A scowling Megumi had done a beautiful job of decorating the lodge with flowers and swags of eucalyptus and evergreens. Dozens of white candles light the way for Ella to walk to me. Yuri stood beside me, slapping me on the back and murmuring, "The chances of her trying to run are much lower this time, eh, brother?"

"It is not too late to assign you a shift at the shit docks," I remind him pleasantly. Even my idiot brother cannot irritate me today, because here she comes.

Tania walks first, grinning triumphantly as if she alone had brought us back together. Unfortunately, this is so close to the truth that I am forced to be civil to her for the rest of her life. And then, my sweet Ella. She's wearing the same wedding dress because, as Tania gloatingly announced, "I picked it out in the first place and I knew Ella would love it."

But this time, her face isn't hidden behind the veil, her eyes aren't red from crying, and her smile, the huge one that lights up her entire face, is very much in place. She is holding Ivan's arm as he escorts her down the aisle, he looks close to weeping with happiness.

"Dearly beloved," grins Patrick, "we are gathered here today to..." My *Obshchak* has a license to perform a marriage in the State of New York. He claims he's had it "forever," but I suspected he ordered it just in time to marry us; I've never seen him so gleeful.

"...Do you, Maksim Aleksander Morozov, take Ella Givens Morozov as your lawfully wedded wife?" Patrick winks at me.

"I do," I say, smiling down at Ella as I slip her wedding ring back on her finger.

"And do you, Ella Givens Morozov, take Maksim Aleksander Morozov as your lawfully wedded husband?"

"I absolutely do," she says firmly with a saucy little grin.

"Then it is my honor to declare you husband and wife. You may kiss the bride."

I sweep Ella up in my arms. "Do you remember how long I kissed you at our last wedding?"

"I do," she put her hand around my neck. "Tania?"

Her best friend laughs and with Yuri, shouts *"Gorko!"*

"Our kiss makes the bitter drink sweet," Ella whispers, "let's make this one for the record books."

Ella...

Maksim raced us through the rest of the evening with an unseemly haste, though no one seemed in the mood to complain.

"Gimme a call tomorrow," Tania whispered as she hugged me goodbye. "That is, if you have the strength to pick up the phone."

"God, you are still sixteen, I swear," I whispered back, hugging her harder.

"Goodnight, sister." Yuri gave me three kisses, left, right, left, and then a kind smile. "I am happy to call you sister again, but I never stopped thinking of you as such."

"If you make me cry, it's going to ruin my fabulous bride makeup and you'll be sorry," I warned. "Thank you for everything, brother. For saving Maksim and me, for being the rock for all of us."

He winked and escorted Tania out the door.

We were alone in that ridiculously large hunting lodge, even a sour-faced Megumi exited the entire region as soon as possible after packing the fridge with meals for the next few days. If only I could be sure she hadn't poisoned them.

I shrieked as my husband swept me up in his arms and took the stairs two at a time until he reached the master bedroom.

"Is Megumi a secret romantic?" I gasped, "Look at this place!" There was a cheerful blaze in the massive fireplace, a distinct lack of dead animal heads, and more candles and flowers everywhere. She'd strung white lights on the headboard of the huge log bed and flickering from the bathroom indicated more candle decor was lit and ready to go in there.

"I'm looking at you, *solnyshko*," Maksim's gazing down at me and the tenderness from the wedding ceremony has passed. He's gone Full Pakhan on me now.

I'm not quite sure what to say to that, which is stunning in itself, so I bite my lip and brace for his next move. Walking behind me, he slowly pulls my zipper down, his bent finger tracing the skin bared as my dress opens. I'm struck with a vivid memory of my husband doing the same thing in reverse with the dress I wore leaving this place last time. With absolutely no idea about what was going to happen to me then.

But as for now, I had a pretty good idea.

Maksim strolled over to the wingback chair by the fire, seating himself, legs spread in that show-offy way I loved. Pulling off his tie and unbuttoning the first two buttons of his shirt, he gave me a little, dark smile.

"Undress for me."

My cheeks flamed. *Why must this man always push my limits?* I thought.

Puffing out a nervous breath, I pulled my wedding gown off one shoulder, then the other, turning with my back to him. There was the slightest groan that sent my confidence right back up. I let the dress fall, knowing he was looking at my corset and lacy undies. I know kicking the dress away from me would go with the whole brazen strip act but I really like this dress, so I bent as gracefully as I could in those alarmingly high heels and picked it up, draping it carefully over the bench at the foot of the bed. Maksim's gaze follows me with a slight smile.

Walking a step or two closer, I know the firelight is doing some flattering things for my body, so I face him again, slowly unknotting the laces on my corset. I feel a little sexy, a few parts sillier, but the admiring gaze of this beautiful man was making this so much fun. Opening one side, and then the other, I let the corset drop.

"Would you like me to remove my stockings, or would you prefer to?" I flutter my lashes madly, making him grin. He gestures me forward with two fingers and I saunter over.

Maksim lifts my foot onto his knee and removes my left shoe, and runs his hands up my leg in the lightest caress until he reaches the top of my stocking and slowly pulls it down. The feel of the silk stocking and his calloused fingertips stroking down my skin is setting off little fireworks along my nerve endings. He repeats the action with my right foot, watching my expression the entire time. How could something so simple be so erotic? Running his thumbs up the inside of my thigh, this wonderfully perverted man says, "How attached are you to this?" He plucks at the strap on my undies, snapping it back lightly against my hips.

"Not unduly attached," I allowed, and he ripped it right off of me with a wicked grin.

"Hold still," he warned, and sliding his giant hands over my bottom, he pulled me forcefully toward him and ran the flat of his tongue all the way along my center and then back again, pausing to push his tongue up inside me.

"Bozhe moy!" I wheezed, and I could feel his shoulders shake as this diabolical reprobate lashed me with his tongue, nibbling gently with his teeth and when he pressed his entire face against me and growled, the vibrations made me come immediately, knees buckling as I grabbed his shoulders.

"You'll give me one more, *solnyshko,*" Maksim growled, and went back to work, squeezing my ass tightly to keep me upright. My head was lolling back as he kept his promise - or his threat, who knows at this point - and I was clinging to the back of his head, lightly scratching his scalp as I tried to catch my breath. But when he tried to lift me and carry me to the bed, I stepped back unsteadily.

"Hmm, tit for tat, honey," I fluttered my lashes again as I sank to my knees, carefully pulling off his belt and opening his trousers. My husband's cock was already hard and the head pushing free from the top of his boxer briefs. Lowering my head, I sucked the silky tip into my mouth, my tongue tracing along it and fluttering underneath. His groan made me grin and I pulled his underwear down to take all of him in my mouth, a skill I took some pride in. Pulling my long hair over my shoulder, I wrapped it around the base of him and tightened it, and a growl erupted from Maksim's throat.

"Enough!" He lifted me off his cock and into his arms, carrying me over to the bed - well, more like throwing me onto the bed - and followed me down, covering me with his giant self and kissing me with a flattering degree of fierceness.

There was always a moment when Maksim first drove inside me that stung sharply, the sudden stretch to accommodate him and I suspected that would always be there. I'd learned to love the feeling; even crave it and I wrapped my arms and legs around him and held on.

Sliding his hands under my back and his fingers gripping my shoulders, Maksim thrust inside me harder, keeping me from moving as his hips jolted me.

"You are mine, you beautiful-" *Thrust.* "Infuriating-" *Thrust.* "Brilliant-" *Thrust.* "Courageous woman."

Laughing, I kissed him, running my hands up and down his back. I had seen each of the scars on his back and mapped each one with kisses, and those on his chest. Some, Maksim would tell me about, others made his expression go blank and I would move on quickly. I knew this constellation of pain went clear back to his childhood and his evil father. He would tell me when he was ready.

I squealed, startled when he hoisted me onto his lap, bouncing me up and down. "I can feel you in my ribs, I swear," I moaned, biting his thick shoulder. He only chuckled evilly and pushed against the small of my back, arching me and I felt his cock slide up even farther, hitting something that made me shriek. The heat of him tearing through me, the way he unapologetically pushed everything aside to make room for his cock... I shivered and moaned and finally screamed, nothing had ever felt so good. His heat poured through me and we stayed pressed together, rocking slightly as we tried to catch our breath.

"I love you," Maksim whispered, kissing my temple.

"*YA tozhe tebya lyublyu,*" I promised, so happy that I want to freeze the moment in my memory forever.

Maksim...

"May I touch your right thigh?"

My sweet bride's tempting - and naked - body is draped over my legs. I look down, trying to focus on something other than her shapely ass, which I'm stroking as I watch her map out my scars, dotting each with a tender kiss.

"Ella darling, you may touch anywhere you like on me."

She looks up at me, attempting to look stern. "Maksim, you know that enthusiastic consent is key to a healthy relationship."

"Well, Ella, I would not wish to venture into the unhealthy region of simply throwing you onto your back and fucking you senseless."

"Oh, Maksim," she says with a cheeky little grin, "that will always have my enthusiastic consent."

EPILOGUE

A year later...

Maksim...

'WHERE IS HE!"

I can hear my wife shout from behind the sturdy door of my office, and she is clearly not pleased. Yuri's shoulders are shaking silently, trying to control his laughter as we hear Ella stomping down the marble hallway.

There is a polite knock and her tone is demure, "Maksim darling, may I speak with you for a moment?"

Rising to open the door, I attempt to control my smile in the face of her seething rage. "Do come in."

She stares at me, unflinching as she calls out, "Hey, Yuri."

I can hear my idiot brother still trying to quell his laughter as he replies.

"So, Maksim," she not-quite snarls, "could we speak in the bedroom?"

"Of course, Ella," I can almost smell her outrage from here. The moment the door's shut, she's on me.

"You chipped me? Like a pet? You chipped me like a runaway cat?"

It takes me a moment. "Ah. The tracker in your arm."

She's speechless, her pretty pink mouth opening and closing helplessly. This is a rare occasion, so I enjoy it while I can.

"You saw Dr. Chang today, correct?" Dr. Chang is an OB/GYN, ruthlessly vetted and background-checked in every possible way.

"I did," she says, "and guess what she shared with me?"

I seat myself. "She likely scanned your birth control implant in your arm and found the tracker placed under it?"

"You chipped me without my knowledge!" Ella's waving her hands helplessly, trying to communicate her rage, I imagine. "Wh- how- when did this happen?"

I rub the back of my neck; it would have been helpful to have remembered this and discussed the tracker at an earlier time. "Before our first wedding, when your birth control device was implanted. This is a state-of-the-art GPS tracker that's no bigger than a pea. It has a battery life of five years and is perfectly harmless, I assure you."

"You chipped me!" Ella repeats, clearly unwilling to move past the outrage.

"Solnyshko," I take her hands and pull her down on my lap. "I am sorry I did not discuss this with you after we vowed to be honest with each other. I am aware you are outraged and knowing that I forgot to mention it is not helping. But how do you think we found you at the Sokolov bunker? They'd taken your phone and purse, which had two trackers. The one in your arm saved your life. Though you would not have been in that position in the first place if it were not for me. And for that, again, I am sorry. Sincerely."

Ella pursed her lips as she thought about it. "You have already apologized for... well, everything. This is like an addendum apology. I accept."

"So, you agree to keep it there?" She shoots off my lap like a rocket and I catch her before she makes it to the door. "It seems my apology needs to be more thorough," I said, pulling up her skirt and lifting her, wrapping her legs around my waist as I press my cock against her.

The Next Day...

Russian Orthodox Easter - St. Nicholas Cathedral, NYC

Ella...

There are two days of the year that Maksim and his family will be in church, no matter what else might be happening. Russian Orthodox Christmas, which we celebrated in St. Petersburg, and Russian Orthodox Easter.

I loved the St. Nicholas Cathedral, with the glorious, soaring ceilings with their gold leaf and exquisite carvings. The wonderful stain-glass windows and the priceless statues of the saints. It was a magnificent, elaborate building, but it was still filled with a sense of humble spirituality.

We were sitting in the Morozov family pew, with Yuri, their mother, and Ekaterina and Mariya, who'd come to visit. There was a moment of silent contemplation, and I leaned over slightly to whisper in Maksim's ear.

"So, there was one other thing I discovered at Dr. Chang's appointment yesterday."

He attempted to frown at me quellingly, the Big, Scary Pakhan.

"It seems that what your tech person didn't know is that the tracker you installed diminishes the effectiveness of my birth control implant."

Maksim's eyes widened. "Are you alright? Are you ill from it?" He's barely managing to keep his alarm to a whisper, and his mother looks over with a frown.

"Yeah, I'm fine," I shrug, "it's not like pregnancy is an illness."

"What?" This time, my husband forgot to whisper.

"Yes," I'm still whispering because I'm responsible like that in church. "I'm twelve weeks along. We're going to have a baby."

Maksim leaps to his feet and I'm torn between laughing and

crying at the look of joy on his face. "You are pregnant? We're having a child!"

There's a long moment of silence as his outburst echoes around the cathedral, then a scatter of applause and friendly laughter.

"It is indeed a blessing from our Lord," the Archbishop finally speaks from the altar with a kind, regal smile, "but now, let us return to..."

My husband takes my face in his big rough hands, thumbs smoothing over my cheekbones. "A child," he barely breathes, "thank you."

It takes another thirty minutes of the service before his utterly uncharacteristic giddiness passes and he whispers again, "The timing of this blessed announcement is your revenge for the tracker implant, isn't it?"

I kiss him on his lovely, high cheekbone. "Yes, it is."

A FAVOR, PLEASE?

If you enjoyed the story of Maksim and Ella, can I please ask you to review it on Amazon? Reviews are the lifeblood for independent writers and mean the difference between success and failure for us. Thank you in advance for taking the time to leave a review.

Thomas And Lauren

Would you like to know more about the story of Lauren and Thomas from the sinister Corporation? Find their story in The Reluctant Bride: bit.ly/thereluctantbride

Free Book!

Join my email list and I'll notify you about upcoming books, freebies and giveaways. The Reluctant Spy is a story of the sinister Corporation and it's terrifying - but hot - leader and the spy he uncovers under his command.
https://dl.bookfunnel.com/6xud62r

GLOSSARY

Pakhan - head of the Brava organization

Sovietnik - the second in command

Obshchak - head of the security branch

Brigadier - a captain in charge of a small group of men

Obshchaka - chief accountant and bookkeeper

BOOKS BY THIS AUTHOR

The Reluctant Bride

Wait. What do you mean, my dad gave me to you?

I was ready for a fresh start in England, a career with the London Symphony Orchestra. But my father's "underperforming" company is bought out by The Corporation. Suddenly, I'm being told I'm marrying the tall and terrifying Thomas Williams, because dad would rather trade me to keep control of his company. Thomas tells me that it "looks better" to be a married man as his organized crime empire starts a partnership with the Russian Bratva Syndicate.

Really?

I'm a wife. I have a giant diamond ring to prove it... and a husband who can be kind in one moment and scary in the next. And there's car chases, and assassination attempts. There's a body in my cello case! Who has a marriage like this?

But by the time we're in St. Petersburg and surrounded by new friends and old enemies, my gorgeous, terrifying husband might just need me.

The Reluctant Bride is a Dark Mafia Romance and is 18+ only.

The Reluctant Spy

Maura MacLaren - mousey, dowdy, and very, very good with technology - is a perfect Corporation employee. Brilliant at her job, smart enough to know to keep her head down, and in debt to the criminal enterprise that gave her a chance when her past left her with nowhere to turn. But this puts her under the watchful eye of the Corporation's diabolical, gorgeous, and utterly unforgiving Second in Command, James Pine.

Pine has been sent by the head office in London to be sure nothing will go wrong with the Corporation's largest deal to date. The last thing a man in his dangerous position needs are feelings, or surprises. Especially feelings for a nerdy underling who is turning out to be full of surprises, including a sensually submissive nature that Pine finds too compelling to resist. But Pine is as cold-hearted as he is handsome and he never denies himself what he wants.

But when Maura's darkest secret puts her life and Pine's deal in danger, they both find themselves shocked at the sensual depths he will drag her to for revenge. And the lengths he will go to in order to save her life.

The Reluctant Spy is a dark Mafia romance and meant for 18+ readers only

Mr. And Mrs. Ari Levinsky Invite You To... The Worst Wedding Ever

Heather's given to Mafia King Ari Levinsky in an arranged marriage to create an alliance with her terrible mobster dad. She's supposed to be touring Europe after graduating from college, but before she can blink she's standing at the altar trying to read her vows in... Aramaic? Heather's new husband is gigantic; tall, muscled, terrifying, and loud. And she doesn't even get to pick out her own wedding dress! Then, it's on to a romantic beach honeymoon, with so much double-crossing, and she finds the only way to outsmart her scary, ridiculously hot husband... is to out-sex him.

Mr. and Mrs. Ari Levinsky Invite You to... the Worst Wedding Ever is for 18+ readers only.

Blood Brothers - Captive Blood Book One: A Dark Vampire Romance

"It'll be good for you," he said. "The stalker will never find you there." My agent sends me to stay on an Oregon mountaintop, cared for by a surly handyman named Steve, who looks like a supermodel ... lumberjack ... Greek God sort of guy.
I'm supposed to feel safe here? I keep having all these dreams ... dreams where Lumberjack Steve is biting me. Now, I'm losing time. Losing blood.
And I think it's possible my stalker is closer than I thought.
Blood Brothers is a dark romance meant for 18+ readers only.

The Birdcage - Captive Blood Book Two: A Dark Vampire Romance

Black Heart keeps me in the Birdcage, high above the blasted remains of the earth after the Night Brethren plunged us into darkness. At the gate of his mansion, the Shadows wait to tear screaming humans into pieces of blood and bone. In the Birdcage, the vampire who keeps me is growing impatient. What does he want? My blood? My soul? I don't have long to decide whether to take my chances with the Shadows or find out what Black Heart intends to do.

To make it worse? He's not the only monster who wants me.
The Birdcage is a dark romance meant for 18+ readers only.

I Love The Way You Lie: Loki, The God Of Mischief And Lies - A Dark Romance

A nameless princess: innocent, damaged and very lethal. A ruthless king with the power of a god. And trouble, lots of it.

When King Loki of Asgard takes the daughter of the Dark Elven Queen captive, he not only strips an enemy of a powerful weapon, but gains for himself a wife. Now the newly named and wed Queen Ingrid must learn to survive the perils of court life, the wages of war, and most dangerous of all, her seductive husband's bed.

"I Love the Way You Lie" is a Dark Loki romance for 18+ readers only.

ABOUT THE AUTHOR

Arianna Fraser

 Working as an entertainment reporter gives Arianna Fraser plenty of fuel for her imagination when writing tales about current-day romance-suspense stories and Norse Mythology - Loki in particular. There will always be an infuriatingly stubborn heroine, an unfairly handsome and cunning hero - or anti-hero - romance, shameless smut, danger, and something will explode or catch on fire. She is clearly a terrible firebug, and her husband has sixteen fire extinguishers stashed throughout the house.

When she's not interviewing superheroes and villains, Arianna lives in the western US with her twin boys, obstreperous little daughter, and sleep-deprived husband.

Have a thought? Wanna share? ariannafraser88@gmail.com